NOAH BODIE

Suneater
Book 1 of the Desert Rose Saga

First published by Highly Caffeinated Art 2024

Copyright © 2024 by Noah Bodie

All rights reserved. No part of this publication may be reproduced, stored or transmitted in any form or by any means, electronic, mechanical, photocopying, recording, scanning, or otherwise without written permission from the publisher. It is illegal to copy this book, post it to a website, or distribute it by any other means without permission.

This novel is entirely a work of fiction. The names, characters and incidents portrayed in it are the work of the author's imagination. Any resemblance to actual persons, living or dead, events or localities is entirely coincidental.

Noah Bodie asserts the moral right to be identified as the author of this work.

This book is recommended for audiences ages 18+.

Being set in my dark fantasy world 'Lusefell,' this work contains darker themes including, but not limited to: frightening creatures, dystopian/grimdark setting, reference to magical experimentation on being/creature, murder, trauma, C-PTSD and PTSD, scars, blood and gore, mental health topics, reference to homophobia, reference to suicide, anger issues, and grief.

Please be safe as you dive into the world of Lusefell.

First edition

ISBN: 979-8-3304-5988-9

This book was professionally typeset on Reedsy. Find out more at reedsy.com

For all of the young creatives who struggle with finding their purpose and believing in their power, you have the ability to make magic. Do not give up. You are seen, you are loved, and we need you.

Contents

Prologue		iii
1	Fate	1
2	Semantics	9
3	The Green Dragon	17
4	Spellglass	24
5	Charming	33
6	Change	40
7	Memory	48
8	Piety	56
9	Understanding	64
10	Confidence	71
11	Family	79
12	Exhaustion	86
13	Hope	96
14	Survival	103
15	Suspicion	112
16	EDEN	119
17	Trust	126
18	Sincerity	136
19	Unknown	150
20	Promise	155
21	Deception	165
22	The After Party	174
23	Possibility	183
24	Light	195
25	Sara	204

26 Agreement	213
27 Slumber	227
The Maps of Lusefell	234
The Six Planes of Existence	240
The Immortal Boundaries	242
The People of Lusefell	244
The Pantheons of Lusefell	249
The Celestial Bodies and Calendar of Lusefell	253
Concept Art	259
About the Author	266
Also by Noah Bodie	268

Prologue

Allow me to tell you the true story of what came before ...

In the beginning, there were **two** *Planes of Existence*.

The first, and the oldest, is that of the **Primals** —*The Primordial Plane*.

The second is that of the **Old Gods**—*The Divine Plane*.

They separated themselves, never interacting or crossing paths. Those of the *Divine* thought those of the *Primordial* to be savage, unintelligent, and lesser beings. Those of the *Primordial* thought those of the *Divine* to be weak, selfish, and lost in far more ways than they could explain. For eons, the two remained equally in power.

Then came the *Era of Expansion*.

The *Divine* had grown tired and sought to create magic far away in the empty spaces of the cosmos. Many **Old Gods** feared that those of the *Primordial* would follow them, jealous of the infinite possibility of the void. The *Divine* then secretly wrote the *Immortal Boundaries* and carved out the four new *Planes of Existence*.

Thus, the **six** *Planes of Existence* were born and upheld by the *Immortal Boundaries*.

* * *

Our world, **Lusefell**, began from the whim of two sibling **Old Gods**. One sought to correct a grievous power imbalance between *The Divine Plane* and *The Primordial Plane*. The other sought to enjoy the chaos such a promise would bring. The brother and sister discovered a vast, barren expanse deep within *The Mortal Plane*. They created star-filled skies, two suns to guide, and two moons to control the tides. By creating a place of infinite potential, they crafted a clean slate that those who received this gift could shape.

Then, the brother—**Braxus**—reached into the heavens and plucked the four brightest stars from *The Primordial Plane*. He granted the four the authority to create and govern a wondrous world as desired, unknowingly initiating an era of endless conflict.

> The first was the Water Primordial **Qella**, The Seeing One.
> From her, mortals gained an understanding of magic, knowledge, patience, and temperance.
> The second was the Air Primordial **Pithus**, The Selfless One.
> From him, we mortals gained an understanding of change, time, punishment, and memory.
> The third was the Earth Primordial **Uldrich**, The Loving One.
> From them, we mortals gained an understanding of healing, growth, prosperity, and sincerity.
> The final was the Fire Primordial **Cael**, The Wrathful One.
> From him, we mortals gained an understanding of strength, justice, truth, and passion.

All was well, and we prospered for a time; our world remained unknown and untouched.

Then came the day that **Illhiea**, the sister, struck down her brother and ended his spark. A disagreement arose because **Braxus** wanted to uphold their kind's exclusion from our world as promised while she grew weary of peace's constant *simplicity*. She sought refuge in another, and they broke her heart, twisted it, and used it as a pawn. It was another being: old, forgotten, and one who enjoyed chaos more than she did.

Lusefell plunged into a divine war, and our existence was exposed.

For **324** years, the **Primal Lords** waged war against the **Old Gods** and those who wished to claim this place outside their purview. The war tore our realm apart and traumatized our ancestors beyond measure. One of our suns, *Celestine*, darkened and faded from the morning sky forever.

… The war slowed, thought won by those who created our world and fought for the life given to them by **Braxus**.

Then, on the eve of the *Festival of Reaping,* **The Smolder Ridge Mountains** were set aflame, and chaos spilled across the continent of *Redirine*.

In a single night, much happened.

A pact between a **Primal** and *Mortal* crumbled: one far older than *The Lady of Water* had undermined her. Furious, **Qella** turned against both her kin and the *Mortals*. Using her power, she revived a felled **Fire Primal** into **Lusefell**. **Cael** fell, slaying the threat to his people, and his soul was bound to *The Mortal Plane* by **Qella**. **Qella** broke and rewrote his memory, flipping our world on its head. **Qella** fractured our history, distorted it, and turned everyone against **Pithus** because of her crimes.

Uldrich was bound to a tree in *The Mortal Plane* after an unsuccessful attempt to free their brother, **Cael**. However, before their imprisonment, they planted a seed that grew into a wondrous gift of undying life. This gift revived **Cael** and cursed him to a cycle of death and rebirth for eternity. This gift ensured our world always had a sword and shield to protect it, so long as we were patient **and had faith**.

Pithus accepted his fate and assumed the mantle of blame cast upon him. He vowed revenge for himself and his broken husband, **Cael**. He struck a deal with **Qella**. She had little faith in the *Mortals,* and he wished to prove that his husband's faith in them had been justified. He vowed the *Mortals* would glorify **Cael**, and **Qella** considered them his undoing. A wheel of destiny was set in motion, manipulated only by time and **Pithus**.

Cael rose from his ashes; in a fit of fire and misunderstood sorrow, he descended over the mountains of *Redirine* for a year. **The Flame King** lamented as he blackened, sundered, and turned the *Smolder Ridge Mountains* into a molten hell. He did not know why he grieved nor what he had forgotten… only that he had lost something irreplaceable. His memories of his family, the truth of his fall, and of his *husband* were empty voids.

Then **Cael** vanished from our history for a time. So long, many forgot about him while others cursed his name. In our time of need, many believed he had abandoned us.

Over **166** years, many wars have taken place. It is now the year **1296**, and organizations of power have risen, fallen, and appeared defeated. A fading organization known as **EDEN**, once thought to work towards healing the wounds of the past, has come under scrutiny and suspicion.

It has been **10** years since an alliance between a group of *Mortals* loyal to **Cael** and a family of unlikely heroes defeated and imprisoned **Qella**. We have restored **Cael**'s memory and our own. We have begun the tedious process of *correcting* our history books. The people have desecrated places of worship for **Qella**, and they have shunned her followers. **Uldrich** has been freed, and **Pithus** has gained more respect and adoration than the **Primal** ever thought possible from we mortals for his faith in **us**.

The world's cogs have started to turn, long-lost villages and towns have rebuilt, and continents have sprung to life. Forests have overgrown charred places of the world, deserts scattered with wildlife, and aquatic treasures brought to the surface. The icy shelves have thawed, and so much life has flourished far and wide.

Peace, long thought lost, has returned. Even so, whispers of old foes and fragments of our terrible history remain across the four continents, along with an unsettling fear.

Peace, as we saw long ago … is impermanent, yet we hold on to hope.

That hope blooms like a Desert Rose.

One

Fate

Looking for an adventurous individual to explore rumors about a distinguished family in Fossy. A strong reputation and discretion are necessary and will be assessed before full job details are provided. If you are considered suitable and complete the task successfully, you will receive a payment of **5,000** gold pieces.

There will be no negotiation of payment.

Interested parties should bring this notice and report to **Cian Dwyer**. Urgency arises as the assignment's deadline nears. Please be honest and professional, as I will evaluate you accordingly.

With the highest regards,
Cian Dwyer

These notices would often suddenly appear out of nowhere and contrasted with the rushed notes on simple parchment that always covered the information board. The paper was crisp, clean, and flecked with gold. The writing, elegant in crimson ink with a flourish, suggested a well-educated and charismatic author. Both were true, for the notice was signed at the bottom in a giant golden script: *'Cian Dwyer.'*

Dwyer wasn't a common name, but most people knew it. It carried a sense of authority and notoriety, especially among the faithful of the Primal Cael. The Dwyer family, after all, was the very family that had assisted Cael's legion, **The Rose Guard**, in overthrowing Qella and reclaiming Cael and the world's memory ten years prior.

The Barbed Rose, previously a dwarven winery, now thrives as Belmare's most famous tavern and inn. The Dwyer family purchased it shortly after the conclusion of the *Second Great War*, and it was now run by Cian and Neil's infamous son, Leon, and his wife.

Not only was it well-known for being a travel hub and a gathering spot for adventurous people, but it stood out within the city of sandstone and terracotta. The pub's artisans gathered mahogany wood from deep within the *Smolder Ridge Mountains* to the south to construct it, which was unusual for buildings in Belmare's desert landscape.

It's a lovely two-story establishment with multiple windows that shimmer in strange ways. Carved with flowers and depicting a flame encircled by a crown, the double front doors add an elegant touch to the pub. Due to the building's history as a winery, the builders constructed it into the rocky sandstone cliffs that border the city. Therefore, its backdoor leads to a beautiful garden within the cavernous space.

Now, the city of Belmare is a gem in itself. Nestled near the ocean on the northeastern part of the continent of Redirine, it stands out as a gleaming beacon amidst the vast sands beyond the mountains. Belmare was set against a backdrop of stunning sunflower fields and was renowned for its lively music scene and diverse culture. For those who follow **The Flame King**, it is both the beginning and the proverbial end. It is a city that has persevered through war hardships and has emerged as a thriving economic center.

Tucked within this city of infamy, just beyond the double doors of **The Barbed Rose**, and peering over the sparkling notice, is where he found himself.

He was familiar with the place. The pub was somewhere he frequented, for he lived there with his family; the notice board was one he looked at more than he could count. Looking, but unfortunately never taking... Someone—one of his parents or his uncle—always seemed to be able to distract him or notice his interest and steer him away. There was always a reason given, and as he'd grown older and watched his sister venture out into the world, he had become more suspicious of it.

There was a reason, yes, for him to be kept safely nestled within the watchful eye of his parents or uncle, but it wasn't the reason they were telling him. Indeed, some wished ill on his family, and the world had numerous frightening creatures. However, his family was less worried about the outside world and more concerned about other unspoken things, as if they were taboo.

Andreas had learned that danger was inevitable as a Dwyer, but his upbringing often shielded him from it. Very purposefully, almost imprisoning, had been the shield cast over him. Often, he wondered if it was his parents wanting more than a life balanced on the edge of a blade or if it was his own self-deprecation wrecking his prospects to prove himself capable. Either way, at least after the war, he'd grown up within the pub's walls in a somewhat stable daily life. Suffocatingly stable.

Andreas read his Papa's posting yet again. He had seen these notices multiple times, read them, and always felt curious about taking one. This nagging curiosity intensified every time he saw one and almost doubled when his Papa (Cian) posted and not his Grandpa (Neil). The two had distinct ways of expressing themselves, and as he had grown, his Papa had always had more influence over his decision-making.

Which, he admitted, was strange.

Cian Dwyer was a very strict, albeit charismatic, man. He favored honesty and structure and often had contingency plans, even for dinner. Neil Dwyer, the eccentric one of the couple, always seemed determined to keep his grandchildren away from the wilderness and more eager to steer them toward romance. Cian disliked this, not because he disliked the idea of *romance* but because he disliked the idea of his **grandchildren** having someone hurt them. While they both were protective, Cian was overbearingly protective.

The half-wood elf bit his lip, brow furrowing as he reread the posting.

Andreas looked around the small room on the lower levels of the pub and spotted the bartop about forty feet away. His uncle was chatting with a patron, but there was no sign of his mother or father from where he stood. They would never know if he accepted the posting. If he departed tonight, he could leave the city undetected. He could even bribe his twin sister to lie about him visiting their grandparents.

He soon realized that now was his only chance.

Andreas' attention returned to the regal notice, and he hesitantly reached out to take it. He didn't know how to define what happened next; perhaps it was bad luck or a strange act of *fate*. Regardless of which it was, another hand grabbed the paper as his fingers locked on it.

An awkward silence hung in the air as neither released the parchment.

Andreas peeked at the individual beside him and realized he had to look up. He wasn't short; he was taller than his human father, but this individual was still taller. Andreas swallowed as his gaze met the mismatched eyes, one warm brown and the other a steel gray.

The two stared, sizing each other up.

Andreas stood around six feet tall, with wavy crimson hair that reached his lower back and framing bangs. He had a warm, carnelian complexion and large, expressive emerald eyes. Andreas had softer features and a more delicate bone structure despite his sturdy build.

The orc[1] stood around six feet eight, with soot black hair cut close to his neck and messy bangs. Compared to the rolling dunes beyond the city's walls, his light, sandy complexion, and sharp eyes stood out in a city filled with sunkissed faces. He had broad shoulders and a boxy appearance, resembling someone in a profession that demands extensive physical labor. He had a visible scar down his right cheek, a few inches from his eye, that

---

[1] For more information about the Orcs of *Lusefell*, please refer to the back matter titled **"The People of Lusefell."**

followed his jaw and golden piercings along his pointed ears, septum, and labret.

Andreas frowned and said, "I grabbed it first."

"I'm pretty sure we grabbed it at the same time," the orc responded.

Their voices contrasted. Andreas' medium tenor was annoyed, while the orc's low baritone was amused.

Silence filled the room again. Neither released the parchment nor attempted to move it from its space on the board. They both waited for one another to propose a solution.

Andreas bit his lip again, eyes returning to the elegant writing.

Fate? Ha, this was no doubt lousy luck. He had lived a life filled with close calls and near misses, even teetering on the brink of death multiple times.

Andreas sighed, defeated, and pulled his hand away.

"I mean, we could split the payment. 2,500 gold is still a hell of a lot."

Andreas paused, his hand frozen, as he met the gaze of the observing orc. He seemed to sort through the words, trying to comprehend them. He appeared startled and confused, as if the suggestion had never crossed his mind despite years of study.

The orc laughed and smiled, causing his tusks to push away from his skin as his lips curled back. He then extended a free hand beneath their occupied arms and said in a chipper tone, "Simon."

Andreas glanced at the hand, swallowed, and nodded. "Andreas."

Together, they both ripped the paper from the wall, leaving the top edge of the parchment attached to it. It seemed like they would fight over it, but Simon let go and nodded in acknowledgment. He didn't seem bothered by the rejection of a handshake and instead turned his attention to the bulletin board, scanning for another job opportunity.

"Are you looking for another one?" Andreas asked, quickly shoving the torn paper into his pocket. He didn't want to chance one of his family members seeing him with it or questioning him about it.

"Yeah, since we'll already be out in Fossy, we might as well grab another one."

Andreas had never considered that either. He never thought he **could** take one, so the plans afterward were uncharted territory. It was an exciting prospect.

Andreas glanced back at the wall and began to scan it with silent, barely contained joy.

Simon noticed the erratic energy beside him and studied the darker features as they focused on the wall. He chuckled to himself and then looked back at the uneven parchment rows. His interest had surged after they first interacted, intensifying as events unfolded and Andreas' excitement built.

"Do you see anything interesting?" Simon inquired.

Andreas acknowledged a posting by Selbi, a familiar woman in the city.

Selbi was an older halfling woman who ran a bed-and-breakfast near the market. The pay was much less, only 200 gold, but the task seemed simple. She needed someone to carry a patron's remains to their family in Fossy, and there wasn't an imposed timetable.

Andreas looked towards Simon and saw him reading over the pointed post.

Simon carefully read the paper, examining the details. A huge smile appeared, and he eagerly grabbed it from the wall.

"Good eye, Red."

Andreas jumped, startled by the nickname, and felt his stomach lurch.

"I haven't been here much, but I think **The Green Dragon** is close to the market. I planned to stay here tonight, but if the bed-and-breakfast owner posted the job, maybe staying there would be better. ... Unless you have a room here already?" Simon looked over, tucking the parchment into the bag over his shoulder.

Andreas pondered the words, letting them repeat a few times as silence filled the small room. He had options but was unsure which one to pursue. Simon seemed oblivious to his identity, which worked to his advantage and was exceedingly rare. Perhaps Simon hadn't visited Belmare much, or he ignored the implications of where he was and who he could be talking to. It was strange because, in most circumstances, Andreas would have been suspicious of it, but he'd been given no indication that Simon was *lying*.

Simon's lack of awareness would prevent his sister from asking many questions and would dispel any assumptions that he was being exploited if he asked for her help. However, Simon likely believed he already knew about this type of work or lacked experience. Both options seemed challenging and unappealing to him. He wanted to satisfy others without facing criticism. Andreas didn't handle criticism well and usually reacted by being overly self-critical.

Andreas swallowed, deciding how to respond to the concerned gaze watching him. He looked up and smiled. "Yes, kind of. I was planning to leave tonight. Going to **The Green Dragon** is fine. I know the owner, so she might give us a discount. I've spent a lot of time in the city."

That was close enough to the whole truth.

After all, a lie of omission was still a *truth*, as his Grandpa Neil would say.

Neil often offered his husband, Cian, this line when he was caught twisting his words to avoid giving others full details. As they grew up, the man had ingrained this phrase in Andreas and his sister's minds to ease their guilt about avoiding discussions of their family or history. Andreas still felt a pang of regret in his gut, knowing that his Papa and father would scold him for technically lying.

Cain and Leon despised liars, and Cian refused to tell lies of omission. To avoid lying, Cian would outright refuse to answer a question.

After the long pause, Simon absorbed the information, and his face still twisted in concern.

"Okay. I can wait outside or meet you at the bed-and-breakfast," Simon said.

"I ... will meet you out front," Andreas stated, despite wanting to say he'd meet the man at **The Green Dragon**. He felt this would only increase the suspicion he had already noticed growing on Simon's face.

"Give me ten minutes," Andreas said.

"Sounds like a date," Simon grinned, excused himself, and bent down to pass through the door frame, unable to fit at his full height. He then started into the main pub.

Andreas struggled to answer, processing the words he'd been left with, and finally settled on a gurgled noise and silence as his gaze followed Simon out the front door. It broke as Andreas moved around and flattened against the wall.

The spark in his gut was back, and he swore he could hear his Papa laughing at him somewhere in the distance. A pleasant heat radiated from his ears, and he was unsure if it resulted from Simon's parting words or the exhilaration of successfully stealing from the job board without being caught. Both seemed impossible to believe.

He needed to grab his belongings and leave the pub undetected by his family. Hopefully, he didn't encounter either of his parents or their friends in the city. Selbi wouldn't say anything about his family by name, at least he hoped, but he could deal with that later.

Andreas reached into his pocket, searched for his coin purse, and counted how much he had to spare to bribe his sister. After a few counts, he nodded and glanced at the pub. There was no sign of his parents, only his uncle cleaning a table with empty mugs in the corner.

Feeling giddy, he quickly swallowed and rushed towards the spiral staircase in the corner of the room. He wanted to gather his things, leave a note, and put the bribe money in his sister's room as quickly as possible.

He had a date to keep, after all.

Two

Semantics

"I want to make sure I have this right. You're planning to do something for Daddy to be *justified* in being annoyed?" The female voice was musical and asked in a tone of near disbelief.

Andreas grimaced as he looked at his twin sister and replied, "Yes, if you want to put it that way."

His sister laughed and fell back, landing on her bed with a slight bounce from the firm mattress.

Lilliana Dwyer was nearly identical to her brother, at least from the outside; they were the same height, but she was much slimmer in build with noticeable curves. The only difference between them, aside from their gender identities, was their eyes. Lilliana had heterochromia and had one eye that was a pale gray and one that was a bright ice blue. Her hair, like Andreas', was wavy crimson and worn long. She, however, had side-swept bangs instead of long, messy ones like her brother's.

Regarding their personalities, both individuals were flirtatious and cared about their outward appearances. They were both proud and stubborn and could be rude if irritated, but that is where their similarities ended. Lilliana was more self-assured and confident. Much to their father's disapproval, she had been venturing into the world, taking on odd jobs. On the other hand, Andreas was prickly and lacked social skills outside of flirting. He attracted their parents' attention like a newborn would.

Andreas grumbled before crossing his arms and looking at his sister. "Are you going to help me or not, Lilli? I told you I would pay... I can spare thirty gold."

"Dear brother, I will gladly help you," Lilliana said with a smile, her laughter fading as she wiped a tear from her eye. She shifted to lean back on her palms and tilted her head. "Seeing Daddy *explode* on you when you get back is worth all the trouble."

Andreas rolled his eyes. "If you *help*, he won't know what I'm doing... will he?"

Lilliana scoffed and laughed again. It took a moment, but she calmed down enough to respond. "This is *Daddy*. He's as capable of sniffing out liars as Papa Cian. Do you think you can avoid them both finding out? Or worse, Momma?"

"I'm less worried about Mom and more worried about Pops, which is why I need **your help**." The last few words were strained, and Andreas leaned forward, anxious.

The two met each other's gaze, and for a moment, it seemed like Lilliana was about to burst into another fit of laughter. She, however, did not. Instead, she sighed and smiled at her brother before patting the bed beside her.

Andreas scoffed but sat and was pulled into a tight embrace. "Lilli!"

Lilliana kissed her twin's cheek and said, "Alright, I'll help for ten gold."

Andreas sighed and handed over the money, saying, "Deal."

Lilli counted the coins, pocketed them excitedly, and asked, "So, the story is that you traveled to visit our grandparents. You hired an escort to ensure you got there without dying, one that *'I've worked with before,'* right?"

Andreas nodded, smiling at the wink he received as the last words left his sister's lips. He bumped her shoulder affectionately and said, "Yeah, that's the story. The name of your 'acquaintance' is Simon. He's an orc, maybe in his late twenties? I don't know his age. Sandy complexion, black hair, and six feet six, maybe eight? Tall enough to duck like Papa Cian in the doorways."

"Ooh, handsome?" Lilliana asked as she raised an eyebrow and nudged her brother.

Andreas responded without hesitation, "Yes."

Lilliana let out a triumphant squeak when her brother answered her without pause. She grabbed his arm and shook him before asking, "So, this is **business**, right?"

Andreas frowned, his brow furrowed in annoyance as he replied, *"Yes."*

Lilliana giggled, feeling giddy, and pulled away from her brother to stand up. She paced back and forth a few times before stopping and leaning forward animatedly. "Alright. I'll do it, but I want to meet him when you return—promise," she said.

"You're not sleeping with him," Andreas stated in mild annoyance.

"I just want to see if your taste in men has improved. Your idea of being attractive is Rhys, and while I adore him, he's a mutt," Lilliana cackled when her brother shoved her playfully. She watched Andreas grumble and mutter about taking back his money. Then she settled back down and bumped his shoulder again, adding, "Be careful. Promise?"

Andreas found sincerity in his sister's expression. He sighed, mustered a small smile, and responded, "I will."

The two sat briefly in silence, neither daring to break it as if it would bring ill will on Andreas' coming departure. They had said farewell several times, but usually, it was Lilliana who was to go off and risk danger. Something about the shoe being on the other foot felt strange and larger than it should have. There seemed to be a heavy implication of something neither could place a finger on.

"I'll send you a message when I arrive, okay? *Thanks*," Andreas said, standing. He spoke with solemnity and overwhelming affection for his sister.

Lilliana nodded and leaned back on her bed. "You'd better," she said.

Before leaving, Andreas paused and added, "Please be careful and don't get in trouble."

Lilliana was mock-offended and exclaimed, "Me? I would *never* do anything wrong!"

The two exchanged grins, and then Andreas turned to excuse himself into the hallway.

"I love you, Anni," Lilliana called out as her brother opened the door.

Andreas paused for the final time, not daring to turn around out of fear of crying. There was a weight on his chest, and he couldn't place why. Instead, he swallowed and whispered, *"I love you too, Lilli."*

Andreas closed the door behind him with a soft tap and searched the area for signs of their parents. Thankfully, he hadn't seen either of them or their dog, Bear. He would have worried about this if Lilli hadn't informed him they had left to visit a family friend's newborn early that morning. The family could keep their parents occupied for hours, and his mother loved children.

He composed himself and stored the familiar weight in his memory.

Andreas lifted his belongings onto his shoulder from where he had left them at his sister's door. He reached down to tuck a folded metallic item into a small pouch on his right thigh. He mulled over the checklist: sister, bag, weapons, food, and Keena.

He adjusted, lifting one side of the teal shawl draped over his shoulders and peering beneath it. Tucked into his shirt was a small bundle of blue feathers, head under her wing and resting comfortably against his chest.

Keena was a blue jay and had been his companion for nearly ten years. He'd found her with an injured wing in the forest when he was sixteen. It had been when they'd lived in the mountains during the war. Andreas had nursed her back to health, and they had become inseparable.

He'd wake her once he got out of the pub and closer to **The Green Dragon**. Keena drew attention and could be protective of him. The last thing he needed was for her to start a scene with Simon.

Andreas sucked in a breath, tapped the pouch holding the item he'd stowed, and then muttered an elvish word. A pale spark of energy appeared like a flicker of a candle before vanishing, and he made his way downstairs. He stayed around the edges of the walls, avoiding the creaky floorboards, and slipped down the spiral staircase into the room holding the notice board.

He pressed against the wall and peeked his head out of the door to check the bar.

Michael, Andreas' uncle, was there, cleaning and looking around as if he suspected something.

Andreas waited, pushing on for what felt like ten minutes. Then he saw the human behind the bar grab a plate from a patron and slip into the kitchen. He dashed out of the doorway and made a beeline for the double doors of the pub in an instant. He held his breath, checking over his shoulder every few seconds to see if his uncle had emerged. He grasped the golden handle of the door and pulled it open. Andreas exited, closed the wooden door behind him, and quickly scanned the area, not for Simon, but for familiar faces. Finding no one, he exhaled and calmly approached the orc leaning against the far eastern wall.

Andreas waved and said, "Sorry, it took a bit longer than expected."

"I thought you had stood me up," Simon responded absentmindedly, his gaze fixed on the large tower shield he had been polishing. He picked up a small vial and a worn cloth, put them in his bag, and effortlessly lifted the worn shield onto his back. Standing up, he smiled when he noticed the emeralds watching. "I'm glad you didn't," he said.

Andreas responded with a sheepish smile, "No, I had to find my bird."

It was true... *almost*.

Simon seemed intrigued, nodded toward the city, and walked forward. "Bird?"

Andreas followed and added, "Yes, I have a blue jay companion. She's my best friend."

A silence fell between them, and suddenly, Andreas wondered if it would have been better not to mention Keena yet. Perhaps it was questionable to mention his close friendship with a bird. It wasn't something he thought much about, but only because it never came up in other conversations, which were solely focused on how to get into a bedroom and how quickly he could remove his pants.

Well, that or **being a Dwyer**.

It had become a sensitive topic as he had grown older because being associated with the name was suffocating. Everyone was curious about your family, their activities, and their wartime accomplishments. *It was a lot to fit into.*

"Are you okay, Red?" Simon asked as he leaned over and waved his hand in front of the other's face.

Andreas was jolted, knocked out of his thoughts, and sputtered, "What?"

Simon squinted and said with a bassy laugh, "I asked where she was, and you were off somewhere, too."

The shorter man's cheeks darkened in embarrassment, and Andreas mumbled, "Oh… um. Here."

Andreas lifted the side of his shawl and pointed toward the bundle, which caused his shirt to stick out. He noticed Simon leaning closer, angling his head to peer down the fabric toward the sleeping bird. Feeling self-conscious, he dropped the shawl and said, "She was sleeping."

Simon stated, "She's pretty."

"Ah, thanks," Andreas responded nervously.

"I guess pets do take after their owners," Simon said, letting the words roll out as if commenting on the weather and turning his attention towards the unfolding city before them. The man beside him made a sound that seemed to be a mix of shock and embarrassment, but he didn't look over and just smiled to himself. Simon had observed that his new companion was easy to tease, and he made a mental note of this for future reference.

Silence settled between them as they continued, a new, uncertain silence that typically lingers when warming up to others. Andreas appeared more uncomfortable with the silence than Simon as he looked over, following Simon's lead as they wandered the streets. He seemed to consider breaking it but did not, mainly because he didn't know how to. His mind was drawing a blank on what topics would be ideal to talk about.

Ten minutes into their walk, he questioned whether Simon knew the way as they had passed the market turn two blocks back.

Andreas asked, "So, you don't come here much?"

The mismatched eyes glanced over, and Simon responded, "Not much. The last time was nine years ago."

The emeralds crinkled at the edges as if smiling, and Andreas remarked, "Ah, that explains it."

Simon looked confused and asked, "Explains what?"

"You missed the market turn two... now three blocks ago," Andreas stated, snickering.

Simon stopped, looking flustered, and glanced around at the surrounding city streets, visibly confused as he reassessed his location.

"The market was closer to the main gate ... unless it changed. *Did it change?*"

"Much of the city was destroyed by the end of the *Second War*, and the market was moved back when they started rebuilding. I think it was finished six years ago," Andreas stated.

Simon tried to recall the last time he visited Belmare. Most places were beaten up due to the fighting, and he remembered it being a mess. "It seems like you do come here often," he told his counterpart.

Andreas laughed and nodded for the other to follow him as he turned around. He waited until Simon matched his pace and spoke, "We moved here ten years ago, right around the time everything ended, and this place was completely different. The city has grown a lot, especially in the last few years. It's common to get lost if you haven't been in the city for a while. Many people do. People have asked me for directions at least once daily for years."

"So, are you from this area?" Simon asked, tilting his head with interest. "Not just 'in the city a lot'."

"I mean ... semantics?" Andreas said, laughing uncomfortably. "Some people here are biased against us because of the temple, so..."

Simon's face showed understanding as he nodded and said, "That makes sense."

He moved closer and bumped his shoulder into Andreas, who was somewhat startled but fully engaged as Simon had hoped.

Simon smiled genuinely and said, "I don't care who you pray to, or if you pray at all, for what it's worth."

There was a look of appreciation, and Andreas returned the smile. He cleared his throat, looked down at his hands, and twisted his fingers before replying, "That means a lot. Thanks. There's a lot of controversy around that these days, especially with those who follow the Old Gods. They can be prickly. They're not too fond of those of us who revere the Primals as a higher power."

"I don't pray, so I don't keep close tabs on what's happening with the followers of the Primals or the Old Gods, to be honest," Simon said, stretching and folding his hands behind his head. "Is there anything else you want to share that's a controversial topic for most folk?"

Andreas chuckled and replied, "I don't even know your age, so we're not at the deep dark secret level yet."

"Thirty-two years old, six feet eight, two hundred thirty pounds on a good day. From Faixte, specifically the city of Sebree on the continent." The older male let the words flow out, his eyes focused on the surrounding streets. He was noting where things were and what streets they walked down. "Mercenary by trade. I've smuggled someone out of a city and killed a few people. Haven't killed someone that **didn't** deserve it, for what it's worth."

Simon glanced back at his companion and saw Andreas watching him with shock. He grinned and asked, "Anything else?"

Andreas stammered and nodded towards the building at the end of the street. "There. We're there."

He quickened his pace, averting his eyes from the watchful orc beside him. He felt his ears burning, and that strange tingling spark in his gut kicked up again. Confused for a split second, he looked up because he swore he heard his Papa laughing *again*.

What he found was Simon following and chuckling to himself.

Three

The Green Dragon

※❦※

If Andreas had to choose a second favorite place in Belmare, **The Green Dragon** would be it.

It was a cozy two-story establishment at the far end of a street leading to the marketplace. The bed-and-breakfast itself had never moved and, thankfully, had survived any desolation from the attacks during the war. It had an old terracotta roof and a faded sandstone exterior adorned with sunflower carvings along the lower parts of it. Over the door was a large plaque of carved redwood shaped like a sleeping dragon and painted green with blooming wildflowers.

The large windows shimmered like **The Barbed Rose** because Selbi, the woman who owned it, was the inventor of a material known across the realm as *Spellglass*. The bed-and-breakfast was once the owner's home.

Selbi was an accomplished alchemist and tinkerer who worked alongside her late husband in her youth. She discovered a method to manipulate glass and enhance its properties, allowing it to eliminate atmospheric distortion and concealment magic when looked through. In her lifetime, she had only sold a few pieces made from the material, which was highly sought after by astronomers and astrologists wanting to study the night sky, as well as by individuals working in fields that required them to see through enchantments that made things or people invisible or illusioned.

Even in Selbi's old age, only four known buildings in *Lusefell*'s realm had been equipped with the magical glass. They were her home, a tiny home in Belmare that the city's Captain of the Guard had inherited, the renowned pub known as **Sídhe**[2] within the city of Fossy that the Dwyer patriarchs owned, and **The Barbed Rose**, also owned by the Dwyer family. Andreas' family and the place he called home.

Occasionally, there were pendants or fragments of broken items that used to be mirrors or trinkets. Local shops would sometimes display these items, and they sold quickly at a high price. Selbi didn't craft these items much anymore, even though she still could. As a result, they were nearly as rare as platinum in some parts of the world.

Andreas gazed around the cozy interior of the establishment, his eyes lighting up as he spotted the banquet table in the adjacent room. Selbi offered buffet-style meals and drinks, which were included in the price of a night's stay. Guests could visit the buffet thrice daily and enjoy as much food as they liked. The place smelled of delicious food and had a comfortable atmosphere, with numerous photographs adorning the walls. Well-maintained antiques were scattered throughout the rented rooms, and the two most popular suites featured ornate claw-footed bathtubs. The bed-and-breakfast was a local gem, and Andreas often found himself within its walls, nestled in one of its beds several times a year.

Unfortunately, his other best friend wasn't welcome at **The Barbed Rose**. When the man came to visit, they took up a room here until he left. Also, having nightly encounters was difficult if his father was home, so he'd taken a beau to **The Green Dragon** several times. Whenever he called, he would reserve one of the suite rooms if it was not occupied. A suite was his aim because the rooms had enough space for two or three, a large bed, a bathtub, and a small sitting area with a comfortable sofa.

"Um, do you have a problem sharing a room? I don't think I could get a discount on two separate rooms," Andreas asked. He looked over his

---

[2] Sídhe (shee): "hill or burial mound under which fairies live, aka fairy hill" OR "the fair folk"

shoulder at Simon as they lingered in the entryway. He kept his voice low, trying not to draw attention from the older woman he heard conversing in the banquet room to his right.

Simon was busy looking at some antique weapons on the wall near the front door. He then inspected a few scattered family photos. He nodded before looking over and responding, "That's fine. It's best to save as much as possible because Fossy is expensive."

He then returned to browsing the family heirlooms.

Andreas fell silent, knowing which accommodation in Fossy Simon must have been talking about. He knew about **Sídhe**, which his grandparents owned, and where they were headed. Not that Simon, thankfully, knew the *grandparent* bit...

"Okay," Andreas said as he walked towards the front counter and rang a bell.

It took a moment, but a halfling woman, standing three feet three inches, soon came around the partition. She took her time, for she was well into her golden years. She had bright blue eyes set into a wrinkled face adorned with many laugh lines. Her complexion was pale, much like her white and gray hair coiled into a braided bun with sunflowers stuffed into it. Selbi beamed when she spotted the half-elf and headed over with her arms extended, exclaiming, "Anni!"

Andreas smiled, knelt, and accepted the hug before adding, "Hi, Ms. Selbi."

The interaction drew Simon's attention away from the walls lined with history. He watched with piqued interest as the two conversed. Andreas glanced in his direction and pointed, and then the halfling woman's eyes turned his way. He didn't know what was said, but the woman laughed, and Andreas' cheeks were darker than Simon recalled. He smiled as he watched the two turn their attention back to one another. They both went to the front desk, and he returned to looking at the walls.

Five minutes passed, and there was a jingle of keys.

Simon noticed the golden key in Andreas' hand and asked, "Did we get lucky with a suite?"

"Selbi had one open one up this morning," Andreas said, nodding towards the stairs. He then waved back at the woman and turned to Simon, asking, "Shall we?"

"There's a patio here, made of that *Spellglass* stuff, right?" Simon asked as they ascended the stairs and looked for a backdoor.

Andreas replied, "There is. It's connected to the dining area; she only allows those with suites access, so it's private. I'd recommend waiting until it was later and the sun was down, though ... it's pretty bright otherwise." He focused on leading his acquaintance up the stairs, making sure not to trip on his feet as they ascended.

He didn't notice the captivated look that Simon gave him.

"Have you been out there before?" Simon asked.

"Yeah, a few times. I often stay here, especially when a friend is in town."

"I see. Is it true that Uldrich stayed here when they visited Belmare? I saw a paper about this place's historical importance on the wall downstairs," Simon spoke up, his hands sliding into his pockets as they stepped onto the second floor, and he followed down the hallway. The orc seemed to enjoy talking, and he was pressing to keep their conversation going.

Andreas glanced back and said, "Yeah, they used to stay here whenever they visited Cael in the city. The main suite has preserved flowers they created displayed in a case. Have you never been here?"

Simon shook his head, a slight frown forming on his lips as he said, "No. When we passed through here, we slept in the desert. We didn't have much money, so we used what we had to buy provisions and things at the market."

"We?" Andreas asked, looking over his shoulder before focusing on the door ahead. He unlocked it and stepped into the room.

"Yeah, my partner and I," Simon responded, and then he followed and nudged the door closed behind them. He looked around, whistling as he saw the room's decor.

Even for a bed-and-breakfast, the room had an elegant design with flawless sage green paint and dark green trimming. The entire room created the impression of walking into a well-maintained forest, with curtains resembling leaves and a bed frame crafted from intricately woven branches with gold and silver accents. A large bay window gave a view of the street below. Beyond that, just around the corner, you could see the ocean in the distance. Above the plush sofa, there were glass-encased flowers displayed on the wall.

It appeared that they received the Uldrich suite.

Andreas watched, his brow furrowed at the words spoken a few moments before, as Simon wandered around, investigating every nook and cranny as if he was soaking up everything he could. There was a childlike sense of wonder about him as if he had never seen anything like it.

Andreas smiled and asked in amusement, "Is it acceptable?"

"Shit, I've never been in a place like this," Simon said, his voice joyful and his eyes filled with excitement as he looked around. A huge smile spread across his face as he inquired, "How much did this cost you, Red? Your discount can't be that good… I can pay half."

"I have a tab, so it's fine," Andreas said and waved a hand, dismissing the words. "Selbi barely makes anything off of me."

Well, not him; his family, though. He ignored the thought and focused on the other figure heading for the sofa. Andreas' gaze widened, and he said, "No, I can take it…"

"Hell no. If you're paying, you get the bed," Simon said, his mismatched eyes narrowed and his jaw set sharply. He seemed unwilling to negotiate the sleeping arrangement.

Andreas bit his lip, shifted on the balls of his feet, and then tugged his hair forward to braid it. He shrugged and stepped forward to deposit his things on the bed, adding, "Not much… like I said, she barely makes any profit off of me."

Simon collapsed onto the sofa and let out a deep breath. Leaning back, he rested his head on the plush backrest. Clearly, he hadn't sat on anything comfortable in a long time. As he spoke, he seemed to relax and unwind gradually. "Either way, I owe you once we get paid. Specifically for *this*," he said.

Andreas glanced over as he reached to remove Keena from his shirt. He paused, noticing that the other man's features had softened, and his eyes had closed as he leaned back. Somehow, Simon looked tired. The man had been animated and solid throughout their interactions for the past two hours, so seeing his large form melt onto the couch was surprising. Andreas looked back at the bed, and his hand smoothed over the silken covers.

"Simon?" he questioned.

"Hm?" The response was more of a grunt than a word from the orc.

"When was the last time you slept in a bed?"

Simon's eyes opened, and he stared at the wall. He noticed that the ceiling was painted with a mural of sunflowers and took in the nuances of the blossoms for a while. He carefully considered the question, then shrugged the topic off. "A few months? That was probably the last time I visited Ransol."

A few months.

Andreas frowned, unhappy with the response. The thought of not sleeping in a *bed* for months bothered him. He knew it was probably common, but he had the option of changing that, of giving a bed to someone who wasn't used to having one. That was important.

"I don't think you'll fit on the sofa. You'd better take the bed," Andreas said as he grabbed his belongings and wandered over to the green-tufted piece of furniture without giving time for a complaint. Andreas dropped his bag on the ground and slumped onto the opposite end of it.

There was a quick chirp of dissatisfaction from the jolt.

Before Simon could protest, a blue jay poked her head from beneath her owner's clothing. She looked around to determine where she was, then spotted the stranger's face. Her eyes grew wide, her pupils dilated, and before Andreas could catch her, Keena fluttered over and landed on the other man's knee.

Keena's head tilted; she ruffled her feathers, then let out a loud squawk.

"Keena! Be nice!" Andreas snapped.

Simon burst into laughter and held out a finger. He watched her jumping around as if she were assessing or trying to intimidate him. "I like you. You're feisty," he said.

Keena chirped once more, tilting her head as if she understood while she watched Simon. She shifted in the opposite direction before pecking at the finger presented to her. It was a small peck, nothing aggressive, but it earned her another deep laugh as she fluttered up and landed on her owner's head.

Keena then nestled into Andreas' hair to watch Simon.

Andreas looked up, frowning. "Behave. He doesn't mean any harm," the half-elf said. He thought for a moment and then smirked at his companion. "So long as he takes the bed and lets us have the sofa, you can peck him all you want if he complains."

Simon's laughter ceased as he noticed the bird's eyes widening as if she expected him to make a move. He asked cautiously, "Are you serious?"

"I wouldn't test her. She's taken out an eye before," Andreas said, grinning.

Keena's beady eyes grew wider, and her feathers rustled.

Simon raised his hands in a gesture of innocence and quickly moved back toward the bed, saying, "Relax. Look, I'm not anywhere near your friend, little lady."

Keena settled down. She chirped in contentment and let out a shiver of joy before standing up and jumping sideways onto her owner's shoulder. She leaped to the left, heading down Andreas' arm until she reached his elbow and tilted her head into his shirt. Another cheerful chirp escaped from her, and she looked up expectantly.

Andreas smiled and patted the bird's head before grabbing a mealworm from his bag. He offered it, watched her snatch it up, and then laughed as she fluttered onto the sofa.

Keena settled down, tucking her head under her wing beside his belongings.

Simon chuckled and asked, "Is she always like that?"

"Most of the time, she'll warm up to you eventually," Andreas snickered.

Simon sat on the bed, watching the little blue bird with amusement.

Four

Spellglass

The last time he slept with a proper roof over his head, he'd heard idiots fighting and hundreds of ruffians cheering them on. However, comparing that roof and that bed to these wasn't fair. This place aimed to cater to a particular clientele, not the entire bed-and-breakfast, but specifically this room. It was more lavishly decorated than the rest and cost a lot, Simon was sure, even with a discount. In Ransol, the accommodation he often stayed in was sentimental and cost nothing.

Simon exhaled and sank into the refreshing water he had been enjoying for half an hour. He looked up, examining the floral mural across the ceiling for the third time, and then glanced back at the door.

Andreas had told Simon that he was heading out to grab something to eat and some wine and to give Simon some time for 'peace and quiet.' Andreas insisted on it, despite Simon's complaints that it was unnecessary. Peace and quiet were unfamiliar concepts to Simon. He had seen others enjoy them but never experienced or thought about them.

Andreas' suggestion made him wonder about the man's background. Andreas hadn't shared much besides his city, a male friend, and his bird. For someone who seemed to have connections in places like *this* and talked about luxuries such as *'peace and quiet,'* ... Andreas wasn't very trusting. The little details were lovely, but Simon was interested in learning Andreas' skill set and general information, such as age and experience in combat. They were details that Andreas adeptly danced around, almost as if it were intentional.

"I wonder what you're hiding, Red..." Simon mumbled, looking towards the bag left atop the sofa.

If he were someone else, he would rummage through it, not for money, but to see if any weapons were stashed. He felt tempted but wasn't known for forcing secrets out unless he was getting paid. He was **not** getting paid to pry details out of an unwilling party, so he would leave it until it endangered his life and see if he got lucky.

Simon yawned and rubbed his eyes. The warm water and essential oils made him sleepy, which he didn't like. Maybe this was one of those dreadful parts of 'peace and quiet.' He needed to get up, dry off, and go downstairs before he fell asleep and potentially drowned himself. He could see if that fancy glass lived up to the hype. He'd heard about it countless times and seen it in a random shop once or twice for an outrageous price, but he had never looked through it. He didn't have that kind of money.

Hell, he didn't have **this** kind of money.

His eyes glanced around the room absentmindedly. This train of thought prompted Simon to reach into the water and pull the chained plug so it could drain. He stood up, grabbed the folded towel from the table beside the claw-foot tub, and started drying himself off.

As he wandered through the room, he dressed, hoping the door would open so he could spook his roommate. He would admit, at least to himself, that Andreas was *attractive*. He had thought this upon their first meeting, and if they hadn't both grabbed the same notice, he had been debating striking up a conversation regardless. Ultimately, he was glad they both grabbed the notice because he had fallen short of suitable topics to bring up.

Simon paused to dry off his hair and looked towards the door. He waited, lost in a daydream. Andreas seemed *jumpy*, and from the few flirtatious quips he'd dropped on the half-elf, Simon wondered just what kind of face Andreas would make if he happened to walk in and catch him naked.

Sadly, no one knocked, and Simon got bored of dawdling.

The sun was setting below the horizon, and he could hear the city coming to life in the streets below. He remembered that Belmare was very active both during the day and night. A myriad of musical instruments swelled from the streets below and caught the orc's ear. It wasn't a terrible place to settle down, he'd admit. The people he'd seen here all believed in the lingering sense of safety, and they seemed willing to enjoy their daily lives without thinking of the danger that sat only an hour or more outside the city walls.

Simon paused, glancing at the tower shield he always kept with him. He considered whether to bring it downstairs but, in the end, decided to embrace the brief moment of 'peace and quiet' he had been encouraged to enjoy. The shield wasn't far away if something happened, and he had other talents; his size made him a difficult target to intimidate.

Actually…

The mismatched eyes peered around, looking at the ceiling, then the doorway's height, before inspecting the furniture in the room. Simon pondered, as he hadn't thought about it before. However, he was confident he hadn't needed to duck to get into this room. The room, which didn't feel stuffy, appeared designed with someone of larger stature in mind. The more he thought about it, the more he recalled Andreas had looked tiny against the sofa's size. For a moment, the man's gaze fixated on the preserved flowers.

"Guess you Primals are big, huh?" he said, his voice strained.

There was a twinge in his gut, and his lips frowned. Something about the train of thought seemed to irritate him. Simon sighed and shoved away the thoughts as he headed out the door and descended the stairs.

*****

As Simon reached the ground floor, the sound of chatting patrons and the gentle strumming of a lute filled the air. He glanced into the spacious room brimming with tables, food, and about twenty scattered faces.

One thing he'd give Belmare credit for was its diversity. There were people from many different backgrounds and with various levels of wealth. They all seemed to mingle with one another without any hesitation. Too often, he had been in cities or towns where an unspoken barrier made it difficult to interact freely, depending on your occupation or place of origin.

He didn't feel anyone would care when he walked into the next room.

Simon scanned the other customers, looking for a flash of red hair and vibrant skin. Surprisingly, his roommate was nowhere to be found. Something seemed suspicious, so the thirty-two-year-old changed tactics and searched for the halfling woman who owned the place. Fortunately, she wasn't challenging to find; he spotted her at the front desk. Selbi sat on a stack of books, inspecting a giant ledger, and appeared to be counting coins.

Simon approached and said, "Excuse me."

Selbi looked up, adjusted the bottle-like glasses on her slight nose, and smiled. "Hello. Are you looking for Anni?"

Simon flashed a smile and said, "You caught me."

The halfling let out a squeaky laugh, closed her ledger, and quickly got down from her seat. After a moment, she walked around the desk holding a ring of keys. Selbi gestured for Simon to follow her and said, "Come with me. He's out back."

Simon nodded and followed the older woman, muttering, "Of course he is."

As they made their way through the room, the mercenary finally noticed the stares from the patrons. Additionally, the lute had fallen silent, creating an awkward atmosphere. Simon's gaze darted from one person to another, checking for signs of hostility and second-guessing his earlier assumptions. To his surprise, he realized that the onlookers seemed genuinely intrigued rather than hostile, which puzzled him more than it concerned him.

"That's not Rhys," muttered a human woman to a dwarven male sitting beside her at a table near the back door.

Simon furrowed his brow. The name sounded familiar, but he couldn't remember why. Somewhere in his gut, he felt he *should* know why... but his mind drew a blank.

When they reached the backdoor, he watched Selbi turn and wave her hands at the whole room, almost purposefully scolding them. Then, the patrons seemed to filter back to what they were doing prior with little fuss.

"That one has a reputation. Not very surprising, Bella," muttered the dwarven male.

Simon glanced at the dwarven male, who responded to the human woman after a short delay. As they resumed their conversation, he heard the door click and felt a small hand patting his leg. Turning his attention to the older woman beside him, he was tempted to ask who they were talking about and why the name they mentioned sounded familiar.

"Pay them no mind, dear. They enjoy gossiping about Anni," Selbi said.

"Should I be concerned?" Simon questioned, daring to take another look around the room. Gossip was one thing, but the reason *behind* it was what interested him more. "He's not planning to kill me in my sleep, is he?"

Selbi chuckled and said, "Anni? No. He's a good boy from a well-respected family. They like to stir up anything about them they can."

"Which family?" Simon asked, feeling both intrigued and concerned.

Selbi smiled at him, saying, "If he hasn't told you, it's not my place."

Simon felt the woman pat his leg once more, and then she pushed him to urge him forward. He paused briefly before entering the patio through the doorway. Simon heard the door click behind him and a lock turn as he examined the stone wall he had just passed through. The door was made of thick wood without any cracks or windows, giving the impression that the owner was selective about who could access the area. He grunted and turned to survey his surroundings.

What he discovered left him breathless and filled his eyes with wonder.

It was a pretty spacious area, large enough to fit a table that could hold eight to ten people and had enough room for other tables to be placed around it. The walls weren't walls; they were glass panels. The entire space was nothing but metallic beams and glass. It seemed situated on the edge of the stony cliffs that partially surrounded Belmare and overlooked the ocean. There was an endless wash of vibrant colors as the dull light of golden hour crested over the space.

The sky appeared flawless, revealing a sea of stars beyond the setting sun's light. The absence of clouds and the dissipation of haze from the surrounding desert's dry heat made the ocean look clearer and brighter blue than ever before. Simon was amazed, unable to move from where he stood as he took it all in, sucking in a breath.

So, this was *Spellglass*? It had a mystical quality that evoked wonder and awe; it was simply beautiful.

"Pretty, right?"

Simon's attention was suddenly drawn away from the stunning sight he had stumbled upon, and he quickly scanned the room. He spotted Andreas sitting in a wooden chair near some sunflowers, gazing at the ocean with a bottle beside him. Andreas seemed *relaxed* as he braided his hair and tossed it over his shoulder.

Simon furrowed his brow; he was sure he had not seen Andreas look relaxed yet. He watched in fascination, carefully observing the details of Andreas' clothes and the nuances of his skin. Andreas had faint freckles, which gave his cheeks a slight golden hue, and his hair wasn't just crimson but had a variety of shades of red. The gold threading in much of his clothing, which Simon hadn't noticed before, seemed to sparkle.

The man appeared entirely comfortable in this setting, as though he belonged there, and Simon allowed himself to think he might never see Andreas the same way elsewhere.

Andreas furrowed his brows and cleared his throat before asking, "Simon, did you die?"

"Maybe," the mismatched eyes watched the emeralds curiously before looking around. Simon stepped forward with his hands shoved into his pockets to keep them from feeling large and out of place at his side. "This is not what I expected."

Andreas replied, "It's quite overwhelming for most people the first time they see it. Do you see why I suggested waiting until the sun went down?"

Simon nodded, found a chair, and pulled it over. He turned it to face its back and leaned against it with his chest. Now, he understood that seeing this in the full light of day would have been blinding. He may *have* died.

"Yeah. I do," Simon said.

Andreas passed the wine bottle and gestured towards another glass before saying, "Just wait until the sun sets. You can see all the stars, even the ones you rarely spot. There's cosmic dust, and I swear you can make out the edge of the universe... It's beautiful."

The words had a sense of wonder, and Simon noticed it immediately. Excitement, much less *wonder*, wasn't something he'd heard in the other's words all day. He'd thought Andreas was a bit on edge. Simon reached down and swiped the glass, filling it with red wine.

"Well, that makes sense..."

Andreas looked over, curious.

Simon gestured at the figure beside him. "You fit right in."

Andreas looked down, feeling self-conscious. "I don't know about that."

Simon tilted his head and said, "You look like you could eat the sun in this place."

Andreas chortled, feeling nervous under Simon's lingering gaze and subtle flirtatious behavior. "I don't think Mithir would appreciate that," he stammered.

Stillness filled the space between them.

When Andreas dared to glance up, he found Simon staring into the sky toward the sea. The man appeared content while watching the large star vanish below the horizon as if he had done it many times before. Andreas tilted his head in thought.

Simon seemed gentle and approachable, unlike his initial appearance. The orc looked as though he belonged in the sun at all times. His sandy skin had an almost faceted appearance reminiscent of gemstones. Even the golden jewelry seemed to glow as if it could melt at any moment.

Andreas took a sip from his glass and said, "Selbi always says you can see others for who they are here. The light that filters through the glass has its properties. I don't know if I believe it, but..."

"If that's the real you, no wonder they gossip. They're jealous."

Andreas swallowed, his shoulders stiffening as his voice cracked. "Gossip?"

"You have a reputation, Red. Not that I could get many details from the lady," Simon smirked and leaned towards Andreas. "Maybe you can help me?" he asked.

Andreas shifted, uneasy.

Of course, others would talk ... he wasn't *unknown* in this city.

His gaze fell, unwilling to meet the two-toned eyes observing him. He slumped back into his chair and fiddled with the end of his braid in his free hand. After a moment, Andreas collected his thoughts and muttered, "I may have a reputation for sleeping around. Just a small one."

Simon snorted, "That's better than being a murderer. If that's all, I can relax."

Of course, that made perfect sense. Why would you be on close terms with a bed-and-breakfast owner? Especially to the point that she gave you a discount on rooms unless you were bringing her business. And looking like **that**... Simon glanced at the nervous face beside him and chuckled.

Pretty was always pretty, and pretty things always drew a lot of attention—some terrible, some wonderful, sometimes even unwanted. Simon let the thoughts linger and swallowed the nasty taste left from the last one. The idea of unwanted attention didn't sit well with him and seemed more than likely correct, considering the whispers in the other room.

Andreas continued to fiddle with his hair, avoiding eye contact. "I don't want to make you uncomfortable or cause trouble with your partner," he said hesitantly.

"Partner? Who said I had a partner?"

Andreas looked up and saw Simon watching with a grin. "You. You said," he said.

Simon laughed out loud. "You thought I meant *that* kind of partner... Selbi's right, you're a good kid."

Andreas blushed in embarrassment, his ears turning red. "I'm twenty-six. I'm not a kid, thank you," he said, sitting up straight and glaring at the man beside him. "Besides, anyone could have that kind of partner. It's not impossible to find someone appealing, right?"

The emeralds grew. It had only been a moment, but Andreas had seen a look cross the other's face. It was challenging to place, but he was sure it sat in sorrow or discomfort.

Simon appeared dull, as if an unpleasant thought had crossed his mind.

Andreas frowned, feeling confused and wondering if he had said something wrong. He had a talent for noticing the hidden, seemingly unimportant details others missed and unintentionally revealed. Maybe it was because his Pops and Papa had influenced him, or he paid attention. Regardless … Simon was trying to **hide** something.

Simon sighed and wiped the sour expression from his face. "I guess… No, though. I **don't** have that kind of partner," he said, rolling his shoulders and leaning closer. "Does that change our agreement?"

Andreas focused on the end of his braid, avoiding the man's eyes above him. He was self-conscious and worried about making the man uncomfortable again. "Oh. Well, good. Great. I don't either," the words came out rushed and chaotic, and Andreas swallowed.

Why had he phrased it like that?

Simon snorted and took another sip of wine. "So, you're twenty-six?" he asked.

"Yeah, my birthday just passed recently," Andreas responded.

"Mmm. Six and a half years then, huh?" Simon pondered over the words.

"Wait, what?" Andreas asked.

"They'll think you like older men now, Red," Simon teased, grinning.

Andreas flushed. "*Of course,* you're talking about age differences."

Simon laughed, his tusks rubbing under his eyes. "Get ready to be teased a lot," he said.

Andreas scoffed and settled down to sulk. "It's a good thing I'm used to that."

Simon glanced over at the other man. It seemed like he was considering saying something else, maybe teasing Andreas further. However, he just laughed and then looked back up at the sky. The light was fading, and the stars were beginning to appear. The edges of the horizon were gradually disappearing from his sight.

Twenty-six. No partner.

Well, it was a start.

Five

Charming

"You know the sun is not even up yet, right?" Simon grumbled, yawning as he followed his companion out of **The Green Dragon** and into the sleeping city of Belmare. It was late, or rather early morning, maybe two hours before sunrise. Andreas had woken him up by shaking him, and Keena had pecked his forehead. He was still pretty sure that she had drawn blood despite her owner insisting she hadn't.

"Yes, that is the point," Andreas rolled his eyes, laughing as he watched the taller man rub where Keena had pecked. "She didn't break the skin… or much of it," he said.

Simon appeared unsure, glanced at his palm for blood, and then readjusted his belongings higher on his shoulder. "You keep saying that, and I continue to doubt it."

When Andreas peeked into his shirt, he found Keena tucked safely inside, still sleeping.

He smiled and led the way toward the main gate. Since a few citizens had seen him the night before, he did not leave anything to chance. He was supposed to be on the way to visit his grandparents, but he didn't want the entire city to see him walking around with a six-foot-eight orc. While it might strengthen the story he and his sister were trying to sell, it could also lead to his father trying to hunt him down for *other* reasons.

Simon was the type of man Andreas usually went for—the kind he took back to the bed-and-breakfast. He might have exaggerated this when he was talking to Selbi. He was trying to keep quiet about these details, as he had already been teased enough for eight hours.

"Have you forgotten that it's better to travel in the desert when it's cooler? You've been there before, so you should know better," Andreas said as he noticed Simon's embarrassed reaction.

"Alright, maybe you know a thing or two," Simon grumbled, rubbing his neck.

"I told you last night. It's not like I've never left the city before, Simon."

Simon sighed. "Maybe, but you certainly haven't given me much to rely on regarding what you **can** do. We're heading out of your safety barriers," he motioned to the enormous walls that wrapped around Belmare and connected to the sandstone cliffs, "out into the desert and later into the mountains. If the weather is favorable, it's a week-and-a-half journey to Fossy from here. There are a lot of creatures between here and there, Red."

Andreas glared. "I'm aware. There's everything from diseased coyotes to sandworms. I've probably seen some creatures you haven't encountered before—" His heated words stopped abruptly before revealing too much.

Simon grumbled and rubbed the back of his neck as he tried to think of what to say. "Look, I'm not implying you can't fight. You just haven't given me much to work with to prove *otherwise*." The heterochromatic gaze fell on the half-elf's hands, and he zeroed in on the fingerless gloves he had still not seen taken off since their meeting. "The gloves. Are you an archer? They typically help with gripping, right? Your fingers look calloused."

Andreas defensively rubbed his calloused fingertips together, not expecting anyone to notice. He frowned and glared at the man walking to his left, grumbling under his breath, "Sort of."

"Sort of?"

Andreas rolled his eyes. "Sort of. I'm just not the best at aiming. My hands shake, so I rarely hit where I mean to."

Alright, they were getting somewhere, at least.

Simon shrugged, saying, "It sounds like you just need to practice more."

Andreas frowned and responded rather dryly, "**Sure,** we can say that."

His eyes fell to his hands, and he stared at the fabric covering his palms and wrists. He fell into silence and chewed on his bottom lip. There was nothing he liked about this topic, and he felt even worse about feeling useless. Simon could change his mind about working with him if he decided he was ineffective in a fight.

"I have a particular skill set," Andreas stated.

"With ... any weapons?" Simon asked.

Andreas looked up and examined the figure following him, annoyed. "I don't see any weapons on *you* either," he snapped.

Simon tapped the shield on his back and grinned. "That's all I need," he stated.

Andreas glared, then focused on getting them out of the main gate. He didn't care if this conversation fell flat and got left behind in the city.

* * *

Andreas inquired, "Do you have a match or a candle? Something you can light with a flame?"

"I have some flint?" Simon narrowed his eyes, confused by the sudden question.

"Alright ... let me try something else then. Stay here."

Andreas quickened his pace, putting some distance between them. He checked to see if Simon had listened, and thankfully, the orc did, despite his confusion.

"I don't know what you're doing, but," Simon started to speak.

"I have a dagger, and a bow. I'm just not good at using them."

Simon jumped and looked around, searching for his companion, who was supposed to be fifteen feet away. He found Andreas standing in the same spot ahead of him and debated whether he was going mad. The mercenary considered the words whispered in his ear, and his brow furrowed deeper. "Either I'm losing it, or you did some funny shit, Red."

Andreas laughed as if he had heard him and tapped the bag on his thigh. He vanished from where he was and reappeared beside Simon in a burst of embers. Simon opened his mouth to speak, but no words came out. Instead, he lifted a finger and pointed to where the other had been and where he now stood.

"*Magic*," Simon whispered in disbelief.

Andreas smiled. "Yes. Magic," he said.

Simon seemed impressed and said, "I can't do any of that, so I think that makes up for the poor aim and not being skilled with a dagger."

"I'm not *that* proficient at it; I can't control it all the time. I only learned I could use it about seven months ago, and it's a rather unpredictable variety," Andreas shrugged and looked down at his hands. He twisted his fingers a bit. "My Papa thinks I've had it since I was born but never had the stamina for it until recently."

"Your dad sounds smart," Simon stated.

"Oh, no. Grandfather. I call my grandfather Papa, and my father I call Pops."

Simon nodded, filing the information away as he absorbed all that had happened in three minutes. He inhaled, held his breath in his lungs for a second or two, and then started walking as he exhaled. "So, has poor bow aim and can't control magic."

Andreas fell in step with Simon and smiled sheepishly. "I'm talented at telling if people are lying, and I could probably steal something out of your bag right now without you even knowing. ... I've also been told I'm *very* charming," he said.

The last few words caused Simon to burst into laughter. "Well, I'll give you the last bit."

Andreas teased, "Oh? Do you think I'm charming?" He sidestepped to bump into the figure by his side.

Simon smirked, avoiding eye contact with the shorter man. He was intrigued by Andreas' charm and found his remark amusing despite his reluctance to acknowledge it.

It wasn't as comforting as knowing Andreas could take out someone from a hundred yards away without being detected, but having someone with a bit of magic wouldn't be so bad. He had seen those who could channel wonders do some crazy things.

"A kind of archer and a sort of sorcerer with a mercenary who only uses a shield," Andreas chuckled. "We make an intriguing duo, at the very least."

"Sounds like you just need to kill things…" Simon met the emerald gaze and grinned. "And I'll keep them from killing *you*."

Andreas tilted his head, pleased with the response. "You sound **very** sure of yourself."

Why exactly he did it, he didn't know. Maybe Simon felt that his abilities were being doubted, or he needed to *impress* the man at his side. Either way, Simon moved; his right foot slipped out to trip the sorcerer, and his left arm grabbed the shield from his back. Perhaps it was because Andreas hadn't expected it, or the orc moved too suddenly for him to react. Either way, it worked.

Andreas fell backward toward the sand as Simon kicked his feet from under him. Before he could react, Simon's arm caught him. The light from the stars and the face of the moon, Karanos, dimmed behind a gigantic shadow. The sandy features that were usually above him suddenly faced him, and the different-colored eyes looked at him with a smoldering enthusiasm.

Simon tightened his grip on Andreas' waist and leaned in with the shield he had raised to block out the fading starlight until their noses almost touched. The pale freckles he had noticed the evening before were visible to him but appeared less vibrant without sunlight. As the crimson wave washed over the face near his, he reveled in the fact that he had effortlessly made Andreas' features match his hair.

"I am **very** confident in my ability to keep you alive," Simon said, his voice deeper than usual.

Andreas' brain stopped working as the man's firm grip caught his waist, and the man's tusks came close enough for him to feel Simon's breath across his cheeks. He swallowed and felt his whole body light up like a firework at a festival at the words. There was a spark in his gut, and he was terrified to move lest he bump the larger body against his uncomfortably. He bit his lip, and his eyes darted from the lips speaking to him, then back towards the eyes, watching him like a hawk.

His thoughts were in disarray, and Andreas blurted out his words without considering their impact. "Reliability is a desirable trait," he said. Instantly, his blush deepened in embarrassment.

Simon's face smirked as he tightened his grip on the smaller waist. His eyes scanned over the scattered freckles, and he noticed the embarrassed realization that flooded his counterpart's face. For a moment, Simon appeared to consider commenting on the reaction or doing something else as he started to lean forward.

Before he could, a blue ball shot up and began screeching. Keena had woken up in time to see Simon looming over her owner as if he intended to harm him.

"Keena!" Andreas called out as the tiny bird screeched, flapping her wings into Simon's face.

Simon grimaced and jolted back from her talons, dropping Andreas.

Andreas struggled to regain his balance, almost falling, and winced as he saw the bird peck at one of Simon's eyes and miss.

"**Keena!**"

Keena chirped, swiveling her head back towards her owner and giving what could only be a look of disapproval. She then looked in Simon's direction, screeched again, and flew to Andreas' head. She landed, settled into his hair, and angrily puffed out her feathers. Once there, her beady eyes zeroed in on Simon, daring him to come closer.

Andreas glanced up with a scowl. "You're being rude," he said before returning to Simon. "Are you okay? Did she catch your eye?"

He found Simon watching, not the bird, but *him* with appeal. There was no hint of disgust or annoyance, only pure and joyful intrigue as the orc put his shield away. Andreas shuddered as the familiar spark in his gut flared up again. He had only experienced this feeling when he looked over the job board at home and contemplated stealing one and going off into the world.

He daydreamed of doing anything outside the shadow of his family name.

... ***This was outside his family's name***.

The interaction just now wasn't about his family. It wasn't about who he was or what could be gained from him. It was about him and Simon, who had chosen to tease him for no reason other than *wanting* to.

Andreas tugged at his braid, feeling warm as he twisted it. His face burned, and he swallowed and started walking as fast as his feet could carry him. "We should keep going. The sun will be up soon," he said, nearly yelling the words out in a hurry.

Simon watched the short interaction with a growing smile as he secured his shield. He let Andreas get a few feet ahead before following, feeling excited. He hadn't expected his playful gesture to elicit such a response, but it was... charming. 'Charming' was a fitting word he would no doubt use to describe his traveling companion again.

Simon snickered to himself and quickened his pace to catch up.

Six

Change

"What the hell is that?" Simon whispered.

He flattened himself against the stone cliff they had chosen to rest on for the night. One moment, they had been huddled around a fire, and he was telling a story about Ransol, and then they heard this annoying yipping. He'd been sure it was a wounded or dying fox. However, Andreas hadn't been too confident and had put out their tiny fire before forcing him to the ground.

He had thought Andreas was foolish, but a mere five minutes later, he had seen the strange creature they were now watching **appear** seventy feet below them on the rocks—a beast he had never seen before.

It was quadrupedal and seemed fox-like despite its large size. Its legs were too long for its body, and the fur covering it was shaggy. Its coloration seemed to change; one moment, it appeared off-white, while the next, it was almost a tawny or sandy color. It moved jerkily, shifting around like it existed in several places simultaneously. The creature's eyes were a bright, icy blue and streaked like they were aflame or moving fast enough to leave light trails. Its maw was vast and oversized, and when opened, its lips curled back and exposed massive rows of teeth with two-foot-long saber-like canines.

Andreas' eyes widened as he swallowed, locking onto the beast below them. His heart rate increased, and without thinking, he reached out and clutched the man's sleeve at his side. *"Mistwalker."*

Simon glanced over, not because of the whispered word but because he felt the hand clutching his sleeve shaking. He observed Andreas, noting his strained features and how he flattened himself down. There was fear and terror; the distinction between the two was a line he had encountered many times. The emotion pouring out of his companion right now was pure *terror*.

"You know these things, Red?" Simon asked.

Andreas jumped and reached over to press his finger against Simon's lips. *"Shhh,"* he whispered. He nodded to the west, into the darker part of the desert, where three more sets of blue eyes were racing.

The creature nearest to them raised its head and looked around. Its ears swiveled, listening to the surroundings. It then barked into the darkness, and a chorus replied.

Andreas focused on the creature's behavior, momentarily forgetting his terror. He had never seen them exhibit a pack mentality before.

"Andreas."

Andreas jerked, and his eyes returned to Simon. It seemed like he had momentarily lost awareness of his body, but now he was fully conscious of the firm grip on his wrist and the arm that had slid on top of him. Andreas tugged on his arm, and Simon immediately released it, but the man's arm remained across his back.

Andreas glanced back, checking if the creature was still there, and felt bile rise in his throat when he saw another one. ***"We need to leave. Now,"*** he whispered.

"We don't have anywhere to go," Simon whispered, nodding to the surrounding space. They were atop a rock formation that soared maybe a hundred feet into the air. They had climbed up around seventy feet to avoid danger. The closest spot to jump from was inaccessible, and descending the rocks without making a sound was equally impossible. *"Are they smart?"* he finally inquired.

Andreas furrowed his brow deeply as he watched the creatures, pondering how one would define intelligence, and whispered, *"Average."*

Simon pressed closer to the ground, his gaze fixed on the creatures below them.

The Mistwalkers sniffed around and let out small yips of varying pitch before wandering around in circles.

Simon was grateful for the magic Andreas had insisted on using as they approached their campsite. It was supposed to make it more difficult for them to be found and to clear out any hints of their presence. From what he could tell, the creatures had a faint scent, but they weren't sure where it led. He knew nothing about them, but based on other pack animals, they appeared to be... *"Hunting?"*

Andreas sank against the rocks and shook his head.

He had never seen these creatures hunt, especially not in a pack. They only followed simple, single-minded orders. He started to speak but felt the arm over his back apply pressure and saw Simon nod towards the ground. He dared to glance up and noticed three beasts circling away from their rock formation and toward the next one.

"Wait it out," Andreas whispered.

***

Simon nudged the figure under his arm, and Andreas jumped. He was still skittish, and Simon noticed another tremor shake his body. This was the main reason he'd kept his arm there. Anxiety gripped him, fearing that Andreas would suddenly spring up and bolt. Simon nodded towards the ground and whispered, *"Your eyes are probably better."*

Andreas cursed his elven heritage, which probably made it true. He sat up, peered over the vast space below, and scanned the scattered desert around him. He saw nothing and couldn't hear anything except the wind stirring around them. *"I think they're gone."*

Simon nodded and stepped away from the edge of the rocks, moving towards the rising cliff face behind him. He preferred to have his back against something and didn't want to be caught off guard. As he looked up and listened, he didn't like the thought of something surprising them from above. However, climbing any higher might attract more attention than they wanted.

Andreas slumped against the cliff, stiff as he pulled his knees up to his torso and wrapped his arms around them.

"Fire?" Simon whispered, wondering if Andreas was cold.

Andreas shivered and whispered back, "*No. Fire scares them, but they might see it.*"

Simon nodded, reached for his bag, rummaged around, and found a blanket. He tossed it over and whispered, "*I'll take the first watch. Sleep.*"

Sleep. He wasn't sure if he could sleep. Andreas accepted the blanket and wrapped it around himself. He wasn't freezing, but it was more for comfort than anything. When he was younger, he had done the same thing when something scared him: he curled up under blankets and hid. "*I'll try,*" he whispered.

Simon looked over. "*Is this a creature thing ... or **them** thing?*"

"*A **them** thing,*" Andreas whispered back, annoyed.

He understood what Simon was suggesting. Simon was asking whether he intended to continue being unreliable if they encountered any other situations, and deep down, he felt angry—not at Simon, but at himself. The fact that the question had to be raised was infuriating and embarrassing.

Simon cleared his throat, breaking the silence between the two. His gaze remained on the world around them as he asked, "*You called those Mistwalkers?*"

"*Yeah ... they're Mistwalkers.*"

"*Aren't those the beasts that abducted children during the war?*" Simon asked and glanced downward.

Andreas grimaced and looked up to meet his gaze. "*Yeah. That's them.*"

A thoughtful expression crossed the orc's face as if he were processing the presence of the creatures and the information that they were still lurking around. He had heard of them but had never seen them up close; any stories he'd heard of them provided little detail. There was always an unspoken terror as if mentioning the creatures by name would somehow summon them.

It seemed odd for Mistwalkers to be so far away from a city and even stranger to be so close to Belmare. He had never heard any stories about Belmare being targeted by those creatures. It had always been poor areas without the means to defend themselves, where most people wouldn't notice an orphan vanishing off the street.

"Are you sure?" Simon asked.

Anger flared within him, and Andreas' voice rose above a whisper. "Yes. I am **sure**. I'm **very** familiar with those nasty shits."

"Okay, okay. Calm down." Simon huffed back, glaring at the sudden outburst.

Andreas fumed, his eyes narrowed in agitation before looking back at the ground. He'd know those creatures anywhere. That's why he had been so frantic about extinguishing the fire. He'd hoped they hadn't noticed it.

… Granted, those things being *here* was odd.

Andreas bit his lip, chewed it in thought, and winced when he tasted blood. He lifted a hand and wiped it before exhaling. "They were acting strange, though. They've never worked together before. Back in the war, they were single-target focused, but not with a joint focus. They just snatched and ran with anything they could sink their teeth into."

"Come again?" Simon questioned, attention drawn to Andreas abruptly.

Andreas carefully chose his words, "I've only seen them follow superficial orders and act independently. I've never seen them act as a pack or exhibit hunting behavior before. They just took kids and killed everyone else," he said as he felt his body grow cold and absentmindedly started rubbing his hands.

"So maybe it's not them?" Simon sounded more skeptical now.

Andreas leaped to his feet, dropping the blanket. He was on edge and didn't appreciate being second-guessed by someone he barely knew, much less about something he knew intimately. ***"I am positive those are Mistwalkers!"***

His voice echoed around the space, bouncing off the cavernous walls and returning. This made the whole exclamation more intense and fueled the manic irritation in his body. A small explosive had been set off within him; the doubt growing in his companion's words made him feel like a child. Why was it so difficult for others to believe he was capable? Somehow, this entire exchange felt like another he'd had with his father countless times. It made him dizzy, and he ground his teeth.

Andreas locked eyes with Simon and exclaimed, "Things can change! People can *change*! I'm not some city boy you have to protect from monsters in the dark! They **are** Mistwalkers!"

Change... **Changed**.

Andreas focused on the words, trying to catch his breath.

Oh no, the Mistwalkers had changed their behavior.

Simon spoke, but Andreas didn't hear the words clearly, only muffled chatter. As his attention settled on the ground at his feet, he realized the weight of his words. His heart rate increased, and his ears rang. His breathing became shallow and labored as panic set in. No, no. If they changed their behavior, that meant something had changed. *Or someone altered them.*

"Andreas!" Simon snapped and shook the other's shoulders. He stood up when he noticed Andreas go pale, and tremors overtook his body as they had before. *Terror.* Something about these things terrified this man, and Simon didn't understand.

Andreas reacted to the sudden shake of his shoulders before he heard his name. His eyes were frantic as he spotted Simon looking down at him in concern. He inhaled; he needed to tell his parents.

Keena. He needed to send Keena.

Andreas pulled away and rushed to his belongings, ignoring Simon's concerned look and mumbled words. He searched for a piece of parchment and some charcoal to write with. After finding both, he started writing, detailing the behavior.

"Keena!"

The small bird chirped as she rose from her nest in his shirt. Keena seemed to hear his tone of voice and recognize it. She ignored Simon and fluttered to look up at her owner, her little eyes focused on giving him her full attention.

Andreas handed her a mealworm and tied a small pouch to her leg. He folded the parchment until it was a square the size of a gold piece and slipped it into the tiny bag. His eyes watched her intently, unblinking. "I need you to take this to Pops. If you can't find him, give it to Mom, and she'll tell him. Do not get hurt. It's urgent, okay?"

Keena fluffed her feathers and chirped in understanding.

"Pops," Andreas repeated, emphasizing who the note was intended for.

Keena chirped and tilted her head to acknowledge, her small eyes determined.

"Be careful," Andreas said as he picked her up and kissed her on the head. Then, he threw her into the air. He watched her catch the breeze and fly off as quickly as her wings could carry her to the south, back towards Belmare.

After a moment, Simon cleared his throat.

Andreas jumped. In his flurry of action, he had forgotten Simon was there. He looked back nervously, unsure what to say or how to explain.

This constant lack of information had become exhausting. This information was too crucial to dance around, impacting his ability to live comfortably with all his limbs. Simon glared with his arms crossed and asked, "Are you about to fucking fill me in?"

Andreas avoided meeting Simon's eye and instead focused all his attention on the end of the braid in his hand. He was twisting it, nervous.

Simon narrowed his gaze. "Remember how I said: 'You kill them, and I'll keep them from killing you'?"

Andreas was startled by Simon's tone of voice and noticed the distance between them had decreased.

Simon's upper lip curled, making his tusks jut out somewhat intimidatingly. He didn't like being ignored for no good reason.

Andreas swallowed and nodded, stammering, "I do ... yeah."

Simon glared and spat, "*I can't do my job if you withhold critical information.*" He forced himself to breathe, trying to maintain his heart rate. "If they **are** Mistwalkers, and they have changed behavior. Then what the fuck are they hunting? Kids? **Out here**?!" Simon's hand swiped the surrounding air.

"I don't…" Andreas shifted as he tried to think the words over. He knew it made little sense because, of course, there weren't any kids out here. If there were children out here, they'd be long dead before those things found them.

So, what were they hunting?

There was a sudden dread as something fell into place, something important that had been forgotten; it was as if a core memory had been pulled from a closet in his mind. Andreas looked up, his eyes wide and his voice trembling. "… **Me**."

Seven

Memory

The uncomfortable silence had settled between them over the past few days. Every time they stopped to make camp, it became more noticeable. It was so unbearable that Simon had wandered around for hours in the trees before returning with firewood many times.

They had found an isolated clearing near the edge of the mountains, far enough off the main road to avoid passersby. They would be heading into the *Smolder Ridge Mountains* in the morning, which meant they were halfway to their destination. The mountains were part of the journey that would either slow them down or force them to encounter something they didn't want to face again.

Andreas watched Simon stoke the fire and sit across from him on the other side of the flames.

Simon grabbed the kettle they'd been using for coffee and poured himself a cup.

Being at the base of the mountains meant that the climate was no longer dry and humid but colder, with snow lingering further into the peaks as you traveled. Winter, after all, had a few more weeks before ending.

Andreas wasn't sure if it was the mountains, the temperature change, or the unspoken tension between them, but Simon seemed more on edge than the night before. As a result, Andreas was in a sour mood. It didn't help that he hadn't heard from his parents, so he didn't know if Keena had made it there safely or not.

Andreas tightened his grip on the mug in his hand and pulled the shawl around his shoulders. He moved closer to the fire, enjoying the warmth from the newly added wood. His gaze fixated on the flickering flames, and he lost himself in their dance. The scent of the trees and the chilly air reminded him of living in the mountains with his grandparents. Before the pub was constructed in Belmare, his Papa used to keep him and his sister hidden away with Bear, their dog, most of the time. He recalled his Papa telling them stories by the fireplace and how his Papa would make the flames dance and flicker into shapes as he spoke.

It had been something wondrous that had amused Andreas growing up.

Andreas moved the cup of coffee to his left hand and lifted his right hand to make a slight gesture. He saw the campfire flames jump, and then sparks of white fluttered around like dragonflies. He heard a soft sigh and looked up to find Simon watching the images within the fire. Then, as if the raven felt eyes on him, Simon looked up and locked his gaze on Andreas.

"That's a neat trick," Simon muttered, sipping his coffee.

Andreas mustered a halfhearted smile and said, "Thanks." He made another gesture, and the dragonflies transformed into sunflowers. "My Papa used to tell stories and do it."

"So, your grandfather uses magic too?" Simon shifted to be more comfortable, leaning against a dead log behind him. His voice was flat, almost tired, as if he were straining to hold the conversation.

"He can. Differently, though." Andreas replied, sensing the tension in the other man. "Both my grandparents can. My parents can't. My sister can't."

"You have a sister?" Simon asked.

"Yeah, twin sister," Andreas sighed, waved his hand, and changed the flames' colors to deep gold before returning to his cup.

"Those things chase her around too?" Simon asked.

There it was: Andreas had been waiting for the conversation to be brought up again, as he had been less than willing to share much information when everything had happened two nights ago. He took a sip of coffee and watched the embers dance. He knew it wasn't fair to expect someone he barely knew to continue working with him under the circumstances, especially at the risk of life and limb. As Simon said, sharing information was necessary when working together. Moreover, Simon had been forthcoming about himself without being asked, at least in the basics—simple things that would provide understanding without delving too much into his past, **without** disclosing his family name. Andreas could do that much in return.

Andreas exhaled. "Probably, but I don't think I've ever genuinely asked her. All I've thought about is keeping my sister away from them. They took her when we were kids, and I've been protective of her ever since."

Simon fell silent, his gaze fixed on the flickering golden flames. He furrowed his brow and let the stillness linger as he pondered the last words. Andreas' understanding of the creatures and his fear of them made more sense. It didn't shed any light on why they were now hunting the younger man, but like everything else, it was a start. The tension gathering in Simon's shoulders the past few days lessened. He felt the ball of anger and irritation unraveling in his chest. "You got her back," he said.

Andreas chuckled. "No, my Pops found her in one of those **EDEN** experimentation facilities that were shut down on Usphra. I didn't do shit, and I don't think I've ever forgiven myself for it."

Simon gazed at the man across from him as Andreas stared into the fire. Andreas was biting his lip and twisting the end of his braid with his free hand. This topic made the half-elf uncomfortable but piqued Simon's curiosity. Simon tilted his head with interest; he wanted to discuss the subject, if only because Andreas seemed to be trying to avoid it. "You were a kid," he said.

"That isn't an excuse for just accepting she was dead, for giving up on her," Andreas spat back, his hands shifting to grasp his shoulders as he curled in on himself.

Simon scoffed, "You were a **kid**. Kids aren't supposed to have to deal with that kind of shit. Cut yourself some slack—it's not your fucking fault the world is garbage."

Andreas looked up, caught off guard, and stared at the mercenary across from him. Was Simon trying to comfort him? He stared, confused by the sentiment. Simon's face was dark; a valley had slowly formed between his brows. Eventually, the orc looked at the cup in his hand as if pondering his words.

Stillness settled between them again, and Andreas' attention slowly returned to the fire. He found himself getting lost in it, feeling guilty about the memories that were coming back and realizing that he had once again left his sister behind.

"Is that why your family moved to Belmare? Refugees?" Simon asked, breaking the silence abruptly. Andreas looked up, clearly startled by the sudden question. Simon watched him, frowning slightly but interested in continuing their conversation even if he had to force it.

"Sort of. When my sister was taken, we became orphans. My Pops and my Mom saved me, took me in, and then I stayed with a family friend in Belmare. My Pops and Papa discovered my sister and brought her home a few years later. They hadn't planned it and just stumbled upon her. We lived in the mountains after Belmare was attacked and moved back when the war ended. My sister and I didn't see our parents much until the war ended," Andreas said, pulling the shawl around himself tighter, trying to shake off the chill in his body.

He didn't enjoy talking about himself.

"How old were you when they took your sister?" Simon asked as if he were trying to emphasize his earlier comments.

Andreas frowned and stated, "***Ten***. They found her when I was fourteen, and we moved out of the mountains and back to Belmare when I was sixteen."

Simon looked at Andreas sternly as if his point had been proven, and Andreas rolled his eyes in disbelief.

"Did you two come from Belmare before she was taken?" Simon asked finally, his voice much softer than it had been previously.

Andreas recalled, "No, we lived in Pirn. Our birth parents were poor, so we lived in the slums: Topside. I don't know if you've ever been there, but there isn't much protection from creatures above the city's third level. The guards there are horrible, and the leaders don't care about anyone but themselves. Attacks in our neighborhood were common, but that night was awful. **Terrible**." Andreas spat the words out in disgust, agitated as he shifted and pulled a blanket from his belongings around his shoulders.

He hated thinking about this. He loathed remembering. He despised that Simon was right. He had been ten years old. What could a ten-year-old do to creatures double their size and strength? Even when he was small, he had been useless...

Simon exhaled in thought: Pirn. Well, that told him several things.

Pirn was a vast underground city carved from stone beneath the deserts of Redirine. It consisted of numerous levels that extended deep into the earth, with access to several levels restricted to those with work visas or lineage paperwork proving high-ranking family ties. The city had only one entrance, apart from the Lightning Railroad that connected to its hub. The sole entrance was a steep stone staircase leading through the interior slums and a massive gate that sealed off the rest of the city.

He had never been there but heard stories about the city and its outdated class system. The deeper underground you lived, the more important people considered you. Being deeper underground also meant you were safer. Generally, anything past the city's third level was considered secure because it was behind thick gates that closed at sundown. You needed papers to get through that gate. If Andreas' family lived Topside, they were nobodies—at least to the people of Pirn. This meant they were sacrificial lambs to the creatures that roamed the desert, just like those on the second and third levels of the city.

Simon let out a long sigh and leaned his head back against the log behind him. He looked at the sky, absentmindedly counting the stars he could see.

He was trying to process the information and find a reason for the same creatures that had taken Andreas' sister to hunt him. It seemed like the family who took him in was pretty active in the war, based on how they found him and his sister and the mention of them not seeing their parents much. Selbi said they were a respectable family in Belmare, so they had to be connected to the city guard or **The Rose Guard**. That was the only connection he could think of that would place them actively in the war and show that they were from Belmare.

Andreas' reaction to the newly discovered information about those creatures made sense now. If the half-elf had grown up in a family that killed those things, any updated information would be worth passing on. That's what Andreas had done, even though he was terrified of the creatures, and for understandable reasons, it seemed. That would also put Andreas and his family on the hit list of those who owned the Mistwalkers. So, it made sense why the Mistwalkers started hunting him if they caught a whiff of him.

Simon adjusted himself to get more comfortable against the log and watched a shooting star cross the heavens. Part of him wished Andreas would tell him outright, but he had to admit that trying to figure it out stimulated his inquisitive nature in a way that rarely happened. It was frustratingly entertaining. If Andreas were part of a family in that hell of a mix, he would be expected to be careful about what and who he shared information with. *The Rose Guard* ties made the most sense to Simon, as they were the army built under the Primal Cael, and Andreas had mentioned the temple when they were in the city.

"I became an orphan at sixteen. It had nothing to do with the war, just family issues. My mother was killed, and a dwarf named Tembor took me in. I lived with him in Sebree on and off until he passed away when I was twenty-six," Simon spoke softly, his eyes still fixed on the sky. "I now have a whole house that's way too fucking small for me because it's dwarf-sized. I constantly hit my head on the ceiling."

Andreas tried to stifle a laugh and failed; it earned Simon's attention. Simon tilted his head in interest and chuckled. Andreas sighed; the awkward tension between them was fading away. He was glad.

"I'm sorry about your mother and Tembor," Andreas said.

Simon smiled in return and shrugged. "My mother was …" His voice trailed off as if he were fighting to find a word to describe her. Instead, he cleared his throat and sat up, swallowing. "She was *something*. Tembor was old. An old pain in my ass that never stopped harassing me about settling down and giving him grandkids, but he was a good man."

Andreas chuckled and took a sip of his coffee. "He sounds like it," he said.

The atmosphere was filled with a comforting stillness. There wasn't the sense of being balanced on a knife's edge, as if either could snap at a wrong word. They both enjoyed it as they watched the fire. Andreas adjusted the flames back to their original color before conjuring a white spark that coalesced into a bird with trailing feathers soaring through the air.

Simon glanced at the looming mountains before asking, "Do your grandparents live in the *Smolder Ridge* or mountains on another continent?"

Andreas nodded toward the towering peaks behind them. "No, these. They go between their primary home and their home here. You can at least expect a night under a roof up there."

Simon whistled and said, "Sounds like money. Are you sure you *need* these kinds of jobs?"

"Technically, no, but I'm not a fan of relying on my family my whole life. They've done a lot for us already, and my Pops is keen on keeping my sister and me out of the world as much as possible. He's overprotective," Andreas said.

"I think he has a reason to be, based on what you said," Simon added. His words drew the attention of the half-elf across from him. Andreas looked confused, maybe irritated at the idea, and Simon shrugged in response. "Good parents care about their kids' safety, right?"

Andreas pondered the words and then shrugged halfheartedly. "He…" He trailed off as if struggling to find the right way to describe the man. In the end, he shook his head and chuckled. "You haven't met my Pops. He's quite a character. **Always**." Andreas looked up, watching Simon with interest, and asked, "Do you … have siblings?"

Simon looked surprised by the question and sat up. He laughed, almost in disbelief. "Gods no. I wouldn't wish my birth parents on anyone else," he said.

"Did Tembor have kids?" Andreas questioned.

"No, Tembor was a lonely old man who never married. He was part of the royal guard in Sebree and retired. He dedicated his whole life to the family and never considered having one of his own until he found a bumbling teenage orc getting into trouble and picking fights," Simon said, laughing. Genuine joy filled his face.

"I was just a few minutes away from getting on a pirate ship and sailing out. Then, this dwarf kicked me in the knee and dragged me home by the ear, grumbling the whole time. I remember my back killed me for two days because I had been bent so low while walking," Simon said, letting out another fond laugh as if he could see the memory.

Andreas stayed silent, listening and watching as the other man spoke. The firelight cast a warm glow on Simon's sandy complexion, highlighting the joy of the memory visible on his face. For a moment, Simon looked soft again, just as he had when they were on the patio at **The Green Dragon**. The mercenary's manner of speaking about Tembor revealed that Tembor wasn't just an old dwarf who had given him a hard time. There was a sense of fondness, similar to the affection Andreas saw in his sister's face when she talked to their parents. Simon didn't just like the dwarf... he respected him. It was evident from his words.

"I like Tembor," Andreas said.

Simon looked up, his eyes shining, and grinned in a way that caused his tusks to move and wrinkle his eyes. He watched the face across from him, lost in thought. Then he laughed again and said, "Yeah? He would have said you were trouble, Red."

Eight

Piety

The howling started halfway through their journey in the mountains. As time passed, Simon became increasingly anxious. They stopped more than once so that he could listen and determine where to continue. The main road through the peaks was difficult to follow. The pair veered off course multiple times due to the snow and uneven terrain. They were now off the main road, trying to find their way as a storm approached.

Andreas stopped, jerking his head to the right when he heard the howling. It was close, and somewhere in his gut, he recognized it. It was a passing thought, one that he wished wasn't true. Regardless, he reached out to catch Simon's shoulder and prevent him from continuing.

Simon stopped and turned around. "What's up, Red?" he asked, focusing on the treeline.

Andreas nodded to their right at a staggered rock trail leading to a lofty peak, recognizing it as the path to his grandparents' cabin, just an hour away. "Do you remember the roof over your head that I promised?" he said.

Simon looked in the direction indicated and nodded, showing that he understood. "Alright."

Andreas maneuvered past Simon and took the lead. He heard the man behind him take a deep breath and looked over his shoulder with concern.

"What?"

Simon shook his head, his jaw set. "Just be careful. If something comes at us head-on, you're easier to target."

"I take offense to that," Andreas said, glaring, but then he turned and led the way.

* * *

It took another half hour before they stopped to allow Andreas to get his bearings. Their family cabin was hidden deep in the surrounding woods to ensure no one would stumble upon it. It had been a few years since he'd been there, and he had to search his memory to recall the proper way to get there. It didn't help that the snow was falling harder; he was sure he couldn't feel his toes through his boots.

He turned to look at Simon, about to ask a question, when he noticed something. Bright red eyes stared at him from the treeline about forty feet away. "*Son of a bitch. They've been following us downwind,*" Andreas whispered, swallowing hard as the eyes continued to focus on him.

Simon glanced over his shoulder and spotted something in the shadows. "Shit," he muttered.

The following events unfolded quickly. First, Simon shifted his focus between Andreas and the beast lurking in the trees, then grabbed his shield. Second, two more sets of eyes appeared and moved through the trees, seemingly attempting to find a suitable flanking position. Third, the *smell* hit as the creatures pushed out of position and into the wind's direction. It was awful and unyielding. It was overwhelming how fast it came. The scent of rotting flesh, maggoty wounds, old blood, and festering disease filled the air. Andreas felt bile rise in his throat from the stench as a creature stepped onto the snow.

They were large, canine, quadrupedal beasts with thick shoulders. They had black, matted, oily fur falling off in specific areas; there were places where rotting flesh and sinew, broken and discolored bone, peeked through and contrasted against their pelt. The eyes were unblinking and burned against the sharp surrounding white. The sounds they made were a mixture of growl and gurgle. It sounded like blood sat in their throats and disjointed maw. There weren't visible lips, only teeth pushing through melted and decayed flesh.

The Varog, now rare creatures, were familiar to many travelers. There was a rumor that these creatures, which had spread far and wide across the continents during the war, were made to do the bidding of the dead if they could come back and walk.

Simon grimaced. "These things usually come in packs of six or more. … Three I can take. Six might push it."

Andreas watched as the three creatures advanced, their mouths dripping with saliva. He began racking his brain, trying to remember how far they were from his grandparents' land; it couldn't be far now—he was sure of it. He could see the tension building in the beasts as they edged closer; they were running out of time to decide. "I need you to trust me," Andreas said.

"What?" Simon snapped, turning his head to look back at Andreas.

"**I need you to run, Simon**," Andreas said. He looked at Simon and the approaching creatures. He seemed to give the man a moment to consider the words before dodging around him without warning and rushing ahead.

He needed this to work because it was the only thing he could think of to keep the beasts away long enough to give them a head start. Andreas lifted his hands as the creatures rushed forward, and he snapped over his shoulder, "**Run!**"

Simon was about to grab and pull the other man back, but flames rushed forward from Andreas' outstretched palms. He saw the creatures run into the fire, and this deafening yowling erupted in response. The smell only got more intense; for now, it smelled like burning rotten flesh. His stomach churned, and far off, he heard more howling. Simon turned and sprinted in the opposite direction.

A few seconds later, Simon heard approaching footsteps, which abruptly stopped. He realized he was faster than the idiot following him. Simon looked back and saw Andreas running as quickly as he could but still falling behind. Meanwhile, the Varog pack chased and gained ground on the half-elf.

Simon groaned, "Teleport over here, now!"

Andreas looked up and saw that Simon was farther ahead, so he tried to figure out the exact distance. It couldn't be more than thirty feet ahead of him. Hearing a snap behind him, he winced. When he turned around, he caught sight of a snarling, charred face in pursuit of him. He was outmaneuvering them but didn't know how long it would last.

"Shit," Andreas muttered under his breath. Then, a burst of embers sparked around his feet. He heard the creature yelp, and the sound of disjointed paws stopped. Then? He was beside Simon.

It worked.

"Good!" Simon spat.

Andreas looked up when he heard the man next to him speak. Suddenly, his feet left the ground as Simon lifted him onto his shoulder. Andreas panicked and exclaimed, "Simon!"

"Easy, you're light, and I move a hell of a lot faster than you," Simon replied, focused on the creatures that had started pursuit again. They were approaching and gaining ground; he didn't like that. He glanced at Andreas and snapped, "How far do we have to go?!"

"I'm not sure!" Andreas snapped back.

Well, it sounded like there wasn't a choice. Simon shifted the shield in his hand, tightening his grip in case he saw a head he could smash in his peripheral view. Then he asked, "Think you can hit them with something while I'm moving?!"

"Maybe?!" yelled Andreas, sounding surprised and flustered.

Simon chuckled at the reaction, finding it amusing despite the situation. He could almost sense the growing embarrassment on Andreas' face as he remained perched on his shoulder. Glancing down, Simon sidestepped as a creature caught up to him and snapped its jaws at his leg.

"Now *might* be a good time to try it, Red!"

Andreas felt dizzy as he realized he could see the ground rushing past like a cart was carrying him. He had been so preoccupied with this that he'd forgotten about the things chasing them and the constant flexing of the other man's shoulder beneath his stomach. He looked up, trying to steady his gaze from the bobbing of the figure beneath him, then grimaced and aimed at the closest Varog, tossing up a hand. An unseen force seemed to hit the creature, causing it to yelp and fall momentarily.

"Hey! Not bad, Red! Looks like you *can* aim!"

"Oh, shut up!" Andreas snapped back and smacked Simon's back with his fist. It only earned him a laugh, and then he suddenly jerked as Simon dodged around another creature's jaws. Then, there was a loud, wet sound of bone impacting steel before a creature howled and stumbled backward. Simon had smashed it in the head and shoved it away. Andreas was prepared to comment on the action when he heard a snap, a loud grunt of discomfort, and then the ground rushed towards him. A Varog bit Simon and forcibly dragged him down.

"Get off!" Simon snarled and swung the shield towards the canine that had closed its jaws around his thigh. It whimpered and let go, but not without dragging its teeth down his leg. His muscles contracted as a sharp burning sensation settled into the wounds, and he gritted his teeth. He'd forgotten about the spicy bits of these things; they fucking hurt. Their saliva was acidic.

Andreas yelped and rolled to the right as the canine he'd hit earlier barreled towards them and snapped. The creature just missed, nearly catching his hair. There was a burst of energy, and several shining, golden rays erupted around him, impacting the beast. The Varog yelped as the flame-like blades dug into its flesh and drew blood before it recoiled.

"Back off!" Andreas snapped, scrambling to his feet.

The ring of steel hitting bone echoed again. This drew Andreas' attention to Simon, who was swinging on another Varog and shoving it off. He saw the third Varog attempt to bite the orc twice, and each time, it was parried off by Simon's hands. It was almost effortless how he caught the creature by the throat and shoved it back. Then, almost instinctively, Simon did it again.

At first, he was impressed, but then teeth came barreling towards him. Andreas jolted, his hand lifting, and a bright barrier of golden light flared, sending the creature back. "Can you stand up!?" Andreas yelled.

Simon grimaced as he hoisted himself up. "Yeah."

The howling echoed again, closer than before, catching the attention of the three canines for a split second. This was long enough for the duo to move out of the small space where they had been cornered. The creatures reacted—one of them slashed out with its claws, narrowly missing Simon. The other two lunged for Andreas, and both of them managed to grab hold of him. One latched onto his hip, and the other caught his arm.

The bite on his hip hurt terribly, and he cried out as he yanked his arm free. The beast's teeth found bone and *crushed it;* he felt something crack. Andreas winced, dizzy, as burning rushed through his limbs from the saliva on his skin as it seeped into his wounds. He hated these things; he reached out, hand shoving into the canine's face still attached to him. Flames crackled, erupting off his palm in a torrent, and the creature yelped loudly before falling to the ground in a burning heap. It stumbled before collapsing into black tar.

Andreas staggered, his vision blurred, and he struggled to reach out and catch something to keep his balance. He found nothing but felt an arm snake around his waist and steady him. Then, the world spun backward as Simon lifted him off the ground. Andreas felt like he was going to be sick. It felt as though his hip had been dislocated, and his skin burned. *"Fuck!"* he screamed.

Simon looked up, his brow furrowing at the exclamation. Andreas was even more limp than before; he couldn't tell how much damage was done, but something was wrong. "Take it easy, Red," he said, trying to offer a comforting word.

Andreas gasped; the hanging feeling was painful on his dislocated limb. Somehow, the world's gravity pulling down on the injury was worse than standing on it. The shifting of Simon's shoulder beneath his pelvis was excruciating. Simon jerked, dodging another set of teeth, and Andreas yelped out in pain from the motion. Then a Varog caught Simon in the arm, and the orc snarled.

Andreas looked around, searching and trying to sort through the flurry of snow and his spinning world. They had to be close. *Please, they had to be near.* He begged silently because he would pass out from this constant motion if they weren't.

"Simon. **Put me down!**" Andreas pleaded, sobbing.

"*Absolutely not!*" Simon snapped and slammed his shield into one of the creatures' head thrice. There was a squelching sound, and bones popped before a final yelp escaped it. The creature melted into tar, just like the last one.

"**How far is it!?**" Simon snapped.

"*I don't know!*" Andreas said, words mixing with a partial scream as his hip slammed repetitively into Simon's shoulder. His eyes brimmed with tears, and his face contorted from the pain surging into his gut. At that moment, he felt the world slipping away from him; he was about to pass out.

Simon felt Andreas go limp, and panic set in. A nagging, festering anger caused bile to rise into his mouth. He swung, finding a foothold on the last creature's shoulder, and shoved as hard as possible. He felt the weight get pushed back and away from him. Instantly, he turned and sprinted as quickly as he could with his damaged thigh. Adrenaline pumped, making his muscles move quicker than they should have. He desperately searched for any sign of a home.

"**You better fucking help one of your people, Primal!**" Simon snarled out the words into the falling snow, directed not in any direction in particular. Although he wasn't religious, it seemed the person hanging over his shoulder was. He had seen Andreas praying with what looked like a holy token in his hands more than once. Specifically, it was a long feather with gradient hues from cobalt to orange, yellow, and finally red. If Andreas came from a family that served in **The Rose Guard**, that could only mean one thing. The phoenix: **Cael**.

Simon focused on running and putting as much distance between himself and the sounds of paws behind him as possible. Suddenly, he saw something like a flicker of light, an energy sphere bursting to life within the trees. It was quick, fleeting, and almost forced his attention. There was a strange familiarity to it that flared deep within him. Simon hurried towards the glimmer he had seen, feeling his shoulders tense as the howls behind him grew louder.

He was determined to follow whatever it was.

Nine

Understanding

It was strange because he was confident that three rotting dogs were following closely behind him when he stumbled through the treeline and nearly fell on his face. The forest abruptly ended, and the reasonably sized clearing caught him off guard when he finally noticed it. Unfortunately, he had already stumbled fifty feet or more into the space before seeing it. Simon paused, his legs shaking from his wounds and the cold of the snow they had spent far too much time in. He glanced around, hearing gurgling, yowling, and then a chorus of howls from behind him. He found three creatures stalking the treeline, watching him and snapping their jaws in agitation but not stepping forward into the clearing.

Simon narrowed his gaze and followed them as they anxiously paced the tree's edge. It made little sense; there was nothing to keep them away, so why were they so determined not to step forward? His head spun, searching for anything that would give him clarity. All he found was a beautifully crafted two-story cabin in the center of the space he had stumbled into. Its windows were dark, and no smoke billowed from the chimney, which was constructed from stone. Unfortunately, that didn't bode well for him or his companion. The cabin's exterior only emphasized the fact he'd contemplated on the day before: *money*.

Understanding

The house had a precisely cut wooden framework and marbled sandstone along its exterior. Massive windows offered a three-sixty-degree view in all directions. Lanterns hung along the outside walls, with brightly glowing shards of red crystal inside them, casting a benevolent light that encased the house. A wrap-around balcony surrounded the second floor, and an eerie melody filled the air, sounding like multiple wind chimes singing in succession.

Simon was panting heavily, his breath forming misty clouds before him. The sun was gone, and the already dreary mountain atmosphere was overwhelming. He looked back at the creatures that refused to enter the open space, recalling what Andreas had said.

Magic. Andreas' grandparents could work magic.

Simon exhaled, a wave of relief washing over him as the fresh air filled his lungs. "Holy shit, Red... What kind of family do you come from?" he murmured. He glanced at the shape slumped over his shoulder and winced. Gaining entry was essential, but breaking into a magically guarded house seemed increasingly hopeless—especially if Andreas was senseless or *dead*.

Simon searched for an open window or a cracked door but found none. However, he noticed firewood stacked against the home's wall and the remnants of a fire pit about thirty feet away. Moving carefully with the body he was holding, he shuffled over to the circle of large rocks. Using his shield, he compacted as much snow as possible in a single area, then threw it aside.

As he fidgeted with his bag, he pulled out the thicker blanket he had given his companion a few days earlier. He carefully spread it over the snow-covered ground and gently placed Andreas on it. Immediately, he began checking for signs of blood loss and felt for his pulse. Andreas was alive and didn't appear to have any severe wounds in the dim light. He was unconscious, but they could address that later.

Simon struggled to move his legs and stumbled towards the front door. After several trips, he gathered enough dry wood to feel comfortable lighting a fire. He searched for flint and a blade, then set to work. It took a few tries, but the wood soon roared to life. Then, he fell back onto his backside and caught his breath as he looked into the surrounding trees.

Simon gritted his teeth. Five sets of eyes peered out of the darkness, watching. The Varog had stopped circling and trying to gain access and instead settled into one spot. Being watched was uncomfortable; he felt like a delayed snack, and the whispering sound of wind chimes added to the discomfort creeping up his neck. He looked down at his leg, and his face twisted in disgust. Upon examination, it became apparent that the bitten and torn flesh still had an oily texture. This caused the lingering burning sensation that flared every time he moved. Simon glanced back at the treeline and muttered, "I *hate* those things."

He had encountered these creatures before. They were scattered across the continents and were a remnant of the prior war. There were various rumors about their origin and why they still existed. The most plausible explanation, in his opinion, was that they came from one of the abandoned **EDEN** facilities, which was also a widespread speculation. When everything went downhill, people discovered the organization had deep corruption. There was a lot to uncover about the organization, from their animal experimentation involving necrotic magic to their use of blood magic on abducted children. It wouldn't surprise him if anything emerged from those horrific places.

Simon wiped some snow over the wound, complaining to himself and growling at the cold, but the burning sensation slowly subsided. The puncture wounds weren't deep, and they were already clotting. He could worry about dressing and cleaning the wound later. His arm could be defined in the same way. Fortunately, his clothing and armor had done their job and kept most of his skin intact. The odd eyes glanced at Andreas, and he gave a quick scan again in the firelight. Andreas' arm was oily, and most of his sleeve had soaked up the substance. There were notable puncture wounds, but the most concerning was the apparent difference in the other's leg lengths.

"No wonder you were ready to curse me to the *Eternal Plane* and back," Simon muttered, turning his attention to the motionless figure on the blanket. He glanced at the other's hip and grimaced at the sight of the

Understanding

puncture wounds, the dried blood, and the stagnant saliva. The raven frowned, his brow furrowed.

Oh, he was about to be on this idiot's shit list.

Simon repositioned himself to securely grasp the dislocated limb and the other man's injured hip. Looking down, he said, "Okay, this is going to be painful, so try not to incinerate me when you flinch awake, agreed?" There was no response, so Simon took a deep breath and shoved with all his strength.

Andreas bolted upright, screaming in pain. There was a sharp pop that sounded slick. Before he could stop himself, he doubled over Simon's back, trembling, as the world spun around him.

"Easy, breathe. Just breathe," Simon said, allowing Andreas to lean on him like a crutch while he reached over to support his back as much as possible.

Andreas' vision was filled with white, yet the pain subsided to a dull ache and a persistent burn. He swallowed, attempting to expel the bile that had seeped into his mouth. "Where are we?" he asked.

"Your grandparents' house, but it seems like they're not home," Simon replied.

Andreas glanced at the crackling fire, then at the familiar cabin. He took a deep breath, feeling tension melt away as he saw the large windows. They had arrived; he had led them in the right direction. *They were safe.*

Simon swallowed, remaining bent over, bearing the other's weight. He had yet to complain and wouldn't until Andreas' breathing stabilized. His gaze drifted to where Andreas' hands clutched his arm. Previously unnoticed, he now observed the charred remnants of the man's fingerless gloves, revealing the skin beneath. Little of the gloves remained, their edges scorched. Apparently, the spell Andreas had cast was one of the difficult ones to control. The skin beneath the remaining fabric then captured his attention.

The sight caused Simon's eyebrows to knit together and his shoulders to stiffen. Old scars marred the surface, evidence of deep wounds that had once torn through the tissue. Around these were more minor, jagged scars, like the flesh had been pulled at odd angles or with great force. It appeared that the marks were made by something that had bitten and then either shaken or dragged its prey... something with *saber-like teeth*.

Simon observed the muscles and tendons in Andreas' hand flex as he shifted his weight and moved his hand downward. Their movement wasn't smooth, indicating discomfort and deep tissue damage. It was the kind of injury that would cause one's hands to tremble when attempting to grip or pull an object.

Simon shivered as the crackling fire and haunting chimes faded into the distance. Only the surface of the carnelian skin was visible, and he didn't dare imagine the condition of Andreas' palms. A deep sense of shame washed over him.

Andreas felt the shoulders beneath him tense and looked down in concern. "Simon, are you okay?" It dawned on him that he was lying on top of the orc. He quickly recoiled, feeling a sharp pain shoot through him from the sudden movement. He whimpered and said, "Sorry."

Simon exhaled and then straightened to sit beside his companion.

He felt guilty as the thought churned in his stomach like the plague. He had told Andreas that he needed to practice and implied that the man wasn't trying hard enough when he mentioned he performed poorly with weapons. Simon had never been fond of laziness and had made assumptions. Over the last few days, he had painted a picture of a well-off kid who didn't want to work hard. In Simon's mind, since Andreas came from a respectable family, was wealthy, and was good-looking, he was likely to achieve much with minimal effort.

A week ago, he would have described Andreas as a spoiled, entitled individual with a poor attitude and poor people skills when he didn't know a ***damn thing*** about him. After all, Andreas had intrigued him when they first met. However, Simon's interest in something usually led to trouble, so he avoided digging too deep by making **assumptions**. ... At least, he had as of eight years ago. Simon's face contorted in irritation, and his chest throbbed with pain. The shame and guilt flared fiercer, and he frowned.

There was someone who came to mind who would scold him severely right now—someone who was incredibly painful to think about.

"It's my fault," Andreas rambled, trying to meet the other man's gaze. "I

Understanding

shouldn't have asked you to run; it probably just made everything worse."

Simon had been motionless and unresponsive for a few minutes, which made Andreas uneasy. He suspected that Simon was angry once more. Andreas feared they had reverted to the uncomfortable silence they had only just managed to escape.

"It's okay," Simon said, shaking his head as his vision cleared.

It was a terse statement, and it caused the emeralds to study the larger form. Simon appeared to be trying to work something out, for he gazed into the fire in disgust. Andreas cleared his throat, eager to dispel the tension, and asked, "Could you help me get to the door? I don't mind the fire, but... it's warmer inside. There's food and wine. There's even a bathtub."

Simon glanced over and asked, " Can you get inside?"

"Yes," Andreas gestured broadly at his surroundings. "Enchantments."

Simon nodded, then stood and helped up his companion.

Reaching the door took them longer than usual, but they finally arrived. Andreas waved his hand a few times to open the door, and they stumbled through. It took Simon only five minutes to help Andreas settle into a plush seat by the fireplace, gather their belongings, and light a fire. Now, he turned to head back out into the snow.

"Simon, aren't you staying?" Andreas looked up, alarmed.

Acknowledging the roaring fire outside with a nod, Simon swallowed and attempted to speak. However, Andreas interrupted him before he could start. Andreas' words were panicked, "I know I'm not the strongest companion, but... I promise..."

Simon turned toward Andreas, cutting his words short with a look.

Andreas caught a glimpse of something fleeting. It was reminiscent of Simon's look at the bed-and-breakfast, yet not quite the same; this time, it expressed shame and uncertainty.

Simon said, "I'll be right back. I need to put out the fire and clear my head," He turned around only to feel something strike his head.

He grunted as he reached out to catch whatever it was before it fell to the ground. The fabric was soft, like chiffon, and featured a mix of blues and teals. The gradient looked as if someone had splashed dye without following any specific method. Golden stitching formed intricate loops around the edges to prevent fraying. However, the ends showed signs of wear, as if they had already been through a lot.

It was Andreas' shawl.

"Why did you give me this, Red?"

Andreas uttered, "Bring it back; it's cold," the words tumbling out in a chaotic rush as if he couldn't say them fast enough. His voice quivered with each syllable as if he were about to cry. He didn't want to be left alone—he was afraid of being left alone.

At first, Simon was confused, but soon he began to understand. He smiled gently and nodded, putting the shawl over his shoulders. He noticed Andreas relaxed slightly, and Simon hesitated as if thinking about making a joke. ...But making a joke didn't seem appropriate at the moment.

"*I'll be right back*," Simon said, dismissing the thought. "If you can, clean your wounds." Without another word, he stepped out into the snow.

Ten

Confidence

Andreas had cleaned his wounds as best as possible, using his magical abilities to speed up recovery. It wouldn't heal them completely, but at least it would help them settle sooner rather than later. Then, he carefully wrapped them in medical supplies from his parents' room. While doing so, he noticed that his gloves were practically nonexistent. He removed the remaining shreds of fabric and wrapped his hands in bandages, covering his palms, the tops of his hands, and his wrists completely. Since he didn't have a spare pair, this would have to suffice until they reached Fossy and he could purchase more.

He then took some of his grandparents' bourbon before returning to the den. From there, he watched Simon through the window that faced out towards the front of the home, sipping his glass in concern. Andreas bit his lip, readjusted to support his weight with the wall, and softly huffed.

Simon had been outside in the snow for nearly an hour. It appeared he was waiting for the embers to die down completely before putting them out. Occasionally, Simon would look up and scan the treeline or glance back at the house as if considering going inside. He never strayed from the smoldering fire.

"Come inside already…" Andreas murmured, his front teeth clicking against the crystal glass in slight irritation. It seemed as though the mercenary was dodging him, which he found displeasing. His gaze sharpened as Simon faced the house once more before turning back to observe the fading fire.

"Oh, for fuck's sake," Andreas grumbled and bounced off the wall without thinking. Pain surged up from his leg to his stomach, making him wince. He finished the last of his bourbon and went to the large kitchen adjoining the open sitting area.

He thought about food, knowing there was an ample supply of preserved meats and fresh ingredients in the cellar due to his grandparents' frequent visits. However, he didn't have much of an appetite. He looked at the ornate bottle he had taken from his grandparents' room, let out a tired sigh, and poured himself another glass. It wasn't nourishing, but it gave him a sense of warmth and dulled the throbbing pain in his hip.

As Andreas lifted the glass to his lips once more, the clink of metal against wood startled him, causing him to spin around too quickly. He winced as a sharp pain shot through his side again.

"Be **careful** with that hip; I don't want to have to push it back into place again," Simon called from the front door.

Andreas clenched his teeth and gave a slight shrug. *"It's fine,"* he hissed.

He was suddenly less worried about the pain surging through his body and more concerned about the very *underdressed* orc in the room. His eyes were locked on the ground, purposefully **not** gazing at Simon.

Andreas' face felt warm, and his ears tingled as the sensation spread throughout his body. He hadn't expected to look up and see the man half-naked. It turned out that the metallic sound he had heard was from the ring mail Simon wore under his tunic, hitting the ground. When Andreas saw him, Simon had been pulling his shirt back over his head. Now, he worried about looking up and seeing the other half of the man in full view.

Not that it would particularly *bother* him if he saw... *No, no, no.* Andreas immediately dismissed the entire train of thought.

Simon laughed, adjusted his tunic, and strolled over to offer Andreas his shawl. "It's warmer than I expected," he remarked.

Andreas said, "I'm glad you didn't burn it out there," he draped the clothing around his shoulders and looked up at the man before him.

"I promised to return it, not return it safely," Simon said with a snicker.

"Usually, that would be implied," said Andreas with a smile despite himself.

Simon stayed silent, observing Andreas thoughtfully. His gaze shifted to Andreas' hands and hips before settling on his eyes. Andreas shifted uncomfortably and pivoted back towards the bartop he had been leaning on. The way Simon watched him was unsettling, almost as if he were being scrutinized. It only made his ears burn more and his gaze lower again.

"Are your hands alright?" Simon finally asked.

"What?" Andreas replied quickly. The hand holding his glass of alcohol jerked back reflexively as if he expected it to be grabbed. Following Simon's gaze, his eyes lifted, and he nodded sharply. "Yeah. Fire spells were chaotic," he said.

Simon furrowed his brow deeply; he hadn't thought about that. He reached out tentatively, gauging the reaction he would get. He wanted to take a look and make sure the damage he'd seen earlier wasn't new, and if that prompted a conversation about the scars he'd witnessed, he'd take it. "Did they get burned?" he asked.

Andreas quickly pulled his hands back and pressed against the bar to create as much distance between them as possible. "Yeah, but they're fine. It's fine," he said, swallowing hard to control the panic in his voice as he noticed Simon's hand stop and then quickly pull back.

Noted: Don't touch the hands. Simon would remember that.

"Alright, sorry," Simon said with an apologetic smile as he limped toward the giant chair where he had first settled Andreas. He needed to look at his leg again because it was becoming painful now that it was warming up. It's funny how that worked: once you got feeling back, all you felt was pain.

Andreas noticed Simon's limp and frowned as he asked, "Simon, did you clean your leg?"

Simon sat down, grimacing. "Technically, *yes*, but probably not in the preferred way. Snow isn't the most sanitary thing, but it works."

"*For fuck's sake.*" Andreas cursed aloud and grumbled incomprehensibly.

Simon jumped, caught off guard, and looked over with confusion.

Andreas furrowed his brow, set his glass on the bartop, and slowly approached the staircase. "There are supplies by the fire; I'll fetch you some clean clothes."

"Are you good to go up?" Simon asked, concerned.

"I'm perfectly fine!" Andreas snapped back, cutting the other man off.

Simon watched as Andreas ascended the stairs; it was hard to watch. He waited until his companion was out of sight before taking the medical supplies and lowering his trousers to get to work on his thigh.

* * *

Andreas took about twenty minutes to return, his steps mingling with the crackling of the fire. He came down with clothes slung over his shoulder, moving awkwardly and slowly. Instead of finding Simon in the chair by the fireplace, he saw him leaning against the wall near one of the main windows, gazing at the sky.

"Here ... these should fit," Andreas said.

Simon glanced back and reached out to take the clothing offered to him. His brow knitted in concern; these clothes were *expensive*. The pants were black, tailored, barely worn, and made of fine linen. The tunic was silken, a deep crimson color, and had intricate golden threadwork resembling interlocking triquetras around its collar and sleeves. He looked up, feeling uneasy, and was suddenly reminded of the wealth disparity between himself and the person he was traveling with. "Are you sure about me wearing these?" Simon asked.

"Unless you want to sleep in soggy pants," Andreas remarked, glancing down at Simon's pant legs, damp from the snow. "Those are old. Papa hardly wears them anymore."

These clothes were not old at all. Simon said in disbelief, "I think we have conflicting definitions of '*old*,' Red."

Andreas' frown deepened, creasing his forehead. He knew his Papa owned fancy attire, reflecting his love for luxury and his inclination for costly commodities. With a nervous shrug and a bite to his lower lip, he admitted, "No, it's just that my Papa is the only one who's about your size... and has specific tastes."

Simon sighed and headed for the oversized chair he had previously used. He carelessly tossed his clothes onto the seat and pulled his shirt off.

Andreas gazed at the faint scars trailing down Simon's back from old wounds, and then his eyes wandered back up to admire the *width* of the man's shoulders.

"Is there any food?" Simon spoke, pausing when he looked over and caught the emeralds watching him. Andreas froze, resembling a startled deer, before almost tripping over his own feet in an attempt to turn around. Simon chuckled quietly and then continued taking off his clothes without saying anything.

Well, at least Andreas had hesitated to *watch* for a little while this time.

Andreas ignored the question and blurted out, "Do you... do you like bourbon?" He had turned too quickly and tried to hide the pain in his leg as he limped to the kitchen to look for another glass. This wasn't good for his heart, let alone his hip.

"Is it good? ... You know, I don't know why I'm asking that. Look at this place," Simon called out over his shoulder.

Andreas chuckled as he picked up a glass and carefully backed towards the bartop. His hip complained loudly about the movement. "*Yes*, it's good," he said.

"Unsurprising, considering all this money," Simon scoffed as he adjusted his updated pants. Then, as if trying to dispel the awkwardness, he added, "You did well earlier. I might even be impressed; I wasn't expecting a sorcerer when I saw you."

"Gee, *thanks*," Andreas said with a smirk, his words laced with playful sarcasm. "I appreciate you carrying me when I passed out," he said before bursting into laughter.

"I'm sure your refined ass is used to being carried," Simon answered, laughing as he pulled on his shirt. Despite the looming risk of death, it had been a *nice* view. With a grin, he mumbled, *"No trouble at all."*

Andreas reached for the bottle and poured them both a drink. He wrapped his hands around his glass and leaned on the countertop with his back to the sitting room. As he processed the words, the frown on his face deepened. The words somehow stung, no matter how he looked at or thought of them. He suddenly became keenly aware of the barrier between them, even though Simon didn't know his last name. He couldn't shake off his family's influence and wasn't sure how to feel about it.

"I probably seem like a spoiled rich brat, huh?" Andreas questioned.

The room was quiet, almost uncomfortable, for a minute. Then, Andreas felt body heat, and the next thing he knew, an arm was reaching over him for the available glass. Simon's chest was pushing into his back, as if Simon had purposely angled himself to reach over, not beside him, for his drink. The weight remained, barely pressing against him, before withdrawing. Simon leaned beside the shorter figure and faced the sitting room in silence.

Andreas couldn't bring himself to look up again. There it was, that scintillating sensation that made his ears burn and his hands clasp his glass desperately. Simon had teased him again, just like in the desert. He felt his knees go weak as the image of the orc's bare back popped into his mind, and heat rose in his cheeks from the memory of the weight that had just been pressing into his back.

Simon took a sip of his drink and swallowed it with raised eyebrows. There was a spice to it that settled in the back of the throat and lingered with a citrus profile. He appreciated it and then looked over, observing the tightness in Andreas' shoulders and the man's utter refusal to look up. He bumped his shoulder against Andreas', took another sip, and spoke casually, "Rich, *obviously*. Bratty ... sometimes ..."

Andreas looked over, glaring.

With a deep laugh, Simon said, "I don't think you're confident enough to be spoiled."

Andreas' glare darkened as he said, "And what do you *really* know about me?"

Simon grinned as he turned to face the man beside him, keeping his weight comfortably against the bartop. "Not a lot. You're a hard one to crack, honestly... Once I think I've got you figured out, you go and *surprise* me."

"Try me," Andreas huffed, attempting to ignore the growing heat in his cheeks.

Simon settled into silence to gather his thoughts. He was torn between being honest and being sarcastic. Part of him wanted to be snarky. "You're charismatic and *charming*," he said, taking another drink and tilting his head. "But not confident, especially not in yourself or your abilities. So, no, I wouldn't say you were spoiled. I think you apologize too much and doubt yourself too often to be spoiled, Red."

Andreas tried to suppress a smile, his fingers running over his glass absentmindedly. He felt relieved, even though he had been insulted in the process. Somehow, being considered spoiled was worse than being insulted at the moment. He didn't want Simon to think he was spoiled ... "Well, it's a good thing that at least **one** of us is extremely confident," Andreas spoke, glancing up to find Simon eyeing him with curiosity.

Simon's eyes crinkled at the edges, and a smile spread across his face. He was suddenly glad that he had chosen to be honest. The look Andreas had just given him was more than worth it.

Andreas' stomach flipped, and he looked down to try to hide a grin. He could feel Simon watching him, almost as if the orc had forgotten their drinks already.

Simon tightened his grip on his glass and moved it closer to Andreas. He didn't dare reach out and touch the other man, but closing the space between them was suddenly important. He had unexpectedly become aware of the distance separating them. Andreas waited, ready to pull back if Simon tried to get closer. Simon put his glass down and tapped the rim as if he were giving himself something to do to keep his fingers from venturing too far into the unknown.

"Are you sure your hands are okay?" Simon asked as he looked down, not at the bartop they were leaning on, but at the distance between them. He felt very far away and was grappling with wanting to be closer. He wasn't sure how he felt about desiring to be nearer or if Andreas *wanted* him closer.

"Yeah… my hip just hurts," Andreas responded quietly, his fingers still running around the edge of his glass. He looked up briefly, only to see where the other eyes were focused. He noticed that Simon was intently focused on the ground, and a palpable tension hung in the air—not uncomfortable but filled with anticipation. It was almost like a storm was coming, and it was a sensation he knew pretty well: *attraction*.

The invisible line was usually easy to cross; he typically just made a few simple jokes, twirled his hair, and gave a look before the other person moved. However, they knew exactly who he was, what they could get, and what he was after. What he was after… right now, Andreas wasn't quite sure what he was after. All he knew was that this magnetic sensation skittering over his skin was new and that he was desperately searching his brain for a way to stop it.

"Be careful. If you push too hard, I *might* carry you down the mountain," Simon said. He gave his glass a final tap before reaching out—not for the fingers close by, but for the shawl draped over his companion's shoulders. He shifted the fabric until it was securely in place and then pulled back, grabbed his glass, and turned to place his back against the bar. His attention focused out the window; he took a deep breath, then chugged down the rest of his alcohol in silence.

Andreas felt a sinking sensation in his stomach, like a wave of disappointment. When Simon first spoke and moved, he felt his toes curl, and his skin ignite. He had been waiting for the man beside him to touch him because the words had been *playful*. He bit his lip and returned his attention to the liquid in his glass. He now understood that Simon had **no** intention of crossing that invisible line between them. The strange part was he didn't know if it was because the orc didn't want to or because he was *waiting* for something.

What, exactly, was Simon waiting for? He didn't know.

Eleven

Family

Andreas left Simon to wander the home as he bathed. As he walked around the place, he was amazed by its beauty and the amount of gold that must have been spent to build it.

He was only allowed to enter four out of the five rooms on the second floor. One room had a thick redwood door with intricate dragonflies and what looked like a phoenix surrounding it. Andreas said it was his grandparents' room and was only open to family members. In the hall was a plain wooden door that Andreas had shown him, the only one not holding an intricate carving. He was told it was the guest room where he could sleep. Aside from these two things, he had been told not to wander outside the bounds of the clearing. Otherwise, he was welcome to any food or drink he found and to roam where he pleased outside the off-limits area.

Simon lingered in the hallway, waiting to hear the washroom door lock and the steady water pouring before heading downstairs and pouring another glass of bourbon.

His eyes lingered on the high ceiling, noticing the intricate metallic carvings hanging around as decoration. Most hanging pieces were crafted to look like stars, giving the large spacious den the look of an astronomy tower. They seemed to have those same strange crystal pieces as the lanterns outside at their core. The furniture was lavish, with several comfortable sofas and oversized plush chairs around the massive stone fireplace. A soft fur rug, the kind of which he couldn't tell, spanned the expansive space and offered a change of texture from the polished wooden floor through the rest of the home. There were several shelves with books and odd trinkets that looked like expensive knickknacks that a collector with a specific taste would enjoy. Most trinkets were insects, some even being once-living creatures encased in polished amber or crystal.

The kitchen had polished granite counters and an island bar they had lingered near earlier in the evening, which held a massive sink. The stove was double and designed for someone who often cooked and knew their way around the kitchen. The many cabinets, filled to the brim, magnified this with pots, pans, dishes, and cutlery. Spices and various oils lined a wall, and above the stone was a metal vented hood decorated with wrought floral blossoms. This family seemed to hold togetherness in high regard because of the size and extravagance of the communal places. The kitchen and sitting room alone spanned the whole of the cabin's first floor, except for the door that led down to the cellar.

Simon took a sip of his drink and glanced around the two rooms. He then headed upstairs to explore further. Passing the bathroom, he noticed a carved waterfall motif, indicating the room's purpose. Upon peering inside earlier, he had observed that the room was constructed with wood and stacked stone, featuring only two small windows. The tub, carved from a large tree and treated to be watertight, was situated in the center of the room. Stone steps on either side led up to a fireplace built into a partition above the tub, with windows above that. The room contained linens, towels, toiletries, a small wooden bucket, and a carved wooden stool.

The next door was forbidden, and he studied it. Part of him wanted to peek inside. After all, how would Andreas know? Simon contemplated, his eyes peering towards the washroom before he sighed and moved on to the next door in the hall. He had promised, and although he was many things, he didn't want to add 'liar' to his list of descriptors.

The door next to it was adorned with carvings of flowers, including sunflowers and lotus flowers. Upon opening the door, Simon found himself in a medium-sized room with a high ceiling, small windows, and wooden walls. The stone half of the room featured a fireplace and a sizable bed, positioned across from each other. Several scattered shelves adorned the walls, displaying a collection of trinkets, books, and several small wooden carvings. By the largest window in the room, there was a table holding a flower vase filled with sunflowers. Two plush chairs were placed on either side.

Simon surveyed the room, pondering out loud, "I don't think this room belongs to you, Red… and I doubt it's your sister's room since you're both the same age. It's not your grandparents' or the guest room… so it must be your parents'?"

He stepped inside and noticed a small nook with enough space for a pet bed next to the wall, with its own small window. On top of the pet bed, there was a rather worn-out teddy bear and a well-used ball. Simon examined the wooden figures: several flowers, what looked like a small dog, and a bird. As he got closer, he noticed many pressed flowers he hadn't seen before. He took another sip of his drink and looked at the wardrobe before opening it and peeking inside. The clothing lacked any extravagance, in stark contrast to the opulent garments he had previously seen: a sea of basic tunics, devoid of any patterns, along with worn trousers and a mix of what he considered fashionable dresses and smaller tunics and trousers.

"Parents seem less extravagant. Father doesn't seem to care for expensive things, judging by his clothes… Mother appears no more concerned about her appearance than any other lady," Simon mumbled. He closed the wardrobe, then turned to leave and closed the door behind him.

Alright, there was still nothing to give him an idea of who this family was.

He walked to the next door and discovered a larger one adorned with carvings of lilies and what appeared to be a dagger. Upon opening it, Simon found a small room with minimal furniture. The room was constructed of polished wood, had no fireplace, and featured two large windows overlooking the wrap-around balcony. Delicate carvings decorated the edge of a desk built into the wall. There was a cozy bed with numerous pillows, soft blankets, and potted plants. Stepping inside, he made his way to the small wardrobe in the corner and opened the door. Inside, he found luxurious clothing more suitable for someone with a feminine build, designed to reveal more skin. At the bottom of the wardrobe were several pairs of shoes, most heeled, and an assortment of jewelry. Apart from these items, the only personal touch in the room was an ancient stuffed rabbit seated on the bed amidst fern-like flora.

Simon closed the wardrobe and clicked his tongue. "Sister seems to like fancy stuff. She appears more confident than you, Red… or maybe she doesn't come here often." He sighed, turned, and left, passing the guest room's and last hallway doors. Since he had run out of doors, this one must belong to Andreas. Simon looked at the carvings and smiled. It also had floral accents, but the depicted blooms were camellias with a small bird carving. He wondered if one parent, from the flowers in their room, loved flowers.

He opened the door and peered inside before leaning against the frame.

The room was barely wider than the one he had been in, which he assumed was the sister's. It had wooden walls, floors, and furniture. The white paint on the ceiling seemed slightly unfinished, leaving stains. On the floor, there was a small table and a large chest, both wicker and white, with a top opening mechanism. A bed without a frame was in front of a massive bay window, settled on the floor. A small wooden bookshelf held old-looking books, a few wooden carvings, and scattered crystals and gems. Large baskets of ivy were hanging from the roof throughout the room.

When Simon stepped inside, he noticed a small wooden perch with a large nest of woven sticks and multicolored fabric. He looked over the bookshelf and saw old storybooks, the kind you would expect from childhood, and carved figures. The oldest figure looked humanoid and appeared to be holding a stick. He also found scattered drawings, including one that seemed to depict the schematics of a bow. Additionally, a few simple paintings of bursts of color were on canvas. Simon paused in the space, taking it all in.

Out of all the rooms he had seen, including the ones on the first floor, this was the only room with a less polished and more lived-in look. To him, this room seemed the most normal, with its patchwork quilts and stuffed pillows of various patterns. It looked lived-in and homey, as if its owner was often there.

"Looks like I've found your room, Red," Simon chuckled. He didn't know the family, but the rooms revealed much about their dynamics. He noticed similarities between this room and the one downstairs, both filled with curiosities. It seemed that Andreas must have had a close relationship with his grandparents, as they likely influenced his interest in collecting things. The room also shared similarities with the parents' room, specifically the carvings. There was evident mutual interest and respect for carving hobbies, but it was clear that different individuals had created the carvings in the two rooms.

Based on the poor skills of the carvings in this room, he felt that the parent who enjoyed carving hadn't taken the time to teach Andreas properly. This probably meant that their relationship was strained. Simon clicked his tongue and remembered how Andreas described his father.

"So, your father likes wood carving..."

There wasn't much similarity between this room and the sister's room; he wondered about their relationship. Perhaps she didn't spend as much time here as he had thought. Simon's eyes landed on the scattered gemstones again, and then he grinned. Ah. The sister enjoyed giving her brother pretty things. She likely adored him and wanted to give him something practical that he would enjoy but also expensive. Considering they were the only items aside from the crafted carvings and the books, he got the feeling that the man he'd been traveling with was sentimental.

Simon chuckled and said, "Alright, good relationship with your sister."

The mercenary flipped over one of the storybooks and nodded as he saw the barely holding-on binding. It was evident that Andreas had read or been read to from the storybook a lot. Most likely, one grandparent liked knowledge, history, and stories. Simon looked over the room, thinking of all the little nuances he'd observed while going through this home and the small comments he'd heard tossed around by Andreas down the hall.

"You spend more time here than at home, huh?" Simon muttered to himself, his free hand running over his lower face in thought. As he investigated the house, he became increasingly intrigued by Andreas' family and background. The minor details were piling up, and he was trying to figure out where they were pointing.

Simon turned to leave, closed the door behind him, and headed down the hall to go downstairs again. He felt strange stepping into the guest room. It was as lavish as the first two he had inspected, with fancy furniture and an enormous fireplace. He was used to sleeping on the ground and maybe an ancient bed tucked into a spare room the size of a small closet. This was when he was in Ransol. He wasn't accustomed to all of this space, nor the eerie silence disturbed by wind chimes. He could hear them in the house, as ten or more must have been hanging outside. Making his way into the sitting room, he walked towards one of the plush sofas by the front door.

Taking another sip of alcohol, Simon sat down and slipped back into his thoughts.

Wealthy, respectable, and most likely influential based on what Selbi said to him. Both grandparents were male, at least from the designations assigned by Andreas. The parents looked simple and polished but not as polished as the grandparents were. The sister was high maintenance but seemed to care enough about her brother to consider his feelings when giving gifts. Someone liked flowers a lot. From what he'd gathered, the father enjoyed wood carving and must have a rather interesting personality based on what Andreas told him. The kids were twins, orphans from the war, which the family seemed connected to via Belmare or **The Rose Guard** under Cael.

Simon pondered, furrowing his eyebrows. He didn't like how all these small details lined up because the more he thought about it...

Simon let his thoughts wander, and his shoulders stiffened when he heard something in the kitchen behind him. He turned his head, his eyes taking in the details of the room to ensure he didn't miss anything new. His breath caught in his throat, and his eyes widened when he saw a figure that seemed to have come up from the cellar, closing the trap door.

It was a figure he had seen before but never *here*.

Turning around, **Neil Dwyer** held a bundle of dried sausages.

"Simon, are you ... **Grandpa Neil**!?"

"Oh, hello, Firefly. I didn't realize you were here," came the playful voice, a musical high tenor full of delight and entertainment.

Simon turned to look at the stairs slowly. His jaw tightened into a sharp line, and confusion and irritation flooded his eyes. He saw Andreas frozen halfway down them, his face contorted in panic and dread as Andreas looked at the man in the kitchen and then at him.

Simon swallowed, trying to rid his mouth of the unpleasant taste. He stayed silent, afraid that speaking might lead to regret.

Andreas appeared to be trying to speak, but Simon looked away whenever the man's green eyes tried to make contact with his.

Neil said, "Anni, are you alright?"

Andreas looked back at his grandfather, pale. "I... I'm fine," he said.

Simon scoffed and went outside into the snow before he could stop himself. He needed to process this.

Twelve

Exhaustion

Neil Dwyer was a slender man, standing at around five feet ten. He appeared in his mid to late forties, with pale, almost snow-white skin. His long, windswept hair was white and silver, reaching just above his shoulders. Longer bangs covered his right eye and the areas of his face above his cheek, while the other was embellished with a long feather of bright blues and reds. A complex, grayish-black tattoo decorated his right shoulder, neck, and arm, disappearing underneath his clothing. He was blind, with one large and expressive visible eye, and wore a teal shawl that matched Andreas'.

Neil turned his head as he heard the front door open and slam. His brow furrowed, and his lips sank into a frown. "Firefly? Did I interrupt something?" he asked.

Andreas closed the distance between himself and his grandfather and took hold of the hand reaching out to him. He squeezed it, and Neil turned towards him. There was a moment of concern as Neil noticed the bandages, and then he ran his fingers along Andreas' arm as if examining it.

"I'm okay," Andreas said.

"What happened to your hands?" Neil asked with concern. His vacant gaze darted around as his hands moved. It seemed like he was visualizing something in his mind, and he rechecked Andreas for any injuries.

"Spells backfired again. I'm fine," Andreas repeated reassuringly.

"Is anyone here with you?"

"Yes, he stepped outside," Andreas sighed, allowing his grandfather to brush his cheek.

Neil's brow rose. "He? *Oh?*"

Andreas rolled his eyes and said, "I accepted Papa's job, and someone else grabbed it simultaneously. We agreed to work on it together. That's all."

Neil paused, then smiled brightly. "Cian will be glad to hear that you accepted the job. He won't have to run through all his silly evaluations; he can trust you. Plus, if you're working with someone…"

"I don't know him that well," Andreas interrupted.

Neil's grin grew, and he said, "Well, clearly, you trust him some. You brought him **home**."

Andreas' face turned crimson. "A bit… sort of. I haven't disclosed my name," Andreas said, ignoring the wave of laughter that broke over Neil's face.

"What?" Neil frowned. "What do you mean, Anni?"

Andreas anxiously glanced at the door, then at his grandfather. "I may have forgotten to mention my last name."

Neil's frown deepened as he scolded, "Cian would be disappointed. Do your parents know you're out here?"

"Not exactly…" Andreas swallowed, allowing a slight smile to cross his lips as he noticed a hint of amusement on his grandfather's face. "I might have paid Lilli to tell them I was visiting you with an escort," he admitted.

A wry smile of approval spread over the older man's lips, and Neil chuckled. "Well, Cian won't be pleased you lied, but…" He reached forward to squeeze his grandson's hand and continued, "I may have received a message from your sister yesterday saying something similar."

Andreas laughed in disbelief. "You came here deliberately, didn't you?" he asked.

"Me? I would **never**," Neil scoffed, mockingly astonished, but couldn't hide the grin on his face as he said, "Cian ate all our lamb, so I came for something to cook for dinner."

They laughed and embraced effortlessly as if the conversation had been rehearsed. Andreas sighed, squeezed Neil, and smiled when it was returned. His eyes closed, enjoying the moment before pulling free. "I missed you," he said.

Neil smiled and stepped back. "I always miss you. How are you? You seem thin," he said.

"We ran into a pack of..." Andreas started to speak, then let his thoughts wander. "Grandpa Neil, did Lilli say anything about Keena?"

"No, is Keena not with you?" Neil asked, looking around as if he could see the tiny bird should she appear. He listened to the house quietly.

"No, I sent her home. We were near the pillars, and there was a pack of Mistwalkers."

Neil stiffened, concern filling his face as he spoke, "A *pack*? They don't roam in packs."

"They seemed to be hunting, and if I'm right, they were hunting me," Andreas replied. "I sent Keena with a message to Pops, but I don't know if she got there."

Neil pondered the words, his expression remaining unchanged. Then, he turned to his grandson. "I will contact your mother to ensure Keena's safe arrival. Are you certain you're unharmed?" he asked.

"Thank you, and no, they didn't see us."

Neil offered a reassuring smile. "Since you took Cian's job, would you like to return with me? It would be quicker than trekking through the mountains and valleys for another four days."

Andreas grimaced and said, "I think I need to talk to **him** first... perhaps if the storm doesn't let up or the Varog pack that chased us here lingers for more than a day?"

Neil's face darkened, his voice losing its toying tone and gaining a frightening edge. "Varog? *Near my home?* I could get rid of them. I'm sure they would be **delighted** to see me."

Andreas swallowed, disregarding the coldness in the man's tone. "I'm sure they'll leave soon."

"Perhaps," Neil's head turned, his gaze focused on the direction of the

Exhaustion

door. He considered the words as if waiting to hear something abnormal. He turned back, smiled, and said, "Well, talk to your companion. Please let me know if you decide to accept the offer, and I will come. Okay?"

Andreas replied, "Alright. Thank you."

Neil sighed and patted the sausage coils in his arms before saying, "Well, as much as I would love to stay and chat, I must prepare dinner. Emhyr can't keep Cian entertained with card bets for long; lying to that man is impossible." He leaned, reaching up until he found his grandson's face, and then tugged down. He kissed Andreas' cheek and said, "I love you. I'll see you soon."

Andreas smiled and said, "I love you too."

Andreas tensed as he looked at the door, dreading the upcoming conversation with Simon. Neil felt Andreas let go of his hand and gently patted the half-elf's cheek, sensing the unease beneath his touch. "Anni, just be honest. If he's trustworthy, he will understand why you're hesitant to reveal your identity."

"I'm not sure… he's…" Andreas paused, biting his lip. "He sometimes has quirks like Papa."

"Oh, I think I will *adore* him, then. I love teasing your Papa."

"Grandpa," Andreas huffed, glaring at the man instinctively.

Neil chuckled. "When I avoid telling your Papa the whole truth, I usually end up being straightforward with him when he finds out. If he becomes upset, stand your ground. His feelings are no more important than your own, Firefly," he explained.

"I'll try to remember that," Andreas sighed.

Neil affectionately patted his grandson's cheek one last time. "You must. I've raised you to be a stubborn thorn in the side of men; remember that," he said. The sound of his grandson's laughter made his smile grow larger. "Inform me within forty-eight hours so you're not late. Do you promise?" he said.

"I promise," Andreas said. He watched the man's nose wrinkle playfully before allowing Neil to pull away and put space between them. He observed a blur of white energy rustling around his grandfather's form as if a wind had picked up within the home. Then, Neil was gone as quickly as he had come.

Andreas audibly sighed, wishing for the ability to use teleportation magic to make his life easier. One day, maybe, but he had to figure out how to control simple spells first.

His gaze shifted from the door to the windows that offered a view of the surrounding property. A few feet from the house, he saw Simon gazing into the forest. Every so often, Simon's hands would flail as though his thoughts were spilling into physical manifestations. Andreas bit his lip, a crease forming deeper on his brow. He had a feeling this wouldn't end well. Nevertheless, he wrapped his shawl tighter around his shoulders, strode to the door, and pulled on his boots. He then opened the door to trudge through the expanse of snow.

Stepping outside, he peered at the treeline, his eyes narrowing to discern the eight figures skulking at the fringe through the thickening snowfall. The Varog were clustered together, their crimson eyes fixed on Simon... and now on him. Andreas' brow creased, memories surfacing of similar gatherings from his youth, sometimes lingering for days. He hoped it wouldn't be the case this time. He hoped their hunger would compel them to feed elsewhere. His gaze shifted back to Simon, noting the rigidity of his shoulders.

"... Simon. It's cold. Come inside."

Simon spun, his eyes wild. "Why the **hell** did you lie about who you were?!"

Andreas frowned. He glared and snapped back, "I didn't **lie** about anything. I didn't say my last name. If I'm not mistaken, you didn't ask for it either!"

A tense silence enveloped them as Simon trudged forward to glare at the shorter figure, his breaths heavy and forming puffs of white smoke in the cold air.

"Don't you understand the impact of being around you? Working with you?" Simon's voice was intense, and he seemed to struggle to control it. "If the wrong person finds out I've been traveling with you, I lose my livelihood. My contracts will dry up in an instant!"

Andreas squared his shoulders; he disliked the wording and felt the heat rising in his gut from offense. He managed to scoff, his emerald eyes nearly

Exhaustion

as deadly as the mismatched ones they locked with. "You mean if **Talien Draper** hears of you traveling with me? Excuse me if I thought you had more class than dealing with that piece of shit!" he exclaimed.

Simon focused on breathing as he processed the words. His frown deepened as he replied, "I don't *deal* with that piece of shit! Some of my contracts go through people who do, however. **You're messing with my livelihood, Red**. The Dwyers ..."

A loud laugh silenced him, one that was dry and seemed to echo back into the vast open area. Andreas glared and spat, "If I fucking hear you *finish* that sentence. I am **so sick** of hearing 'The Dwyers this' and 'The Dwyers that'! You **knew** it was our job, yet you nearly fought me for it, right?!" He shoved Simon's shoulder as he continued, "What? Are we only worth working with if it's profitable? Or are you saying your problem isn't with the Dwyer family but **me**?!"

Simon roared back, shoulders squared, "You're damn right; my issue is **with you**! **You're** the one who pissed off a powerful man who controls half a continent!" He'd been trying to maintain his temper, but it wasn't going well. Andreas was instigating him. "I didn't sign up to babysit a rich **brat** who chose to work for his grandfather on a whim! You didn't give me a *choice*! I didn't get to choose if working with you was worth not being able to feed myself for the next three months!"

Another moment passed, and Andreas stepped closer, nearly closing the space between them completely. His eyes were wide, and his features contorted into an annoyed snarl. "Well, here's your chance to *choose*. Do you want to keep doing jobs that *mostly* involve guilty people, potentially resulting in the death of innocents? Or do you want to work with **us** instead of that piece of shit, **Talien Draper**?!"

Simon scoffed in disbelief, "I don't think asking me *now* is the same thing! Ransol may have a lot of questionable shits and jobs that skirt the line, but the people there haven't been blamed for the war ten years ago! How can I be sure that working with your family is better than working for him!?"

Andreas hadn't planned for it, but his body reacted before his mind could tell him not to. Before properly registering what he should *not* do ... he punched Simon in the jaw. Simon didn't stumble, but the impact forced his face aside, leaving him mildly shocked. He wasn't expecting to get punched.

Andreas shook his hand, wincing off the pain caused by clenching his fist. He shifted, grabbing tightly onto the other man's tunic before pressing against Simon's body. He slipped onto his tiptoes, forcing as little space between them as possible. His ears rang; he was furious, and his face cramped from frowning.

"Don't you **dare** mention my family as the cause of that again, Simon!" Andreas snapped, eyes manic and hand trembling. He shoved Simon's chest and continued, "My mother almost died! My sister was tortured! My father has to live with the pain that bitch caused him every day! My grandparents had years of their lives stolen from them! … If you *ever* insinuate that my family has any positive ties to **EDEN** again, *I will fucking kill you!*"

The rumor was that his family had staged an elaborate scheme to gain authority and reputation during the war and played sides for their benefit. Some blamed his family for the wars and held a heated hatred for his father because of his past connections—ones that his father, Leo, never agreed to. They blamed his father for being abducted and tortured by **EDEN** when he was a child—for being one of their experiments. Like his Pops could fucking control that!

Andreas had heard insinuations about his family's credibility before, but this time it felt different. His family weren't saints, and he would never say they were. Still, they had lost and suffered *so much* while trying to protect the very people who wanted to cast doubt and blame on their names.

He was fed up with it, and hearing it from Simon was more painful than the hushed conversations he often overheard at the pub. It struck a nerve and sent him into a blind rage. Andreas knew he was physically weaker than the mercenary, so if Simon retaliated, he might end up worse for wear. Nevertheless, he wouldn't let this man *insult* him or his family to his face without doing something about it.

Simon stood in silence, his eyes wide and his jaw clenched. His anger was evident as he processed the words and the sudden strike to his face. He didn't move or try to escape the limited space between him and Andreas.

A mix of guilt and agitation made him uncomfortable as it gnawed at his gut. He knew they both had reason to be angry; somehow, knowing that was more infuriating than him being completely in the wrong. The most disappointing thing was that some part of him felt *excited* about eliciting such a strong reaction from Andreas.

His heart pounded loudly in his ears, and his eyes fixated on the golden freckles on Andreas' cheeks. The memory of the bed-and-breakfast patio and the other's relaxed demeanor came to mind, just like the earlier conversation in the kitchen. *Something about Andreas reminded him of* … Simon felt a lump in his throat as he tightened his fingers and ended his thoughts.

He had been searching for connection all his life because, growing up, he had never experienced much of it. His clan valued strength and combat over meaningful conversations, a mindset he could never fully comprehend. He often found himself around others with similar views as his clan, so when something sparkled, when something was *different*, it caught his attention instantly. In just a few days, Simon had witnessed many things that piqued his interest in Andreas. Many of the half-elf's traits reminded him of someone *important*.

These similarities sparked Simon's desire to communicate with and understand Andreas, even if it meant raising his voice to be heard by this man.

Andreas hissed and broke the silence, "I didn't tell you because I'm **tired**. I am so sick of hearing about being a Dwyer. I'm sick of others knowing my identity and only being interested in what they can get from me. I'm **fed up** with having this massive name hanging over my head every second of every day!" Andreas' words tumbled wildly as if he were nearing a panic attack. His hand trembled as it held fast to Simon's tunic, his brow so tightly knit that his eyes strained to focus as he continued, "But do you know what I'm **most** tired of?!"

"What?" Simon whispered, his pupils dilating as he pinned Andreas' wrist against his chest. He leaned down, centimeters away, and fixated on the panicked green eyes that looked near tears.

Andreas exhaled as if Simon's nonchalant reply had stolen some of his momentum. The casualness of the response had taken him by surprise, and the limited space between them made his thoughts stall. Andreas stared wide-eyed, and the tension in his hand eased. He seemed disoriented suddenly.

He didn't remember what he was planning to say or know how to respond. He was too focused on the orc hanging on his every word—the heat of Simon's breath on his cheeks and the intensity of the man's stare. Andreas' stomach was filled with butterflies, and he felt his determination waver as the scent of oud from the man before him encompassed him like the warmth of a fire.

"… *What are you tired of, Andrea?*" Simon whispered, not daring to pull away.

Andreas' stomach churned as soon as he heard the nickname. Only two people had ever called him that; they were both important to him. They were Rhys, who was his only friend besides Keena, and his father. His Pops called him 'Andrea' unless he was in serious trouble.

Andreas recalled asking his father why he liked that nickname. They had been sitting in the garden after an incident, and his mother had encouraged the talk. Leo was not very good with words, so he needed to be prompted to start a conversation. He remembered the man being unusually calm—or trying to appear that way. His father was a terrible liar and hadn't been able to hide the fact he'd been worried the whole time they'd talked. They'd discussed Andreas' feelings and why he'd done what he had. Why Andreas had walked into the ocean, knowing he couldn't swim, and just **… let himself sink**.

It hadn't been the first time something like that had happened, and it was one of the reasons his family kept such a close eye on him. Andreas was more of a risk to himself than the world was to him most of the time.

> *'Andreas and Andrea have similar meanings, but I prefer the concept of you being brave and strong without the overwhelming need to fight. You can possess bravery and strength without being a warrior. I like*

*you best when you don't feel like you have to fight, kid. ... So can you promise to say when you're tired? We can't carry the weight of your feelings, but we can sure as hell carry **you**, okay?'*

Andreas' grip on Simon's shirt broke as he recalled his father's words. He saw Simon's face contort from anger to concern as his vision blurred from tears. Andreas' knees buckled, and he felt the world shifting as he fell to the ground. Everything was slow, and Simon seemed to move simultaneously, following him down. Simon's arm steadied him as Andreas landed on his legs in the piling snow.

Andreas gasped, barely recognizing his voice as the words tumbled out mid-sob, "**I'm so tired of fighting, Simon.**"

Thirteen

Hope

Simon thought about the night before, dissecting the events.

Every time he recalled them, the memory of a half-orc woman scolding him came to mind and made his gut twist in guilt. Gitah had always told him he was too nosey and quick to judge. In the beginning, he thought she was trying to curb his grief and make him stop running out night after night, chasing dead ends and contradicting information. Eight years ago was an awful time for him, as well as for her. He had been chasing answers and trying to make sense of the ball of sorrow embedded in his being.

When the war ended ten years ago, that was supposed to end the hard times. It was supposed to begin the realm's new and promising future. Confusion, anger, and chaos were rampant ... but there was hope. Hope was something that this world was lacking for a long time, and he'd dared subscribe to it back then.

Dared, and one night, he was reminded that hope wasn't worth it.

Hope was temporary, for individuals' opinions and feelings were chaotic in the world at large. Hope couldn't grow without becoming twisted by the people's festering wounds. When everything he had known his whole life was revealed to be a web of lies, societies crumbled, and families disintegrated. The upheaval of the foundations of entire cities and cultures had caused as much chaos as the war. In that chaos, *good* people ... were **broken**. Lost. Blamed.

Simon's gaze drifted to the sleeping figure on the bed as he contemplated.

He had helped Andreas up the stairs to his room and made sure he went to bed the night before. Andreas had been incoherent and cried so much that he couldn't understand what he was saying. Simon stayed until the crying stopped and attempted to leave when he thought his companion was asleep. Andreas had grabbed him, reminding Simon of when he'd been tossed the shawl. There had been an unspoken fear in Andreas' face, so Simon had settled on the floor with one of the older quilts.

Occasionally, he would wake up to see Andreas' fingers hanging off the bed as if they had reached over to ensure he was still there. That was where Simon found them again, as his thoughts lingered on the words he'd considered only moments before. *Good people were hurt and unfairly blamed for things that were not their fault.*

Simon took a deep breath, filling his lungs with the faint scent of ivy and the lingering smell of amber cologne. Perhaps, he thought, the Dwyer family were good people who fit into that category. He had never followed up on the common suspicion of them, if only because he found it very hard to believe that a lone family caused all the world's sorrows. He was confident the family had its dark aspects and had blood on its hands, but if you were living in this world, it was tough not to, especially during wartime.

Simon saw the darker fingers stir, and Andreas' hand shifted as if looking for something. Simon reached up and placed his hand close enough to touch. It took a few seconds, but when the bandaged hand bumped into his own, Andreas grasped and squeezed his index finger. It was as if Andreas wasn't sure of what he had found. After a moment, Andreas tapered off and returned to sleep, and his hand slacked.

Simon exhaled as he held his hand in place, inches away from the dangling fingers. The past few times Andreas had grabbed him, he'd been aware of the varying sensation of his grip. Even through the bandages, he could feel the ridges of scars and how the hand seemed to seize if Andreas squeezed too tightly. He dared to extend a finger and brush it along the side of the limp wrist beside him. It was the same even there, where the other's hands connected to his body ... small ridges of scar tissue.

Simon frowned.

He'd gotten some answers, but they prompted many more questions. It was something that always happened because he could never have enough answers. Simon had been born a curious child, which had been seen as debilitating to his clan. The more he wanted to know, the more unfortunate things came to pass ... and the more he lost. Perhaps that's why he'd started making assumptions eight years ago. If he assumed and answered his own questions, then there was no chance of trouble.

There was no chance of him losing anything again ... but there was no chance of him *gaining* anything either. It was a deafening realization he came face to face with the longer he was around the man lying only a few feet away from him.

A valley formed in Simon's brow, and he found himself biting the inside of his cheek so roughly it bled. *"You remind me of Olur, Red ..."* he whispered, his gaze fixed on moving his finger as it reached the end of Andreas' index and lingered. He'd heard his throat close, and he forced the name out like it was a foul taste. He hadn't spoken that name aloud in *years*. It almost seemed wrong to do so with how it sliced his throat like broken glass.

Simon's attention shifted to the faint light pouring through the window. It was early morning, and he couldn't tell if the snow was still falling from his place on the floor. He followed the light rays as they filtered through the glass pane and out of sight onto the mattress beside him. His hand retracted, and he sat up to peer over the nest of quilts and pillows.

Andreas was curled into a small ball and deep in slumber. Blankets covered him, and his hair was spread out in tangled waves, obscuring his face.

Simon's head tilted, taking in the sight. Despite being sound asleep, he'd never seen someone look so distinct or *alive* in natural light. His attention settled on the fragments of skin visible in the mass of crimson, and he started following the freckles as they spread over and off the other man's cheeks. They appeared on the visible pieces of Andreas' throat before vanishing beneath the blankets and red hair. There was this wild, chaotic beauty around the sleeping half-elf.

Simon could see why Andreas would be a popular bedmate, and he'd be a liar if he said he hadn't thought of just how far *down* those freckles persisted. He'd often wondered if they made the rest of the coppery skin luminous in the sunlight.

*Of how Andreas would look naked and **writhing** underneath ...*

Simon swallowed and returned his attention to the bay window to end the introspection. He focused on calming his breath and ignored the tingling sensation settling into his belly. The thoughts persisted, and his mind's eye wandered, imagination blossoming without even looking at his counterpart as it had several nights before. His head was already a mess without adding half-drowsy morning fantasies.

Last night, mixed with the giddiness of eliciting a reaction from the sleeping man, Simon had been fighting the realization that he found the whole explosive argument *desirable*. He didn't have a very passive personality, and more often than not, when he was angry, others were intimidated to the point of silence. Arguments weren't rare, but being challenged so animatedly during them was **exceedingly** rare. He wasn't used to caring about being told he was wrong, much less continuing the quarrel to the point it escalated into blows.

Last night, he was fueled by this unsolicited, enchanted anger; he'd been drawn to Andreas' overflowing words like a fly to honey. It had been *intoxicating*.

Simon's eyes flickered back to the sleeping form and froze when he saw an emerald eye peering back at him. He swallowed again, still trying to chase off the wandering thoughts his mind clung to; a chill rolled down his spine, and he dared wonder if Andreas could hear his thoughts with how intently he watched.

"*You stayed ...*" Andreas whispered, moving his hair from his face. He adjusted to reach up and tilt the orc's face. Simon's wide jaw tensed, and his teeth gritted as Andreas angled his sandy features. Andreas inspected the swollen area just under the man's left eye. "Sorry," he said.

Simon focused his gaze on the wall just above the other's head. He swallowed as his face shifted, and the bandaged hand lingered under his chin. *"I deserved it ..."* he whispered. The same unnerving silence settled between them as the night before.

Andreas tapped Simon's chin and pulled his hand back as he said, "You did."

Andreas saw the odd eyes that had been focused off, unwilling to look him in the face, shift to meet his gaze. Andreas moved under the blankets, and he eyed his companion. Simon was leaning forward, putting more weight on the side of the mattress than he had been when looking out the window. The orc seemed more interested in *him* than the sky, and the man's body gave him away. His stomach twisted; the tension **had** returned from the night before—all of it.

"Simon?" Andreas whispered.

The mercenary's brows lifted, and his nostrils flared when he heard his name. Simon shuddered, ignoring the buzzing in his ears and throbbing in his gut. He was still attempting to dispel the thoughts from earlier and failing. The way his name was called was enticing and made his words whisper out heated, *"Hmm?"*

"Why did you stay?" Andreas asked.

Simon took a deep breath and replied, "You wanted me to stay, so I did." He nervously played with the edge of his tunic, trying to keep his hands occupied.

It reminded Andreas of the previous night in the kitchen when Simon had started fidgeting with his glass. Andreas bit his lip and chewed it as he processed the response.

Was it that simple? Was Simon waiting for him to **ask**? Andreas felt his stomach flip. If that was all ... *he could do that much.* He had never had someone attracted to him go out of their way to keep their distance. Initially, he questioned whether there was interest or if he had made Simon uncomfortable in the past week. The past twelve hours, however, gave him more certainty.

Andreas tucked some hair behind his ear and asked, "Aren't you cold?"

Simon stared at the blankets and the concealed figure beneath them before meeting the emerald eyes watching him. He mentally groaned and shifted where he sat. The question was loaded, and he knew it. "No," he said.

Andreas leaned on his arm and let the blanket loiter around his elbows. His head tilted, hair falling like a curtain to block the sunlight. Simon's gaze followed the blankets as they slid down, then snapped back to Andreas' face as if the orc had caught himself doing something vile. Andreas' toes curled, thrilled by the response, and he fought to keep from smiling at the action. "You're sure? It's warm here in the sunshine," he said.

The beams of light caught the freckles across Andreas' cheeks, and Simon watched them glitter like fragments of gold. He lost himself for a moment counting, following them from one to another as if he were playing a game. Then, Andreas bit his lip and looked from Simon's eyes to his mouth.

Simon's thoughts came to a screeching halt, and he had to swallow to rid his mouth of pooling saliva. This wasn't safe for his heart and only made that nagging sensation in the pit of his stomach more vicious. It seemed like Andreas was poking at it, and Simon came to the startling realization that ... *he was now the one being teased*. A small smile appeared as he looked away from his companion. He was almost ashamed at how captivated he was by this man.

"Is it?" Simon finally asked, voice husky.

A smile blossomed over Andreas' lips as he caught the expression on Simon's face. He tilted his head and teased, "It is. There's plenty of room *if you're cold.*"

Simon chuckled, the tension that had built over the last few hours of thought fading into one of a far different kind. Sitting was becoming uncomfortable, and the captivated smile on his face grew as he thought about it. Andreas knew what he was doing; this sorcerer was toying with him like a spider would a fly. Finally, Simon returned his eyes to the face across from him and gave his full attention. "Are you *inviting* me over there ... or just passing on information?" he asked.

"Inviting... if you can forgive me for being a Dwyer and..." Andreas patted the mattress and smoothed the blanket back to reveal the space beside him. The sunlight flooded onto the sheet. "If you're willing to piss off Talien

more," he said.

A heavy sigh hit the air; Simon seemed to have come to terms with something.

An excited sense of accomplishment settled into Andreas' gut when he felt the space beside him occupied, and he squirmed. A rough hand brushed his jaw and tilted his face upwards. The hetero-chromatic eyes were as they'd been the night before, inches away and fully invested. Simon's hand slid, trailing down Andreas' arm till it found his hip. It was hauntingly slow—as if the orc were trying to regain some control over the situation. Andreas felt a chill creep down his spine when Simon's hand finally fell to rest over him, and the man's fingers teased small circles on his lower back.

"You're right. It is warm," Simon whispered, a smile creeping up.

Andreas laughed and leaned into Simon's chest. Simon's heart thumped wildly in response. *"You'll learn I'm right often,"* Andreas whispered.

Simon laughed, teasing, "Oh yeah? Look who's confident now."

Andreas leaned in and whispered, *"I'm pretty confident you want to **kiss me**."*

The arm on his hip tensed. The fingers that trailed over his lower back spread as if they were determined to keep him close. Simon chuckled again, looking from Andreas' eyes to his lips and then back. There was lingering uncertainty in the man's face, and Andreas didn't know where it came from.

"Andrea ..."

"You can," Andreas whispered back, waiting.

It wasn't long before the space between them closed, and Simon kissed him desperately. Andreas' mind reeled as the other man's weight pressed on top of him, and he forgot how to breathe. All he knew was that it was warmer than it had been in a ***long*** time.

Fourteen

Survival

The scent of bacon and pancakes tugged at his nose as if he had been thrust into a memory from his childhood. It was so familiar that Andreas smiled and buried his head in the pillow he leaned on. After the smell always came thundering feet and his sister and dog jumping on top of him. He waited, but the weight of his family trying to wake him up never came. Instead, he was left in silence to listen to the wind chimes from his cracked window.

Andreas breathed deeply, verifying he wasn't dreaming up the smell, and slowly opened his eyes. He found himself alone in his room, the window still cracked and the door open to reveal the hallway.

The light was bordering on dusk, and the warmth of the sun's sinking rays washed over him in waves as they dipped below the treeline. Reaching over, he felt the space beside him that had been occupied before he fell asleep. It was still faintly warm, the pillows bearing remnants of another body that had altered them for a time. Simon couldn't have gotten up too long ago if the orc was why he smelled breakfast.

He shifted and instantly regretted moving. His hips were sore, mainly the one that had been injured—nothing unbearable, but enough to make him pause and maneuver his leg to stretch it out. Andreas let out an extended sigh, closing his eyes and wandering off absentmindedly. What surfaced was a recollection of the previous night, causing his face to flush and his eyes to widen in an attempt to suppress the memory. After clearing his throat, Andreas got up to find his clothes.

The longer he smelled food, the more he realized how *hungry* he was. The longer he lingered on that memory, the more his hunger may change to something else entirely.

***

It took fifteen minutes to crawl out of bed and locate his clothing, the last piece tucked underneath his mattress. Then, he loosely braided his hair as he started down the stairs, humming an idle tune to himself. When his feet touched the ground floor, he secured the black ribbon he often used as a hair tie. He spotted Simon in the kitchen. The older man caught sight of him, and Andreas lingered on the stairs before waving.

Simon smiled back and said, "Evening."

"Is it really evening?" Andreas asked, looking out at the surrounding forest through a window. He stepped not toward the kitchen but toward the window beside the door. He was starting to lose track of time here, as he always did when he came to his family's cabin.

"Are you looking for them?" Simon asked as he poured hot water into a teacup.

"Are they still here?" Andreas asked, fiddling with the platinum dragonfly on his necklace. He glanced up when he noticed a presence beside him and reached out for the cup of warm liquid he was offered. Hands moved and encircled his waist, and Simon leaned against him before he could react with more than a small smile.

"They aren't. I walked out about an hour ago for firewood and looked around," Simon said, head turning so his tusks brushed his companion's exposed neckline.

Andreas tried to stifle a smile when Simon left a token of affection against his jaw. "That tickles," he said, shifted his attention downward, and leaned in to return the kiss with one on Simon's forehead. "That's good. We can leave at first light," Andreas continued.

Simon squeezed; the kiss had pleasantly surprised him. He smiled and focused his attention on the snow. The sky was cloudless, and stars could be seen brightening in the fading sunlight. It drew his attention not further out the window but to the man in his arms. Closeness. He hadn't realized he missed it, for it had been so long since he'd had it. His face then buried in Andreas' neck, and his tusks brushed against his skin again. Simon smiled as if he'd thought of a joke and whispered, "*Hey, Red ...*"

Andreas looked down absentmindedly, laughing, "Hmm?"

Standing up, Simon surveyed the man he had been holding. He studied the carnelian features before smiling broadly and teased, "I was going to compliment you, but I don't know. ... I think you looked prettier *naked*."

"Really?" Andreas questioned, laughing. His face heated, and he elbowed Simon in the stomach playfully.

Simon pulled away, laughing, and then headed back towards the kitchen.

The green eyes watched, following the orcish form as it skirted the island bar and returned to where he'd been plating food. Andreas bit his lip and shifted his body weight onto his healthy leg. He'd never had someone cook him food ... at least not someone he'd slept with. Hell, they rarely stayed to say good morning, much less anything else.

"Come eat, Andrea. You've barely eaten in two days," Simon called from the kitchen.

Andreas felt his heart jump, and he looked down at the mug of chamomile tea he'd been given. Being called that nickname by someone else was unfamiliar, and its inexplicable power over him was mind-boggling. He turned and headed toward the kitchen. As his stomach growled loudly, he settled against the cool stone bartop.

Simon laughed and pushed a plate over. "Here," he said.

Andreas glanced at the plate and noticed the absence of bacon. Instead, there were fresh red berries and four pancakes with honey. He placed his cup of tea on the countertop and glanced up with a smile. "You remembered," he said.

Simon was chewing bacon when the comment caught him off guard. He swallowed prematurely and then made a slight face of discomfort.

"That you don't eat meat?" Simon asked, trying not to choke.

"Yeah," Andreas laughed.

"I've been around you all day for a week and a half … if I didn't notice it by now, I'd be concerned about my intelligence," Simon said, shrugged, and grabbed another piece of bacon.

Andreas snickered, and the two settled into silence to eat.

* * *

Simon gathered the dirty dishes and walked them to the sink. He then started cleaning up, ignoring the small protests he received about help.

Andreas sipped his tea before saying, "I'm sorry for not telling you who I was sooner." He heard the dishwater noise stop, looked up to see the other figure still, and focused on the items in his hands. Simon remained this way momentarily before looking up and catching his eye.

"It's not alright that you did it, but I understand why you did." The mercenary spoke carefully, trying to put his thoughts into words properly, "I'm sorry for insulting your family."

Andreas gave a stiff smile, looking guilty. "It's not okay … but I accept your apology. I know my family and I don't have spotless reputations, so …" he said.

"I'm more likely to make my own judgments and assumptions than listen to others. You don't have to worry about that," Simon responded quickly, then focused on a dirty skillet.

"Reliable and free-thinking… you *are* desirable," Andreas said and sipped his tea.

Simon stopped what he was doing. His face burst into a nervous, almost skeptical grin as his eyes lifted, and he noticed the other man watching him. There was a tinge of warmth in his cheeks as he laughed and replied, "If this is payback for the desert, I think we're even at this point."

"What? Don't you like the taste of your own medicine?" Andreas hummed playfully.

"Careful, Red. Keep it up, and I'll haul you back upstairs."

"I'll have to try harder then," Andreas replied. He smiled as he saw the orc grin but remained focused on his task. He took another sip of tea and asked, "… Will Talien mess with your contracts?"

"If he finds out, yeah. He's pretty hell-bent on making your life and anyone interacting with you's life a living hell. Whatever you did, you pissed him off," Simon glanced up and shrugged before continuing, "I don't care; he can't ban me from the city because I have ties to other folk there."

Andreas rolled his eyes, "I did nothing to him. Ironically, you would think he would be happy to hear that I *didn't* reciprocate feelings for someone he cares about … but that wasn't the case. He's been pissed for years because I *hurt* the person, not happy for me giving him the open door to where he wanted to be," he complained.

Simon laughed loudly and asked, "Is that why you're banned from Ransol?"

"I swear on my mother's life. That's why he hates me," Andreas said, laughing at the stunned look he'd been given. "I wish I were lying because it's a pathetic reason to have an entire city barred from you if you ask me."

"I knew he was insane, but that's …" Simon shook the water from the skillet he'd washed and set it atop a towel to dry, "I thought you had stolen something from him," he said.

"No. Depending on how you look at it, I *gave* Talien something," Andreas shrugged. The noise of the water stopped again, and Andreas looked up to find Simon watching him. "What?" he asked.

"Rhys," Simon said in disbelief.

Andreas frowned, "What about Rhys?"

"You didn't return Rhys' feelings," Simon sighed as realization dawned on him. That was why he recognized the name when it was mentioned in Belmare. Rhys was the man Talien was infatuated with and why the whole of Ransol was on the lookout for Andreas. It was also the name said at **The Green Dragon** when the two patrons mentioned Andreas' reputation.

Andreas' face wrinkled in confusion.

"Rhys, is your friend that isn't allowed in **The Barbed Rose**?" Simon asked. Andreas nodded, saying, "He is. Why?"

"In Belmare, I overheard two folks talking about you. They mentioned his name. At the time, the name sounded familiar, but I didn't make the connection to Talien," Simon replied and shrugged. "I just connected the dots and realized why his name was familiar now. ... Isn't he a Lycan?"

Andreas nodded as Simon returned to washing the dirty dishes. "He is. He's natural-born, not bitten or cursed," he said.

"Is that why he can't go to your family's pub?"

"No, my Pops dislikes him because we used to fool around. He's tried to kill Rhys twice; the last time, he nearly broke one of Rhys' horns clean off his skull," Andreas said, frowning.

"Horns? Is he an Ifreann[3]?" Simon asked, glancing up momentarily.

"Yeah."

"That's quite the combination. A natural-born Lycan and an Ifreann... does he have horns when he shifts?" Simon asked.

Andreas finally laughed and said, "He does, actually."

Simon smiled, nodded, and then focused back on the dishes.

Andreas sat silently, observing the man across from him as he completed his task. He couldn't help but notice the sharpness of Simon's jaw and how the man's septum ring added a subtle elegance to his rugged face. A smile crept onto his lips as he watched Simon until he had to look away and focus on the cup of tea in his hands. The longer Andreas thought about their small conversation, the more giddy he felt. It was unusual for him to have casual conversations with someone he had been intimate with, especially about other men. He, however, found it *enjoyable* to talk with Simon.

... To be *with* Simon.

"Have you decided if you're going to finish the job with me?" Andreas inquired without looking up.

The sound of water flowing filled the space, and Simon dried his hands. He saw the other leaning forward on the counter, observing it. Instead of responding immediately, he rounded the bartop and reached out to take

---

[3] For more information about the Ifreann of *Lusefell*, please refer to the back matter titled **"The People of Lusefell."**

the cup of tea from Andreas' hands. The green eyes widened in surprise and looked up in confusion. Simon then reached down and angled Andreas' sharp features toward him; he kissed him. Andreas relaxed and then slowly returned the kiss.

Simon pulled away from the smaller figure, leaned forward, and boxed his counterpart against the bartop with his body. "I think Talien would be more pissed that I slept with you than helped you with a job, Red."

Andreas' cheeks turned pink as he stifled a smile. "That's... fair," he said, reaching out to toy with the hem of his companion's shirt, "If he finds out ... he may not find out."

"True, I don't think we like Talien enough to brag to him," Simon smirked.

"That's true ... and if that's the case ..." Andreas let his fingers tiptoe up the orc's chest, "What's the harm in doing it again? Or a few more times ... He'll never know, *right?*"

Simon chuckled in disbelief and leaned down to kiss Andreas' cheek before drawing his lips along it and to one of his long, pointed ears. He felt the man against him squirm, grip his shirt, and exhale. "I'm not complaining ... but we have *a lot* of walking tomorrow," Simon teased.

Andreas appeared flustered and muttered, "I *hate it* when you're right."

"Don't you like sharing the spotlight?" Simon asked, tilting his head.

"I'll share it sometimes. *Maybe*. If you say please," Andreas said and smiled. He felt a hand shift from the bartop to his lower back; Simon leaned in, closing the distance to one of his ears again. Andreas squirmed more and whispered, *"Simon, if you keep doing that ..."*

"You can keep the spotlight. You look better in it," Simon whispered, drawing his tusk along his companion's ear before pivoting to leave a token of affection on the other man's neck. His other hand moved to trail down Andreas' arm. He felt the man tense the closer to his wrists and hands he grew. His fingers stopped just above the bandages, and Simon turned to bury his face in the crook of Andreas' neck. Once there, his brows furrowed, and his lips frowned. "Andrea?"

Andreas exhaled. The actions were enticing *and* terrifying the closer Simon's fingers got to his own. His hands trembled as he forced them to stay where they were. He swallowed, trying to calm down, and replied, "Yes, Simon?"

"You mentioned your family … what they'd been through in the wars …" Simon felt Andreas tense and clutch his shirt, "Those things we saw at the pillars. *Did they do that to your hands?*" he asked.

"*You saw.*" The words were barely whispered. Andreas almost seemed angry.

"Not intentionally. You lost consciousness the night we arrived," Simon said, his grip on Andreas tightening as though he feared the other man might flee. He had come to understand one thing: Andreas liked to *run*. He would create physical space or engage in distractions before redirecting the topic of conversation if it was something he found uncomfortable. "When I was fixing your hip …" Simon continued.

Andreas swallowed and turned his head to rest on Simon's shoulder. Simon wasn't asking for information other than 'yes' or 'no.' He didn't have to dive into details; he didn't have to … Andreas closed his eyes, trying to push a hazy, creeping memory back into his subconscious. "… *Yes. They did,*" he said.

Simon released a breath he hadn't known he'd been holding. The arm holding Andreas' waist gave a rough squeeze, trying to reassure him that he wouldn't pry. He'd been right, and there it was again: an answer and another string of unanswered questions. "Can I grab your hand? To show you something …" he asked.

Andreas remained quiet for a long time before nodding and whispering, "*Don't squeeze.*" Simon grabbed his fingers and lifted them gently. Andreas leaned back, pulling away from the man's chest when their hands crossed into view. Simon positioned them against the old scar from his temple to his jaw. Simon pulled Andreas' index finger along it, and the half-elf's brow furrowed.

"Simon?"

Simon let Andreas' hand fall against his shoulder, and his eyes found the concerned green ones watching in confusion. "My …" Simon started and cleared his throat. The word was raspy, "My mother gave me that the day she died; she tried to split open my skull because she found out I'd fucked another man ..."

Andreas' green eyes widened and grew glassy.

Simon smiled, leaned forward, and nudged the darker features with his nose. "She tried to kill me, so *I killed her*. ... Then I ran. I don't regret killing her because she'd have walked into Ransol and tried to kill the man I slept with, too," he said.

Andreas swallowed, reaching up to Simon's cheeks; he squeezed them gently, then tilted Simon's head down to press their foreheads together. "*You were **sixteen**,*" he whispered.

Simon nudged Andreas' nose with his own and closed his eyes to breathe in the scent of amber cologne, saying, "I've survived. ... *So have you.* Please don't be ashamed of surviving because I won't judge you for what's happened that led you to this point. Alright?"

The hands holding his cheeks trembled, and he pulled Andreas close. Simon settled into the warmth, enjoying the physical contact. He didn't know how long he had this man's radiance to enjoy, *but he would bask in it while it lasted.*

Fifteen

Suspicion

They still had a day of travel before seeing Fossy's tall stone gates in the distance. However, he could smell the salty air rolling in the breeze from the sea nestled against the port city. Unfortunately, the city waiting for them wasn't what Andreas was thinking about. He was focused on the gathering of tents off the side of the road, as he had been since he spotted them.

He hadn't liked the look of the small gathering of tents as they descended from the edge of the mountains and ventured into the valley beyond. He recalled seeing them the day before and had considered contacting his grandparents; they had *not* been there when he visited six months ago. Now that they passed the encampment of five tents, he regretted not reaching out the day before. The more he looked at the gray canvas, the more uneasy he became.

The camp was not big or close enough to the city to be militant. However, the few individuals he saw moving around within it were all in similar garb. The cloaks and armor were all black, covering as much skin as possible. It reminded him far too much of **EDEN** soldiers' clothing over ten years ago, even if it was less defined and leather back then.

Andreas jumped when he felt a hand brush the small of his back, and Simon looked at him with concern. He forced a smile and replied, "Sorry.

Just interested in the encampment. They weren't here the last time I came this way."

"*Should we be worried about it?*" Simon whispered, stepping closer. His eyes lifted to drift over the tents a hundred feet away.

Andreas looked back at the tents and shook his head. "No ... not yet," he said.

Simon let his attention linger momentarily, almost as if he wanted to memorize the armor of the individuals walking around. Then, he nodded to the road ahead. "I'm scoping it out to see if there is anything worth seeing," he murmured, leaning close enough that his lips almost brushed Andreas' ear, hidden from the view of the tents. "*Don't linger too long, or you'll look suspicious,*" Simon whispered, kissed Andreas' temple, and pulled away.

Andreas pulled the shawl closer around his shoulders, crossing his arms under the fabric as Simon moved forward. Simon's behavior changed, reminiscent of his actions in the mountains. Andreas remembered how Simon's attention sharpened at any sound or sight, his shoulders tensing significantly. Simon often seemed poised to react instantly, a response to uncertainty Andreas found strikingly similar to his Papa's. This made him smile as his concentration returned to the camp.

Andreas jumped again, spotting a figure about forty feet away and closing in. It was a slight figure wearing a black cloak that obscured most of its form. Its hood was pulled low so that only the lower half of its face was visible. Andreas' hands unwound from beneath his shawl and fell to rest at his side, ready should he need to react. He inclined his head slightly before stepping back onto the road and asking, "Can I help you?"

"Perhaps I can assist you? You appear interested in our camp," said a woman with a beaming smile.

Andreas swallowed, disliking the gray coloration of her gums and the black residue around her teeth as they flashed. "I didn't see you all last time I went to Fossy," he said.

"No, our minstrels have only just reached this far. Times have been tough for the faithful, as I am sure you know," the woman said and beamed again, gesturing to Andreas' necklace.

Andreas' brow furrowed, "Pardon? I don't know of any faith that dresses like you." He reached up reflexively, almost grasping the long phoenix feather and dragonfly on his necklace. He didn't like this. Something about this seemed *strange*. He turned to walk and noticed the woman matched his stride but never stepped forward on the road. It made him uneasy, and he picked up his pace and caught her match it again.

"No, we follow not the Old Ones, but the Primal Ones. *Like you*," the woman hummed, hands swinging freely at her side.

"Pardon?" Andreas' eyes narrowed, daring a glance ahead to see if he could spot Simon and then immediately returning to the woman following him. Something told him not to look away from her.

"*The Lovers*. You follow the Primal Lovers, yes?" she asked, almost giddy.

"Cael and Pithus?" Andreas asked and glanced down at his necklace. He'd never heard them referenced in such a way. He slowed down, interested in what was to be said, and asked, "Is that who you mean?"

"Indeed," the woman stopped abruptly and approached the road's edge. She did not step onto the gravel that made it nor allow her presence to reach over it. "Do you know who they've **forgotten**? Would you like to hear our story? For you are so lost, you do not even know yourself," she said and laughed; it was almost a cackle of delight.

"What are you talking about?" Andreas' face twisted in confusion, and he swallowed. His stomach was screaming, telling him to keep moving. This woman wasn't right ... *There was something wrong here*—from how she spoke to how she moved and refused to step onto the road. "I'm not lost at all," he said.

It happened quickly, so quickly that Andreas could not react. The woman's hand jerked forth and grabbed one of his tightly, and upon crossing over the edge of the road, it *burst* into flames. He smelled rotting, charred flesh and felt the fingers around his hand squeeze. It was painful, not because of the fire but because of the sheer pressure of her grip. As Andreas struggled to free himself from her grasp, his eyes were locked on the fingers that held him. **He** did not burn; the flames did not touch him. They felt warm, almost comforting, as they brushed against his skin.

"**You are more lost than you realize, little spark**," she said.

Andreas' gaze lifted, and he saw the other half of the woman's face staring back at him. She looked unphased by her burning limb, and the flames concentrated only on the piece of her body above the road. Ashen and heart-shaped, her face was pretty in an unsettling way. Her eyes captivated his attention, making it almost impossible for him to turn away. They were pitch black, pupilless, and had markings that flooded out of the sockets of a black and gray coloration. Andreas recognized the markings, which bore a resemblance to the peculiar tattoo of his grandfather, Neil.

There was whistling and a wet squelching.

Before Andreas realized what had happened, he saw a dagger tumble onto the ground, covered in coagulated crimson. The woman's fingers that had clenched his hand loosened, and he pulled his arm back, shaking it free. The woman's arm had been cut in half, and the growing flames had done the rest. Half of her arm fell to the ground in a burning heap. Andreas felt a heavy hand grab his arm and pull him backward, and he watched the woman in stunned confusion.

Simon maneuvered Andreas behind him and snarled, "**I suggest you head back to camp.**" His voice was acidic and growled out in a way that caused his lips to curl and his tusks to flare menacingly. He looked like a starving animal that was hell-bent on keeping an intruder away from its last scrap of food.

The woman's head bowed to hide the upper part of her face, and another smile spread. She seemed unbothered by her arm lying smoldering on the gravel road and resumed her stance on the edge. She giggled and said, "Of course." Her attention turned to Andreas, and another toothy smile appeared, "Mind the road, little spark. Don't want to get lost on your way home."

Andreas watched her leave. "*What the fuck?*" he whispered and looked at the blackened arm cut free at the elbow.

Simon grabbed Andreas' forearm and started inspecting his hand. "Are you alright?" he asked through grit teeth, glancing back towards the retreating figure. He looked as if he were debating chasing her down and snapping her neck.

Andreas directed his gaze downward. He noticed the bandages were untouched but could see the edges of a burn scar he bore on his palm glowing faintly beneath them. Andreas muttered in confusion, "What the … yeah. Yeah, I'm fine."

"We need to leave," Simon hissed and tugged Andreas forward, eyes locked on the encampment. Upon the woman's return, several figures paused what they were doing and looked in their direction. Not moving, not threatening …just staring like they were watching a performance play out. It made his skin crawl as he grabbed the dagger he'd thrown and shook the blood free.

Andreas looked over and started to speak but paused. As they walked, his brow furrowed. He pointed at Simon and muttered incomprehensibly under his breath.

> **"She wouldn't step on the road, Simon. Her arm burst into flames when she reached out to grab me. It's like she *couldn't* step onto it."**

Simon looked over as the words magically echoed in his ear as if whispered. He looked down, inspecting the gravel, before muttering back incomprehensibly under his breath.

> **"Looks like we're sleeping on the road tonight. Have your grandparents ever mentioned this road being enchanted? Guarded? Anything?"**

Andreas shook his head at Simon's response. No, he'd never heard of anything other than the shattered beacons years prior. "There used to be beacons—enchanted crystals—scattered along the road. They were all destroyed in the wars, though. There's no way they could have lingering effects, right?" he asked.

Simon shrugged, still on edge. "I hit shit. You do the magic—you tell me."

Andreas looked back down at his palm in confusion. The dull light from beneath the linen bandages had faded off. He could only trace the scar beneath them because he knew where it was. "I ... *I don't know,*" he whispered the last words, at a loss.

"Your grandfather's notice said something about investigating a family ... Do you think that has anything to do with it?" Simon asked and glanced over his shoulder, watching the fading tents as they put more ground between them and the encampment.

"I don't know. Either way, I wouldn't say I like it ... We need to tell them what we saw. I've never seen armor like that, even with cities growing and changing after rebuilding," Andreas said and fidgeted, his arm falling between him and Simon as they walked. With a shaky hand, he brushed the orc's wrist. Simon's hand reacted and bumped back immediately.

"I've never seen them either; they didn't have insignia or markings of family membership. That woman stunk ... like rotten flesh, Red," Simon glanced over. "*Like Varog stink,*" he whispered. He sounded like he was getting agitated again.

"*That's what I'm worried about,*" Andreas whispered back, his face pale and focused on the road ahead.

"Would **EDEN** be that overt?" Simon whispered, his pinkie nudging Andreas' hand.

"Usually no ... but ..." Andreas reached out absentmindedly with his pinkie and caught the other man's. He looped them and let his finger remain; he felt Simon's small finger squeeze reassuringly as if Simon felt his hand shaking.

"*Something has changed. Remember what I said at the pillars?*" Andreas whispered.

The mercenary nodded, shifting his head to inspect their surroundings. "**Yeah. I do,**" Simon spat and dared a look back over his shoulder. His pupils had grown small, barely visible, as if the more he thought about the woman, the more he wanted to turn around and *kill* her. The moment he'd seen her grab Andreas popped to mind, and his temple throbbed as his blood pressure rose. His nostrils flared, and his little finger tightened around Andreas' as his attention turned back to the road before them.

He shouldn't have left this man's side; he knew better than that. He knew that straying too far with unknown factors at play was a poor choice on his part, and thankfully, Andreas hadn't paid the price for his foolishness.

He would **not** make that mistake again.

Sixteen

EDEN

He'd admit that camping on the physical *road* wasn't exactly what he'd thought they'd be doing—even though Simon said they would be. Regardless, Simon started making camp under the path marker when they reached where the route split in two.

"You weren't kidding about sleeping *on* the road," Andreas said.

Simon looked up, frowning, and replied, "No, I wasn't. I'm not risking getting my throat slit in my sleep, even with us this close to Fossy."

Andreas dared a look over his shoulder, back towards the mountain path they'd traveled down. He could make out the flickers of firelight far in the distance, and it reminded him that the strange encampment was still closer than he had hoped. "Do you think whatever happened would happen again?" he asked.

"What part are you talking about?" Simon asked as he focused on starting a fire.

Andreas bit the inside of his cheek in thought before responding, "The flames."

Simon's hands stilled, and he looked up at his companion, scrutinizing him. Andreas was shifting on the balls of his feet, his gaze locked on the worn path they'd walked all day. The half-elf's face was twisted in thought, and his shoulders tensed as if he were on edge.

"Are you *positive* you didn't do that?" Simon asked.

Andreas looked up, confused, and replied, "I don't think I did. I didn't *try* to, anyway."

Simon shrugged and returned to striking the flint in his hand against his dagger. "Your magic is unstable, though, right? Could it have just reacted?" he asked.

That had happened before, Andreas would admit. Focusing on the place beneath the bandages where he knew burn marks were concentrated, Andreas looked at his palm. "Maybe. That's how I found out I could use it after all," he said.

"I feel like there's a story there; you want to elaborate?" Simon asked, chuckling.

The fire roared to life suddenly, and Simon jolted back in shock. He hadn't expected it to light so abruptly or with as much force as it had. He watched it, noting the embers had barely taken time to grow and were already jumping high into the air as if they'd been given oil. Simon looked at the road they were on, and he frowned. It was strange, and he wondered if some enchantment *was* at work.

Andreas slipped over, settling beside the fire to warm his hands, "It's not much of a story. My Pops was out of the city when some rumors were getting stirred up about children going missing. There's a cave on the beach near the *Theron-DeLeon Estate*—the leader of Belmare's home. I was worried for obvious reasons, so I talked two folks looking for a job into helping me investigate," he said.

Simon settled on the ground and searched their bags for food. Their rations were running thin, and he was pleased they were so close to a warm bed and a full meal. "You didn't think to investigate the leaders?" he asked.

"No. Aunt Yuena wouldn't do that; neither would Aunt Kamille."

Simon's head tilted, and he asked, "Aunt? You're related to them, *too*?"

"Not exactly," Andreas responded, laughing aloud. "They're family friends, so we just call them that. When I was saved during the war, Aunt Yuena's aunt, Remi, took care of me."

"As in Remillia Villieu? The *Speaker*?" Simon blurted out, eyes wide.

"Oh? You know Remi?" Andreas asked.

Simon choked on his spit before managing out, "Even those of us who don't keep up with the Primals know who she is. I've never met her, but O—" Simon stopped, silencing himself.

Andreas snapped his head up, thinking perhaps Simon had seen something along the path. Yet, he found Simon staring into the fire with a look of disconnect; somehow, the mercenary looked paler than usual, and his shoulders were as stiff as a board.

"Simon?"

"I know who she is. Yes," Simon answered mechanically, eyes not leaving the fire. He jumped when he felt a hand brush against his.

Andreas watched, tempted to question the sudden shutdown because it wasn't *like* Simon to shut down without cause. "Are you okay?" he asked.

"Yeah. *Speaker*?" Simon asked, changing the topic, and looked up.

Simon was a terrible liar. Andreas let his hand linger, concerned, before he nodded. "Yeah. I didn't know who she was when I was younger; she made good cookies, and her kitchen always smelled like cabbage," he said.

Simon snorted.

"She always made this stewed cabbage; I think she just wanted to tease my Pops with it, from what I remember," Andreas spoke, laughing as a fond memory surfaced. "Anyway, Aunt Yuena and her wife, Kamille, wouldn't harm kids. They're good people; one works for **The Rose Guard** under my Papa. If anything, Aunt Kamille got a lot of kids *out* of really terrible places. She runs the spy network in the organization."

"Are you allowed to tell me that?" Simon asked, breaking apart a piece of bread and handing half of it to the man beside him.

Andreas took the offered food with a smile. "Probably not, but I'll vouch for you with my Papa if he tries to kill you for knowing too much," he said.

Their fingers brushed, and Simon smiled back before leaning against the road sign to watch the world around them. He studied the mountains and asked, "What happened then? Regarding your magic?"

"Ah. Sorry, I got sidetracked," Andreas smiled, blushing and looking away.

"There was some weird ... *rift*? If you can believe me about that?" he said.

"Rift?" Simon asked, brow furrowing.

"I don't know how to explain it, but based on what my Grandpa Neil said, it was most likely caused by magic. He said powerful spells or people can sometimes tear open rifts between here and other places in the *Mortal Plane*. Sometimes, it's a different plane altogether. It's extremely rare, but ..." Andreas said.

"So someone with a lot of power did something they weren't supposed to. Do you think they were trying to target Belmare?" Simon questioned.

"That's what we think. Mistwalkers were in the cave, and when I saw them, I panicked and ran. They cornered me, of course, and I nearly died, but before they could finish me, my hands ..." Andreas paused, looking down at his palms.

"You did the same thing then as in the mountains with the Varog," Simon said.

"Yeah, just not on purpose that time. I had no control, and my hands were burned because of it," Andreas replied.

Simon digested the words before clearing his throat, "You didn't get hurt on the road, though. Do you think that's what happened again, but you had control?" he asked.

"No. This fire was different. It was almost cool against my skin. It wasn't a spell I did or a knee-jerk reaction by my magic," Andreas replied.

Simon leaned forward, listening, before asking, "You think you know what happened?"

"I don't know. I know there used to be beacons along the path on this side of the mountains. Do you remember seeing the crystals outside my grandparent's cabin?" Andreas asked and looked up expectantly.

"The weird-looking red things?"

"Yeah. They were like those, but smaller and worked more like torches along the road; they kept dangerous things off it so travelers were safe. Just before Cael regained his memory of everything, Qella destroyed the magic on them and shattered them. Belmare was almost destroyed when it was attacked then," Andreas said.

Simon nodded, vaguely recalling the stories of the event. "You think they have lingering effects now that Cael is back to full power?"

Andreas shrugged. "I wouldn't think so because they got destroyed, but… maybe?" He let his mind wander for a time. Then, remembering something, his brow furrowed, and he continued, "I know my grandparents were gifted crystals from the Holy Isle for their work in the war—that's why the cabin is such a safe place."

"That's why the Varog wouldn't walk into the clearing," Simon muttered.

Andreas nodded and replied, "Yeah, there's a lot of protection magic *and* beacons. Those things are terrified of Cael, and it would take someone on par with him to destroy them now that he's at his full strength again. So …"

"You think it was him?" Simon asked.

Andreas looked up, confused, and asked, "Who?"

"Cael. Your family is a big deal with him, right?" Simon responded.

Somehow, this made Andreas laugh uncontrollably for a few moments.

Simon watched, observing how Andreas' face lit up, and his whole body shook from some unknown joke. Usually, not understanding would have annoyed him, but at the moment, he felt happy to see that the anxiety that had been growing was lifting from Andreas' shoulders.

"A big deal is … one way to put it. I don't think he's paying that much attention to me, much less enough that he's reigning down flaming punishment on others. If that were the case, he'd have killed Talien Draper long ago," Andreas managed through chuckles.

Simon snorted, nearly choking on his bread, "That's fair." The older man dusted off his hands, ridding his tunic of any remaining crumbs as he looked over the dark skyline. The temperature was plummeting, and the stars were overtaking the sky. "I'm assuming **EDEN** isn't gone then, or your family would have retired. Or am I wrong, and you're all just paranoid?" he said.

Andreas sighed and shifted so he could lean against Simon's shoulder. Simon maneuvered to allow him more access and reached out to twirl a few loose crimson strands that brushed his fingers.

"No. They're weaker, and the woman who leads it is less powerful if she's still alive, but they're not gone. Some people still believe they were victims of bad luck and deceived by Qella, just like the rest of us. Some still believe the organization is trustworthy. My Papa is determined to prove that wrong and is doing everything he can to strip the organization's remaining power before more kids vanish."

Simon looked down towards Andreas and nudged him. "So, you all know that **EDEN** was behind the kids vanishing *without* Qella's influence?" he asked.

Andreas looked up and bit his lip. "... Yeah. We do, but it's complicated."

"Your family has reasons that are keeping it from being proven."

"Yeah ... big ones," Andreas replied and sighed.

Simon gave another nudge and asked, "Ones ... I can't know?"

Andreas frowned, his brow furrowing. He started twisting his fingers, and within a few moments, Simon grabbed them to stop them.

"It's okay. I know enough about your family now to understand why you can't tell me *everything* ... just don't let it kill me, alright?" Simon said, and he squeezed the fingers within his own.

"That's why I can't tell you," Andreas replied, gave a small smile, and then settled back against the other's shoulder to watch the flames of the fire. "... I can't tell you much we know or about **EDEN** unless my Papa says I can."

Simon noted that the man sounded almost ... sad. Maybe that was why he didn't press the issue more—Andreas sounded like he genuinely wanted to tell him but couldn't without risking himself, his family ... and Simon's safety. It made a small knot in Simon's stomach twist as a wave of affection rose for the half-elf. He'd let it be for now and focus on proving himself *safe* to tell. He had a nagging suspicion that he would have to prove himself to more than just Andreas.

Simon reached over and pressed against Andreas' once-dislocated hip. Andreas winced, and Simon frowned before asking, "Tender? It hasn't popped out again, has it?"

"No, just uncomfortable. The joys of healing magic—won't bother me for long," Andreas hummed.

"You're sure your hands didn't get burned?"

"I'm sure, Simon," Andreas smiled and then nudged the man he was using for support. "What? Are you *worried*?" he asked.

"Worried you're going to hurt yourself with how much you want to bone," Simon teased. He saw the man against him turn red and redirect his attention to the fire. Simon settled into the silence that followed and allowed his thoughts to consume him as he digested the information he'd been told.

Yes, though he wouldn't say it aloud, he *was* worried … but about a lot more than simply Andreas' dislocated hip. He wondered just how many more times Andreas would be targeted, like earlier, if **EDEN** were still big players in the darker aspects of the world.

How many more times was Andreas going to need to run or fight?

Simon's face darkened as he looked back towards the mountains and recalled their argument in the snow. It seemed much heavier a burden to bear now.

He didn't want Andreas to fight to live his life.

Seventeen

Trust

"Emhyr, where are my grandparents?" Andreas huffed out the words, a look of contained annoyance filling his features.

The individual in question was an Ancara[4], the bestial people of the realm; specifically, they looked like a leoprine variation.

Emhyr had a humanoid build overall; however, the fingers on their hands were longer than a human's with finely sharpened claws. Their features were tanned and oblong, and they had a flatter nose than most humans. Atop their head were two three-foot-long brown rabbit ears that seemed on a constant swivel. A fluffy cotton tail was apparent through their clothes, where their lower back met their backside.

They were short, barely five feet three inches, and had straight shoulder-length hair. It was a mousy brown with golden highlights that seemed perfectly placed to catch the light of the chandeliers above them. They wore fine, though simple, linen clothes in colors ranging from dark brown to dark blue.

Emhyr grinned, twirling a finger around a hair strand, and said, "*Simon.*

---

[4] For more information about the Ancara of *Lusefell*, please refer to the back matter titled "**The People of Lusefell**."

You never told me you knew Anni."

Simon chuckled, leaning forward against the bar towards the leoprine figure. He shrugged. "That's because I *didn't* last time I was here. ... Your hair's longer. It looks nice."

The Ancaran's eyes fluttered, the cobalt irises reflecting the male across from them. "You could learn decency from him, Anni. He notices the small things, see?" Emhyr said, grinning at Andreas when his face darkened in response.

"**Emhyr.** *My grandparents?*" Andreas asked, the words strained.

Emhyr huffed and pushed off the bartop animatedly. "Busy. Neil ordered me *not* to bother them. Something about Cian promising him a night to themselves?" they said.

"Of course. My grandparents returned to the cabin, didn't they?" Andreas sighed audibly.

"The cabin? *That* cabin?" Simon spoke immediately.

"Oh? *You've seen the cabin?*" Emhyr replied, and they folded their hands excitedly. "This is a thrilling development, but be careful, Simon. Andreas will break your heart faster than you can move those *lovely* hips."

"Emhyr!" Andreas shouted, his face red from the chorus of laughter from the barkeep and Simon. "We're working together; outside of that, it's none of your business."

"Is that what you're calling it?" Emhyr asked and leaned forward, folding their hands to rest their head atop them. "Darling, I can smell him all **over** you, and I am *intimately* familiar with how he smells."

This caught Andreas off guard, and he looked at Simon for confirmation. Simon shrugged in response. Andreas huffed and said, "You've *smelled* a lot of individuals."

"You're certainly one to judge. Last I checked, your reputation preceded you, **brat**." Emhyr clicked their tongue and then popped up. "I won't disturb your grandparents till they return in the morning. So, you want a room, or are you planning to pack your cute ass up and head down the road?" they asked.

Andreas gritted his teeth. "A room," he replied, watching the Ancaran look at Simon and lean back across the bartop.

"Two rooms? Or one? I can pop by for room service *anytime* if you want your own," Emhyr said. Their cobalt eyes fluttered, and a broad grin grew on the barkeep's face.

Simon smiled, eyebrows raised. "As cute as you are ..."

"Two rooms!" Andreas yelled, cutting Simon off before he could finish. He earned a look of irritation from Simon and amused intrigue from Emhyr.

"Red ..." Simon spoke again and felt a finger press against his lips. Emhyr had raised a hand to silence him and earned a look of confusion.

"Nope. The brat has spoken. Let Andreas sleep in the bed he's made," Emhyr said, pushed off the bar, and bent down to rummage through a storage bin holding keys. They popped back up shortly after, two in hand; one looked larger and ornate as if it were a suite room, and the other looked plain like a shared room's key would.

Emhyr handed Simon the ornate key. "Here you go, on the Dwyer tab," they said.

Simon smiled and grabbed the key, and then before Andreas could grab the other, he snatched it from where it was being held aloft. He slammed the simple key down and roughly slid it back towards the barkeep. "Thank you, Emhyr," he said. His voice was strained, and without waiting for either response, he seized Andreas by the upper arm and pulled him away.

"Oh, ho ho ... *the plot thickens*," Emhyr mumbled and earned a look of annoyance from Andreas as Simon tugged him to the stairs.

"Simon!" Andreas snapped, trying to pull back from the heavy hand yanking him upstairs.

Simon ignored the man's complaints as he stepped onto the third floor of the building and then pulled his hand back in annoyance. "What the hell was that?" he asked.

"What? I figured you might want your own room; we're in a large city, and *clearly*, you know Emhyr well," Andreas huffed, fixing his shawl where it had come untied around his shoulders.

Simon stared with a look somewhere between annoyance and amusement on his face. "So, you want your own room? Because you're welcome to take this one. It might be more private to snag up a patron," he said.

Andreas glared. "That's not what I said! You're putting words in my mouth!"

"Oh, you mean like you just did downstairs!" Simon snapped back, eyebrows raised.

Andreas started to speak but closed his mouth and looked guilty. He twisted his fingers and mumbled under his breath, *"Alright, that's fair ..."*

"Look, if you want your own room, you can have it. If you want to share a room with me, I won't object. **Do not** decide for me; if you're unsure, ask me," Simon said, trying to keep his voice even.

Andreas peered up, biting his lip, and found Simon had put a few steps between them. "I just don't want you to feel pressured. We're working together and ... Just because we slept together, I don't want you to feel like ..." he said.

Simon frowned as he digested the words. "We slept together. I enjoy your company. We're working together for this job. That's it. I already told you I'm not here to judge you, and I'm not expecting anything to come of it besides another job," he said flatly.

Andreas fell silent, his gut twisting at the words. It wasn't much different from the point he was trying to get across, but somehow, it didn't sit well with him. The way Simon had phrased it was—It *bothered* him. He bit his lip harder and twisted his fingers rougher. He heard footsteps and glanced up to find Simon looking down at him.

"But ... if you're planning to get *jealous* about someone else ... it seems a little counterintuitive to have separate rooms, Red," Simon tilted his head and reached out to nudge Andreas' chin up. He grinned when he saw the other's face darken, and the emerald gaze refused to meet his eyes. "What? Not used to someone calling you out on your bullshit so quickly?" he asked.

"I *wasn't* ..." Andreas let the words taper off, eyes rolling, "I wasn't **that** jealous."

"Looked like you were ready to make rabbit stew," Simon laughed when Andreas hit him in the gut.

"Well, it is *Emhyr*. ... Really? **Emhyr**?" Andreas looked up and frowned deeply.

"They're a friendly face from Ransol; that's it. Besides, they don't like tall men," Simon smirked, amused. He'd never done more than drink with Emhyr, but he'd quite enjoyed the clever stunt the leoprine bartender had set up downstairs.

Andreas looked taken aback by the comment. "What? They don't like tall men?"

Simon briefly assessed his companion and then laughed, "You know, I'm not surprised you don't know that. Emhyr doesn't fit your type, and I feel that you're pretty off-limits, seeing how they work for your grandparents," he said.

"My type? And what is my type, Simon?" Andreas hissed, crossing his arms.

Simon scoffed, his fingers tapping Andreas' chin before releasing, "Tall."

Andreas grinned when Simon stepped closer, and he stepped back, "Tall?"

"Ruggedly handsome," Simon grinned, stepping closer.

"Mm. Is that all?" Andreas giggled, stepping back and hitting the wall.

"I also remember you saying that being reliable and free-thinking were **desirable** traits," Simon tilted his head and leaned forward to block Andreas between his arms and the wall. "You're fond of being picked up, too, so they gotta be strong enough to do it," he said.

Andreas snickered, his face warm. "Oh? Anything else?" he asked. He looked up and found the mismatched gaze watching him playfully.

Simon dipped down and let his lips linger a few inches away. "You seem pretty fond of directness..." he said quietly, leaned in, and closed the space between their lips. He lingered a few beats before pulling back and whispering, "Based on the criteria... **I might be your type, Red.**"

"Mm, I don't know. I'm considering taking Emhyr up on that second room," Andreas murmured, looking embarrassed. He fiddled with the hem of Simon's shirt, shifted on his heels, and continued, "I might enjoy your company... just a bit. Plus, you're not bad on the eyes," He looked up and found the hetero-chromatic gaze still observing him, almost as if it hadn't turned away. "No pressure... right?"

Simon forced a smile and said, "Business associates with benefits." He pushed off the wall and handed over the key before nodding down the hallway. The words were terse, almost forced, as he spoke them and continued, "If you want to head to the room, I'll be there in a second. I think I'm going to ask Emhyr for some alcohol."

Andreas nodded, took the key, and headed down the hall. "Don't take too long!"

"I might need rescuing if I do!" Simon tossed back as he descended the stairs and disappeared onto the lower floors. It didn't take him long to slip through the crowd and back to the bar to tap it. He saw the Ancaran turn, their eyes bright, and they frowned upon registering who it was.

Simon breathed in. "I don't want to hear it, Emhyr," he said.

Emhyr stepped over, frowning deeper, "He's going to break your heart."

"Can I get the top-shelf bourbon and two shot glasses?" Simon asked and pulled out coins to slap them on the table. He ignored the other's words.

Emhyr huffed, grabbing the half-empty bottle and two glasses before setting them on the counter. They snatched up the coins and frowned, "I mean it, Simon. Andreas doesn't do feelings ... **you do feelings**. It will *not* end well."

"Thank you, Emhyr," Simon said, tapped the table, and turned around to walk away. He didn't get far.

"Olur wouldn't like you setting yourself up to get hurt, Simon!" Emhyr yelled after him.

Simon froze, his back tense. He breathed in, trying to calm the rising sorrow that had built up in his throat. Then he snapped over his shoulder, "Don't you **ever** talk to me about what Olur would or wouldn't like! Do you hear me?!" He turned to look at Emhyr behind the bar; Simon's eyes were wide, pupils constricted so much they were almost invisible. "I may know you from Ransol ... but you don't have the right to say that name! **Are we clear**?!" he hissed.

"*Just be careful,*" Emhyr whispered, their brow furrowed. "I mean it."

Simon waved them off angrily and continued on his path upstairs.

The mercenary rushed, taking the stairs two at a time as he ran around the wooden spirals. He wasn't sure if he was running away from Emhyr or to the room waiting for him. Regardless, when he reached the third floor and found the correct door, he paused, seeing it cracked so he could slip in without trouble. Just outside the door, Simon breathed in, waiting for his face to stabilize and calm. Tension coiled in his body, tightening his muscles with an iron grip, and Andreas had a knack for noticing even the slightest disturbance.

Simon focused on his breathing, eyes locked on the ceiling.

He didn't mind old friends, but sometimes they were troublesome. Sometimes, they brought up things he didn't want to think about, things he would rather push off and remain apathetic about. The mismatched eyes shifted towards the cracked door. Soft music came from within the room, chime-like, like a music box playing.

After stepping through the door, a lavish room of warm wood tones greeted Simon. It had a massive bed with silken sheets and heavy curtains of fine fabric with thick red and gold cords. There was a table with two chairs, a vase of roses, and a partition blocking what looked like a bathtub and washing basin. A cozy sofa was near a roaring fireplace and a balcony with two glass doors across the room. The fire's warmth filled the room, and the light almost lovingly reflected off the shades of red and gold. There was an orchestrion playing music, small enough to fit on the bedside table.

Simon spotted Andreas as he slipped into the room and closed the door. Andreas was on the balcony, peering over the wooden railing and looking out into the main square of the market district. Andreas hadn't noticed him enter, so he paused at the table and deposited the bottle and glasses. He then placed his bag and shield at the end of the bed.

Simon stepped out to the balcony and slid his arms on either side of his companion. He grabbed onto the railing and leaned against the other man's back. Andreas chuckled and leaned back into him as though he had decided to use Simon for support.

"Are you okay?" Simon asked and settled his head on the twenty-six-year-old's shoulder, his eyes focused on the city below them. The market was busy and lit by strings of arcane lights that gave it a welcoming glow.

Andreas inhaled for some time before wrapping his arms around himself, "I will be." His voice was soft, almost distant, as if he were thinking of something.

Simon's brow furrowed, and he asked, "You sure, Red?"

Andreas nodded and let his head fall against Simon's shoulder; his eyes closed, and he listened to the faint chimes as they carried out onto the balcony in the wind, "Thinking about that woman, those creatures ... my grandparents. It made me remember things from years ago that I'd rather not remember," he said.

Simon turned his head, and he kissed Andreas on the temple.

That was something he understood intimately.

Andreas smiled and said, "I'll be alright."

"Do you want to talk about it?" Simon asked, eyes following a firefly as it fluttered above the city street.

Andreas inhaled as he felt Simon's heartbeat through his heavy chest. It wasn't fast, but almost slow when he thought of it. He'd noticed it when they'd slept in the cabin in the mountains. "No ... not now," he replied.

Simon didn't want to pry, but somehow, it made him dislike what had happened on the road into Fossy more. He fell quiet for a time, matching Andreas' energy and listening to the music as it cascaded into the open air. There were several songs he recognized and several he did not. However, they all sounded serene when played on the bell-like instrument.

Simon adjusted his weight onto the balls of his feet as the next song started and whispered into Andreas' ear, *"Do you want to dance?"*

Andreas opened his eyes slowly. He felt the shoulders supporting his weight tense with nervousness. It was strange because Simon was never nervous when flirting or in these simple moments. The orc always had an air of confidence, like he was so sure of himself that no one else needed to be.

Dancing ... He thought about the word long and hard as if searching for a memory of dancing. Andreas recalled a story his mother told him about her and his father. He also remembered seeing his grandparents dancing in their kitchen and the pub below when it was quiet. Although he tried repeatedly, he could not remember when he had danced, or someone had asked him to do so.

Andreas felt Simon's shoulders shift again, like the orc expected to be turned down, or Simon thought he'd fallen asleep. Simon had reached to grasp his waist as if preparing to pick him up and carry him off to bed. Andreas chuckled, and the man supporting him paused.

"I'm not great at dancing. I don't think I've ever danced," Andreas said.

Simon smiled and replied, "I'm not either, but I learned it can be fun. ... I'll have to hold your hand, though." Andreas stiffened, and Simon pivoted to look down and see the green eyes gazing up at him. "Can you trust me to do that, Andrea?" he asked.

The song faded off and changed to another slow melody. After a moment, Andreas stood up from leaning against his companion and turned. His hands shook, and his teeth clamped nervously on his bottom lip. Simon knew what his hands looked like ... *Simon knew.* Part of his fear of others touching his hands was people feeling the scars covering them, and part was them *hurting* when touched. It was partly shame and partly sheer self-preservation from pain.

Andreas tentatively held out his hands. Simon placed one on his shoulder and took the other into one of his hands. Heat flooded Andreas' face as Simon pulled him close enough for their waists to crash together. Then, Simon settled his empty hand on his companion's lower back to steady him.

Simon leaned to whisper in Andreas' ear again, *"Relax. Just follow me, alright?"*

Simon then started to lead, swaying as they turned bit by bit. Simon held his hand gently and made it pretty easy for him to follow the steps, causing the tension in his body to fade with every movement they made. Andreas thought about his grandparents dancing in the kitchen at the cabin, how they'd looked, and how his grandpa Neil leaned into his Papa tenderly every time.

Andreas leaned against Simon's shoulder and felt Simon rest his chin atop his head. A calm stillness settled over him, dispelling the uncertainty surrounding the earlier action. It was soft, sweet ... *new*. Dancing. If this was what dancing was, he felt he could do it more often. He didn't think it was that simple, though. No one but Simon would know not to squeeze his hands tightly because it would be painful. No one but Simon would know to hold on to him because he leaned on others too much when he could.

Not everyone would ensure he knew where to put his feet like Simon was.

Andreas concealed a smile that curled his lips, his eyes locked on the older man's tunic. His stomach twisted like it had been since the notice board at home. After closing his eyes and relaxing into the dream-like music and the motion of them spinning, *he heard it again.*

Andreas opened his eyes and listened instead of trying to figure it out immediately. It was louder than he'd recalled before, more joyful; perhaps it was because of where he was. ... He swore he could hear his Papa *laughing* like the man was watching him.

Eighteen

Sincerity

Simon had always found Cian Dwyer intimidating. Now, Cian stood in the room where he had been sleeping just thirty minutes earlier, curled up with the man's grandson. It was a bit unnerving, to be honest.

Andreas had woken up five minutes before his grandparents knocked on their door and was frantic. He had slapped Simon awake, shouting about his grandparents and saying they were coming to chat. Simon had never gotten up, dressed, and splashed his face with water to wake up so fast. The dread of the two older men finding him *naked* and curled up with their *grandson* was a powerful motivator. Why? Well, he was still contemplating that.

He shouldn't have cared; they were his employers and outside the contract …

Simon looked up and locked eyes with Cian, whose sharp golden gaze met his from across the room. Like Simon, Cian stood by the wall near the fireplace instead of sitting on the sofa. Simon's attention then shifted to Andreas and Neil conversing on the couch. The Dwyer patriarchs were highly respected but had distinctly different personalities and physical traits. While Neil could be intimidating, Simon always found him entertaining.

Cian, however … Simon inhaled as the realization sank in again: **Cian was terrifying.**

Cian Dwyer was a human who stood at six feet eight inches, matching the height of the orc across from him. He had a sturdy build with broad, muscular shoulders and shocking crimson hair that matched Andreas. His hair was cut short in uneven and messy layers, giving the impression that it had been cut in battle, but Cian never fixed it. Unlike Neil's, his face bore a well-cared-for beard that was neatly trimmed to hug his square jaw. With warm chestnut skin covered in old scars, he looked to be in his early to mid-forties. Despite his current stoic expression, he was, in all honesty, a handsome and charismatic man.

Cian's clothing fit him perfectly and was made of expensive fabrics. He had many golden trinkets on his person, most notably rings on his large fingers. His eyes were expressive and the color of polished gold as they stared over the three in the room with him. Their hue seemed to change with his mood as they lingered on his family... and then on Simon across from him. They were brighter when he glanced toward his husband and grandson and seemed molten when they found Simon, as if he found the orc irritating.

Simon noticed the golden eyes once again before taking a third look at Cian's clothes. The two patriarchs were usually very neat individuals. However, it seemed that Cian had been in some altercation. Neil was spotless when they arrived, but his husband had dried *blood* splattered all over his hands, white shirt, and boots. This merely intensified the overwhelming unease Simon felt creeping up his spine. He wanted to ask questions but was hesitant to delve deeper.

"Cian, are you going to sulk over there like an irritated child, or do you intend to come and talk with Anni?" Neil asked dryly, his head shifting in the general direction of his husband before a teasing smile brushed his features.

Cian sighed, "I am **not** sulking," His deep baritone voice had a rustic charm and a heavy accent, a stark contrast to that of his husband. Unlike Neil's, his speech was formal, and he used a heavy cadence to ensure clarity. "I am respecting your conversation and assessing Andreas' new companion," he said.

"Assessing. Quietly. From over there?" Neil said in an amused tone, "Darling, that sounds like you're trying to *intimidate* him."

"Nonsense. I have no control over his reaction to my presence, mo stór[5]," Cian said, his voice tapering off to a tender nature as he spoke the words of endearment.

Neil suppressed a small laugh, pressing his lips together to prevent a smile. He breathed in quickly, rolling his eyes, as if stuck between scolding his husband and enjoying the entertaining banter. "Cian. I love you deeply. *Please* behave," he begged.

Andreas chuckled to himself from his grandfather's sheer adoration and amusement. He glanced over at Simon and spied a small smile retreating from the man's lips. Despite the situation, Simon appeared to have also found the exchange entertaining.

Cian huffed, turned his attention to Andreas, and said, "Neil told me you encountered several creatures on your way here. Are you well?"

Andreas nodded, putting down the cup of coffee he'd been sipping. "Well enough. Simon … is reliable, so he got me out of a tricky situation near our cabin. I passed out from an injury, and if he hadn't been there, I wouldn't be here now," he replied.

Simon shifted, slightly uncomfortable, when Cian looked back towards him.

Cian glared at Simon and whispered tersely, *"I see."*

"You were lucky. It sounds like *The Flame King* guided you. Thank you for protecting Andreas, Simon," Neil said, a smug smile curling as he sipped his coffee. Both Cian and Simon turned to Neil. Simon looked confused, but Cian appeared almost unamused by the comment. Andreas, however, started laughing, attracting the three's attention. Neil looked pleased with himself and patted Andreas' hand.

"It's pleasant to hear you laugh, Firefly," Neil said and smiled when Andreas clutched his hand.

"Simon isn't religious," Andreas said and gave Simon an apologetic smile.

---

[5] mo stór (muh stohr): "my treasure"

"Clearly," Cian huffed and drew the hetero-chromatic eyes to him.

"What's that supposed to mean?" Simon asked, his voice terse.

Cian shoved off the wall and stood to his full height, his golden gaze darkening back to the previous near-molten gold. "I do not see any paraphernalia that would suggest that you pledged yourself to an Old God *or* a Primal. I only state an obvious fact, *Simon*."

Simon pushed himself off the wall and stood at full height, matching Cian's posture. He didn't like the way Cian said his name. "I didn't know it was necessary to boost a god's ego or champion something older than the rocks we're standing on. One doesn't deserve it, and the other gets on just fine without it, as always," he said. Surprisingly, he saw Cian's golden eyes soften and return to their polished gold color. He watched a broad grin spread over Cian's face, brightening it considerably from the stoic frown of the past few minutes.

Cian laughed. The sound was deep and bassy as he looked at Neil. "You were right, as usual. I *do* like him," he said.

Andreas released a breath, but Neil looked amused as he sipped his coffee. "When will you stop doubting me? I'm always right," Neil said, placing his cup on the tiny coffee table. Cian walked over, leaned down to kiss his husband's head, settled beside him, and reached for coffee.

Simon snickered and locked eyes with Andreas. "I see who you got it from," he said. This drew the attention of the three on the sofa, and Andreas frowned.

"Got what?" Andreas asked.

"Your annoying knack for being *right* all the damn time," Simon scoffed and walked over to sit across from the trio on the floor.

Andreas' face heated; he cleared his throat and looked at Cian. Cian was beaming, earning him a roll of his grandson's eyes. "Are you satisfied enough to tell us what we're looking into now, Papa?" Andreas asked.

"Yes, he has at least met my expectations so far," Cian said, sipping his coffee and ignoring Simon's confusion. He adjusted a ring on his finger before folding his hands. "I need you to investigate Prince Wyatt Richard. I suspect someone unfavorable is trying to coerce him into an alliance with

Pirn. Can you do this?" he asked, looking at Simon and raising an eyebrow.

Simon furrowed his brow. "Do you think someone in Pirn is trying to gain power in Fossy?"

"Precisely. An individual who has had much power stripped from them politically," Cian responded with a frown.

Simon took a deep breath as the implications of the family's history and the phrasing of the words sank in. **EDEN** was led by a woman who also held power in Pirn. He remembered that Elaina Sylvester, the human mage who founded **EDEN**, had claimed that followers of the Water Primal had corrupted the organization. It was later discovered that Qella had manipulated history and deceived the other three Primals, betraying the mortals of the realm. Elaina's story had little support despite the events in the wars and the fall of the Water Primal.

"Is she still alive?" Andreas asked, his voice trembling.

"Of course she is, little one. That **witch** does not die so easily," Cian responded, irritated.

"What do we have to do?" Simon asked.

Cian turned his attention to Simon, a grin on his face again. "I *do* like you. To the point, detail-specific, and capable, it would seem. Should you prove yourself worth your weight in gold, I may have more to ask of you later," he said.

"Well, that's the hope, considering my other contracts are dried up now," Simon sighed, eyes glancing up in thought, before returning and finding the golden pair watching curiously.

"If there is going to be a meeting, it will take place during the ball on the evening of the queen's remembrance ceremony. Unfortunately, we must attend and keep our faces in the spotlight throughout the event. There is etiquette to uphold and nonsensical bureaucracy to entertain," Cian scoffed, annoyed at the thought of the event before continuing, "You and Andreas will attend the event with us as you have come: as a member of our family and that member's escort from Belmare. When those in attendance are loosened by drink and tired from their full bellies, you two will leave under the pretense that Andreas has had too much to drink. Then, you will find a way into the palace backdoor and the prince's study. That is the most likely place for them to talk privately away from the King. You will need to do so quickly and quietly and ensure that you are **not** discovered under any circumstances. If someone found you, little one, it would cause quite a stir."

"You don't think **she** is coming, do you?" Andreas asked.

"Elaina may be a fool, but she would not dare set foot in **my** city again," Cian spat, nostrils flaring in agitation at the thought. "She does not have a death wish."

Simon shuddered, noting the hatred that pooled off Cian in palpable waves as he mentioned the name. It seemed like he was right; they suspected **EDEN**'s leader. He cleared his throat and asked, "If she's after political influence, then what does Fossy's monarchy gain if they agree to be friends with her?"

"How familiar are you with **EDEN**, Simon?" Neil asked, raising a hand to quiet his husband as Cian began to speak.

"Very little that isn't common knowledge. I know they claimed to want to fix food shortages by manipulating crops with magic and were trying to figure out how to extend life with blood magic. I know they were fucking around with animals and necrotic magic, too, like anyone who's seen the Varog knows," Simon said, thinking over the words before continuing, "I know when everything came out at the end of the *Second War* that Elaina was blaming Qella for the corruption in the organization, and saying that the Primal was trying to manipulate her people and research to get rid of mortals."

"Lies! Elaina wished to make a silk purse of a sow's ear!" Cian snapped.

Simon jumped when the flames in the fireplace surged to his left, and he was sure part of his eyebrow was singed by the sudden heat. He looked back to Cian in time to see Neil place a hand on the man's knee and squeeze roughly. The flames slowly died down, and Simon fidgeted uncomfortably in his spot. He glanced at Andreas and found him watching in mild panic; he looked ready to jump off his seat.

Simon recalled what Andreas had said about his grandparents' magical abilities and felt he was slowly beginning to understand what he'd meant by 'different.'

"It is all true—at least the parts you stated about what they were doing and what Elaina **claimed**," Neil said, pausing to glance in his husband's direction and offer a sharp look of disapproval.

"I am *behaving*," Cian huffed. Then he leaned back against the sofa and sipped from his cup of coffee in silence.

A ghost of a smile brushed Neil's lips, and he said, "We are quite certain that Elaina is attempting to rebuild the organization, but a few pieces are missing. Her movements are different than before and during the *Second War*, so we ask for some assistance. Please excuse my husband's outburst—when his temper flares, the gift *The Flame King* gave him tends to get a bit out of hand."

Simon gave a curt nod of acknowledgment, paused to scold himself mentally, and then said, "Understood."

Neil smiled and folded his hands back in his lap. "What Fossy is to gain has, no doubt, been exaggerated on **EDEN**'s part. The Richards never gave us the impression that they were *against* their people, so they were most likely promised a way to fill depleting grain stores or cure diseases. ... Of course, they could wish to line their pockets, or the prince has different views on ruling the Kingdom of Midwind than his father and late mother."

"You're not sure then?" Simon asked.

"No. We are not," Cian said and sat back up straight before continuing, "Do you now understand the importance of what you are to do? The consequences if you are discovered, and the expectations if you succeed in this endeavor?" Cian spoke not to Andreas but to Simon. His head turned, eyes wide as they studied the mercenary. Cian seemed to look for the slightest nuance that would give away deception or the need for him to deal with the orc within his presence. It was an icy, calculated look that teemed with intimidation.

Simon took a deep breath, his gaze fixed on the steaming coffee cups on the table between him and the trio. As he let the words sink in, he carefully considered the details of the job. If they were successful, he would not only receive payment but also have the opportunity to establish a working relationship with a highly influential and wealthy family. However, this family was closely linked to major global conflicts and their potential repercussions. When he first came across the job posting and learned about Andreas, he hadn't fully grasped the gravity of the situation. He had expected something more trivial, perhaps less significant than what was now at stake.

Simon rubbed his hands together, his brow furrowed as he deliberated. If they caught him and Andreas, the monarchy of Midwind would likely put a price on his head. They would also target and exile the Dwyer family from Fossy for infiltrating the palace. This wasn't a simple information-seeking contract, nor was it even in the same league as what he was used to taking on within Ransol. This job was much bigger than anything he had previously undertaken.

"Maybe we should think about it..." Andreas began, but the mismatched eyes across from him silenced him. He swallowed, gripping his pants legs.

Simon nodded at Cian as he said, "I understand and accept the consequences, whether we succeed or are discovered." Simon's brow furrowed, and he swallowed. For a moment, he thought he saw the older man transition from a look of uncertainty and tension to an overwhelming sense of something else.

Cian smiled broadly, and another deep chuckle bubbled up. There seemed to be something different about the way Cian carried himself and the look in his eyes. Cian, infamous for his role in the war and the many casualties he caused, looked **proud**. Simon didn't know why since it was the first time he had spoken to Cian.

Simon recognized Cian by his face. He knew that Cian was the leader of the order that followed the Primal Cael and had an influence on all four continents, even surpassing the royal families. Simon felt insignificant and unknown compared to those who usually interacted with Cian. He would have been like a copper piece in a sea of gold that flowed through the world. Yet, at this moment, Cian gazed at him with the pride a father would show for his **son**.

"Do not use it where you can be seen, but this will take you back to our cabin, and we will meet you there at the end of the event," Neil said, shifting his clothing to withdraw a bound scroll. "We can discuss what you've discovered then and return together secretly. I've already arranged a cover story for the two of you with Emhyr should anyone get nosy: you will have returned here to the pub after Andreas got too drunk and turned in for the night in your room. I will place magic around this room to ensure no one gets any ideas about peeking in while you are not here," he said.

Andreas listened, nodding his understanding, as he reached for the scroll and tucked it quickly under his shawl.

"I have a request," Simon interrupted.

Andreas and Neil fell quiet.

Cian nodded, listening, "I shall hear your request."

"There is a woman in Ransol. Your son knows her; her name is Gitah," Simon said.

Cian nodded and replied, "Yes. I think highly of Gitah Vellin. Continue."

"If we are discovered, ensure her protection," Simon stated.

Cian nodded, as if he had agreed even before Simon asked. "You have my word that I will ensure her safety if you are discovered. She has done much for my family, and it will be an honor to return the favor to a member of her family."

Simon's throat tightened at the words as if they stung and held great meaning. He nodded, looking down at his clenched hands. "Thank you, sir," he said.

Cian smiled, then patted his thighs and said, "Well, now that all is settled, please excuse me, as I must rid myself of this viscera. It smells of rot, and it is unpleasant." He stood without waiting for comment, kissed his husband's cheek and the top of his grandson's head, and then excused himself.

Andreas broke the silence and looked at his grandfather. "Grandpa Neil … *why* was Papa covered in blood?" he asked.

Neil smiled and replied, "Ah. He investigated the encampment you two stumbled upon. I told him of it last night after you told me, and he wasn't met with as **warm** a welcome as you were by those who were there."

Simon looked at Andreas, his face stern. "So, you were right?" he asked.

Andreas nodded and replied, "It would seem so…"

Neil patted his grandson's arm, "You won't have to worry about them being there again. I don't know if Cian left any of them alive. … We are also looking into who they are, or, well, your father is. He's added it to his list of things to investigate after what happened at home the night before last," he said.

Andreas looked over and asked, "Is Pops alright? Did you hear about Keena?"

Neil nodded and said, "Yes, he's as alright as he can be," Neil smiled, "Keena is safe at home in her cozy nest. Your mother sent her regards. She meant to contact you but didn't have a chance with everything happening. I popped by to help your father last night while Cian looked into the nearby encampment."

Simon looked at the man incredulously and said, "*That* was your night for yourselves?"

Neil chuckled. "Yes, it's easier to tell Emhyr we're enjoying each other's company than investigating undead matters. Better to omit the truth and keep them out of trouble," he said.

Simon's lips curled into an amused grin as he looked at Andreas. "You two are *definitely* similar," he said.

Andreas scoffed, blushing in embarrassment. "That's not a *terrible* thing."

Neil smiled as he listened to the small exchange, and Andreas noticed an almost melancholy look come over him. This made the redhead pause before reaching out and squeezing the man's hand.

"Yes, Firefly?" Neil asked with a warm smile.

"What happened back home? Is Lilli okay?" Andreas asked.

"Lilli is safe. She was at home with your mother when Leo was out. He and your uncle investigated that cave again—the one you stumbled into a few months back." Neil replied.

Andreas furrowed his brow and dared to glance at Simon, catching a look of confused suspicion on the man's face. He shrugged in response and then turned his attention back to his grandfather. "I remember, yes. Did something else happen, or did he find a lead into who made the rift?" he asked.

"There was another rift ... and this time, it brought out some strange creatures we haven't seen before. From how Leo described them, they were not part of this *Plane*, but the question is which one they are from. He said they were humanoid, blind, and reacted to sound; they were very slow-moving and made insect-like noises. There were a few that, well, for lack of a better word, *exploded* when you killed them," Neil sighed, conveying the information as if it were nothing more than a dull report. "While Cian was bathing in viscera, I popped by Belmare to see if I could figure anything out about the rift and help seal it," he continued.

"Seal it? ... You can do that?" Simon asked, staring slightly in horror at the implications of the word. Maybe he had been underestimating Neil Dwyer, at least based on the limited information Andreas had shared with him about such magic.

Neil smiled, "Certainly. It naturally takes time, but it is a power I possess. I can't exactly aim anymore, but I was also quite talented with a bow in my youth. I have this uncanny knack for sniffing out portals to other *Planes*. As a matter of fact..." He patted Andreas' hand before continuing, "Anni also has quite the knack for detecting them. I taught him well."

Simon looked at Andreas and watched him, slightly amazed, "You can *learn* something like that?" he asked.

Andreas avoided Simon's eye. "I did. It's kind of like a sixth sense. I guess a knack for incredible things runs in our family," he said. It was strange because he wasn't sure which reaction to what he said caused him more alarm. Simon's brow furrowed, and he looked as if he was suddenly thinking deeply about something, as if the comment made him question its very basis. Neil, however, seemed almost sad. It was a minor, nearly imperceptible flicker across his face before his usual coy smile returned. However, the man's expression had a brief, almost suffocating sense of sorrow.

"Fate has a funny way of bringing people together," Neil said and hugged his grandson. "Well, let me go and let Emhyr rest. Give us a day or two, and then we can shop."

Never had Simon known a word could jar him from his thoughts so quickly. Simon looked at Neil, concerned and confused. "**Shop**?" he asked in disbelief.

Neil grinned playfully and cooed, "Well, of course, dear. You can't show up to a royal event without looking the part. You're escorting a *Dwyer*, remember?"

Simon shifted his gaze to Andreas, feeling so uncomfortable that he forgot about the previous conversation and his thoughts. He hadn't expected to dress up. He saw Andreas laughing and jumped when a hand squeezed his shoulder. It had much more strength than he expected from the frail-looking human. Simon looked up and found a blind gaze peering down at him. "Yes?" he asked.

"Be sure to take care of Anni, alright?" Neil smiled and continued, "I expect *many* excellent things from our arrangement."

Simon nodded as Neil paused before leaving. He instantly scolded himself for forgetting that Neil was blind *again* and started to speak. However, Neil ignored him and headed to the door to excuse himself, leaving the two younger men alone.

Andreas laughed and leaned back on the sofa. "They like you," he said.

Simon exhaled audibly and fell backward onto the floor. He rubbed his face in embarrassment before groaning under his breath, "They're... something." He heard shifting and felt a weight on his chest after a few moments. Simon glanced down and found Andreas had slipped to the ground to rest his head on him. He gave a giant smile before playfully asking, "Can I help you?"

"They're different from how most people think they are," Andreas replied, laughing when an affirming look crossed his companion's face. "They *do* like you, though. Papa was on the fence, but you impressed him."

"By insulting the Old Gods and saying the Primals were fine on their own or by pissing him off because I mentioned someone he really fucking hates?"

"By being honest and not letting him intimidate you," Andreas stated matter-of-factually.

Simon rolled his eyes, chuckling in disbelief as he recalled the sudden surge of flames from the fireplace. "He is intimidating, no question," he said.

Andreas hummed, then shifted, dragging his fingers along Simon's chest in circles. "He can be, especially when angry. He's protective of his family," he said.

Simon sighed and rested his arm lazily on Andreas' tiny waist, using him as a pillow. "Well, I can't call that a flaw," he said. Caring about your family and wanting to protect them, no matter whose toes you stepped on or how much blood you had to smear on your hands, was understandable. It was a quality he respected and could relate to. His brow lifted, and his attention shifted to the face on his chest. Simon felt the small circles trail down towards his stomach. "What are you doing?" he asked.

"Hmm? Me? Nothing," Andreas chimed back and let his fingers slowly spiral toward Simon's hip.

Simon sighed in disbelief but could not hide the entertainment tugging at his features. "You're liable to get into trouble if you keep doing that," he said.

The green eyes flashed upwards, and Andreas grinned, "Oh? Am I?"

Simon tried to hide his grin, his hips shifting as fingers trailed down his thigh. "Your grandparents were *just* here … they could come back. You realize that, right?" he said.

Andreas shrugged, "Probably not. They're busy…" He waved his hand as one appeared near the door, glowing and looking to be made of shifting flames. There was a click, and the magical hand vanished into thin air. "Plus, I'm pretty sure someone has locked the door," he said.

Andreas chuckled as Simon grabbed his arms and flipped him over, positioning himself above him. His feet tapped the coffee table, and a cup shifted before liquid spilled. His face beamed, pleased at his success, when Simon's face came into view centimeters away from his own. "Hi," he said.

"You're unbelievable," Simon huffed, his body pressing into the one under him.

Andreas fidgeted, ignoring the minor complaint that flared in his hip from the pressure. His eyes wandered over the face above him, taking in the faint wrinkles under Simon's eyes and the smile pulling at his lips. *"You're handsome,"* he whispered.

Simon's face showed a mix of flattered disbelief and playful annoyance earlier, but now it softened into a tender, enamored expression. Andreas felt Simon's hands loosen on his arms, so he grabbed Simon's face. Simon seemed torn between wanting to kiss him and wanting to pull away and put space between them. Andreas frowned and furrowed his brow. He felt an overwhelming urge to close the space between them. It was as if a weight of fear and uncertainty was pushing down on his chest.

Instead of waiting for Simon to move, he leaned in and kissed him. He feared Simon would pull away if he didn't take the initiative. Something was *terrifying* about Simon possibly pulling away from him.

Nineteen

Unknown

─── ⋆⋅☆⋅⋆ ───

"Fix your face."

Simon's attention was suddenly drawn to the Ancaran across the bar. Confused, he saw Emhyr roll their eyes and tap the bar with their claws.

"What are you talking about?" Simon asked.

"Your expression... You looked like you were trying to take a shit," Emhyr snorted. Simon jolted in offense at the words. Emhyr leaned forward, cupped the taller man's jaw, and turned it back in the direction Simon had been looking.

Simon turned his chin away and looked back at the brunette. "What?"

"You seem to be deep in thought, and from the way your nose is scrunched up, I assume it has to do with your lovely friend over there," Emhyr said with a smile, nodding towards Andreas, who was curled up in one of the oversized chairs near the fire, reading.

Simon huffed and nudged a lump of meat in the stew he had been tending to for the past twenty minutes. "I'm just getting stir-crazy," he said.

"Ah, I partially believe that; your clan was nomadic, right?" Emhyr hummed and leaned forward to rest against the bar. Their eyes scanned the main floor of the pub, taking the time to observe the few patrons there. They would make a round in a moment, but it was the slower part of the morning, so they could take some time to chat with an old friend.

"Yeah. Even when I left, I moved back and forth between Sebree and Ransol."

"That's right, you moved between the two every three months," Emhyr spoke, seeming to think over the words. "Quite a predicament you've gotten yourself into. They never let him go anywhere. How *will* you manage that?"

Simon frowned and asked, "Why don't they let him go anywhere?"

"Why are you asking me? Ask him. I couldn't care less because he doesn't pay me, nor does he keep a roof over my head," Emhyr said, smiling sweetly, with their ears shifting around to listen.

Simon's face darkened, and he glared.

He would admit that Emhyr had a point, but he wasn't keen on letting them *know*. He looked over to where Andreas was curled up and observed as the man turned a page and shifted more comfortably into his seat. Andreas had seemed more content here than he'd seen him in the month they'd been around one another. There were fewer moments of the younger man being stiff, and he'd not seen him lean on behaviors he often did to help with anxiety, like pulling on his hair or fidgeting with his hands.

"What *are* you going to do, Simon? You look like you need to shit again."

Simon growled and turned his attention back towards his acquaintance.

"You're going to leave, right?" Emhyr cooed, leaning against their arm in a lackadaisical fashion. They looked to be enjoying this round of interrogation.

"If they don't give me another job after this one, yes. There's no reason to…" Simon's words trailed off, and he glanced back toward the man sitting near the fire.

Andreas was looking up this time, glaring at Emhyr. His face calmed and shifted to a pleasant smile when he met Simon's gaze. Simon returned the smile, his brow knitting, and slightly waved. Andreas waved back and then returned to the massive tome he was perusing.

"Oh, I told you that you were going to fuck yourself over, old friend," Emhyr said.

"Shut up, Emhyr." Simon snapped and looked at his stew.

"Touchy, touchy," Emhyr tapped the bar again with their claws. "You could always stay; granted, I would warn that a few here sneer."

"What do you mean by 'sneer'?" Simon asked. "The Dwyers don't sneer."

"No, they don't, but people sneer if you're affiliated with them. The Dwyers have my respect, which was earned, so it's quite easy to ignore. Neil got me out of a rather dicey situation in Faixte. Anyone who sneers at those men is a fool."

Simon was intrigued. "What were you doing?"

"Me? I was living, and as it goes, some people like to earn a living by using others against their will," Emhyr scoffed, their voice almost sing-song. "You know how it is. Men love fulfilling fantasies when you have cute ears and a tail, and they will pay a heavy price to do so, even if you have a collar around your neck."

Simon's face darkened as he asked, "Trafficking?"

"Indeed. I was caught while sleeping, and the next thing I knew, I was being sold to the highest bidder in a little village near Westfort. I got lucky that Neil was in the area; we all did." There was anger simmering in the Ancaran's usually carefree voice. Their eyes were focused on the pub, not locking onto anything. They appeared to be trying to avoid letting their mind linger too long on anything. "Do you remember Shima?"

Simon hissed under his breath as if the name were foul. "I do."

"She's still alive, and they are all in serious trouble now," Emhyr said, returning their attention to Simon. They stared at each other. "She was part of the group that caught me. It seems they pivoted from theft and murder to trafficking. They had some very worrying clients, which is why Neil was even involved."

Simon pushed the bowl of lukewarm food away, realizing he had lost his appetite. Shima was a high-ranking member of a mercenary guild, to whom he had agreed to help on a job and had been considering joining. He had been told the job was simple: take back some stolen cargo and only harm anyone if they got in the way. It seemed like a quick and straightforward job until they actually started doing it.

The stolen 'cargo' was unpaid taxes that the village people didn't have the coin to pay, and it seemed that simply being *alive* was enough to get killed. It was a massacre that the guild leader had agreed to with a broker Simon hadn't known at the time. All they were supposed to do was kill the villagers, take the money, and capture anyone that Shima deemed valuable. He didn't want any part in it, so he left, stole half of the guild's money from their coffers, and skipped town while the others raided the village.

He may have tipped off someone in Pirn about what was happening, too, and many of that guild's mercs probably died that night. Deserved. He had done a lot for money, but he had some standards. Harming people to benefit a greedy bastard didn't sit right with him. He had grown up with less, at least if you measured a fulfilling life by wealth. Looking back on it now, with more information, he should have been suspicious because the village was near *Pirn*.

"They're mixed up with **EDEN** shit then, huh?" Simon scoffed, angry.

"Seems so, but let's keep our voices down," Emhyr said, looking around the room. They leaned closer to whisper, satisfied that no one was listening too closely or paying them attention. *"Neil killed quite a few of them then and saved around twelve of us. Shima got out, along with a few of her idiots, but they're on Pirn's payroll publicly now."*

"Neil freed you?"

"He did. He offered me a job, a warm room, and food. I'm no one's pet, and I can come and go as I please, do what I please, so long as I watch the pub while he and Cian are preoccupied. Compared to the life I had for eight months and the one I was facing for the rest of my life, it sounded too good to be true. Probably the best deal I've ever made," Emhyr said.

Simon offered a look of sympathy, which Emhyr brushed off with a smile and a roll of their eyes. "They seem like alright people to me," he said.

"Cian and Neil?" Emhyr chuckled and nodded. "They are. Much to my surprise."

Simon looked back over to Andreas and watched him silently for a moment.

"Which leads us back to our topic of importance, Simon."

Simon sighed and then looked back at Emhyr. "Which is?"

"What are you going to do about *that?*" Emhyr asked. They pointed, and Simon's eyes followed in the direction they indicated. Andreas had looked up again, watching the two curiously. At first, he looked like he was glaring at Emhyr again, but his face softened when he spotted Simon turn and look in his direction.

"He keeps stealing glances at you. He really **hates** that I'm talking to you," Emhyr said. They smiled, waved toward Andreas, and chuckled when the redhead glared and returned to his book. "Are you going to keep following him around like a puppy, or will you stop pretending to be his pet and let him find another? He's very good at finding pets; I promise he won't be lonely long," they continued.

"*I'm not his pet,*" Simon hissed as he looked at Emhyr.

"Then what are you?" Emhyr asked, chuckling as they pushed off the bar. Simon fell quiet, unable to answer the question.

Twenty

Promise

He never understood what people with money could spend it all on. However, he now understood after visiting the local tailor with Andreas and Neil a few days prior. Those with money spend a lot on clothing, specifically clothing they wear only once. At least in his case, it would be once because if he had to put this outfit on again, he might off himself. Simon fiddled with the neckerchief around his neck for the twentieth time. It was difficult to breathe, and the fitted shoulders of the long coat he wore made his range of motion smaller. The damned neckerchief wasn't helping.

Simon muttered, "I'm never wearing this thing again," as he loosened the fabric from his neck and tossed it over to a chair. Glancing around, he stepped away, hoping no unfamiliar faces would notice his actions.

The clothing he received as a gift was superior to anything he had ever owned, and much to his dismay, it fit him perfectly. The color palette was black, crimson, and gold. He never would have chosen these colors, but he had been told he needed to match Andreas. He realized that the Dwyer family loved palettes of gold and red or teal and white. He believed this was because of their devotion to the two Primals, Cael and Pithus.

He wore black trousers with a high waist and a double-button design featuring thin red striping. His fitted trousers were tucked into black boots with gold striping along the sides. This was paired with a crimson poet shirt made of silk and adorned with golden chain trimmings, revealing his neck and clavicles. Over the shirt, he wore a long black overcoat with stiff cuffs, golden buttons, and crimson trimmings, open with a twin tail. Despite the loud outfit, he blended into the crowd around the sprawling stone palace. Occasionally, he would catch a look of interest from passersby as they headed deeper into the building. However, other than this, nobody paid attention to him.

"*Where the hell are you, Red?*" he whispered, peering over the countless faces scattered around the entryway. Simon shifted, moving to the side as an elven couple passed by. He angled his head to peer out into the garden. He felt out of place, especially since he was alone. Andreas had told him to wait here after arriving, as Simon had to run to the tailor to get a last-minute repair of his jacket just before it was time to leave the pub.

Simon winced as he remembered trying on the heavy fabric earlier. He realized his shoulders were broader than the tailor had planned, causing the fabric to rip. Ultimately, they sent him on his way with a completely different jacket than he had ordered. Simon had only arrived at the palace ten minutes ago and was anxious. He started to wonder whether he needed to track down Andreas. Simon shifted over, turning to ensure he hadn't missed the arrival of the half-elf.

A click of heels approached, and then Andreas called out, "What happened to the other coat we picked?"

Simon said, "My shoulders had other…" His words faded into silence as his eyes locked on the approaching man, following him as he closed the distance.

Andreas reached over and fussed over Simon's sleeves, complaining about them being too tight and incorrectly folded.

Andreas wore ankle-length black heeled boots, which made him three inches taller than average. His clothing emitted a regal vibe, as though it had been designed for a prince rather than the grandson of war heroes. His trousers were black, made of satin, and fitted with a classic front and high waist. He wore a chiffon poet-style shirt, buttoned, with billowing sleeves.

It was red and slightly duller than his hair, with dark trimming and golden embroidery accenting the sleeves and chest. Around his waist was a black corset with gold trim, with long pleated sections of fabric on his lower back that trailed like butterfly wings. He had secured his hair in a thick braid, except for the framing sections that were too short around his face. There were flower additions of actual gold tucked into his braid's plaits.

"Other?" Andreas looked up, confused by the prolonged pause.

"Plans. It's ruined," Simon said as he finished his thought and turned his face away.

Andreas smiled as Simon's sandy features focused on the tile floor, purposefully avoiding eye contact with him. There was a faint tinge of pink on Simon's face. Andreas snickered as he looked back at Simon's sleeves and said, "I clean up pretty well when I want to, don't I?"

"You do," Simon muttered, looking back at the man before him.

This made Andreas smile, and his eyes glanced upwards bashfully before settling on where he adjusted the cuff on his companion's sleeve. "Yeah, well, you certainly do," he said.

Simon smiled and replied, "I don't know how you always wear this stuff."

"I haven't dressed up in two years," Andreas laughed, patting Simon's chest. "All done."

Simon glanced down, adjusted his arms, and realized the cuffs had been loosened, allowing him to move his wrists more freely. He sighed and asked, "Do you think you can let this whole thing out?"

"Unfortunately, no," Andreas complained. He then reached up and wrapped his arm around Simon's. "Are you ready to take on the world of bureaucracy?"

Simon grimaced but shifted his arm to lead the man attached to it. "Do I have to talk to people, or can we just mess around until you get drunk?" he asked, grinning.

Andreas glanced at a couple who dodged around them and passed by, then to the orc at his side and smirked. "Well, I do **love** parties."

Simon noticed the loud and enthusiastic tone in which his companion spoke the words. He also noted Andreas' catlike grin as they walked forward.

He leaned in, his lips brushing Andreas' ear, and whispered, "*So, we don't have to talk?*"

Andreas leaned closer, arching to whisper, "*If they approach us, yes. My grandparents will try to keep the usual suspects away. Unfortunately, if they see me with you, the nosy money here will want to know who you are.*"

Simon looked over and mouthed 'nosy money' in confusion. He felt Andreas squeeze his arm and nod forward to the small line of six couples they were behind to enter the ballroom. The people were stopped and spoken to, and then a halfling announced their arrival.

Andreas leaned in and whispered. "*Alright, we dodge **that**. Once the halfling announces that human couple, follow me—quickly.*"

Simon's eyes shifted downward, and he spied Andreas tapping his arm lightly. There was a bulge under one of Andreas' sleeves, and Simon immediately understood that the man had hidden his bow—folded in its pouch as it always was—under the fabric. He chuckled and nodded. A sensation washed over him, almost like a warm embrace that started at his feet and enveloped him as if a magical flame had brushed him. It was a spell Andreas had used before, meant to help them move about unnoticed as long as they didn't attract too much attention. Thankfully, he had nothing metallic except for the embellishments on his clothes to risk making too much noise.

Andreas sidestepped as the halfling turned and pulled Simon to the right. It was effortless how he maneuvered them into the shadows of the hallway and then down a nearby corridor, out of sight. Glancing back to ensure no one had noticed them, he smiled when he was confident they had escaped. He pointed at Simon and whispered under his breath.

"Follow me. There's a side door that leads to a small balcony above the garden patio. We can slip down onto it without being noticed."

As Simon listened to the magically whispered words, he turned his head and followed Andreas to a simple door that faced the outside, just off the main corridor. When Andreas opened the door, they could hear music and see bright light filtering from open double doors onto a stone balcony. The balcony overlooked a small garden with no windows in the larger hall. Small, shaded recesses below the stone wall were covered in ivy on either side, which would make climbing down easier as long as it supported their weight. It appeared that Andreas knew precisely where he was heading.

Simon glanced at the man beside him and whispered, "I thought you've never been here before. Are you sure about that?"

Andreas smiled and whispered, "I may have peeked when I left you with Grandpa Neil on our shopping trip. Invisibility can be quite useful."

Simon chuckled before stepping away from Andreas and grabbing the vines to check their security. There was no way in hell they would hold him—they were giving just from being pulled on. With a grimace, he leaned down to assess how far it was to the balcony below. He estimated that it was no more than fifteen feet down. Gripping the edge of the railing in front of them, he hoisted himself over and draped over the edge. It took a few moments, but he shimmied down before dropping with a thump.

Both Simon and Andreas froze.

Andreas pressed into the shadows of the upper balcony while Simon moved closer to the edge of the balcony he had landed on. They both held their breath, waiting, but no one had noticed them. The music played by the band and the chatter of voices from within the ballroom masked the sound Simon had made when he'd landed. Simon looked up, extended his hands upward, and made a grabbing motion. *"Jump,"* he whispered.

Andreas looked at the ivy, then at Simon, uncertain about what to do.

Simon frowned, his brow furrowed, and whispered, *"I'll catch you."*

Andreas nodded, looking at his hands. He couldn't climb well because they didn't allow him to grip tightly or for long, often making him feel like a liability. This was especially true when he helped his father with minor jobs requiring a quieter touch than Leo could deliver alone. Andreas peered into the open doors behind Simon, checking them for movement, and then into the open arms, waiting for him below.

They didn't discuss this, but Simon appeared to have considered it all on his own. Warmth rushed over him and settled into his stomach. Andreas suddenly felt intense *appreciation* for the man. A small smile spread across his lips as he nodded, and Simon returned it with a gentle smile.

Andreas maneuvered to sit on the balcony's edge. He took a breath, then pushed off the stonework. He reached out, his body tensing as if expecting to fall, and then Simon caught his waist almost effortlessly. Andreas flailed, his arms catching and wrapping around the other man's shoulders as his feet stopped a few inches from the ground. He hadn't noticed until he was in Simon's arms, but he was shaking.

Simon put his arms around Andreas' waist and carefully set the man on his feet. "*I told you I'd catch you, didn't I?*" he whispered.

Andreas gazed up at the face a few inches above him and smiled. He then popped up on his toes to kiss the orc's cheek. "*Thank you.*"

Simon's hands lingered on Andreas' waist, and he looked like he debated leaning down and kissing his companion. Andreas rolled his eyes playfully, patted Simon's chest, and pulled away. "*Come on,*" he whispered.

Simon huffed and then gathered Andreas' arm in his so he could slip back into the character he was playing. He often played the role of a bodyguard, but he wasn't used to the extravagance of where he was currently working. The polished stone walls were adorned with bright red and gold banners, and the room was filled with well-dressed people talking and dancing. The number of people and the flurry of activity with trays of food and drinks was more than he was used to.

This wasn't his element, and it made him slightly self-conscious. Despite the clothing he'd been given, Simon felt underdressed, as if he were a street urchin playing dress up in hand-me-downs from a theatrical performance. He wondered if the multitude of faces could see through him, and his grip on Andreas' arm tightened. When Andreas returned the squeeze, Simon glanced over and whispered, "*Here we go, Red.*"

"*This is the easy part,*" Andreas whispered back and then turned his attention to the party. Andreas waved down a waiter, an elven male with long dark hair and pale features, and asked for a glass. "Actually, could I have two?" he smiled and batted his eyes.

The elven male paused, looking at the tray he carried. "I'm supposed to allow one per patron at a time... If one is for both of you..." He glanced at Simon, almost for help.

Andreas pulled away from Simon, tapping the elven man's chest. "He won't drink, on duty and all that ... but we can just say it's for him. It can be our secret."

Simon frowned as he watched the scene play out, studying the subtle nuances as Andreas angled his hips and pushed the limits of space between him and the elven man. Simon watched the waiter crumble under the unending attention and small, playful touches. The waiter's face turned red. Simon swallowed, his jaw tightening as discomfort and *jealousy* settled into his belly and twisted.

Andreas had a reputation, and he had often seen the man use his charisma to his advantage. This was different. In a way, it felt like Andreas was pushing the boundaries of the setting. Seeing how easily Andreas could slip into this character made him uncomfortable. It was almost an intricate act, as if the other man used it to...

Andreas regained his composure as he returned to Simon and downed one of the champagne glasses. Like the man before, a woman walked by with a tray; he handed her the empty glass. After she continued with a slight bow, he linked his arm back through Simon's and nodded towards the less crowded side of the room. "Let's go over there. I don't want to draw more attention than I have to," he said.

Simon followed, his eyes scanning the crowd. "You're *too* skilled at manipulating others with your appearance."

Andreas laughed, saying, "It's a learned talent that has kept me alive."

"Seems more like a survival technique to keep others at bay to me," Simon muttered, feeling the arm in his slack. He looked down and saw a far-off look settled into the green gaze. He seemed to have hit a nerve, or made Andreas uncomfortable. Simon frowned.

"Maybe so..." Andreas responded, sipping his glass. "It works. " He looked around, almost as if he had to study the faces in the room. He took another sip of champagne and asked, "Does it make you uncomfortable?"

Simon sighed, his eyes locked on the room and the multitude of people. "It makes me wonder why you need to display this flirty, entitled brat persona," he said.

Andreas choked on his drink and looked over to glare. "I am *not*..."

Simon locked eyes with Andreas and said, "**I know**. That's my point. Why are you trying to be?"

Andreas bit his lip in thought. He avoided thinking about why he had put so much effort into upholding the facade. He never cared what others thought about the person he presented to them; after all, Andreas knew who he was... sort of. *Maybe*. Andreas let his gaze fall to the floor and focused on the dull sound of the music as it faded into the background. Simon shifted, most likely observing the surrounding room. He had never considered why, nor had anyone asked.

Silence filled the space between them.

Simon observed the bodies spinning around the dance floor and noticed the Dwyer patriarchs weaving through the crowd. The longer he watched them, the more his eyes were transfixed on them.

There was something regal about them, almost overpowering, as they moved together. Somehow, they outshined the people here in a way he couldn't explain. He'd seen them several times in their pub but had never seen them both so well-dressed or moving in unison. It held his attention, if only because he appreciated it. He'd often heard how inseparable the two were but never witnessed it firsthand. They loved one another so much that it wrapped around them as they walked. There were subtle nuances to their movements: Cian held onto his husband's arm and leaned in to speak, while Neil's face lit up whenever his husband brushed his cheek or tugged him in any direction.

Simon furrowed his brow in thought and wondered, from an outside perspective, how he and...

"I don't know why," Andreas said, barely above a whisper.

Simon's train of thought abruptly halted, and he looked down, asking, "What?"

Andreas swirled the liquid in his champagne glass, his eyes locked on the floor. He looked deep in contemplation, as if he had been racking his brain for the last fifteen minutes for an answer to an impossible question. "I think, maybe..."

Simon watched in confusion, but leaned his head down to hear.

The emerald eyes looked for the two patriarchs in the crowd and found Cian and Neil as they slipped off to a corner to chat. Andreas took a deep breath and said, "I'm afraid I can't live up to them, to what others expect me to be." Andreas shifted uncomfortably and continued, "I'm not as strong as they are. It's easier to be known as their bratty son and grandson; people expect less of you when you're an entitled brat."

Simon noticed the change in his companion's face as it flickered from shame to doubt and then *helplessness*. The topic rattled Andreas enough that he forgot to hide his emotions, which was unusual for him. Simon swallowed and said, "Andrea..."

Andreas interrupted him, "That's why I did this. *I'm tired of it.* I want to be someone they can rely on and protect them when the time comes." He watched his grandparents across the ballroom as they talked. He'd realized it in the cabin, maybe even before; it was just magnified at the cabin. It was this intricate knot of many things at once. "I don't want to be compared to them; that's stifling. That's impossible because I can't ..." Andreas looked down, laughing dryly before continuing, "I can't even compare to them or my parents, but ... I don't like the idea of others seeing me as this *useless* brat either. I feel lost no matter where I turn. I don't know what to do, or what I want to do ... because I can't tell the difference between what *I* want and what's expected of me."

> "What am I supposed to do? Everyone expects me to settle down with some girl, have kids, and inherit the fighting ring. What if that's not what I want to do? What if that's not **who** I want to settle down and have a family with, Simon?"

Simon took a deep breath, absorbing the sweet scent of the air into his lungs. He had recalled a conversation with someone, not in such a luxurious setting, but on the quiet edge of a dock in the evening. He swallowed, trying to calm his breathing as a wave of sorrow washed over him. It didn't seem fair. He grasped Andreas' fingers, feeling them tense from shaking. He tried to clear his vision as he blinked, focusing on the blur of colors and sounds.

"I don't know," Simon's voice shook, and he paused to remedy it. He felt himself ready to say the same thing he had back then. "I can't tell you what to do, but I'll help if possible, and I won't judge you for your choices, no matter what they are," he said.

It was strange, almost as if the man had heard the words. As soon as they escaped Simon's lips, Neil Dwyer turned and stared him down. Simon froze, unable to look away. There was no way that Neil could hear him, let alone know where to look; Neil was blind and standing far across the ballroom. He knew this. Yet somehow, it felt like Neil was staring into his soul, almost judging him by his words.

Neil grinned and turned his head back to whisper something to his husband. Simon shuddered, and the emotion associated with the memory he had recalled faded. The water that had crept at the edge of his vision retreated, and he could see the room.

"Are you promising that we can work together again?" Andreas asked Simon.

Simon glanced over and saw the large green eyes, almost hopeful. He smiled despite himself and replied, "I promise I'll help if I can… and if that means we work together again, that's what it means."

Twenty-One

Deception

"Oh dear, is he alright?"

Simon looked up at the sound of a woman's voice and found a human woman in her late thirties standing before him. She was beautiful with dark red lips and heterochromia - one bright blue eye and one amber eye. She was short, barely five feet tall, with fair skin, freckles, rosy cheeks, and a square jaw. Her brown, wavy hair was shoulder-length with a slight side part and no bangs. She was dressed in regal attire with a dark color palette and many golden trimmings on the cape fastened around her shoulders.

Simon looked at Andreas, who he supported with an arm over his shoulder, and then back at the woman. "He had too much to drink. He's fine."

The woman looked concerned and frowned. "Should we take him to rest?" She brushed Simon's arm before glancing toward a door leading into the palace. "I'm sure there's a spare sofa we could use."

Simon shook his head stiffly. "I'm taking him back to his room. I've informed his grandparents."

The woman tilted her head slightly to see Andreas' face better. Her eyes widened, and she stepped back. "Oh, the Dwyer boy. I see," she said, looking up and smiling.

Simon locked eyes with her and forced a smile. "Yeah," he replied. He noticed her pupils constrict and eyes narrow briefly before returning to normal. Perplexed, he furrowed his brow. This woman seemed peculiar, almost familiar. He didn't appreciate her lingering. "Was there something you needed?" he asked.

"No, do I know you?" The woman's head tilted, and she stepped forward as if studying Simon's features. "You look very familiar," she said.

Simon adjusted his grip on his companion's waist. "I'm not from around here," he said.

"No, but I…" The woman's face twisted in thought, and then a broad smile spread over her lips like she had figured it out. Her voice was coy, as if she had already known it but pretended otherwise. "Ransol. I've seen you before in Ransol, yes?" she asked.

Simon tensed as he replied, "Possibly. I get a lot of contract work there… I'm sorry I didn't catch your name?"

Her eyes narrowed again before returning to normal, and she smiled. "I did not give it," she said. She grasped the hem of her dress and curtsied. "Does *Talien* know your current job is babysitting the Dwyer brat?"

Simon felt the man in his grip shift slightly, and he squeezed Andreas' waist. His gaze narrowed, locked on the woman. "I couldn't care less about what he knows." He saw a look of interest and amusement flood the woman's face before she tried to suppress it. Ignoring it, he started walking past her. "Excuse me, I need to get him back, or I won't get paid. **Have a good night.**"

The woman sidestepped, folded her hands, and called out as Simon turned to leave, "If you're ever looking for a job, or simply want to upset Talien, you should consider working for me. I'm also more fun than that *brat* in bed, Simon."

Simon froze, and his head jerked back. She was gone as if she had stepped back into the crowd. Whoever she was, she knew his name and had seen, or heard of him, in Ransol. He felt Andreas bump against his side, trying to hurry him along. He hesitated for a moment longer, searching for the woman, and then sighed in irritation and started forward.

* * *

Fortunately, they were only stopped a few more times. Each time, Andreas intervened by pretending to have woken up and flirted ceaselessly. As annoying as it had been, his believable performance had been impressive. When they were safely tucked into a back alley and certain no one had seen them enter it, Andreas huffed and stood up fully.

"That was annoying," Andreas said, stretching out his back.

"You're telling me?" Simon replied, maneuvering his shoulder, which had been locked for nearly an hour.

Andreas looked up and adjusted one of the butterfly-like tails on his waist to reveal a hidden bag. When he opened the bag, half his arm vanished as he rummaged inside. "Who was that woman?" he asked.

"I don't know, and that bothers me more than knowing," Simon said as he pulled his coat off his shoulder. He rolled his shoulders, thankful for his renewed range of motion. "You haven't seen her before? Her voice sounded familiar, but I couldn't place it."

"No, I've never seen that woman before," Andreas said as he unfastened the corset around his waist and took a deep breath as it fell free. He stepped out of his heeled boots and withdrew his old boots from the magical bag. He placed Simon's and his more expensive clothing within it. "I'm leaving your shield in here unless we need it; the less we have to worry about making noise, the better."

Simon nodded, watching Andreas discard the golden adornments he had been wearing and slip into his worn boots. He grinned, tilting his head in thought. "Somehow, you look better without all the frills, Red."

Andreas rolled his eyes and tapped the small pouch hidden beneath his sleeve. Once more, the warmth of sparks filtered over their skin and settled into a comfortable sensation. He looked up. "I only have one more free spell from my weapon enchantment. After that, I will start getting tired from casting magic. We need to get in and out within an hour, got it?"

Simon nodded, still not fully understanding the nuances of magic or how precisely the enchantments on the weapon worked. Andreas had tried to explain it, but all he had gathered was that the bow allowed him to use magic thrice daily without getting tired or needing anything to use as a reagent or catalyst. However, it was limited to the specific spells inscribed on the bow. "Alright."

They began circling back, moving faster than before and staying within the city's back alleys. It took the pair ten minutes or more to reach the castle's outer wall. Another five minutes passed as they slipped into the interior garden without being noticed. After that, they moved to the side of the building opposite the balcony connected to the party.

Andreas looked around, checking for anyone, and whispered, *"Alright, I have a—"* He let the words fall off as Simon grabbed him by the waist and hauled him over his shoulder. Simon peeked around and backed up slowly.

Andreas panicked and whispered urgently, *"What are you doing?!"*

"Trust me, and don't wiggle around. You'll throw me off," Simon whispered. He tightened his grip on the other man and bolted towards the wall. Andreas tensed and grasped Simon's shirt. Simon closed the distance between the wall and himself, then jumped as high as he could and reached out. He grabbed onto the second-story balcony and hoisted them up without much effort. *"Get up there,"* he said and nudged Andreas.

Andreas glanced over his shoulder and saw the balcony's ledge, even with his shoulders. He quickly scrambled over it. Shortly after, Simon was pulling himself over to join him. He looked from the orc to the ground over ten feet away. His mouth opened in awe; this man was terrifying. Simon had outrun a Varog pack while **carrying him**. Now, he had jumped sixteen feet or more while holding him.

Simon grinned at the look he received, shrugged, then backed up a few steps. He jumped without any problems, grabbed the stone railing above them, and hoisted himself quickly. Then he reached down. *"C'mon, Red."*

Andreas gazed upward, his eyes wide with awe. *"That was... how did you..."*

Simon glanced down, noticing the rotation of the guard starting to move from the torchlight against the darkened ground. *"Andreas! Now!"*

Andreas was startled and jumped when Simon grabbed his forearm and pulled him onto the third-story balcony. They pressed themselves against the ground near the wall and waited as two guards passed by, searching leisurely. After the guards moved on, they stood up, and Simon tried to open the door. It was locked, and he hissed in frustration.

"*Move,*" Andreas said as he reached into his bag and pulled out a leather pouch containing metallic instruments. It took him a minute or less to insert the correct metal rod, maneuver it, and hear the lock turn. He then gathered and stowed his things in the small bag on his hip. "*Come on.*"

"*Are you used to breaking and entering?*" Simon whispered.

Andreas smiled, shrugged, and peered into the building, cracking the door just enough to see the dark hallway. There were no guards in sight. He led Simon down the hallway to the left, looking for the office at the far end with a small balcony facing the ramparts. The plan was to get into the office before the meeting began. They would enchant the door so they would know if someone else entered and then hide on the balcony to eavesdrop. The only thing Andreas worried about was that someone on the ramparts would see them, but Simon had assured him that he would handle it.

Andreas reached the door and pressed his ear against it, listening for a moment. "*It's empty,*" he whispered.

Simon nodded and turned the doorknob. Fortunately, it was unlocked, so they could slip inside easily. The office was relatively small and made of stone, like the rest of the castle. The walls were covered with maps, banners, and paintings. The room held bookshelves, a small globe of the realm, and a single polished oak desk in its center. Simon maneuvered to the balcony door as Andreas closed the office door.

Andreas started drawing a symbol on the wood with his finger and whispered an elvish word. The spot he touched lit up briefly with a bright teal light before fading away. Andreas moved closer, scanning the scattered papers on the desk, hoping to find something that would make this worthwhile. Unfortunately, there wasn't much to see, and he didn't want to risk touching anything.

"*Red. Out here, I can't hide us for more than an hour,*" Simon whispered and nodded towards the balcony door.

Andreas looked up, nodded, and quietly followed Simon onto the balcony. He found a spreading fog that looked like it had rolled in from the sea. His face lit up, and as the balcony door clicked, he whispered, "*I thought you couldn't do magic?"*

Simon leaned forward, settling against the door to listen. *"I can't. Tembor left me a gift he used: a ring that could do this,"* he whispered, waving at the fog.

Andreas chuckled and whispered, *"I stand by what I said when I stated I liked Tembor."*

Simon smiled as he looked at the ramparts. A few torches were lit, but most of the stone wall was obscured. When he had peered out and let the fog loose, he hadn't seen any figures on this side watching. He turned his attention back to Andreas, who had positioned himself on the other side of the door. *"Do you think there will be a meeting?"*

"I don't know," Andreas replied as he shrugged. *"I didn't see any paperwork."* He froze and lifted a finger to his lips to silence Simon.

The enchantment had gone off, mimicking a wind chime within his mind. He saw Simon lean against the wall, ensuring his silhouette wasn't visible through the door's windows. Andreas listened as footsteps filled the room.

"Thank you for coming. I received your correspondence a month ago and was worried you hadn't gotten my reply," a male voice spoke in the office.

"Discretion was necessary," replied a female voice.

"Of course, please make yourself comfortable," the male voice said.

Andreas and Simon stared at each other, wide-eyed. They recognized the woman's voice. Andreas pointed to his companion, and Simon soon heard words echo magically in his head.

"That woman. From earlier. Am I wrong?"

Simon shook his head and immediately responded to Andreas via the spell.

"No. You're not wrong."

The man in the room asked, "So, you're Lady Sylvester's liaison?"

"I serve the one she does, and I am here at their request and hers," the woman replied.

Deception

"I see. So, are the rumors of her working with Qella true?" the man asked.

"I do not serve Qella, nor does she serve anyone. The Primal was merely a scapegoat," the woman chuckled.

Wyatt clicked his tongue. "Well, who do you serve then, if not Qella? Is that not what the *Remembrance* proved? What do you mean, scapegoat?"

"Of course. Elaina did serve Qella until she was no longer useful. There's someone older pulling the strings now."

"You do realize your vagueness is not giving hope to an alliance, yes?" Wyatt scoffed, clearly annoyed.

The woman huffed, also annoyed. "Listen, little man, I owe you *nothing* until we are allied. If you wish to keep your dick safely between your legs, then I suggest you show me more respect."

The tapping of heels filled the room, and then a faint click of nails on wood. "Now, either you want to sign the treaty and give us access to this place so that we can gather test subjects, or I kill you and leave without loose ends," the woman said.

"Test subjects? What are you talking about? I thought this was a means for Lady Sylvester to regain some of her lost political power. What is she planning with our subjects?" Wyatt sounded genuinely concerned.

The woman let out a cold laugh. "A prince, but a fool. Do you think of the beggars on the street more than an insect beneath your boot? Would you notice if a few orphans disappeared? Fossy is one of the few cities *without* an orphanage. I'm sure your streets would be the better for getting the riffraff off it."

* * *

Andreas and Simon had been listening for at least twenty minutes, and as the conversation continued, Andreas' face grew increasingly anxious. It seemed like he understood more of the conversation than Simon did. However, there was genuine confusion when specific details were disclosed, especially regarding the orphanages.

Simon understood the importance of having an orphanage in the city.

However, he was confused and anxious about why it was so important *not* to have one in Fossy. As the woman spoke, he became increasingly sure he knew her voice. This realization weighed heavily on him, and it began to grind at his resolve like thought-out torture. Simon finally leaned forward slightly and peered into the room.

He found two figures facing each other near the desk and angled towards the door. Unsurprisingly, he recognized the male as Prince Wyatt Richard, the son of the King of Midwind. However, the other person caught him off guard. It was not the woman they had seen earlier in the evening but a woman he recognized. Seeing her made malice churn in his stomach, and his hands gripped against the side of the wall lest he burst into the room.

She was a high-elven woman with dark copper-colored hair reaching her mid-back. Her hair was straight as a board. She had fair skin and wore darker clothing with several pelts hanging from her shoulders. Her features were sharp, and she had sunburst lines tattooed beneath her green eyes.

Simon felt a chill as if ice had formed in his veins, and he hesitated. He couldn't decide whether to stay put or enter the room. Looking up, he saw Andreas look at him with confusion and mouth words. Simon couldn't focus on the words. His ears rang so badly that he didn't hear his foot scrape the ground as he moved back. The room fell silent, and in an instant, Andreas looked at Simon horrifiedly.

Then the woman spoke, "Wyatt, were you always planning to deceive me?"

Wyatt panicked and asked, "What are you talking about?"

The woman laughed coldly and said, "Guards hidden on the balcony? How unoriginal."

The prince sputtered, "No! No! Wait, I—! What are you talking about?"

Andreas pointed, and Simon heard the voice in his head. It cut through the pain throbbing in his temple and the static filling the world. He looked up in surprise.

"We need to go. Now."

Go. Could he go? Could he *leave* when she was **right there**?

Andreas' brow furrowed, and he mouthed, begging, '*Simon!*'

Simon swallowed the lump in his throat. He had to go. If he didn't go, Andreas would get hurt, and that was less favorable than him letting that woman keep breathing. Simon nodded, looked to the balcony to get an idea of how much room he had to work with, and then looked towards the ramparts. He had no choice; he'd have to make it work. Without speaking, he reached over and grabbed Andreas, then backed up to the wall as far as he could move.

There was a sudden forceful sound, almost like a spell had been unleashed within the office. A scream from the prince reverberated.

That was all Simon needed to hear. He was running at full speed towards the railing and using it as leverage to jump. He felt Andreas grip him tightly, shaking, and watched as the ground passed beneath them. If they fell, they would both be pretty fucked up, so it would be better *not* to fall. He began pleading with his body, wishing for enough momentum to reach the ramparts in one piece.

Simon held onto Andreas tightly and leaned forward towards the approaching wall. It was a close call, but he made it; fortunately, he had estimated the distance correctly, as it was only about forty-five feet away. As soon as they hit the ground, Simon winced, feeling a cramp in his legs as pain shot up from his feet to his knees. He was starting to feel too old for this.

Andreas scrambled, hearing yelling as another loud blast came from the office they had just escaped. Whatever had happened inside hadn't been simple, and for that, he was thankful. That bought them time, and he grabbed Simon and bolted down the rampart, ignoring his throbbing hip. "*Move! Now!*" he hissed under his breath.

Simon did as asked, peering back towards the balcony to see an obscured figure step out to look around. He saw the woman's figure linger, then vanish. His eyes narrowed into slits, and he felt a growl work up his throat.

He would kill that bitch the next time he saw her.

He promised.

Twenty-Two

The After Party

Guards yelled across the ramparts, "Someone attacked the prince! Fan out and search!"

Andreas struggled to control his breathing, desperate for air to fill his lungs and ease the burning sensation within them. However, he was terrified of making noise as they hid in a small supply closet. It was barely spacious enough for both him and Simon. Because of the slanted roof, Andreas found himself in an awkward position with a broom pressing into his back and a crate of unknown items pressing into his knees. Simon, who was too tall for the space, had to lean against the wall with his arms on either side of Andreas' head for support just to fit.

They were both pinned, unable to move without risk of alerting anyone who may be loitering outside and watching the closed door in mild terror. They waited until the sound of rushing feet and yelling faded into the distance before Simon dared to whisper, *"You saved my ass."*

Andreas sighed and leaned his head forward to rest on the chest in front of him. *"I did. You were almost seen."*

They had been running far ahead of the commotion that erupted moments after they landed on the ramparts. Andreas heard the guards approaching before they were in sight. He'd cast invisibility on Simon and pushed him against the wall, then closed the supply closet door with himself inside. Luck was on their side, as Simon had not been seen. Thankfully, during their search, the four guards hadn't considered the closet, and Andreas wasn't sure if it was pure dumb luck or simply because they were in a hurry. After they had passed, Simon had nearly broken his neck when scrambling into the storage closet and bumped his head so hard that it bled on one of the metal shelves above them.

Andreas peered up to where blood trickled down Simon's cheek from his hair. He frowned and asked, *"Are you alright?"*

Simon sighed, *"Yeah. I'm fine."*

Andreas struggled to pull his hand up and caught his sleeve so he could dab at the other's wound. Simon winced as the gash on the side of his head was brushed.

"Be still," Andreas scolded in a whisper.

"That hurts," Simon hissed, surprised when he felt a familiar warming sensation ignite over the wound. *"… Thanks."*

"That should, at least, stop the bleeding," Andreas said with a smile and shifted to get more comfortable.

Simon tensed and breathed sharply as their hips brushed, and his mind nosedived into the gutter.

"Sorry," Andreas winced, guilty.

Simon grumbled, trying to focus on the present moment and not the heat growing in his gut from the sudden stimulation. He looked at the door and whispered, *"Should we try to leave or wait?"*

Andreas listened for movement, *"I need to check in with my grandparents, but we have the scroll. Can you reach my bag?"*

Simon sighed and shifted his weight onto one hand to reach down and pull on Andreas' bag. It wouldn't budge, so he reached for Andreas' hand instead of forcing it. He felt Andreas tense as he moved his gloved fingers to the cinched opening and shoved them inside. *"There. Better?"*

Andreas swallowed, let his fingers fumble until he found the scroll, and withdrew it. Then he unfurled it as best he could with one hand and nodded toward the door. *"Take a peek outside,"* he whispered.

"What?!" Simon replied immediately, giving his companion a bewildered look.

Andreas whispered, glaring and nodding to the door. *"If anyone sees the light under the door, we're fucked. Peek.* **Out.***"*

Simon grumbled as he returned the glare and began the delicate dance of shifting his weight to open the door. It took him a few moments to move around and a few more to refocus his mind on the task at hand. They were standing too close, and he couldn't deny that he had been distracted by the faint freckles on Andreas' face and the sensation of their hips brushing against each other again. Simon cracked the door open and peered outside. He could see torches moving across the way, not on the ramparts, but out on the balcony of the prince's office.

"They're investigating the office."

"No one is nearby?" Andreas asked.

"No, not near us," Simon whispered back, still focused on the balcony.

"Alright, close the door. We need to go," Andreas said. Simon shut the door gently and looked down at the scroll between them. Instantly, Andreas grabbed Simon's waist tightly, startling him.

"What are you...?" Simon's voice trailed off as he glanced down and heard not elvish escaping the other man's mouth but another language. He couldn't help but notice that it sounded older and reminded him of Cian's accent. Although it was a language he hadn't heard before, he was drawn into it—it was strange because it felt like he should know it.

Andreas' eyes brightened, and then a flurry of energy started swirling around them. It felt like a cool breeze, and the electricity took on a soft teal color as it encircled them like wisps of smoke. Simon felt an unfamiliar phenomenon in his gut, as if his intestines were being tied in knots. The whole thing made him feel like puking.

Simon and Andreas fell straight down as the closet suddenly vanished. Simon fumbled, trying to brace himself against the oncoming floor so he didn't crush the slight form under him. Andreas clenched his eyes, almost expecting it, as the scroll he held disintegrated into nothingness. Simon caught himself, taking most of the impact on his palms and knees. He let a few curses escape, his knees still aching from the long jump earlier in the evening, and clenched his eyes.

Andreas peeked from behind his eyelids when he heard Simon complain and found tusks barely an inch from his face. Simon's face twisted in pain, and he felt tremors running up the orc's arms on either side of his head. "Sorry, I can't control where we land or change our position during transport," he said.

Simon exhaled as discomfort shot up his limbs before subsiding enough for him to roll onto the ground next to his companion. He took a deep breath, focusing on the floor against his back before opening his eyes. They were back in the cabin they had left over a week ago. The space was dark, and he could hear thunder outside.

Andreas shifted, wincing from the pain in his back. He had landed hard enough to knock the wind out of him momentarily, and it had only made the spot where the broom had shoved into his spine more tender. "Stay there… let me get some supplies for your head."

Simon watched as Andreas struggled to his feet, momentarily unsteady, and then wandered off. He let out a groan of complaint and let the adrenaline that had been pumping through his body for the last hours ease off. His joints throbbed, and he closed his eyes to focus on their dull ache. He knew he was going to be sore for a few days. "I'm getting too old for this…" he mumbled.

"You're not old," Andreas huffed.

The crackling of a fire bursting to life filled the space, instantly warming the large sitting room. Simon chuckled, his eyes still closed, and savored the moment of peace. "I don't know," he said. He felt old, almost stretched thin from the events.

Andreas smoothed Simon's hair back and gently brushed the gash on his head. He muttered under his breath, and a warm glow illuminated his hand and the wound again. It was still pouring blood.

Simon inhaled and closed his eyes. "Fancy tricks," he muttered.

Andreas chuckled as he grabbed a wet cloth in his lap and dabbed it over the edges of the laceration in an attempt to clean it. "I wish I knew more healing spells, but I'm not meant to help people but to harm them."

Simon opened his eyes and furrowed his brow. Andreas looked concerned, which made him feel uneasy. "You've helped me a lot. I can't do what you do. Without your tricks to make me invisible or read whatever language was on that scroll, I would have been **screwed**, Red."

Andreas smiled and pressed the cloth against the wound to try and finish damming the blood flow. "I guess," he said.

"Hey." Simon sat up suddenly, reaching out to grab the wrist close to his head. He wasn't used to Andreas acting like this. In the past few weeks, as they got to know each other, he had experienced firsthand how stubborn Andreas could be. Andreas also had an annoying habit of hiding his feelings. Seeing the uncertainty on his face made Simon feel restless. He didn't know if he liked it or if it made him uncomfortable. The mismatched eyes tried to find the green ones, but Andreas avoided his gaze.

Simon's brow furrowed, and he refused to release the arm in his grasp when Andreas tried to pull away. "Andrea, look at me."

It happened instantly. Andreas glanced up when he heard his nickname and bit his lip. He suddenly looked like a frightened, cornered animal.

"Considering that we just broke into a prince's study, overheard him talking to a woman about sensitive information, and managed to escape unharmed... don't doubt yourself now," Simon said with a frown, anticipating an objection. It made his gut tremble; he didn't like being able to read this man so easily. "If you dare say it was all me, I'll put you in a headlock."

Andreas chuckled as he felt the hand on his wrist loosen, then moved his hand down to rest on Simon's knee. "Since when can you read my thoughts?"

"Since you started letting your face do whatever it is," Simon replied; he still felt unsatisfied despite the tension easing in the carnelian features.

Andreas laughed again. "I don't know what you're talking about... Let me see your head." He pulled his hand away and reached up to ensure Simon's wound hadn't started bleeding again. Simon was watching him cautiously. Desperately wanting to change the topic, Andreas fidgeted uncomfortably and searched for something to say. "That woman. You seemed to know her when you looked into the office... Did you remember her?" he asked.

Simon filled with rage as he hissed, "**Yeah, I fucking know her**. She wore a face before."

Andreas' face twisted in concern. "You mean she altered her appearance?"

"Yeah. Whatever the hell you call it," Simon pulled his head away, batting at the hand that still wanted to inspect it. "I'm not surprised she's poking her nose into that **EDEN** crap. She has a questionable history, but why is she trying to establish alliances with royalty?" he asked. He saw confusion in the emeralds watching and breathed to settle his thoughts. Simon huffed and said, "Her name is Tsara Falgor. She's a rogue pirate... she can't even come within a few leagues of Ransol. The pirate monarchy has a price on her head."

"There's... aren't all pirates rogues?" Andreas looked confused and settled down to lean against the sofa. "There's a *monarchy*?"

Simon chuckled. "Yes, and no. Even in the pirate community, there are certain things you ***don't*** do ... she's done a lot of them." He shifted to face Andreas and held up two fingers. "Sort of. There are two pirates: **The Two Mothers**. They're the most powerful and have the most influence in the community, so there's a pseudo-monarchy with those two. They have some terrifying people around them, especially Malika. ... Have you ever seen an emblem with two mountains and a body of water before them? Depending on its placement, one would be black and the other pale gray, almost white."

Andreas thought, trying to recall anything from his studies or the odd jobs he'd helped his father with. "I think I remember seeing something like that once... In Belmare, one of the dock markers had something similar. It was a black mountain with a lightning bolt striking its peak. Does that sound familiar?" He looked up.

Simon nodded. "That's the *Warden*'s mark. Malika, the black mountain, has a man sailing within her fleet known as the *Warden of the Seas*. He's the go-between for **The Two Mothers** and acts as their liaison. The *Warden* also enacts any judgments or punishments they dole out. He's a powerful man. Redirine doesn't usually allow pirates at the port, so it's surprising that his mark is in Belmare."

Andreas thought again, his head shaking. "I don't recall ever seeing a pirate vessel at port. I know there is a ship that looks more like a trade or entertainment vessel that comes maybe twice a year, but…"

"That sounds like **The Waning Moon**, his ship," Simon sighed, his brow furrowing. "That's interesting. I didn't know they docked there. You don't have an orphanage in Belmare, do you?"

"Not that I'm aware of," Andreas shook his head in mild confusion. He didn't understand. "Why?"

"It's complicated, but the *Warden* has connections to the orphanages; he's the benefactor of **The Storm's Embrace** locations on the continents. Tsara wouldn't be able to go to cities with them in it, or he would know, and she's on his kill list," Simon waved the conversation off. "Regardless, Tsara was the one who met with your prince and blasted him to death. Her magic was off, though."

Andreas nodded, understanding the significance of the lack of an orphanage in Fossy now. He looked up curiously and asked, "What do you mean her magic was off? I didn't think you knew much about magic."

"I don't know much about it, but her magic usually smells like saltwater and rotting fish. It's so strong that you can smell it a block away when it's used. … I smelled nothing like that tonight." Simon saw Andreas' face contort in disgust, and he laughed. "She worships the Old God of the sea—the crazy one. I've heard she got her magic from a pact with him, but I don't know the specifics. I know she likes to use her bedmates as sacrifices for him, which hasn't gotten her many friends in the pirating world. The **Mothers** don't like folks that fuck around with sea magic if it risks their people or the freedom of the community."

"So, that's what she meant when she said she was more fun in bed than me. … *She wanted to use and abuse you.*" Andreas' tongue clicked his teeth. He sounded annoyed.

Simon chuckled at the tension in the words. "Oh? Are you getting upset on my behalf?"

Andreas flushed and scoffed. "Maybe I'm just upset that a woman would even compare us, considering I don't sacrifice people."

Simon grinned. "Better up the ante … just not with me."

Andreas rolled his eyes and gathered the cloth he'd used on Simon's head.

Simon chuckled as he watched his companion, then asked, "Did you talk to your grandparents?"

"I talked to Grandpa Neil briefly ... he said there was a commotion at the party. They were trying to help the guard calm everyone down and investigate. The prince is dead."

Simon furrowed his brow. "Well, we knew that. No one saw us, did they?"

Andreas shook his head. "No. He said that a woman matching the description of Tsara's disguise was seen leaving the castle, though."

The mercenary lay on his back, hissing quietly. "Any idea when they'll arrive?"

"No, it could take longer than my grandparents expected due to bureaucracy and all. Papa hates it, but he dislikes senseless death more," Andreas lingered, fiddling with a string on his sleeve. "One thing I don't get... Why would a blacklisted pirate work with **EDEN**? Much less Elaina?"

"I don't know much about **EDEN**, but knowing Tsara?" Simon's jaw stiffened, and he fought down the urge to scream. "Power. She likes to think she's the biggest fish in the pond. If she got more power, she'd do whatever the one who gave it to her wanted. Even if it meant fucking her old God over."

"That's what I don't understand," Andreas furrowed his brow. "Qella is imprisoned, and Elaina is powerful, but she doesn't possess godlike abilities. She couldn't top the power of an Old God, so..." he said, trailing off in thought.

Simon glanced over. "Maybe they both found another power source. She mentioned that someone older was pulling the strings."

Andreas looked up, concerned. "I mean, I know, but... as in a replacement for Qella? Do you think she meant it that way? I thought maybe she was insulting Wyatt for being young or foolish."

"It sounded to me that someone else is now at the top, or maybe Qella isn't as imprisoned as we think?" Simon said, shrugging. "Granted, she made it sound like the **EDEN** woman used Qella as much as Qella used the other Primals."

"If she weren't sealed, I would have heard about it," Andreas said more confidently than he had about anything else they had discussed. He saw Simon's brows lift slightly, and he glanced away. "I know she is. Papa is the head of Cael's following and **The Rose Guard**. He would know if she wasn't sealed still."

"... Would they tell you, Red?"

"Yes. Papa would tell me. He doesn't lie," Andreas replied.

Simon observed the other man, noting the nuances of his face. Andreas appeared convinced, which Simon admired, but he still wasn't sure. Qella and Tsara were both topics he disliked and trusted even less. He had seen firsthand what could happen to people when… Simon swallowed, pushing the thought back. "Alright. Then maybe a replacement?"

"Well, that is a *fascinating* discovery," said Neil Dwyer. His icy, calculating tone suggested displeasure.

Suddenly, Simon and Andreas looked up the stairs in surprise as Neil's voice echoed from above. The room fell silent.

Twenty-Three

Possibility

"Simon."

Simon grumbled, unsure if he was dreaming or half-asleep. Although he didn't remember dozing off, a slight shake of his shoulder woke him with a start. The thirty-two-year-old sat up from where he had been lying on the floor beside the sofa and rubbed his eyes before forcing them open. Instead of Andreas, he found Neil sitting beside him, withdrawing his hand from his shoulder.

Simon jumped, surprised. "I must have fallen asleep. I'm sorry."

Neil smiled, his vacant eyes fixed on a point beyond the mercenary's features, and said, "That's alright. You both are most likely exhausted."

Simon frowned, his brow furrowed. "I'm fine. ... Did Andreas fill you in?"

Neil nodded and smiled again. "He did. I've relayed the information to my son, who will investigate this pirate. Thank you for the details."

"Of course ... she's not my favorite person, so ..." Simon saw the human nod, then reached out a hand to feel for the sofa. Neil lifted himself gracefully, looking around the room as if listening for something particular.

"Is Andreas asleep?" Simon asked.

"No. Andreas ran upstairs to get something from his room." Neil looked back down in Simon's direction. "Once he returns, I'll take us back to **Sidhe**," he said.

Simon stretched, wincing at how stiff his legs were. "Your husband returned?"

"No, not yet. After the attack, there was quite a commotion, and Cian offered to investigate the castle and grounds. I said I would check on you two. After I ensure both of you are safe, I'll return to the castle to bring my husband home," Neil chuckled and glanced at the ceiling, listening, before returning his attention to Simon. When Neil locked eyes with Simon, he felt overwhelmed by the same sensation from the event. It seemed as if Neil had been searching for his soul.

"Yes, sir?" Simon asked.

Neil remained quiet for a time, clearly thinking about what he wanted to say. "If I may ask, what *is* your relationship with this Tsara woman?"

Simon stiffened and started, "She..." He looked up, watching the eyes peering *through* him. Neil's face had settled, devoid of emotion save for this odd *calmness*. Simon looked away, focusing on the ground and feeling extremely vulnerable. He didn't like the question. "She helped spread misinformation about someone once; it led to their death. The only relationship I have with her is wanting her dead."

Neil adjusted himself on the couch so that he was closer to Simon. There was a silent understanding as if he had gleaned all he needed from their conversation. He reached out his hand and asked, "May I see your hand?"

Rather than his other hand, Neil had extended the one that looked to have tattoos spiraling over it. Simon hesitantly extended his hand and placed it in the older man's palm. Neil shifted Simon's hand until his palm was up. Simon first noticed that the skin felt like parchment, and the dark lines running through it felt raised like veins rather than intricate artwork. The limb felt *dead*.

"Sir...?" Simon muttered, slightly confused.

"Put this person in your mind. Remember the one who was lost. ... If you can," Neil instructed.

Simon furrowed his brow, feeling a sense of sorrow wash over him. This was a topic he often pushed aside and ignored when it flared up because he didn't *like* remembering it. Suddenly, a wisp of energy rose from his palm, chilling the underside of his hand like a gust of wind. The mercenary's eyes widened as he observed the energy settle and writhe. It was a soft white, almost bluish, and it didn't take the form of a face or figure but of an item—a heart. It was nearly as wide as his palm and appeared made of diamond cut to glitter like starlight.

He recognized it immediately, for it was the main symbol those who followed Qella used. Simon would recognize it anywhere. Bile rose in his throat, and unsolicited anger mixed with the sorrow that began to course in his veins.

Simon exhaled as Neil's hands clasped around his instantly, and the wisps of smoke vanished. Neil squeezed, trying to stop the tremors that had begun in Simon's extremities. "What kind of magic is this?" Simon asked, clearing his throat as his voice shook. He didn't know how to respond to what had happened.

"Memory and sentiment are important catalysts for magic. The stronger the emotion or memory, the stronger the reaction," Neil's voice sounded strained, as if he were fighting to keep it level, like he was **furious**. "I am sorry for the pain *she* caused," he said, offering a small sympathetic smile.

Simon exhaled and pulled his hand back. "Sorry, for *who*, exactly?"

"For whichever of the two, you need to hear it more," Neil said, voice soft.

As Simon looked up, he was struck by the sincerity in Neil's words. Initially, he had thought it was a joke or an interrogation tactic, and he had been on the verge of barking out a string of insults. However, Neil's gaze comforted rather than intimidated him this time. Despite his initial urge to be furious, he couldn't muster the strength to feel anger. Simon sighed and reached up to wipe his eyes, checking for tears. Then he whispered, "*Andreas takes after you quite a bit...*"

Neil laughed. The idea alone seemed to bring him joy. "Is that so?"

"You're both difficult to read, and neither of you misses a damn thing, do you?"

Neil laughed wholeheartedly before falling silent. The silence lingered for a few moments before the older man exhaled loudly. He looked like he was processing something—something that both appeared to make him happy and **sad**. "Thank you for looking after Anni," he said, smiling tenderly. "He has done nothing but speak highly of you and told me about all you've done thus far, including this evening. From my family: *thank you*."

Surprised again, Simon scoffed and said, "He's done a lot on his own." He saw Neil's face light up like he'd hoped for such an answer. "I don't think he's fond of believing that, though," he grumbled.

"No, Anni has a *complicated* nature. He's had a hard life the past sixteen years, and I wish I could say it helped him more than hurt him. He can be a handful, and from what I've heard, you're doing well." Neil folded his hands in his lap, chuckling when he heard Simon's sudden intake of breath. "If I may be so bold, I quite like you, Simon, but that may be because you remind me of my husband."

Simon was at a loss for words and stammered before uttering, "It's a tremendous compliment... wasted on me. I'm **not** Cian Dwyer."

Neil chuckled, his eyes shining as he said, "You would be surprised. Would you believe me if I told you that my and Cian's first meeting resulted in me being screamed at after I attempted to bully him? I'd never had a man humble me before... Sound familiar?"

Simon couldn't help but laugh, his face heating from the comparison. Neil apparently had been told about their fight regarding Andreas' identity in the mountains. "Slightly... though I can't say I believe your husband could scream at you. He looks at you with adoration, like you put the stars in the sky."

Appreciation filled Neil's face before giving way to sorrow. "**Does he?**" he asked.

Simon furrowed his brow and mentally scolded himself. Neil was blind; he didn't know how long the man had been blind, but of course, mentioning something that would have been *obvious* to anyone who could see so bluntly ... He should have chosen his words better, or elaborated, or... His thoughts trailed off when he heard thundering footsteps descending the stairs.

"I'm sorry. It took me a minute to find the book," Andreas said with a smile, his eyes flitting toward Simon. "Oh! You're awake!"

Possibility

"Yeah..." Simon grumbled and looked back at Neil, ready to apologize. Before he could form the words, a hand patted his leg and cut him off.

"Well, let's go. The longer I allow my husband to overwork himself, the more he'll expect me to continue to do so," Neil chuckled, standing and reaching out for Andreas' hand. He then reached out his other hand for Simon and waited. Simon watched, remembering a few moments prior as he stood and dusted himself off.

"I simply need to hold on to you so I don't lose you in the void of time and space, darling. I promise," Neil grinned, his face teeming with mischief.

Andreas chuckled and glanced at Simon before gesturing towards the fingers his grandfather was offering. "He doesn't bite... at least not the people he likes."

This brought Neil's wide grin back, and he said, "Well, that's debatable ... not you, though. That's reserved for my husband."

Simon choked on his saliva, and Andreas groaned uncomfortably.

Then, without hesitation, Simon clasped the older man's hand. Wisps of white and teal smoke encircled them, reminding him of the scroll Andreas had used earlier that evening. It wasn't long before he heard the same strange language uttered under Neil's breath. Intricate runes illuminated under their feet, and energy surrounded them. Simon felt the same gut-wrenching sensation; once again, he felt like puking.

Simon blinked, and suddenly, they were no longer in the cabin but safely within the room they had been assigned in Fossy. The room was dark, with tightly drawn curtains, and it was filled with magic. An odd sensation pricked his skin and sent a chill down his spine. It felt like he had entered a forbidden place, and a massive beast was watching him from somewhere in the shadows. If he had to name the thing that lingered here, it would be fear or **death**. There was a looming sense of stillness, contrasting the warm and welcoming feeling he had gotten used to over the past few nights. It made his skin crawl.

Simon looked down as Neil's hand released him. He watched as the man stepped forward, moved his hands over the door, and repeated this over the windows. In a strange, unknown language, Neil mumbled under his breath.

Glyphs lit up every corner of the room before visibly shattering. The room **exhaled**, instantly becoming a haven of comfort and hospitality. The sense of impending doom had faded away into the warmth he was used to. Simon let his breath slow down and relaxed his muscles.

"Alright, my darlings, I need to go get Cian. Please behave, stay in the room, and do not light a fire. You're *supposed* to be sleeping off a hangover," Neil said as he pulled the curtain open enough to allow moonlight in.

Andreas laughed. "I promise to behave."

There was a small smile before the same magical energy surrounded the man. Neil vanished as quickly as they had all appeared a moment before.

Simon rubbed his face, attempting to rid himself of the slight embarrassment he had gained from being called 'my darling.' "Your family is still … **a lot**."

Andreas laughed as he approached. "You like them, though."

Simon raised an eyebrow. "Oh? Do I?"

"You're pretty vocal about what you *don't* like," Andreas smirked.

Simon laughed, his eyes darting around the room absentmindedly. "I suppose I am… they're alright," he said. He looked down as Andreas entered his space and found emerald eyes looking up at him with concern. "What?"

Andreas frowned, arms crossed, as he asked, "You looked shaken up when I came down earlier. Did Grandpa Neil say something?"

There it was: Andreas' annoying habit of reading *everything*. Simon shook his head. "He asked me something about Tsara, which brought up an unpleasant memory. No big deal." He wouldn't bring up the conversation that followed, not now. He'd find Neil and speak to him privately later so he could apologize for being foolish. Andreas watched Simon, clearly unconvinced.

"If you're sure…" Andreas said, sounding skeptical. He bit his lip, observing for a while before moving towards the door. He reached out, mimicked a sigil, and spoke an elvish word as the mark faded. This sigil looked similar to the one on the prince's office door, but it seemed more intricate as if it included specific conditions. "In case someone other than you or my grandparents calls."

"Smart," Simon said as he watched Andreas walk toward the wardrobe near the partitioned bath area. Andreas began to remove the golden trinkets and unbraid his hair. Simon shifted, his eyes following Andreas as he appreciated the view for the first time since seeing him earlier that evening. It was a silly thought, but he was almost disappointed that they hadn't gotten to dance at the party. They had been so focused on playing their part that neither had relaxed.

"You really **did** look nice ... so that you know ..." Simon muttered.

As the half-elf finished the last plaits of the braid, his green eyes peeked over his shoulder. Simon felt his stomach lurch when their eyes met, and Andreas appeared to search for something. Andreas bit his lip hesitantly, then flushed in embarrassment. Simon tilted his head, smiling, and asked, "What?"

"Just... *nice?*" Andreas whispered, sounding almost unsure. He let his fingers run through his hair, releasing it and tucking it behind his ear to rest over his shoulder. He seemed uncertain about what to do with his hands and finally settled on wrapping his arms around his waist. He didn't move and kept his eyes on the floor. Nice was ... *nice*.

Even though others at the party repeatedly complimented him with words like 'lovely' and 'stunning,' it wasn't exactly the word he sought. In retrospect, it was a silly thought considering their evening, but 'nice' wasn't the word he wanted to hear from **Simon** regarding his appearance. He wasn't sure what he wanted to hear. It was probably a selfish thought, and it scared him because it meant he cared what Simon thought about him. He didn't know how to handle that.

Simon exhaled and sat on the edge of the bed. "If I say more than nice..."

Andreas looked up, almost hopeful at the words.

"Won't that complicate the *no-pressure* thing between us that you're insistent on?" Simon asked. His shoulders stiffened as a wave of disappointment, almost agitation, surged through him. What had he been expecting? Appreciation? He should have known better than that. It wasn't appreciation he'd seen on Andreas' face ... it was *expectation*. Simon scoffed in disbelief at the realization.

Andreas tensed up, hunching over and leaning against the wardrobe doors. A feeling of unease washed over him as he sat with a contorted expression. He seemed torn between staying put and moving; sometimes, he leaned forward like he wanted to walk over to Simon. Then, clearly second-guessing himself, he would lean back against the wardrobe.

Simon fidgeted on the bed, and anger plunged in his stomach. He felt exploited—like a babysitter for a brat who wanted more attention than they were willing to give back. He scoffed again and looked at his hands; he was anxiously picking at the skin of his thumb. He wasn't sure when he'd started doing it.

"You know, that bratty personality of yours is showing," Simon said and winced before continuing, "You can't get what you want from me just by batting your eyelashes and twisting your hair; that doesn't work on me." His gut shifted in displeasure; that was only half true. He just had self-control. "If you're just looking for someone to fuck you or distract you—I'm **not** that person," he said.

"*Simon...*" Andreas whispered, his head hanging in mild shame.

"What do you want from me, Andreas?" Simon spat the words, panic rising as he continued. Simon was met with silence, which fueled his anger.

"You scream about what you want from everyone else, but when I **ask you** ... nothing. You can't even pretend to want to tell me," Simon said, pausing to try to steady his voice. He looked at his thumb and noticed it was bleeding from how much skin he'd torn away. His hand shook with rage as he continued, "I don't need your money or your pity or your fucking connections, and to be completely honest, I don't **need** sex from you either."

"Simon..." Andreas said, trying to speak and failing to find words.

"What do you want from **me**, Andrea?!" Simon interrupted, and the words echoed around the room. He had yelled, just like at the cabin. He needed a reaction, clarity ... *something*. There was a *mutual* attraction between them. He was sure of that. Without that, they wouldn't have ended up in bed together. Maybe Andreas could do that, but **he** couldn't. There were also small, seemingly unimportant things; there had been genuine moments of connection between them.

Simon sat in silence, picking at his finger nervously. Andreas still didn't answer him, and his thoughts started to spiral. Simon's brow furrowed, and a look of painful malcontent settled over him.

He felt burdened by the unspoken expectation of being a lover … without receiving acknowledgment, direction, or reciprocation. Andreas would say there was no pressure—that it wasn't complicated… and then look at him like a wounded puppy if he didn't get exactly what he wanted. If he tried to pull away, Andreas would pull him back in, and if he tried to lean in and care … Andreas made a point of reminding him that he wasn't necessary.

It was oppressive and painful.

Simon was jarred from his thoughts, and his attention shifted to the warm sensation against his palm; his eyes locked on the carnelian fingers gripping his hand. He was unwilling to look at the figure invading his space.

"*Stop hurting yourself,*" Andreas whispered, focused on stopping the bleeding.

"If that's what you want, you need to get away from me," Simon hissed.

Andreas froze when Simon yanked his hand away. A wave of terror tore through him, both at the sudden physical distance between him and Simon and at the weight of the spoken words. "… What do you want me to do?"

"Quit acting selfish!" Simon snapped, suddenly furious. "I just told you what I needed from you, and what was your response?! You ignored my question *twice*. Why the fuck is it so hard for you to just tell me what you want from me?" he asked and locked eyes with the man before him. Simon clenched his fist and felt blood spurt over his palm from the wound he'd inflicted on himself. "If you're not going to tell me what you want from me, then at least let **me** make a fucking choice! You're not giving me the option to choose anything, either!"

"You made a choice! You told me to get away from you! What if stepping away from you hurts me!?" Andreas snapped, finally getting angry. He glared and continued, "I don't want you to be hurt! To **get hurt**! Do I not get a choice!?"

"I asked you what you wanted *from me!*" Simon snapped, then reached out and grabbed Andreas' shirt. He pulled him to eye level and snarled, "If I gave a shit about getting hurt, I never would have slept with you to begin with! I'd have walked the fuck out of this room already! You're **choosing** to be fucking difficult!"

"If I'm so fucking difficult, then why the hell does it matter what I want from you!?" Andreas yelled and shoved Simon's shoulder. He didn't try to break free, but it looked like he was angling himself away. He looked like he was trying to run away ... but was unwilling to move. He looked afraid of actually doing it.

"Stop pretending to be a fucking brat just because you're **scared** of someone giving a fuck about you!" Simon snarled, jumped to his feet, and tugged Andreas closer. His grip on the man's shirt tightened as he leaned down, loomed over him, and continued, "If you want me to get my money and leave, tell me to **leave**! If you want me to be your *friend*, say it plainly! But if you want me by your side—if you want to let me *care* about you—then you better fucking **kiss me** like you mean it!"

Andreas' eyes grew wide, and he suddenly looked afraid. He seemed to want to continue to argue but couldn't find a response. "That's ... I ..." he stammered, frantically trying to find words to argue anything said to him. He was failing.

"*What do you want from me?* **Please**," Simon whispered, nearly begging.

He should have just left. He usually would have, but when he realized that Andreas was *purposefully* trying to be difficult ... he couldn't just leave. Simon was tired, and his body hurt from the night's events. His head was pounding from this argument, and he felt he was wasting his breath. The issue was that he **liked** this idiot. He *hated* how much he *wanted* Andreas— not just sensually but to *know* him, to mean something to him. Simon **hated** how irrelevant he was to this brat.

Andreas fell silent again, his eyes locked on Simon as he *begged*. Somehow, it was overwhelming. His gut was twisting, both from fear and adoration.

Simon always talked to him like a person, not like a Dwyer. Simon had never once cherry-picked his words or spared his feelings in lieu of honesty. Even when the words were hurtful, there was still this overwhelming sense that the man wanted to talk to him ... **wanted to be with him**. How Simon treated him was *intoxicating*. Andreas craved the small looks of heated thought and trailing touches along his skin … the *sincerity* in how Simon regarded him.

No one had ever seen him, let alone desired him for being *himself*, and it was both horrifying and thrilling. It made him want to run *and* hang onto every ounce of affection he was given because he was **terrified** of it being taken away from him. He was a selfish, spoiled brat, and … Andreas took a deep breath, recalling the conversation at the cabin—their exchange at the party.

No, Simon didn't think he was *any* of those things. Even when he tried to pretend he was. Even when he tried to **make** Simon see him that way.

Simon released Andreas' shirt with a sense of defeat. He looked *exhausted* as he sat back on the bed and crumpled in on himself. Simon's face was pale, and his gaze fell to rest on the floor as he leaned forward and buried his face in his hands. He looked as if he were in pain as he took a ragged breath and settled into silence.

Andreas felt ashamed and looked down at his hands. He noticed the gloves covering them and started to trace the outlines of scars hidden beneath them with his eyes. Andreas felt his thoughts spiraling, and desperate to regain control, he bit the side of his cheek so hard it started bleeding. He wanted to run and avoid answering Simon. This wasn't the first time someone had confronted him about his emotions or asked him to clarify them.

This was why he avoided spending too much time with the same man back home and instead cherished the moments of solitude when they left. He found solace in being alone, as he had become used to it. He didn't want to risk losing anything or causing harm to anyone just because they knew him. The thought of needing someone, and the pain of potentially losing them petrified him. *He had experienced loss so many times*. Andreas let out another shaky breath, and he blinked to try to rid his eyes of the tears that were starting to gather within them.

It used to be easier than this. It was always more straightforward to turn and leave, to walk away. Simon didn't make it easy to run, though. Somehow, the idea of running and **not** having this man to tease or laugh with scared him more than the alternative. The thought of it made his feet remain planted and his stomach lurch like he was going to vomit. Andreas closed his eyes to calm his mind. He knew what he needed to do … now he just had to convince himself to do it.

He knew what he wanted from Simon.

Simon froze, clearly startled, as gloves fell to the ground and landed in his line of sight. Before he could react, Andreas was pulling Simon's face from where it was buried with his bare hands. A look of disbelief rushed over the orc's face. Before he could say anything, Andreas yanked him forward into a desperate kiss. Andreas' hands shook, and he clung to Simon's cheeks as if he thought it was the last time he'd touch them.

Simon's skin was warm, and the feel of his scars brushing over the one on the orc's face was strange. He'd never touched anyone with his bare hands, and something about *feeling* Simon's skin was … His thoughts fell off as Simon finally reacted, returning the kiss momentarily before pulling away enough to turn his head. The following action was incredibly tender because Simon did not kiss his lips again … *the man kissed one of his palms.*

An emotion welled up, and Andreas was confident he was going to choke on it as a whimper broke from his throat. When Simon kissed his other palm, his knees buckled and he lost the ability to stay standing. Simon caught him, yanked him into a heated kiss, and dragged him onto the bed.

Twenty-Four

Light

The bed was warm, and a body lay beside him. It felt unreal because it differed from Simon's previous experiences sharing a bed. Nostalgia washed over him, filling his heart with uncontainable happiness. Then realization struck, and thinking this might be just a *memory* was terrifying. A memory formed in his sleep-deprived mind. A knot of unease twisted in his stomach, causing him to hesitate to open his eyes and face the reality that he may be alone.

Simon took a deep breath and turned his head, burying it into what he recognized immediately as hair. There was no scent of linen or the lingering salt of the sea within the strands. Instead, the smell of amber and oak filled his senses. The memory he had begun to ponder and cling to faded away. He felt nervous, desperately hoping it would return, as he had been so close to seeing something he hadn't seen in *years*. Then, slowly, he opened his eyes, and fear subsided as he realized he was **not** alone.

The body next to him was not Olur, but deep down, he had known this even in his dream-like state. He knew it was impossible as sleep slowly released its grip on his consciousness, and the world became focused. **That man** being here was unattainable, but this one. *Andreas wasn't*. Simon was suddenly faced with the staggering realization that Andreas may be the only substitute he could ever accept. This caused a new wave of worry to wash over him.

Simon inhaled the scent of cologne lingering on the skin against him. It was his third time in this position, nestled comfortably beneath a mass of red hair and carnelian skin. This time, though, felt different, from the events that led to him being here to the hand resting *naked* on his chest. He lifted Andreas' palm gently, not wishing to wake the man, and started to examine it in the dim twilight. Andreas' muscles twitched in response to his touch, but he did not wake.

Simon could make out the scars he'd seen before but found ones new to his eyes. There were continuations of puncture wounds he'd not seen at the cabin, but also **burn marks**. The burn scars were so large that they nearly encompassed Andreas' palm. Simon drew his fingers over the skin, appreciating the injuries' leathery texture and raised edges.

His fingers slid down, following the burnt surface until they stopped above another scar. There was one on Andreas' wrist. It was thick, with wide borders, and wrapped around his limb. It looked like a cuff, as if something had tightly bound the man's wrist and caused a permanent scar. Simon's brow furrowed as his finger felt the sides of it, probing the surface. It was jagged as if it had been cut and not caused by pressure for an extended period. As his finger passed over the central part of the scar again, he noticed several defined, smaller lines.

Simon ran his fingers over the edges one last time before halting. His stomach sank, and he tasted metal as he tightened his jaw and nipped his cheek. He carefully returned the hand to its resting spot and then moved the crimson strands out of the way to fully see Andreas' face. Andreas was still sound asleep, only shifting from the change of light.

Simon leaned down and kissed Andreas' head as he cradled it carefully. He had realized something about those scars, something he hadn't considered when he saw them for a split second outside the cabin. The ones on Andreas' wrist looked *intentionally* made, and the thought weighed heavy on Simon. … When Neil said that Andreas was complicated, *he meant this*.

Simon sat in silence, processing the revelation, holding his companion and occasionally placing another kiss in the mix of red hair. He couldn't imagine how difficult the times had been over the years. However, he was smart enough to know that things like that left scars—physical and mental.

Simon looked down when he felt the body against him stir and soon found green eyes peering up at him, half-lidded and exhausted. He smiled and angled his head to gaze into them. He tucked the red strands behind the other man's ear and said, "Go back to sleep."

Andreas inhaled, his attention turning towards the partly open curtain and then back to the man he used as a pillow. He grumbled, half-lucid. "What time is it?"

"An hour before dawn. Sleep," Simon leaned down and kissed Andreas' forehead. Andreas physically crinkled in on himself in response as if he hadn't been expecting the affection. Simon chuckled and pulled back, letting his head rest on their pillow. "I mean it."

Andreas grumbled, "Do you want me to go back to sleep?"

"If you're tired, then yes," Simon said, tenderly dragging one of his hands down Andreas' arm. "You look pretty when you're sleeping."

"Am I not pretty when I'm awake then?" Andreas asked, half-lucid.

Simon chuckled, saying, "No, you're radiant when awake."

Andreas gave Simon a playful tap on his cheek and laughed sleepily. Simon grabbed his arm before it could pull away, then placed a token of affection on Andreas' palm.

"You took off your gloves," Simon remarked.

Andreas freed his hand and let it fall back to Simon's chest. "I wanted to show you that I trusted you. Did it work?"

"It did. Clearly," Simon replied, grinning.

"You were *very animated*," Andreas said, snorting and trying to hide a laugh.

Simon maneuvered to lie beside Andreas instead of under him and felt the bed frame brush his toes. Blushing cheeks and a beaming grin were waiting for him when he settled. Simon gently tucked a few more strands behind his bedmate's ear. In the end, he couldn't help but return the smile, and Andreas locked eyes with him in response. The interaction made his heart jump.

"What?" Simon asked.

Andreas blushed even deeper and scooted over until their noses touched. "You make me feel exposed when you look at me like that," he said.

Simon chuckled as he glanced down at the blankets. "Well, you *are* naked, Red. Undeniably so, because on my hip, I can feel—" He burst into laughter when a hand was shoved into his face again to silence him. Andreas' head ducked down into his neck in embarrassment.

Andreas chuckled, battling through the tremors. "Shut *up*," he said as another wave of laughter engulfed him, much like the arms that had reached forward and pulled him close. "I'm trying to be serious, and you're **ruining** it."

The two let the laughter die off slowly. Sometimes, one or the other started a fresh wave by making eye contact. A whimsical stillness settled in and wrapped around the entire room.

After the two quieted, Simon cupped Andreas' cheek. His thumb began to drag over the faint golden freckles absentmindedly. In response, Andreas hid part of his face in the pillow; he seemed embarrassed from the constant attention.

"Thank you for trusting me with them," Simon whispered, his hand resting on the pillow between them. Andreas turned to face him, and Simon saw a look of anxious terror in his green eyes. Simon leaned his forehead against Andreas' and gave a reassuring nudge. There would be no prying, unnecessary questions, or unwarranted judgments on his part. Though he had his thoughts, he could wait to see if they were true.

Andreas smiled, his brow furrowed. *"Simon ..."*

"Not yet. We can talk about it when you're ready."

Andreas grew misty-eyed and nodded with a sigh and a tiny smile. He nudged Simon's forehead and closed his eyes, saying, *"Okay."*

The silence between them returned and lingered so long that Andreas wondered if Simon had fallen asleep. He opened his eyes and found the hetero-chromatic gaze still watching him tenderly. The silence was not from sleep, just from quiet observation and patience. Andreas pulled back a few inches and settled his head against the pillow to see Simon's face better. Simon's eyes darted restlessly as if searching for something that wasn't there, with a look of near sorrow. Simon's jaw tightened, and his lips formed a slight frown.

Andreas was reminded of the look and feeling he had when he convinced Simon to pin him to the ground a few days ago. He couldn't quite identify the emotion on Simon's face, which bothered him the more he tried. He let his fingers drag down Simon's cheek, passing over his facial scar. Andreas paused to rest his thumb on his companion's jaw and said, "You look sad."

Simon pondered for a while, his furrowed brow deepening.

Andreas frowned, looking concerned. "Is something wrong?"

Simon shook his head and then gently grasped Andreas' cheeks. Andreas, in turn, held onto Simon's wrists near his cheeks, his brow furrowed. Something was on Simon's mind, as he seemed nervous and hesitant. It felt as if Simon was contemplating pulling away, just like when they were on the floor. Something had spooked him, triggering his fight-or-flight response.

This was surprising, as Simon had shown little fear of anything, not even the risk of death or injury, in the past few weeks. Andreas had seen the man angry and agitated but never *frightened*. However, that's what it was: fear. Andreas bit his lower lip and asked, "What's wrong?"

Simon exhaled and forced a small smile. "You just scare me, Red."

"You're scarier than me," Andreas laughed. "Why?"

Simon hesitated, seeming to be considering whether to express his thoughts or remain silent. Andreas gently nudged Simon's leg with his foot, and Simon responded with a small smile. Then, Simon sighed. "I'm afraid I'll get lost again," he said, looking down, embarrassed by his words.

"I don't understand," Andreas said, meeting Simon's gaze.

Simon removed his hands from Andreas' face after a brief silence. He shifted to lie on one of his arms and used the other to hold Andreas' hand. He lifted Andreas' hand to his lips and kissed it. *"I'm not ready yet,"* he whispered.

Andreas moved closer, releasing Simon. In response, Simon wrapped his arms around Andreas, and Andreas tucked himself into Simon's chest. A deep, forced breath hit the air from Simon's lips. Then Andreas nodded in response and closed his eyes comfortably. *"When you're ready,"* he whispered.

Simon exhaled, closing his eyes to let the sensation of the skin against him soak in. It was grounding, and he let his thumb trail small circles on his bedmate's lower back. As his breathing calmed, his mind drifted, and he started to focus on the scattered freckles that covered the body beside him. Curiosity sparked in him again as he wondered how many there were, how far they extended, and if the freckles were all the same golden color. He pondered it often, so much that Simon had lost count of the glances he'd dared and his heated daydreams.

His mind often wandered off during sleep, causing him to wake up feeling uncomfortable too many mornings. They had been out in the middle of nowhere, probably being followed more than he wanted to admit, and all he could think about was the patio at **The Green Dragon**. In every daydream, Andreas was as if he'd been on that patio—shining but with *less* clothing. The thoughts were tempting and impure, and Simon would never deny that.

As Simon swallowed, he focused on the light trickling in from the partially open curtain; dawn was breaking. He pressed his thumb into the other man's skin harder, feeling the muscles beneath it writhe. The feeling was gnawing. The memory captured Simon's attention, and he focused all his energy on it. Again, he recalled the memory of Andreas' skin shimmering like gold dust and his hair blazing like an inferno. Simon suddenly realized he had never seen this man naked in direct sunlight.

He wanted desperately to know what Andreas looked like naked and wrapped in the full glow of the morning sun.

Simon's thumb stopped abruptly, and he slowly unraveled himself from the other figure. Andreas grunted in complaint but was ignored when he called out in confusion. Simon got up, overlooking the chill from his lack of clothing. He aimed at the window across the room with a focused purpose, then wrenched the fabric open as far as possible.

"Simon, what are you doing?" Andreas sounded slightly annoyed and winced at the abrupt change in light. "If you wanted to get up, you should have just said so."

Simon took a deep breath. He wasn't sure if the window panes were made of *Spellglass*, but he had a sinking feeling that they were. He tried to remember if this pub had it installed in any of the rooms… He was pretty sure he had been told that it did. As he turned around, excitement and prepared disappointment rose in his stomach. His hand instinctively reached up to cover his mouth, and his heart jumped.

This *was* Spellglass.

Squinting, Andreas was unsettled by the sudden changes in lighting and motion in the room. He propped himself up on one of the pillows with his elbows, the blanket barely covering his hips. "Simon?" he asked in confusion.

Radiant. That word had never occurred to Simon in this way before, but he had used it a mere hour ago. As he leaned back against the window frame, he bit his lip. Andreas *glowed*. As the hundreds of golden freckles on his body reflected light, they seemed to magnify even the tiniest glimmer tenfold. Dust particles swirled around the half-asleep man, creating the illusion of a fine golden mist. Andreas' skin now had a metallic sheen resembling polished copper, and his hair blazed like an unrestricted flame.

"Simon? *Did you die?*"

Simon laughed weakly. "Maybe so. That would explain a hell of a lot."

Dead. Dreaming. Hallucinating? Maybe he had been experiencing vivid hallucinations for the past few weeks. Perhaps he'd been tucked into a bed in Ransol while unknowingly fighting a fever. Perhaps he had been poisoned? It wouldn't be the first time he had bought something from the oddities shop in the port town only to discover that Clapper had sold him something spoiled. Somehow, that half-baked idea made more sense than what sat only a few feet away, staring Simon in the face. The man he gazed at didn't seem *real*.

Andreas extended a hand, causing the misty light around him to shift with his movements. Simon blinked a few times, trying to determine if his eyes were deceiving him. They were not, and death seemed to be the most accurate explanation of what he was presented with.

"If you don't return to bed, I will **drag** you back. It's cold," Andreas grumbled and reached up to tuck his hair over his shoulder and out of his face.

Simon felt lightheaded as his locked knees finally gave out, forcing him to step forward. His heart was racing, and he couldn't focus on anything as he crossed the room. His gaze jumped from Andreas' hair to his shoulders and then to his eyes. The emerald eyes held his attention, causing his stomach to flip as Simon slowly sank onto the edge of the bed.

Andreas reached out and interlocked his fingers with Simon's. Simon pulled away, almost as if he were trying to encourage Andreas to chase him.

Andreas laughed, looking confused. "You're acting so *strangely*. What?"

Simon positioned himself so he could lean against the head of the bed and keep himself from blocking the sunlight through the window. His eyes remained locked on Andreas as he grabbed his hand and said, "Come here."

Andreas slowly emerged from the covers, looking delighted and perplexed as Simon pulled him onto his lap. Something was alluring about this whole charade. "What is it?" Andreas asked.

Simon's gaze lingered on the other's blushing cheeks, basking in the joy directed at him. It wandered slowly, taking in Andreas' form as his hands gripped the copper thighs straddling him. *This would be a hell of a last thing to see if he was dying.* Simon's heart twisted as the wave of awe shifted into this intense **desire** that settled into his bones. "Are you tired, Andrea?"

"That sounds like a loaded question," Andreas said, his lips twisting coyly as he wrapped his arms around Simon's shoulders. "If I say no, what does that get me?"

Simon leaned forward, placing bare centimeters between their lips. His hands gripped greedily onto Andreas' thighs as they both fidgeted, and their bodies pressed together like second nature. Once again, Simon caught the scent of amber and oak before running his tusks along Andreas' lips, jaw, and then ear. He murmured, "The same thing that *'yes'* got you last night."

A tilt of Andreas' head revealed his neck, and he closed his eyes contentedly. Simon left a small trail of affection along his exposed skin, and his breath caught. "*No, I'm not tired,*" Andreas whispered.

It was tender, unlike the night before's frantic touches and overwhelming longing. In his head, Simon counted as he kissed Andreas' neck. He was taking it one by one. He intended to appreciate every golden speck of light on this man's body.

Twenty-Five

Sara

"Pardon me, but is your name Simon?" The voice was a soprano, soft, and kind. It seemed apprehensive, almost as if its owner was worried they'd gotten the wrong individual. Simon looked up from where he had been focused on the sea and saw a petite human woman beside him. She appeared to be short; if he was being honest, he doubted she was over five feet tall. She didn't look much older than him, probably in her late thirties.

Her features were fair, and her face had a lovely heart shape with large sea-glass green eyes. Her eyes were strange; they shimmered in the sunlight in a peculiar way he had never seen before. She had wavy, chestnut brown hair that hung around her shoulders with side-swept bangs. She wore well-made, fitted clothing that resembled a flowy blouse with a dressy suspended romper.

Simon studied her, his shoulders tense, and said, "It depends on who's asking."

She laughed aloud; the sound was musical. "My husband would appreciate that response. He says it a lot," she said with a grin. Then, she unfolded her hands from behind her back and extended one forward. "My name is Sara Dwyer. I believe you've been traveling with my son."

Startled, Simon stood up from where he had been sitting on the edge of the dock. He wiped his hand on his pants and reached out to shake the hand that was offered to him. "Um, yes. I have. I'm Simon," he replied.

Sara's eyes sparkled, and she beamed when she received assurance that she had found the right person. "It's a pleasure to meet you," she said.

Simon felt her squeeze his hand, shake it, and then release. He managed a small smile and inclined his head respectfully. She seemed almost smaller with him standing. He was right; she couldn't have been over five feet tall. "If you're looking for Andreas... I think he was shopping with Neil," he said.

Sara smiled once more and replied, "He is. I dropped by the pub, and Emhyr mentioned I could find you here. I wanted to meet you first."

Simon's face twisted in confusion, eliciting another small laugh from the woman before him. "Um... why?" he asked.

"I wanted to put a face to the description my father-in-law gave me and to meet the man who finally convinced my son to run away from home."

Simon winced and looked off to the side sheepishly. It wasn't entirely *untrue*.

Sara laughed and waved her hands, saying, "I'm not here to interrogate you. I've questioned Neil enough; if I were wary of you, I wouldn't have alerted you I was here. I promise."

"That sounds like a threat," Simon said, furrowing brow.

"It would be if I didn't trust my father-in-law's judgment," Sara answered matter-of-factly. She smiled and then nodded toward the sea. "I'm very good at discreetly getting rid of people, and the ocean is rather convenient."

Simon felt a chill run down his spine as the woman locked eyes with him, and her eyes narrowed ever so slightly. For a moment, they looked cold, and her face looked much more severe than it had during the initial part of the conversation. He glanced down, noticed the daggers attached to her thighs, and then looked back up at her face. He shifted uncomfortably before muttering, "Noted."

Sara smiled and folded her hands behind her back. "Would you walk with me back to **Sídhe**? Anni and Neil should be heading back, and I thought **we** could chat before I join you all for dinner and then head home," she said.

Simon wanted to ask if he had a choice, but considering who this was, he figured that would be seen as rude. He had no desire to be seen as disrespectful by this woman, and it had nothing to do with the threat she had just loomed over him. Simon nodded slowly, looked to where he had been watching the ships enter the harbor a moment before, and then fell into step with Sara without fuss.

She started leading them in what appeared to be the long way back to the pub. Simon noted this detail for later and mentally groaned about it. This interaction felt awkward for many reasons. He reached up absentmindedly and rubbed his neck—he was nervous. "Was there something you wanted to talk about?" he asked.

"Yes," Sara hummed, looking around at the city as they walked.

"Which is…?" Simon asked after a brief pause.

"The Mistwalkers that you two encountered at the pillars. Neil told me that Andreas seemed to believe they were hunting him. Is this true?" Sara asked and looked over with a sense of seriousness.

Simon shrugged. "I don't know. He seemed to think so, and based on what Andreas told me about your family, that makes sense to me, if I'm being honest. They were hunting something," he replied.

"So they were working as a unit? You saw this, too?"

Simon frowned, suddenly offended in Andreas' place. "You sound like you're doubting him. I saw them. They were hunting together," he said.

Sara seemed to pick up on the tone in his voice and smiled. "I understand," she said.

A brief silence fell, and Simon's jaw clenched as he ground his teeth.

"I believe Anni thinks he saw that. It's nice to know he **did** see that," Sara finally spoke, her eyes locked on the street before them. "I ask because he's afraid of those things, and when he was smaller, he used to have nightmares about them hunting him. I wanted to be sure before I asked anything further."

Simon met her gaze when she looked over. He frowned, clearly unsatisfied with the answer, and replied, "I see."

Sara sighed, "I appreciate your concern for my son. As a mother, I'm glad he has such a loyal individual by his side."

Sara

Her words seemed genuine, and Simon's tension eased slightly. He offered a minor smile that faded quickly before replying, "He *is* terrified of them, but the first thing he did when they acted strangely was send Keena to you. Your son feels his duty **heavily**." Simon hadn't meant for his voice to tense again, but the last few words came out strained. Again, he sounded judgmental and offended on Andreas' behalf, and he knew he did.

Sara took a deep breath, as if carefully considering her words. "He does. Quite heavily," she muttered. Simon observed her; she seemed sad and determined not to meet his gaze. "Did you see them again? Hear them again?" Sara continued.

"Not that I know of. If Andreas did, he said nothing to me."

Sara nodded and asked, "Can you describe the armor and the tents you saw at the encampment? The one on the road to Fossy?"

The sudden change of topic unsettled Simon. Sara's rigid tone and pointed questions made him feel as though she was seeking *specific* information. Her earlier threat and how she interrogated him reminded him of someone skilled at extracting knowledge. Was she a spy? An assassin? Perhaps a combination of both. He hadn't heard much about her during the war, and either option would explain the lack of details. She was undoubtedly excellent at her job if her expertise and existence were meant to be a mystery.

"The armor was black; most of it looked metallic with some leather accents here or there. The cloaks were also black, and none of the people showed any skin save for the lower half of their faces. The woman who talked to Andreas was very particular about hiding her face from me. The tents were simple gray canvas with no logos, symbols, or family designations," Simon said.

"You're used to giving reports," Sara said with a smile.

"I'm used to getting paid to do shit. Sometimes that's getting and giving information."

"That's right. Neil and Lilliana said you were a mercenary," Sara replied. Simon looked over, confused. "I don't know a Lilliana…"

Sara's kind demeanor returned, and she laughed. "Forgive me. My daughter's name is Lilliana, but we call her Lilli sometimes."

Simon nodded, a realization crossing his face. He recalled hearing the name 'Lilli' tossed around, but he had never been told who she was, nor had he ever met her. "I see. I remember Andreas saying her name, but ... I've never met your daughter, so how does she know me?" he asked.

Sara laughed, "Of course, you wouldn't know. Andreas paid her to tell us she knew you, and my husband caught her lying a few days after you two left. Anni told her your name and what you looked like, and Neil told her your profession."

"Of course he did," Simon stated incredulously.

"She also immediately confirmed that Anni thought you were handsome." Simon's face grew warm, and he stammered, "I ... see."

Sara grinned.

Simon cleared his throat and changed the topic. "Do you know why those creatures were hunting Andreas?" he asked.

"Yes and no," Sara sighed. "Anni and his sister were targeted when they were younger, as I'm sure you know." She paused, looking at Simon, and he nodded in response. Sara smiled slightly before continuing, "They were just one of many victims. A lot of kids have been taken by those creatures and thought killed. But before the *Remembrance*, we couldn't publicly link **EDEN** with the creatures. No one would believe us because we didn't have solid proof, and the proof we had couldn't be told to the public because of our allegiances with *The Rose Guard*."

"I take it there were some Primal secrets mixed in," Simon scoffed.

"Exactly," Sara said with a forced smile. "Now those creatures are targeting my children just because they're *ours*. Powerful people get angry when you disrupt an entire organization focused on researching blood magic and its potential to **enhance** life. ... And if you are an escaped test subject like my husband, they get even more furious. That woman is rather obsessed with getting my Leo *back*."

"Got it," Simon muttered and pondered the last piece of information, storing it away. He had heard various stories about Leon Dwyer's involvement with **EDEN** during the war, ranging from being an undercover spy to an assassin sent to infiltrate *The Rose Guard*. Learning that he was just another kid who was abducted and mistreated before going rogue was intriguing. This also clarified Andreas' statement from the night they argued in the mountains. Simon finally glanced over and asked, "They've been on Andreas' trail for a while then?"

Sara nodded as they turned the corner. "They have been targeting our entire family for a while. Anni doesn't go out as much as Lilli does, especially not *alone*. We've tried to keep him, as much as possible, at home or with one of us or his grandparents."

Simon remembered how Andreas suddenly became upset at the pillars. Something had triggered the redhead, and Andreas had started ranting about change. Simon thought he was beginning to understand why Andreas was so testy and jumpy all the damn time. "Why? Don't you think that's unfair? Do you trust him less than his sister or something?" he asked. The more he spoke, the harsher the words were, and the more he had to pause and keep his voice from rising.

Simon saw Sara stop beside him, watching him, not missing a beat. He now understood that whole 'suffocating' thing Andreas talked about, and it made him grind his teeth in agitation. Sara sighed, and Simon's gaze narrowed.

"No, it's never been fair, but we've done our best with what we have. Yes, we *can* trust his sister more than him ... at least in **one** regard." Sara said, and she sounded sadder now, far more than she had earlier. Her voice was strained and fearful, and her hands had fallen to her sides and clenched into fists. "Leo and I are good at protecting Andreas from *physical* things. Things we can see—things we can kill. We are good at protecting him from the monsters that go bump in the night," Sara took a deep breath, her voice growing eerily calm. "However, Simon, it has come to my attention that you are very good at protecting my son from **himself**. We have tried many times to do this but have never succeeded. Our failure and fear of losing him have made us overprotective, probably sometimes to his detriment."

Simon's throat tightened, and his breathing stalled as the woman beside him glanced up. Her eyes were piercing, and her face seemed on the verge of tears. He stayed quiet, absorbing her words.

"So, first and foremost, thank you for allowing my son to go out and live. He truly deserves that; he always has," Sara gave a strained smile, which quickly faded before she continued, "However, I want to clarify **one** thing. Anni holds you in high regard, and if there's even a tiny chance that you think this is just a *game* or a passing fancy—if there's even a thought in your head that you might disappear one day or say something so cruel that it sends my son **spiraling** back down into that dark place I've been trying to pull him out of for years…

I want you to understand that my husband will hunt you down to the very end of existence, and when he finds you … you will be **nothing** but bones and dust on the wind. Leo may be unyielding. He may be stronger. He may be a little crazy … but *I* am **unforgiving**. I will take *everything* you are and destroy it piece by piece until you are *begging* me to tell you who you were. **I do not forgive those who hurt the people I love**."

Simon stared, his blood going icy. This was not an idle threat—this was a promise. These were the words of a woman who meant everything she said and then some. There was a lingering sense that someone had tested her patience and the strength of her resolve on this matter. She was making it extremely clear that she had dealt with something or someone before and would do it again without batting an eye.

Sara's eyes were wide, manic, and void of tears. Her fists clenched tighter, and she asked through gritted teeth, "Do I make myself perfectly *clear*, Simon?"

Another shiver ran down his spine as Simon processed the words and the dark shadow that seemed to have fallen over Sara. This conversation confirmed that he was right—Andreas had intentionally made those marks on his wrists. With this confirmation, his heart throbbed painfully, and his stomach twisted as if he were going to vomit. It was a staggering realization, causing him to fight to calm his emotions and avoid reacting disrespectfully. The Dwyers had stifled Andreas because they feared he would leave them, not in the way he did, but *permanently* by his own hand.

"Completely clear," Simon said and felt his heart clench.

"Good," Sara responded, the finality of her tone closing the topic.

Sara

Simon chewed on his cheek, pondering the sudden shift in conversation. Sara, a concerned mother, feared that her son might get hurt and spiral into suicidal tendencies again. He empathized with her worry, but the threat didn't sit well with him. It almost made him angry because it implied that neither he nor Andreas had a choice in their actions. That was unacceptable.

"With all due respect, as we're clarifying things," Simon said, and Sara looked up at him with a critical eye. He frowned and continued, "I want to be clear that if I stay by your son's side, it has nothing to do with you or any threats from you. You don't get to make that choice for me **or** him. You're going to have to trust me and trust **him**."

Sara's eyebrows raised, making her look like she was about to tear into him. He knew his words would either make this woman hate or approve of him. It didn't matter because he didn't like being told he *would* do anything, and he certainly didn't like Andreas being told what he could or could not do, especially not after their conversation a few nights prior.

"I suggest you pick—" Sara started.

"I'm not finished, ma'am," Simon cut her off, causing her eyebrows to raise and a frown to form. He swallowed, and his face darkened. "I have **zero** intention of purposefully hurting your son, but I will *not* dance around him like he is a child. He is a grown man, and from what I have seen, he is a *good* man. He is far stronger than you are giving him credit for, and it's insulting to me on his behalf. If I *am* a passing fancy, and you think he will **crumble** because of *me,* you are either blind or unwilling to see the truth. Give the man you raised more credit than that because Andreas is stronger than you seem to think he is."

Sara remained silent, carefully studying the orc next to her. Her lips were slightly downturned, and her unusual prismatic eyes didn't blink. Simon swallowed, catching his breath in an attempt to calm himself.

"Are you done?" Sara asked.

"I am," Simon answered, anxious.

Sara's face relaxed, losing the sharp edge it had gained during their conversation. Simon tensed up again when Sara reached out, as if he were expecting to be slapped by her. Instead, she grabbed his hands and squeezed them. Sara offered him a genuine smile, her eyes glassy, and said, "... I am very *thankful* that Andreas met you."

Simon stared, shocked at the reaction he'd garnered.

"Let's go to the pub. I want to see my son and remind him that he should *treasure* you, Simon," Sara said with a smile. She squeezed Simon's hands and pulled away to lead them back towards **Sídhe**. Simon swallowed, confused, but followed her in silence.

Twenty-Six

Agreement

Fossy was built of stone and arranged semicircularly around the sea, with arching bridges crossing canals that ran through it. It was easy to get lost in. It had taken Simon far too long to locate the small cottage tucked between a fishmonger's shop and what looked to be an antique store. He had headed out sometime after noon, and it was already far past midday. Simon had promised Andreas that he would deliver the urn they were tasked with by Selbi, as the half-elf had been arguing with Neil. Andreas' father had found something, but Cian and Neil were not keen on sharing any more details than had been already.

Simon was restless and didn't want to get involved in family arguments. He wasn't accustomed to staying in one place for long, especially after completing a well-paying job and having a few days off. It didn't help that no matter how much he insisted on paying for something at the pub, Neil always managed to return the coin he left **with interest**. It drove him mad.

He left three gold coins for food and the room on the bartop every morning. He hoped it would be taken as another patron's payment so that he could repay the men for their hospitality. Then, in the evening, he would find not three gold coins but a *platinum* piece on the table beside the bed. A piece of coin that he had rarely seen, for those with wealth often owned it, and

Simon was not wealthy. It was a single coin worth ten gold coins; now, he had six rare coins. *Six platinum.*

Simon had never even had **one** platinum to his name before. All he'd been trying to do was repay the men, and they had paid *him* forty-two gold for his attempt to settle them **eighteen**. Wanting clarity on the situation, he asked Andreas about it and was met with hysterical laughter.

Simon sighed, feeling slightly overwhelmed as he thought about the situation again. He had not encountered anyone who was both generous *and* wealthy for years. At first, he had been unsure about the Dwyer family. Now, he was at least confident about a few things. They were honest people.

He had even seen Cian reprimand the city guard two days earlier. The guards had come over to ask for the man's help in concealing information about the prince's murder from the public. They were concerned that the city would go into a panic. Cian called them useless pigs and physically escorted them out of his pub. Cian had been screaming that he vowed to reveal *every* detail without hesitation if he was asked, including the castle guard's incompetence in preventing the attack or apprehending the assailant.

The Dwyers were also generous people. Simon's ever-growing personal wealth from trying to pay for room and board was a testament to that. He had never met a wealthy person, much less a family, that was so willing to provide for those who aided or assisted them *or* those they cared for. They paid fairly for jobs, more than fairly if he was being honest, and offered any help they could. In only a week, he understood why they were such a loved and respected family, and his opinion was that they did not deserve the ill will they received.

Cian and Neil were kind, honest men who had endured hardships and made the best of their situation. Now, he understood the reason behind Andreas' anger when the accusations against his family were mentioned.

As Simon walked, he absentmindedly spun a daisy chain around his finger. Even though it wasn't big enough to fit Andreas' head, he thought he could convince the man to wear it on his wrist or tuck it in his hair. He had accepted the flowers as payment when he dropped off the urn so he could give them as a gift. Turning the corner, he saw a shield-shaped sign swinging in the breeze, and the golden lettering on the Dwyer's pub sign welcomed him.

Sidhe was a beautifully carved, three-story wooden structure that stood out among the famous stone masonry of Fossy. The exterior matched the warm tones of the inside with finely crafted gold and red decorations. It was a large building with a spacious bar, multiple tables, and a cozy fireplace. In the center stood a massive central pillar, seemingly the backbone of the structure. Both the exterior and the interior exuded warmth, creating a humbling and welcoming atmosphere. The place was always bustling with music and the delightful aromas of fine wine and roast lamb, accompanied by wind chimes. There was always the sound of wind chimes, like in the cabin.

Simon slipped into the pub, whistling as he searched for Andreas. Navigating the busy bar, filled with laughter and chatter, was difficult, and he made his way to the bartop.

He eventually spotted Andreas and Cian in a corner of the room. The two were sitting at a table with ten books piled high. They looked through two books; one was propped open, leaning against the stack, and the other was on the table. Occasionally, they exchanged a few words or stopped to flip through another book before returning to the two they were comparing. Neil had brought up a job that morning and said they would discuss it over tea that evening. It made Simon wonder if the books on the table had anything to do with it.

Simon tossed the daisy chain, caught it, and tucked it into his bag. He leaned against the bartop quietly to watch the two in the corner. He had observed Neil and Andreas together countless times, mainly because Neil was in the pub more often than Cian. Cian was usually out running errands or busy in the kitchen preparing food for the guests that came through their doors. He had not had the chance to watch Andreas with Cian. Simon's brow furrowed as he focused intensely on the two, and the sounds of the pub faded into the background.

As he observed them together, alone, and interacting, he noticed how similar Andreas and Cian were. They both seemed to possess an intense love for knowledge and stories. As they delved into the books, joy was evident on their faces. They smiled and laughed as they discussed something from them, occasionally furrowing their brows and turning to another publication. They handled the pages delicately as if afraid of damaging the parchment. Additionally, they both chewed their bottom lip when they were deep in thought.

Simon crossed his arms, his brow furrowing deeper as he focused. They had very similar quirks, and it wouldn't be the first time he'd noted their similarities in appearance. Cian's skin was slightly darker, but they both had a warm red undertone to their features. They both had this wild, vibrant hair color and strange flame-like appearance to their magic. The similarities were striking, especially considering that Andreas and his sister were **adopted**.

Simon's head tilted, and his face screwed up in thought.

He wondered...

Cian's eyes flickered towards Simon, staring him down unblinkingly. Simon shifted uncomfortably in his seat as his thoughts stopped **immediately**. Unlike when Neil had suddenly looked at him before, Cian's way of doing so was more than uncomfortable. It was unsettling. Simon felt as if a predator had abruptly cornered him. He lifted a hand and waved halfheartedly at the man, who inclined his head and leaned over to say something to Andreas.

Andreas immediately looked up and burst into an enormous smile when he saw Simon sitting at the bar. He waved enthusiastically and motioned for him to come over. Simon felt his stomach flip, and despite the unease lingering in his mind from the golden eyes watching, he smiled as he stood and crossed over.

"When did you get back?" Andreas called, leaning on the book he was reading.

"Only a few minutes ago, I didn't want to intrude," Simon said, waving at the books.

"No intrusion. We were comparing the updated historical volumes released this morning to the old ones written before the war," Cian said with a smile as he collected the heavy books. "Please join us. My husband will join us soon."

Simon smiled tensely, still feeling uneasy from Cian's earlier glance. He settled into a chair and peeked over the books as they were closed and gathered. Most of them were historical, but there was an enormous book of stories—the one that he had seen the two reference quite a bit. It seemed they were comparing the recorded text with ancient myths. Interesting. The two had eclectic tastes.

"Did you find the house to deliver the urn?" Andreas asked, tilting his head.

"Oh, yeah," Simon nodded and dug out the daisy chain from his bag. He slipped it onto his finger and extended it playfully. "We got a tip for wonderful service… but I think you'd treat them better than me."

Andreas beamed and eagerly grabbed the flowers. "I don't know. I think he could wear daisies. What do you think, Papa?"

Simon looked up and spotted the man standing with books in his hands. Cian's golden eyes lingered on Andreas and then shifted to Simon. Simon noticed a smile tugging at the corners of Cian's mouth.

"I agree, but I'm certain Simon gave them to you as a gift, little one," Cian chuckled.

Andreas' face turned red, and he bit his lip to suppress a growing smile.

Cian chuckled louder. "Excuse me, I shall return with my husband," he said, effortlessly carrying the books away and excusing himself.

Andreas peeked up, still embarrassed, as he fiddled with the chain. "Were they?"

"They were a tip from the halfling, but…" Simon grinned, leaning back in his chair. "I braided them on the way here. So, I guess it's a bit of both?"

Andreas grinned and reached back to gather the end of his braid, tugging it over his shoulder. He began to fashion the flowers around the leather thong holding the strands. "I was wondering… it looks like a five-year-old chained them together," he muttered.

"Hey," Simon said, frowning and looking offended.

Andreas laughed at the orc but did not meet his gaze. "I'm kidding."

"If you don't want them, I can always take them back. I'm sure they'd look flattering on my shield," Simon said, crossing his arms smugly. Andreas looked up and glared at him, then defensively tugged the end of his braid farther away as if the idea was out of the question.

"I'm just saying... you insulted them," said Simon.

Andreas wrinkled his nose and stuck out his tongue as Simon lifted a hand, signaling for silence. Simon's face darkened as he looked around the space.

"... What?" Andreas asked.

"Do you hear that?" Simon asked, turning his head around the pub.

"Hear what?" Andreas listened, his brow furrowed. "I don't hear..." His words fell off again as he realized what Simon was implying, "... Anything."

A bubble was raised around them, blocking the sound and creating an eerie silence. All around the pub, patrons carried on with their lives as if nothing had changed, blissfully unaware of the phenomenon.

"I'm going to ask that you behave normally," Neil spoke, breaking the silence. Andreas and Simon looked to the right as Cian helped Neil sit beside Andreas. As the two men settled on either side of the table, Andreas and Simon remained quiet, waiting for further direction.

Cian spoke calmly, saying, "Tonight, Neil and I will be attacked."

"What?!" Andreas snapped, his eyes widening as his head yanked over.

"*Normal*, Firefly," Neil spoke, his voice chastising.

Andreas swallowed and looked down at the table uncomfortably.

"We were correct in assuming that the prince contacted certain individuals in Pirn. That individual assumes we are behind the meeting complications. It is only a matter of time before we are suspected of having assassinated the prince or accused of attempting to usurp the monarchy of Midwind," Cian spoke again, reaching over to grasp his husband's hand tenderly.

"We have arranged a performance. Well, I have. Cian, of course, dislikes this whole idea," Neil smiled almost smugly and received an unnoticed agitated frown from his husband. "Cian thinks we should only react to the situation as it unfolds, as we have done nothing wrong. However, it would be more pertinent to draw attention away from us. We won't accomplish much if we can't even get into places where we can weasel out information. Unfortunately, the Richards can bar us from events within Fossy and influence our ability to attend events *outside* their kingdom. Our whole family and all those associated with us."

"**The Rose Guard** and the Temple are at risk now, too," Andreas spoke quietly, biting his lip. "That's what you mean."

"Precisely. I agree that my people would be annoyed if they could not perform their duties… Which is the *only* reason I will compromise about this," Cian's words were terse.

"*Normal*, darling," Neil said, smiling.

Cian scoffed.

Simon cleared his throat. "The job … *You're not paying me to attack you …*"

Neil laughed genuinely. "Absolutely not. No offense to you, but it would take much more than you, Simon, to attack us."

Simon exhaled and whispered, "*I will not disagree with you there.*"

"Your father, Anni, found out about another attack in Ransol," Neil said, his empty eyes looking at Simon. "Gitah is well. Do not fret."

Simon huffed, relieved, "*Thank you.*"

Neil smiled. "Someone murdered Chetan Lucis. I'm sure you know him, Simon."

Simon nodded automatically, then gritted his teeth when he remembered Neil's blindness. "Ah, yes, sir. I do," he said.

Andreas furrowed his brow and asked, "Who is that?"

"Chetan is, or was, the leader of the monster hunter organization there, **The Order of Nightmares**. They hunt unnatural creatures that threaten the peace of the people. There are distinct orders, all with various abilities. Chetan was one of the three pseudo-leaders of Ransol as well … if you could claim that place *has* leadership," Cian spoke quietly, thinking.

"His death is complex. I won't give you all the details; old magic was used, and a creature from another *Plane of Existence* was summoned," Neil said calmly.

When Andreas looked at Simon, he noticed the man's jaw clenched. Simon appeared annoyed, almost as if he wasn't surprised by the information regarding Chetan's death.

"There is ample evidence to suggest that Tsara is responsible for his murder," Cian said, managing a sympathetic smile in Simon's direction despite the distaste on his face.

"As a result," Neil continued, "It's the perfect time for us to be targeted—two more people with influence in a city."

"A fake attack to throw the politicians off your trail and put more fire on the ones that want you dead. Smart," Simon reached up to scratch his chin in thought.

"I thought so too," Neil grinned and turned towards his husband. "See, darling?"

Cian scoffed, "It is a *lie*."

"It is using the climate to our **advantage**," Neil sighed and gave his husband a sharp look.

"What does this have to do with me?" Simon interrupted.

"... Do I have to go home?" Andreas asked.

Cian and Neil laughed.

"Patience, little one," Cian said with a smile as Andreas sighed and fidgeted with his hands.

"Our son is worried that our family will be targeted," Neil said, his words trailing off as he looked in Andreas' direction. He reached out until he found the young man's hand and squeezed it affectionately.

Andreas furrowed his brow. "Do you think she will hunt Lilli and me again?"

"Yes, we do," Cian answered, turning his head not to Andreas but to Simon.

Simon focused on the half-elf in front of him, his brow furrowed. He didn't notice Cian watching him until he felt a sense of being cornered again. It felt like a predator was threatening or *judging* his reaction to the information. He looked at Cian, his jaw tense, and said, "I suppose this is where I come in?"

"If you wish it to be so, yes," Cian paused, observing Simon's reaction. "We will pay, but I believe Andreas' safety matters to you... **unless I am mistaken?**"

"That's unfair," Andreas said, frowning deeply.

"I did not say he had no choice. I stated I thought he would care about your well-being," Cian retorted.

"What do you need me to do?" Simon cut Andreas off before he could say more and held up a hand to silence him. Andreas bit his lip and then looked down at his hands.

"Lilli will travel with Remi to Lahmar this evening, and she will hide there with the Grannor family for the time being," Neil spoke, turning towards Andreas. "I think you understand what I'm saying?"

"... I do," Andreas nodded.

Neil sighed and offered a small smile. "You will go with Simon; do not publicly show your face. Where you go though..." Neil trailed off, looking around to remember where he had last heard Simon at the table. "I will leave it up to Simon, as he would know where it would be common for his presence and safe enough to stay for a long period."

Simon replied within seconds, "I own a home in Sebree that someone gave me, and only three people know I still own it. One of them is Gitah."

Andreas looked up immediately at the words and watched Simon.

"Very well, I will take both of you to Sebree while my husband finishes his *preparations* for this evening," Cian grumbled, rolling his eyes at Neil's grin.

Neil shifted and pulled a coin purse from his shawl. It appeared to be made of black silk with white threaded embroidery. He placed it on the table and pushed it toward where he had heard Simon speak. "This is enchanted with a spell to alter the weight of items placed within it—specifically coins. It weighs a pound and holds up to fifteen thousand gold pieces."

Simon choked on his spit.

Neil smiled smugly and said, "Inside are fifteen hundred platinum pieces. You will take them and not argue about taking them. You will use them as payment for watching over Anni and for buying anything you need. Do you understand?"

Cian laughed with joy, clearly finding the whole situation amusing. "I will meet you in your room in twenty minutes," he said, grinning. He stood up and kissed the top of his husband's head before departing and heading upstairs.

"That is *very generous*, but I …" Simon started, the coughing fit tapering off.

"**I said you will not argue**," Neil's voice turned icy, and his smile vanished.

Simon froze and looked from the coin purse to the man on the other side of the table. Neil had suddenly lost all patience and gained a frightening edge in his voice. This was not something Simon could refuse. He swallowed, shrugged off the chill down his spine, and gingerly reached for the purse. "Yes, sir," he said.

"Good," Neil smiled, and the pleasant atmosphere that often surrounded him returned. "If this becomes a long-term arrangement, we will provide you with additional payment as necessary. When Andreas or Lilliana are concerned, money becomes insignificant, and I am willing to pay whatever it takes to keep them safe. … **Do we have a deal**?" He drew out the last few words playfully, and a smile spread across his pale face, revealing his teeth. Neil looked almost giddy.

Simon furrowed his brow when he saw Andreas' eyes narrow, and his head jerked toward his grandfather. The half-elf appeared angry as if he wanted to say something about the situation. Simon looked at the wispy hand extended towards him and locked eyes with the empty ones staring intently in his direction. He took a deep breath and cautiously extended his hand to shake Neil Dwyer's peculiar tattoo-covered hand. "Sounds like a deal," he said.

Neil grinned widely and said, "Wonderful. *I'll hold you to it.*"

Simon looked down at his fingers as Neil withdrew his hand and he flexed them. His fingers had been squeezed tightly, with unnatural strength, and now they felt cold. It was the same freezing sensation as when they'd been in the cabin, and Neil had worked that eerie magic. As he looked back up to the fading grin on Neil's face, he suddenly realized that the man looked more like a predator than his husband often did at that moment.

Another chill ran down Simon's spine and settled deep into his bones.

"There isn't much time. Off you go," Neil waved his hand, and then the whole pub's sound returned.

Agreement

Simon put the coin purse into his pocket and stood up. He looked at Andreas, slightly confused. Andreas was staring at his grandfather with a look of frustration and disbelief. "Red, are you ready?" Simon asked.

Andreas sighed, "**Sure**." He leaned over, kissed his grandfather's cheek, and quickly left the table to head up the stairs.

* * *

There had been an uncomfortable silence as the two left Neil alone at the table and headed to their room. Once safely within the walls, with the door closed, Simon had started to gather their things.

Five minutes later, he noticed Andreas was still standing by the door, his eyes on the floor and arms wrapped around his shoulders.

Simon called, concerned, "Red?"

Andreas didn't respond. Simon sighed, tossed his shield onto the bed beside their bags, and approached the smaller figure. He reached out to tilt the other man's chin affectionately, "Hey," he said.

Tears gushed from the emeralds as they were forced up. Andreas bit his lip in shame when Simon jolted in mild panic. "Hey, hey. What's wrong?" Simon asked softly, wiping at the droplets rolling down Andreas' face.

"You don't have to go," Andreas said, the words fumbled out between sobs. He tried to turn away but found Simon's fingers holding his chin. "You don't have to go if you don't want to. They didn't give you a choice, and it's not fair!" he continued, not quite a yell but more of a panicked plea.

Simon was initially confused and searched Andreas' face, looking for any sign that might give him insight. He then exhaled in realization, and his hands moved to cup the carnelian cheeks before him. Andreas attempted to pull away, but Simon held firm. "Andrea. Look at me," he said.

Andreas tried to look everywhere, but. "*You have a choice, Simon*," he whispered.

The whispered words made Simon's stomach drop, and his heart started racing faster. An emotion he hadn't felt in several years bubbled up and tickled the edges of his consciousness: *affection*. Suddenly, he felt an overwhelming urge to kiss the man who was throwing a tantrum on his behalf. It was ridiculous but sweet. Simon squeezed Andreas' cheeks and shook his head, saying, "No, I don't, Red."

Andreas frowned, his eyes wide, and yelled, "Yes, you do!"

Simon chuckled, his tusks wrinkling his eyes as he started, "If you're in danger ..." His words faded off when the green eyes locked on him. "If you're being targeted," He paused and kissed Andreas' wrinkled forehead. Simon continued, his words strained, "I don't have a choice, Andrea."

Andreas attempted to pull away, his brow furrowed. "You do. *I won't let them bully you into...*" he muttered.

"They aren't forcing me to do anything," Simon said with finality, abruptly cutting off the whispered words. "Cian was right. Your safety concerns me. If they sent you off to someone else, I'd follow you, not because I don't trust them, but because I ..." His voice tapered off, and he bit his lip momentarily in thought. It was as if he had just realized the meaning behind the words that he was ready to belt out without care. Simon then continued, "I need to know you're safe. I **want** to go with you ... *Alright?*"

Andreas appeared to want to speak but gripped Simon's arms instead. Simon squeezed his cheeks in response. "... *Alright,*" Andreas whispered and looked as if he were about to say something more before a loud, shuddering explosion emanated from beneath their feet. Both looked at the ground, their brows furrowed in concern.

Before they could say anything, Cian flung open the room door and slammed it behind him. "Get your things **now**," Cian hissed, his eyes furious and seething like molten gold.

"Papa, what's happening?" Andreas panicked as Simon pulled away and grabbed the bags he had been packing for the past few minutes.

"**Come**," Cian said, ignoring the question as he looked toward Simon.

Simon stumbled over, hoisting his shield onto his back and handing over Andreas' bag. Andreas took it, threw it over his shoulder, and then reached out to grasp the hand offered by his grandfather. Simon didn't wait to be told and immediately grabbed Andreas' other hand.

Cian watched Simon, deep in thought, as if he was trying to decide what to say. As another explosion rumbled beneath them and screams echoed through the floorboards, he closed his eyes and tried to calm himself. Tension built up in his body as he visibly fought the urge to go downstairs. "You **will** take care of him. Do you hear me? Do you understand me, mo leanbh[6]?" he said finally.

Simon shuddered as the golden eyes opened wide and seemed to pierce through him. A sense of authority flared there, and he suddenly felt as if he were gazing into a vast inferno that threatened to burn him alive. He felt genuine terror as Cian watched him. Simon nodded, confused by the words he didn't understand. "*I promise*," he whispered.

Cian took a slow breath before the man gave a quick nod.

Simon felt a surge of warmth unlike anything he had experienced before. It enveloped Simon, and suddenly, he felt as if his whole body had been tossed onto a pyre. A bright red energy consumed him and the other two men. Andreas squeezed Simon's hand tightly, and Simon squeezed back, feeling a gut-wrenching jerk. Instead of feeling like he would vomit, Simon felt like he was being charred. He nearly called out in pain before it subsided. In seconds, the room disappeared, and he found himself unharmed on a grassy plain.

Cian pulled Andreas' shawl over his head, forcing him to conceal his face. "Be watchful and avoid being seen."

Andreas nodded, but his voice shook as he asked, "What's going on?"

"You are loved, little one, and I will speak with you soon. I must return to Neil." Cian's words were brief, and he ignored the question once more. He looked at Simon, glared, and then nodded. "Call for me if you need me. I **will** be listening." Then, Cian pulled back and vanished into a burst of red and orange energy without further explanation.

Andreas squeezed Simon's hand, and the orc turned his attention from the space Cian had occupied just moments before to the half-elf at his side. Andreas was visibly shaking, and the worry emanating from the young man was palpable.

---

[6] mo leanbh (muh LAN-uv): "my child"

"Something happened," Simon stated.

"Yes, something happened," Andreas said, swallowing hard as he yanked his hand free and tugged the shawl off. He dug through his bag, shoved the vibrant fabric into it, and pulled out a heavily worn cloak. He put it on to obscure his clothing and pulled up the hood. "Where are we?" he asked.

Simon let his eyes linger on the man beside him before looking at the horizon. He could see the outline of a city far in the distance—one, maybe two days' journey. "We won't get to Sebree tonight, but hopefully tomorrow. We're in the **Plains of Tenresa**."

Andreas replied, "All right." He tucked the bag on his shoulder and stated, "Let's go."

"You're not worried?" Simon asked when Andreas took his hand.

"Of course, I'm worried, but I trust them," the green eyes looked over, and Andreas smiled. His bloodshot eyes and tear-stained face still showed signs of distress. He barely contained his panic. "And I trust **you**. So, I'll focus on what we need to do for now. We need to get to Sebree," he said flatly.

Upon hearing uncertainty, Simon's stomach twisted. Andreas was worried more than he wanted to admit, once again unable to hide his feelings. As Simon watched the man's exhausted face, he saw tension growing from unanswered questions. However, he also saw a need for control and handling something small and manageable. Simon offered a small smile and said, "Right."

Twenty-Seven

Slumber

He heard cicadas, loud as if they were locked in a song that ebbed and flowed in waves. Knowing that the creatures did not live in the part of the world where he had fallen asleep, he thought it was a dream for a moment. He felt something light on his face and, with it, a low buzz of wings vibrating his ears. Andreas' eyes wrenched open, and he gazed up at the stars, but not where he last laid his head.

There were trees of all sizes, tall and ancient, in every corner of his vision. They soared higher than he could comprehend. Quickly, he understood it was not stars he saw but thousands of fireflies flitting beneath the canopy, mimicking them. He glanced over when the insect that had landed on his cheek lifted. He watched as a dragonfly the size of his palm fluttered off into the surrounding woods. Andreas sat up and searched for the orc that had been watching the fire when he'd nodded off. Simon was nowhere to be found, like the camp they'd made, and panic set in.

The forest he found himself in was beautiful yet terrifying. The trees were numerous, and there was a wide variety of flora. He saw different species growing together, which he never thought was possible. Their diverse needs made him wonder if he was still dreaming. The ground was soft, covered in thick grass and thriving moss. Despite the darkness, insects were glowing as they sped around, and many plants seemed bioluminescent.

Andreas glanced into the woods once more. He realized he had never been to this place, yet it felt familiar in his memory. The twenty-six-year-old jumped when he felt something wet touch his hands in his lap, and looking down, he found he was crying. A deep, unending sorrow surged from within and enveloped him like an old friend. Despite its beauty, this place made him profoundly sad.

Something rustled behind him, so he jerked around to see what it was. What he saw made his eyes widen, and his body instinctively pulled back in apprehension. The wave of sorrow that had already latched onto him grew, and he blinked to stop the tears cascading down his cheeks. He reached up and wiped them away but found no end in sight. He heard movement but could not see to determine what to do.

"So, you remember this place?"

The voices were overwhelming. It was as if multiple individuals spoke interchangeably. They were rich and bassy for a moment, then they shifted to a tenor, followed by an alto, before the last words were whispered in an angelic soprano. There was no way of knowing if they were masculine, feminine, somewhere in between, or simply all at once.

"Do not cry. I wish to speak for a moment."

Andreas felt something touch his head, and warmth spread over him. It was the feel of the sun's rays through a dull tree canopy, the soft breeze as it rolled in from the ocean, the embracing carpet of grass and flora beneath his feet, and the comfort of a fire safely in his room. All these things at once and more, and the sensation immediately made his attention gravitate upwards as the tears slowed and his vision cleared. He did not know this place or this person, but both were painfully familiar.

The figure he found standing over him was massive, well over eight feet tall. Their face was delicate, with lovely features and large, expressive eyes of liquid gold. Their skin was cool, welcoming, and ebony like the surrounding soil, covered in faint iridescent green freckles. They had long hair worn in locks, intricately arranged over massive multi-pointed antlers into a high half-ponytail. They wore fine clothes made of silks and linens, varying in color from deep green to cream. A massive mantle of leaves seemed to change in color and shape like the many trees and seasons they would witness. Spiders spun webs on their antlers, and geodes glittered like starlight in various places on their skin, as if they wore the earth as jewelry.

They were both beautiful and handsome at the same time. They were neither male nor female and yet they were both. Their changing voice emphasized this even more. Their smile illuminated the entire space, bringing sudden light into it. Sunshine shone through the dense canopy, filling their surroundings and the object of their attention with a soft, evergreen glow.

> **"Hello, dear ———."**

Andreas choked, feeling another rush of sorrow and adoration. There was a word, something said that he could not hear, and it made his stomach twist uncomfortably. His brow furrowed, for it was something he wanted to remember. Then, he realized the figure did not speak, at least not from their mouth. It felt like someone said the words directly to him in his mind.

Andreas took a deep breath and said, "I know you."

The figure smiled and reached forward, gently pressing against the half-elf's forehead. They then pulled back their hands and brushed them over their long, elven ears. Their hands then shifted to form words in sign language as their voices responded in Andreas' mind again.

> **"Think about your words ... or use my brother's language."**

Andreas watched, his eyes wide. How could he have forgotten the old stories his grandparents told him as he grew up? Andreas nodded and lifted his hands to converse. Instead of speaking the words aloud, he mouthed them slowly and signed with his fingers, "I know you."

The figure beamed, and the small clearing they took up burst into bright light again. They nodded, their hands folding back into their billowy sleeves.

"You remember?"

Andreas shook his head momentarily before his hand lifted and covered his mouth. He did not remember, but he felt he *should*. He remembered what his Papa told him: the tale of the earth being silenced. In this story, Qella rendered Uldrich, the Earth Primal, deaf and mute. Somehow, he felt this tale was not what the question meant. He saw their brow furrow, and the light in the space dimmed as the broad smile faded to a simple, sad one.

"You will soon. When you are ready, ——-."

Andreas furrowed his brow, feeling more panicked than before. He couldn't comprehend the words in his head, nor did he seek an answer to the questions they brought with them. As more memories accumulated, the sorrow from this place welled up inside him like a sickness. *He wanted to leave.*

Uldrich smiled, and their slender figure sank in front of Andreas. They reached out, placing a hand on the tangle of red hair.

"Do not be afraid. I wanted to see how much you've grown, and tell you not to worry about your sister. She is with my people, and safe."

Andreas jerked his head up. Lilli. Another wave of emotion hit him: relief. He had fallen asleep while worrying and wondering if he should attempt to find her, trying to hide the guilt of leaving her behind. Tears welled up, and he bit his lip to suppress a sob. Unable to speak, he nodded his thanks.

Uldrich smiled, and the sun spread out in a green wave.

"Do you wish to return? —— sleeps."

Andreas followed Uldrich's gaze as they turned to the right, and the faint light of the clearing spread. The area slowly changed to the dry plains where he had fallen asleep, a spot of reality in this otherworldly place. He saw something familiar: Simon was leaning against the tree they had claimed, fast asleep. Andreas watched momentarily, then looked back at the figure beside him.

There it was again. Something, a word, he could not understand.

Andreas gestured and signed slowly, "Please."

Feeling large arms wrap around him, embracing him, he felt close to understanding—close to remembering. Then, he jerked upwards, sniveling, and looked around in panic. The forest was gone, and the dull color of the **Plains of Tenresa** was all around.

Simon jolted awake and exclaimed, "Andreas?!"

Andreas felt the man's hands grip his cheeks and force them up to look at him. He found Simon's face swollen with panic, his eyes wide with worry. He exhaled and smiled. "I'm alright… it was just a dream. I just had a dream," he said. He reached up to clasp Simon's arm but felt something heavy in his hand. He squeezed and looked down. There was a metallic oak leaf with red and orange gradient hues—a dream. He doubted the word's truth.

"I fell asleep. I'm sorry," Simon replied, still concerned. He turned Andreas' face, inspecting it as he noticed its tear trails.

Andreas looked up and teased, "How dare you sleep like a regular orc?"

Simon laughed and then knelt, whispering, *"The audacity of me."*

Andreas observed as the tension dissipated and the cautious look faded from the other man's face. He had seen it many times before: a readiness as if the orc was preparing to attack anything that moved or approached. It made his stomach tingle and twist. "Sleep," he said.

Simon sighed, released Andreas' face, and instead of returning to the tree, he shifted and sat beside Andreas. Then, he leaned back and placed his head on the other man's lap. "Alright."

Andreas laughed, allowed it, and leaned against the tree behind them. He maneuvered the oak leaf and placed it beside him on the ground, out of sight. He tenderly shifted through the black hair in his lap, moving Simon's bangs from his face. "The audacity of you using me as a pillow," he teased.

Simon's eyes closed, and he smiled. He seemed to relax.

Andreas smiled and dared to glance up at the fire to check it. Something beyond the firelight caught his attention, drawing his eyes into the faint darkness. There was a fox with bright golden eyes. Its body appeared made of tree bark, with areas covered in moss and intricate swirls carved along it. It reminded him of one of his father's carvings, and he watched it quietly for a time.

The fox remained, its golden eyes locked in place.

Andreas mouthed slowly, silently, into the darkness. *"Thank you."*

The fox's tail wagged, and then the creature bounded away, leaving bursts of green leaves before vanishing like an arcane illusion.

Andreas glanced down and saw a gentle gray and brown eye watching him. He smiled, "I remember telling you to sleep," he said.

"Now that I'm all tucked in, I need a goodnight kiss," Simon said with a smile.

Andreas laughed, beaming. He leaned down and placed a token of affection on Simon's nose. "If you don't sleep, you'll only get a good morning kiss."

Simon chuckled and then rolled onto his side, snuggling closer to the tree and Andreas' body. It wasn't long before Simon's breathing evened out, and Andreas absentmindedly ran his hands through the man's hair. His eyes looked out towards the fire, watching the flames flicker and dance as he had done many times before. A stray spark jolted upwards, flickered to an ember as the breeze carried it, and then fizzled, capturing his attention.

Andreas furrowed his brow, trying to remember the words he had just heard in his dreamlike state. …Then he remembered the words spoken, not by the Primal, but by the woman near the encampment. His hand shifted to clutch the leaf beside him, assuring himself that it was real and he hadn't imagined it. His other hand paused in its movements and rested over Simon's waist. He latched a finger on the man's belt, ensuring he would still hold Simon if he fell asleep.

Andreas' mind reeled as he focused on the darkness where he had seen the fox. Confused, he longed for understanding. He wanted to remember whatever he was told he **would** remember.

He wanted to understand how he could lose himself without knowing it.

The Maps of Lusefell

The Maps of Lusefell

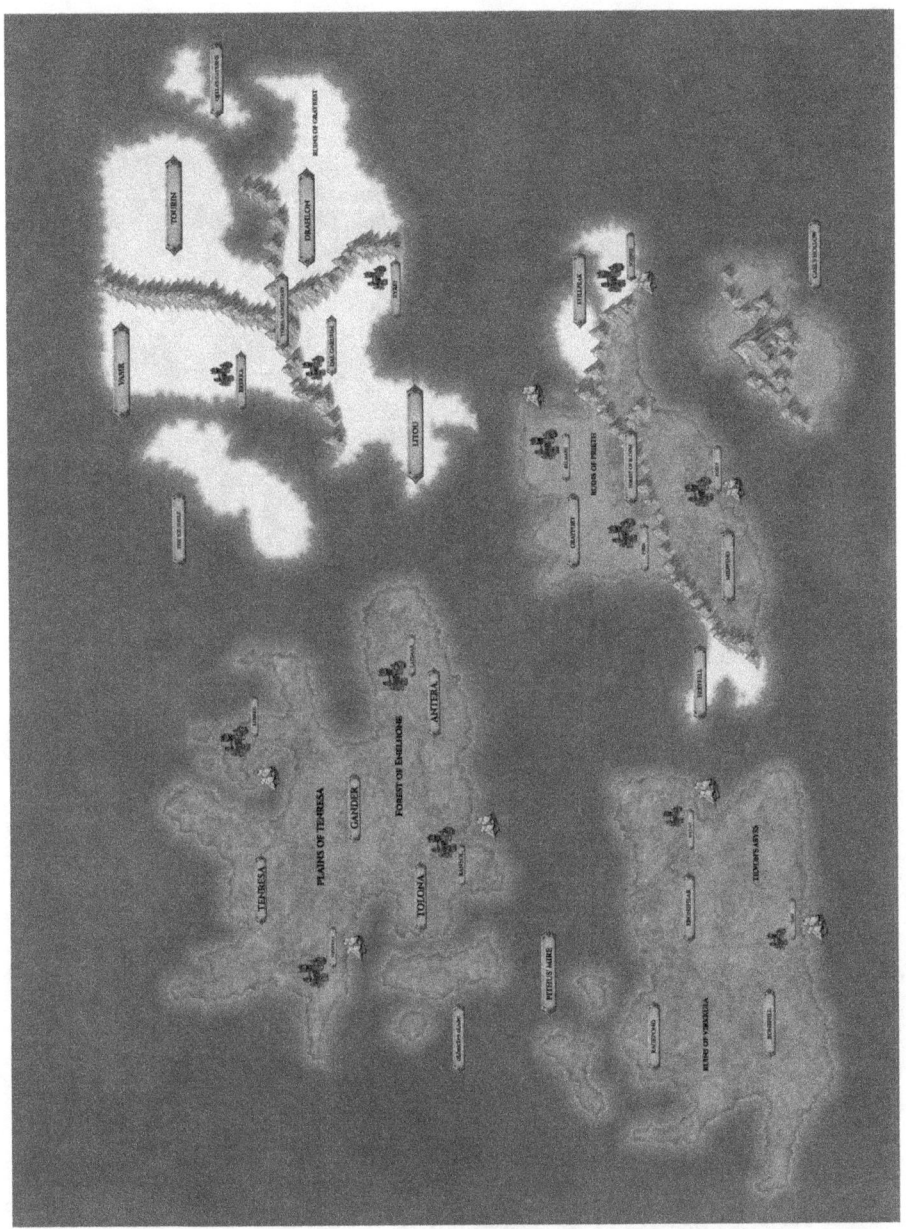

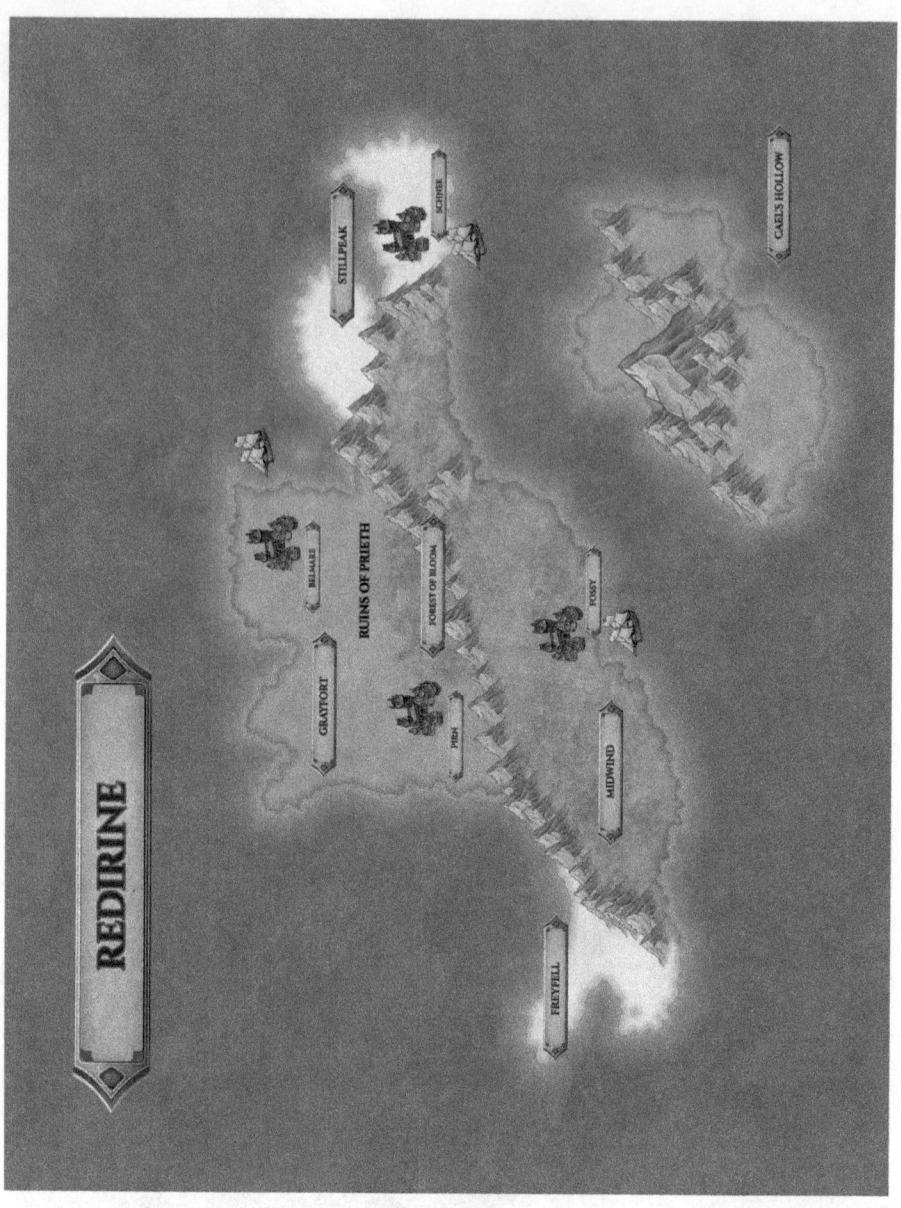

The Maps of Lusefell

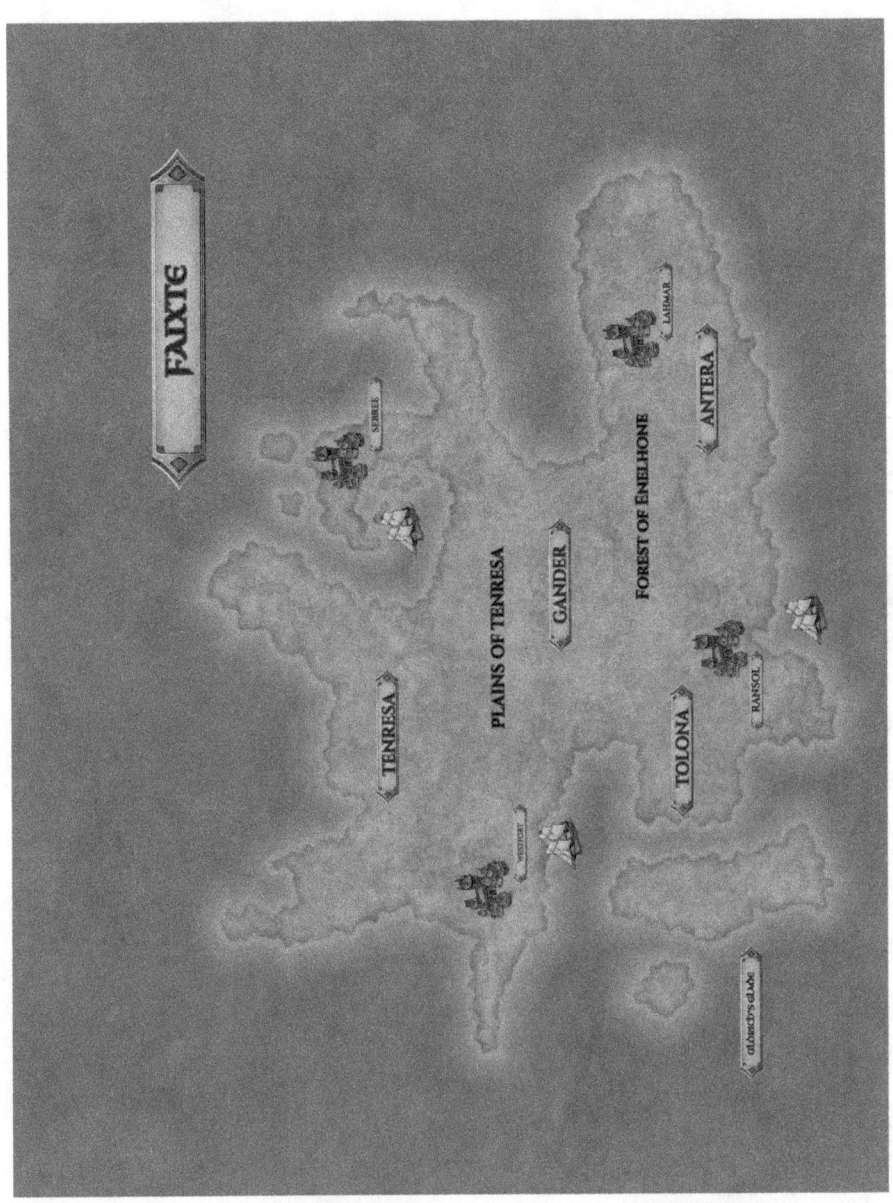

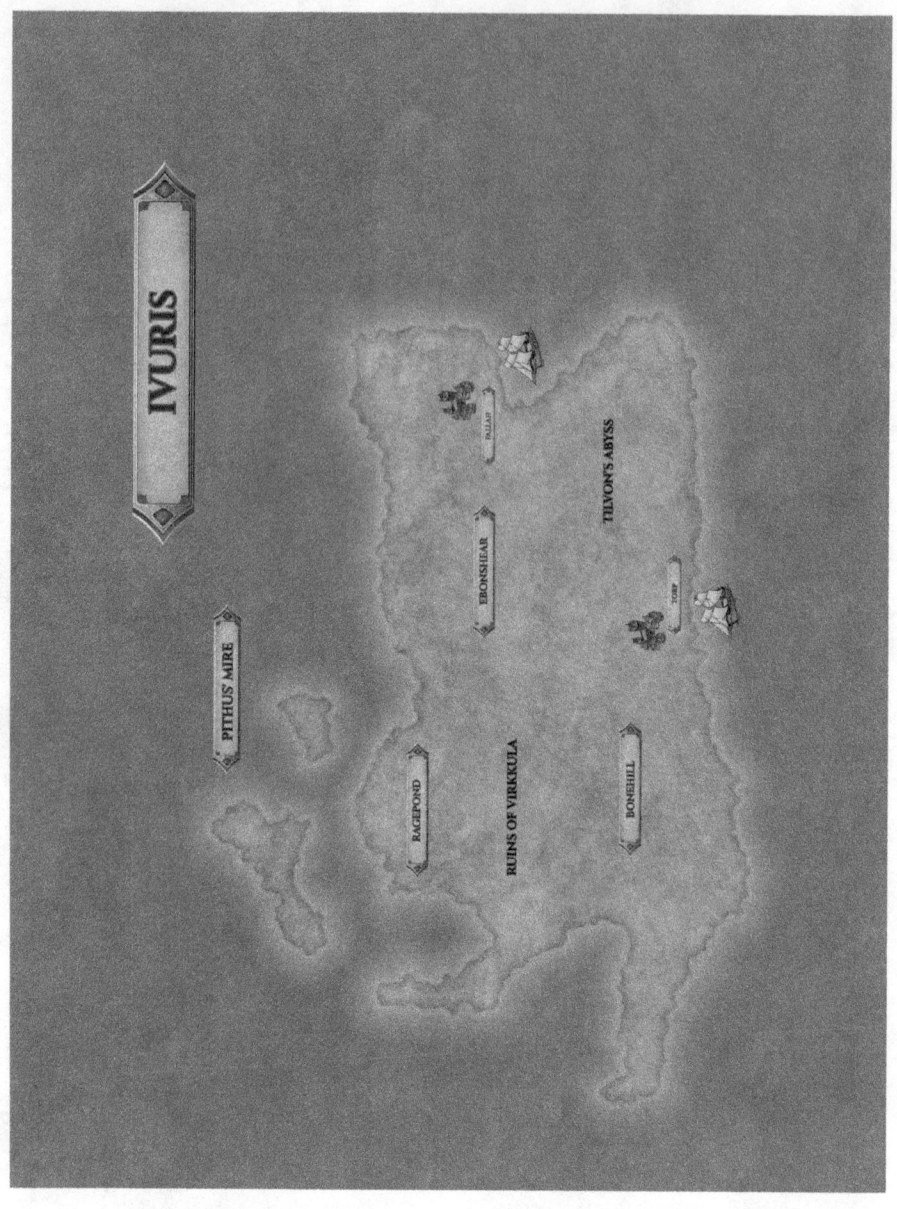

The Maps of Lusefell

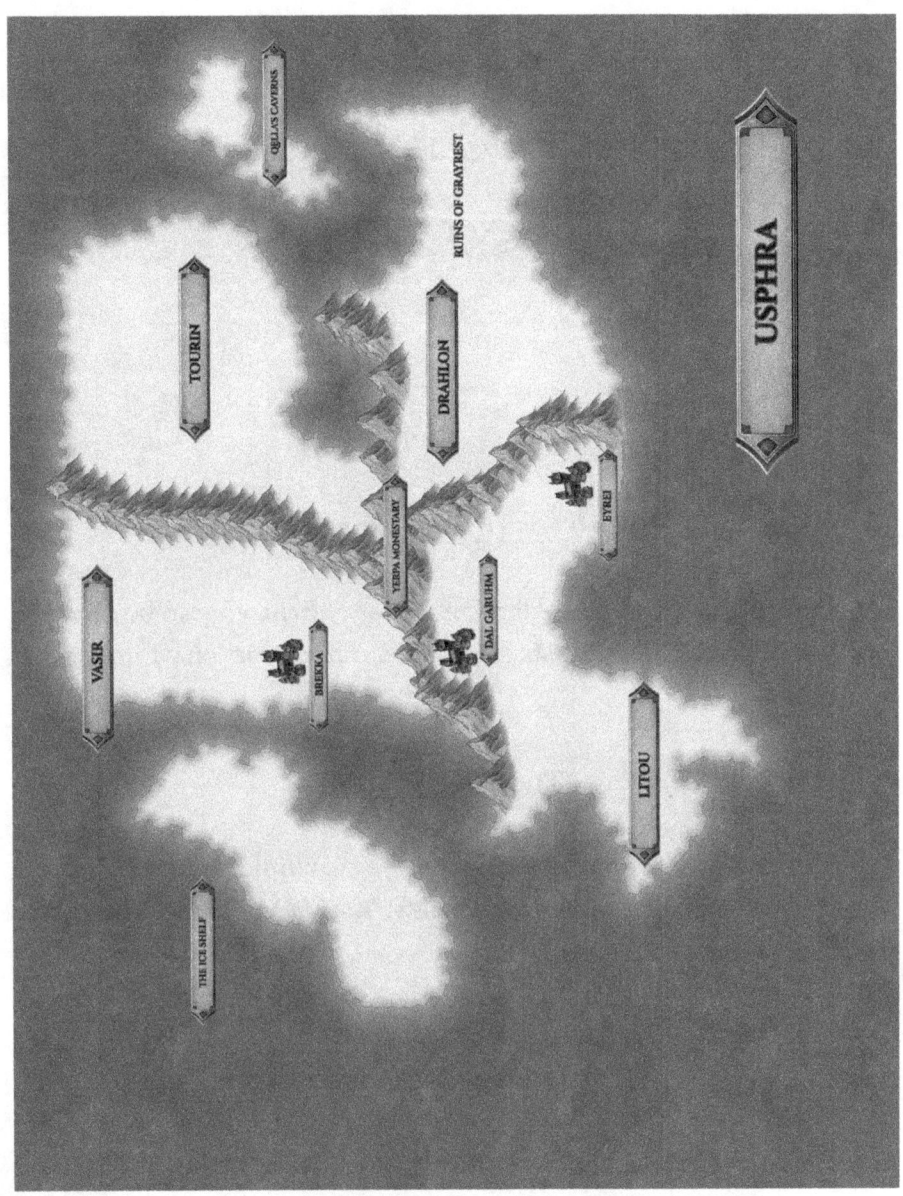

The Six Planes of Existence

The Divine Plane

The home of the **Old Gods**. All other *Planes of Existence* can be seen and heard from here. The **Old Gods** can contact other *Planes* on whims.

The Astral Plane

The home of those who have learned more than others dare, and where heroes are lifted to be glorified for eternity. *The Mortal Plane* can be viewed from here but not contacted.

The Primordial Plane

The home of the **Primal Lords** and all of their elemental children. This *Plane* is cut off from the others. It cannot be contacted or reached save by one from *The Primordial Plane*, one from *The Divine Plane*, or magically endowed individuals on *The Mortal Plane* who have harnessed the ability to borrow from it.

The Mortal Plane

The home of the *Mortals* has various spaces that run simultaneously disconnected. Timelines may branch and bend but never intersect; known intersections by higher powers have left lasting impacts on the separate realms of this *Plane*. The other *Planes* may be contacted without promise of response unless otherwise specified.

The Eternal Plane

The home of the damned and cursed. The place where souls are ferried when they have fallen beyond salvation. It is a *Plane* of eternal atonement, no matter what form that may take for the transgressor. Those in this Plane may succeed in their atonement and be reborn within *The Mortal Plane*. Where in the *Plane of Existence*, they are reborn, however, is a gamble. Once reborn, they hold no memory of their previous existence. This *Plane* can only be contacted by those from *The Divine Plane* and *The Primordial Plane* with direct permission from one who hails from *The Divine Plane*.

The Forgotten Plane

The home of those who are incapable of atonement. It is a place of imprisonment where creatures and beings alike are sent to remain for eternity. Within this *Plane*, the memories of those trapped here are harvested and conveyed to those in *The Divine Plane* to be passed on to their chosen devotees. Many of the **Old God's** teachings, lessons, and laws have been born from lessons unlearned by individuals within this *Plane*. Only those of *The Divine Plane* and **Pithus** may contact this *Plane*.

The Immortal Boundaries

1. Only those who hail from *The Divine Plane* may view, contact, influence, interact with, or enter **any** of the six *Planes of Existence;* as such, only those who hail from *The Divine Plane* may enter *The Divine Plane.*

2. Only those who hail from *The Divine Plane* may grant permission to view, contact, influence, interact with, or enter **any** of the six *Planes of Existence*; only the grantor may revoke this permission once instated.

3. Those who hail from *The Primordial Plane* may not enter any other *Plane of Existence* unless placed there by one who hails from *The Divine Plane;* however, lesser creatures of *The Primordial Plane* may be summoned as **temporary servants** to those who hail from *The Mortal Plane* with the means to do so.

4. Those who hail from *The Mortal Plane* may not interact with others who hail from **different** timelines within *The Mortal Plane.*

5. Those who hail from *The Mortal Plane* may not enter any other *Plane of Existence* unless allowed entry by one who hails from *The Divine Plane;* they may attempt contact with any other *Plane of Existence* without guarantee of reply and at risk of unknown consequences.

The Immortal Boundaries

6. *The Eternal Plane* shall act as a means of **atonement** for souls from all *Planes of Existence*, of which rebirth into an unknown timeline upon *The Mortal Plane* may be granted after death; all memory of previous life shall be forfeited upon rebirth.

7. *The Forgotten Plane* shall imprison **any** deemed unworthy or incapable of atonement who hail from **any** *Plane of Existence*; memories of those imprisoned shall be harvested and passed on to those who hail from *The Divine Plane* to influence history, customs, and atonement within *The Mortal Plane* and *The Forgotten Plane*.

The People of Lusefell

The Ancara

The Ancara are the beast people of the realm. Their race is large and varied, and its members are as numerous as the world's creatures.

Some look like anthropomorphic versions of their bestial lineage, while others have minor features such as ears and tails. Some appear humanoid but have the heightened senses of their lineage.

Some have both bestial and fey lineage and, as such, will classify themselves as one or the other.

The Asir

These people are extremely rare across the whole of The Mortal Plane.

Asir are typically born when an **Old God** or **Primal** meets the following criteria:

- When the life of an **Old God** or **Primal** is at risk, a spark of their essence attaches to a *Mortal*. This spark can remain dormant for years without the Mortal knowing its existence.

Once the spark is attached to the *Mortal*, one of three outcomes may come to pass at any time:

1. The **Old God** or **Primal** will remain dormant, seeking to continue their life in peace. When the *Mortal* dies, though their life is extended beyond average life expectancy, the **Old God** or **Primal** also dies with them.
2. The **Old God** or **Primal** may be awakened naturally or by the *Mortal*. The **Old God** or **Primal** sacrifices the soul of the *Mortal* to be reborn within *The Mortal Plane*, and the *Mortal* whose body they inhabited ceases to exist.
3. The **Old God** or **Primal** may relinquish their spark to give the *Mortal* who houses them their abilities, knowledge, and station. The *Mortal* will replace the **Old God** or **Primal**, and the former will cease to exist.

All Asir resemble the **Old God** or **Primal** that attaches to them in some way by look, temperament, or ideals. The spark of the **Old God** or **Primal** is drawn to the host, who resembles them **most** within *The Mortal Plane*. Not all Asir reside in **Lusefell**, as *The Mortal Plane* is vast and expansive despite its disconnected nature.

The Shapeshifters

Said to be the direct descendants of **Pithus**, Shapeshifters (also known as simply Shifers) roam the world, flaunting their gifts or hidden away. Most can trace their lineage back to *Ivuris* as early as the creation of the continent in year **44**.

It is widely argued that those with *Lycanthropy* are distant cousins of Shapeshifters; many scholars seem to think that the Air Primal created the curse to test *Mortals* in the years of **Qella's** deception.

The Dwarves

Sturdy and hardworking, the Dwarvish people have persevered through the realm's various ages. In recorded history, many cities can owe their existence to the crafty folk.

Thanks to their hearty bodies and stout spirits, these people have adapted to living in many climates and areas. Depending on their origins, some classify themselves as *Imperial Dwarf, Mountain Dwarf,* or *Deep Dwarf*. All, however, are considered Dwarves.

The Dúilí

Directly linking their lineage to *The Primordial Plane*, many were brought here by the four **Primal Lords** for a better life. On their *Planes of Existence*, they were considered high-ranking, extremely loyal, or masters of their field. They were gifted humanoid forms that would better suit them in *The Mortal Plane* without losing their elemental affiliations.

Most call the *Holy Isles* home, but others can be found scattered across the land and sea, seeking adventure.

The Elves

Some are as old as **Lusefell** itself and have witnessed the whole of history played out firsthand. They are innately magical people, often more attuned to the natural world than most. Much like the Dwarves, they have spread far and wide across the land and found homes in various places. Depending on where they are from, some classify themselves as either *High Elves, Wood Elves, Starlight Elves,* or *Astral Elves*.

Within recent years, as early recorded as **1256**, *Astral Elves* have been found walking in *The Mortal Plane*. Those asked and willing to tell how they came here are as varied as the stars. More often than not, these people are considered *Ifreann* at first glance; they have 1-2 sets of horns upon their heads that can vary in shape, size, and coloration. It has been noted that they share a striking resemblance to **Qella**.

The Fey

Otherworldly and often linked to *The Primordial Plane* in ancestry by means of **Uldrich.** They are rare folk who can sometimes be found wandering *The Mortal Plane*. Some by choice, others by misfortune. Many within this classification fall into other origin categories across **Lusefell.**

Those who are **full** *Fey* origin are rare.

The Giants

Distantly related to *Earth Dúilí*, they are a people who split off from the *Holy Isles* and ventured out into the continents. They are large, sturdy people who can handle harsh elements and high altitudes. Over the people's history, many have lost their towering stature that rivaled trees, and most, even those of mixed origin, max out at eight feet tall.

The Gnomes

One of the little people often found sheltered alongside their Dwarvish kin. They are in the most unlikely places, just like their Halfling cousins. Many are skilled tinkerers who have helped advance the realm's arcane technology.

Due to their varied skills and small stature, they have made many places their home. Depending on their origins, some classify themselves as either *Hill Gnomes*, *Mountain Gnomes,* or *Deep Gnomes*.

The Halflings

One of the little people, they are often found sheltered alongside those who reside in the forests of *Faixte*. Some, however, have a knack for adventure and wander off into the most unlikely places. They are straightforward, down-to-earth people who enjoy luxuries.

The Humans

Hearty, adaptable, and ambitious, they outnumber most other races by 2:1. They are the most widespread, with one of the shortest lifespans in **Lusefell**.

The Orcs

Mortals that were deemed to have dauntless courage and fearless spirit were blessed by **Cael** long ago. Most can trace their lineage back to the creation of *Redirine* in the year **497** or the beginning of the first *Great War* in the year **813**. Though they are one of the *Mortals* in the realm that have a shorter lifespan, they are the fiercest survivors of **Lusefell**.

Depending on their origins, some classify themselves as either *Nomadic* or *Stationary*. Values and traditions vary by tribe and are greatly influenced by whether the tribe is *Nomadic* or *Stationary*.

They are very proud and stubborn people.

The Ifreann

They are people who can trace their ancestors back to *the Eternal Plane* and souls who have nearly achieved atonement within *the Eternal Plane*. They have been tasked with a final lesson to learn. Something was not fully grasped in their time in *the Eternal Plane*, or there is a lesson that can only be taught to them within the *Mortal Plane*.

Most have a single set of horns and skin that can vary from natural colors to jewel tones. They often have tails of various types and lengths and can have hooves.

The Pantheons of Lusefell

The Old Gods

Athos

- Alias: "The Young" or "Summer King"
- *Youth, Summer, Love, Inspiration*
- **Iconography**: Cats, Ensnared Hearts

Braxus

- The "brother" of the two that helped create the realm.
- Alias: "The Lifebringer", "The Bright One", "The Noble One"
- *Creation, Life, Luck and Light*
- **Iconography**: Starry Hammer, Halo with Stars

Illhiea

- The "sister" of the two that helped create the realm.
- Alias: "The Forgotten One", "The Lost"
- *Death, War, Destruction, Chaos*
- **Iconography**: Clenched Fist, Demonic Eye

Mali

- Watcher of the dead. Works closely with **Pithus**.
- Alias: "The Dark Lady"
- *War, Death, Shadow, Sovereignty*
- **Iconography**: Ravens/Crows, Black Feathers

Caius

- Alias: "The Horned One", "Lord of the Hunt"
- *The Afterlife, The Hunt, Wealth*
- **Iconography**: A Stag, Bow and Arrow

Gisreius

- Alias: "The Divine Smith"
- *Smithing, Brewing, Hospitality*
- **Iconography**: Smith's Hammer of Gold

Cozasis

- Alias: "The World Breaker"
- *The Sea, Chaos, Nightmares*
- **Iconography**: Tentacled Figure, Runic Eye

Lilith

- Alias: "Mistress of Lies", "Destiny Weaver", "Fleshcarver"
- *Trickery, War, Murder*
- **Iconography**: Spider, Bloody Dagger

Ikas

- Bastard child of **Lilith**. Large vendetta against her mother.
- Alias: "The Seething One", "Lady of Flies"
- *Vengeance, Forgotten Places, Envy*
- **Iconography**: Centipede, Moth

Yam

- Alias: "The Illusioned One", "The World Eater"
- *Illusion, Madness, Malevolence, Destruction*
- **Iconography**: The Evil Eye, Darkened Sun

* * *

The Primals

Aodh

- Father of **Cael** and **Uldrich** – Former King of the Realm of Fire
- Defeated and imprisoned by his son, **Cael**.
- Alias: "The Ashbringer", "Prince of the Underworld"
- *Fire, Wrath, Death, and War*
- **Iconography**: Flaming Eye, Fractured Skull

Cael

- **Fire Primal** that **Braxus** pulled from *The Primordial Plane*.
- Son of **Aodh** and brother to **Uldrich**. Husband to **Pithus**.
- Alias: "The Flame King", "The Wrathful One", "The Phoenix"
- *Strength, Justice, Truth, and Passion*
- **Iconography**: Phoenix, Hand with Flame

Qella

- **Water Primal** that **Braxus** pulled from *The Primordial Plane*.
- Felled and imprisoned in *1286*.
- Alias: "The Lady of Water", "The Seeing One", "The Betrayer"
- *Magic, Knowledge, Patience, Temperance*
- **Iconography**: Diamond Heart, Waves

Uldrich

- **Earth Primal** that **Braxus** pulled from *The Primordial Plane*.
- Son of **Aodh** and sibling to **Cael**.
- Alias: "The Loving One", "The Prosperous One"
- *Healing, Growth, Prosperity, Sincerity*
- **Iconography**: Hands Holding a Sapling, Marigolds

Pithus

- **Air Primal** that **Braxus** pulled from *The Primordial Plane*.
- Husband to **Cael**.
- Ferries souls to final resting places for **Mali**.
- Alias: "The Fair One", "The Deceiver", "The Selfless"
- *Change, Time, Punishment, Memory*
- **Iconography**: Dragonflies, Winged Snakes, Fireflies

The Celestial Bodies and Calendar of Lusefell

The Heavenly Bodies

- **Celestine** - The sun darkened during the *Great War.*
- **Mithir** - The active sun of the realm.
- **Karanos** - The moon that *Lycans* and tides are linked to most heavily.
- **Peola** - A small, always crescent moon with more magical properties than **Karanos**. Many think this moon was created by **Qella** and influences **Magic**.

***

The Calendar and Days of the Week

Time in **Lusefell** is managed in a 12-hour format. **There are 6 days in a week:**

- Samue (Monday)
- Selah (Tuesday)

- Sielyr (Wednesday)
- Zabez (Thursday)
- Binem (Friday)
- Sielel (Saturday)

Months of the Year:

- Solaria (January) - 22 days
- Zephyr (February) - 23 days
- Tempestas (March) - 18 days
- Aquamare (April) - 20 days
- Brumal (May) - 22 days
- Bacus (June) - 18 days
- Glacius (July) - 20 days
- Vernal (August) - 20 days
- Sonnet (September) - 16 days
- Kett (October) - 18 days
- Bellarune (November) - 20 days
- Kismet (December) - 23 days

* * *

Notable Holidays and Festivals

Festival of Repentance

- **Solaria 7th**

A festival first started in *1287* within *Belmare, Redirine*. It was a festival begun by the **Villieu** family on behalf of **The Temple of the Flame King** to represent **Cael's** sorrow and repentance to **Pithus** for the years of unwarranted contempt. Each year on this day, the whole of Belmare is awash in bright teal, white, gold, and red. Many banners showcase a Phoenix embracing a large Dragonfly to commemorate the day **Cael** could recognize and embrace his husband again.

It is said that the two **Primals** always attend this festival, sometimes in the form of the Phoenix and the Dragonfly and sometimes in disguise.

Festival of Lovers

- Zephyr 14

A festival of love, life, and procreation! Most cities and towns across **Lusefell** are awash in flowers, reds, and pinks. Most have barrels of ale and bottles of wine along city streets. Lovers are often connected at the hip, and it's one of the more popular days for courting; several unions in the realm can be dated back to this festival's attendance.

The Bloom Festival (Spring Solstice)

- Zephyr 16

It is a large festival that usually has two main points of celebration: *The Forest of Bloom* and *The Forest of Enelhone*. It's often said that *Fey* can be seen more regularly during this festival as they are drawn to **Uldrich's** magic from *The Primordial Plane*. The forests are alight in carpets of blooms and naturally lit by bioluminescent flora and fireflies. **Uldrich** can be seen traversing both of these forests at some point during this day, heralding the coming season and aiding the growth of the realm's natural elements.

The Festival of Embers (Summer Solstice)

- Brumal 15th

A festival is held every year within the depths of the desert of *Redirine*. There is usually a magic circle that allows attendees to depart from both *Belmare* and *Fossy,* as the location within the desert changes every year. It is a space filled with colorful tents, poles of winding ribbon and flowers, and desert delicacies, and it ends with a breathtaking display of fireworks. Fire elementals from *The Primordial Plane* are often drawn to *The Mortal Plane* during the festival by **Cael**.

Cian Dwyer has planned it every year since the man rose within the *Temple of the Flame King* and began to fill the shoes of the late *High Cleric,* **Cecil**.

Festival of Homecoming

- **Bacus 1st**

A festival centered around family, home, and hearth. Most can be found within the walls of their homes on this holiday instead of within taverns and wandering street markets. It is a time to appreciate the home one has and the doors we can always return to. Many taverns across the realm are known to welcome those without places to return, and ***The Storm's Embrace*** locations within the continents open their doors to those without family or means to celebrate.

Their patron, **Hawke**, is known to visit each one on this day and spend a few hours telling stories of the seas, helping to prepare food, and passing out gold to those in need.

Festival of Rebirth (Autumn Solstice)

- **Vernal 15th**

A festival now held regularly in the growing town of *Fallah* within *Ivuris*. The city is built on floating planks and barges within the marshes of the continent, and the town is awash in teal, black, and silver colors. It is a festival to celebrate the souls that succeed in their atonement within *The Eternal Plane* and rebirth within *The Mortal Plane*'s life cycle. While large, almost arm-sized, Dragonflies can be glimpsed throughout the continent, they seem to gather around the festivities on this day.

It is often said that the giant insects are messengers of **Pithus** that carry good wishes to the reborn and lost souls across **Lusefell** from those gathered.

Festival of Reaping

- **Kett 4th**

It is a festival that was started to celebrate the ending of the season, fruitful harvests, and the coming chill of the cold. It now also marks an essential part of history. Across the realm, you can find at each larger celebration for this holiday an altar of which food, mementos, letters, and drink are left for the dead. Many died on this day in ***1136***, and the realm suffered much from the events. It is often said that **Cael** can be seen venturing into **The Smolder Ridge Mountains** to the summit to mourn on this day.

Festival of Yule (Winter Solstice)

- **Bellarune 20th**

It is a festival to celebrate the bitter months of cold and snow. There is usually a large festival awash with ribbons, bright lights, and decorations in the city of *Dal Garuhm* within *Usphra*. Gifts are often exchanged between family and friends, large feasts are usually prepared, and it is said that the *Winter Lights* can be seen on this night across *Usphra*. The *Winter Lights* were a recurrent phenomenon before **Qella's** imprisonment; however, they seem to have only appeared on this night since ***1286***.

Some speculate it is a means to remind those of the realm she still watches and consider it an offer of atonement; others speculate a more sinister tone to their presence.

Festival of Lights

- **Kismet 23rd**

It is a festival whose host city changes every year; it is a festival of games, fireworks, and celebration of the year past and the coming new one. Often, there are areas for gambling and carnival games within the celebration space. No matter where the festival is held, the night is a constant splash of fireworks and ends with a ceremony known as the *Lantern Lighting*. Paper lanterns of all shapes, sizes, and colors can be seen both set off into the air and floated out to sea. They often hold wishes for the coming year, thanks for the previous, and prayers to the **Primals** written on them.

Concept Art

Simon — 2023

Andreas — 2023

Neil (left) & Cian (right) — 2023

Andreas (left) & Simon (right) — 2023

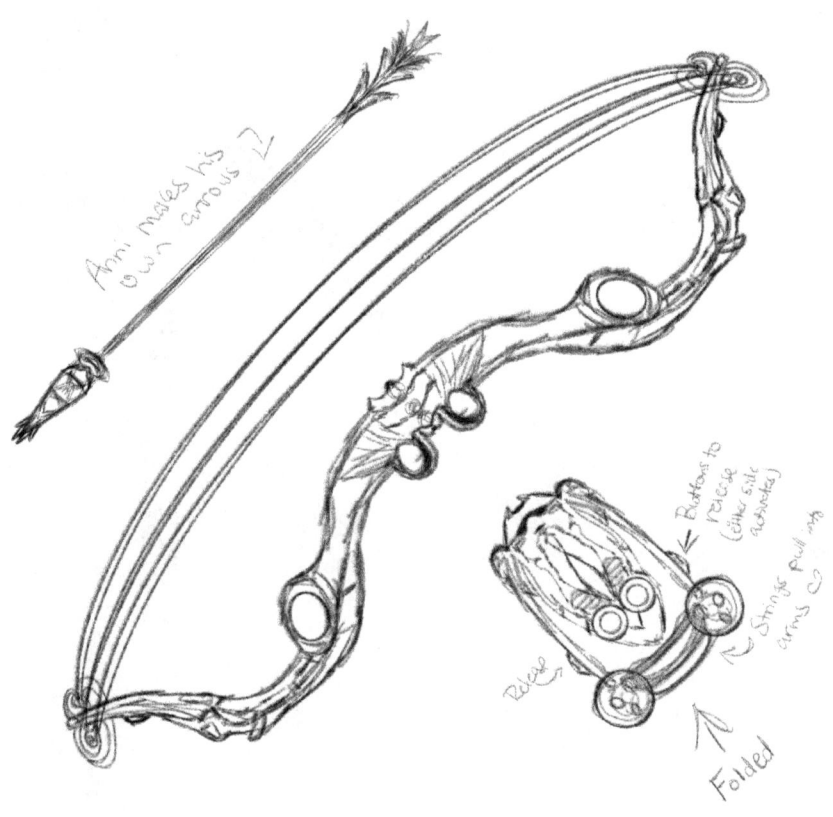

Andreas' Bow — 2023

Simon (left) & Andreas (right) — 2024

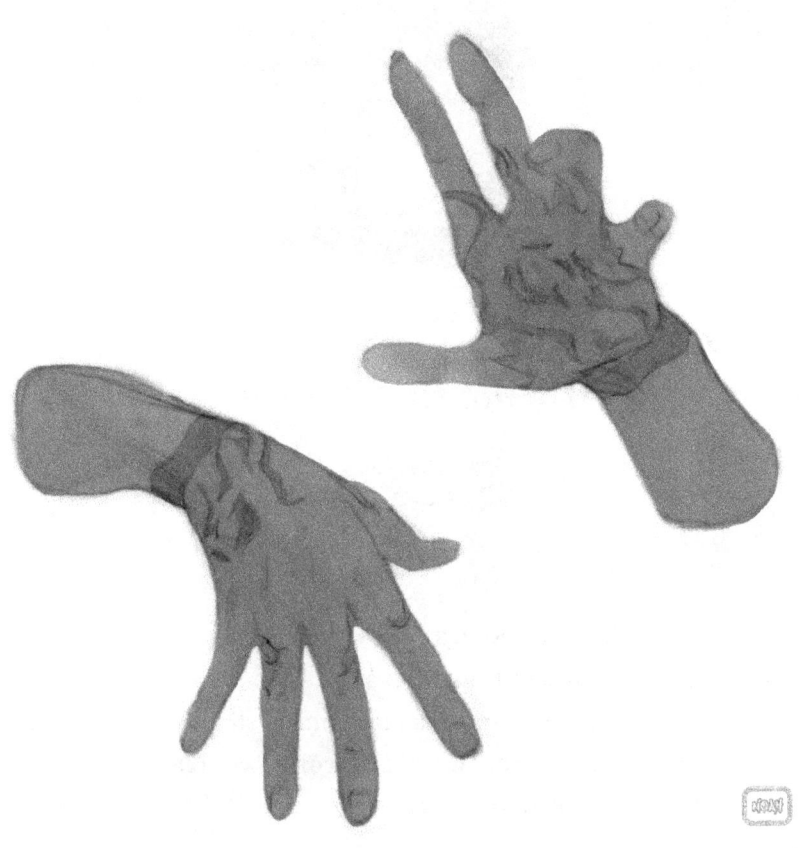

Andreas' Hands — 2024

About the Author

~~~~~

I'm a level 32 He/They located in a little city in South Carolina. I live there with my son, our cat, and our dog. I'm a proud member of the LGBTQA+ community and a single parent. In my free time, I sling coffee for folks, and I'm always caught up in the characters and world I've created over the years, which have become dear to my heart.

I'm a self-taught Illustrator and writer who has been in the game off and on for about 10 years. I create with pencil, imagination, and watercolors—be it traditionally or digitally—and pride myself on fantasy characters and worlds. I love character design, concept art, and all things of the imagination. When not consuming too much caffeine or watching Godzilla movies, I love playing D&D and other TTRPGS, cake decorating, and spazzing over shiny rocks, old bones, and astronomy.

You can connect with me on:

🌐 https://www.highlycaffeinated.art

🔗 https://www.threads.net/@highcafgoblin

🔗 https://open.spotify.com/playlist/2fObiZugTHiTELY5anLM3w?si=55ccdea63ec44e7c

Subscribe to my newsletter:

✉ https://mailchi.mp/794462004bd4/email-sign-up

Also by Noah Bodie

The Desert Rose Saga

Andreas Dwyer struggles to establish his identity outside of his family's notoriety. A chance meeting with an orc mercenary named Simon propels the half-elf on a journey of self-discovery, laughter, and romantic tension. Can they let down their guard and foster a budding romance? Will Andreas discover the meaning behind cryptic messages concerning his future? These unlikely heroes may hold the key to changing the world's fate, and they don't even know it.

The Novellas of Lusefell

This is a series of novellas set within the world of **Lusefell**. Some will be referenced in more significant series, such as the **Desert Rose Saga**. Treat these as little blips of history, giving context to the world, its history, and its rich characters. Together, they and the series weave an intermingling story that explores the fantasy world of **Lusefell** created by *Noah Bodie*.

"The Captain and the Guppy" - A Lusefell Novella

In the underground city of Pirn, Cedric, the enigmatic second-in-command of the feared pirate ship **The Waning Moon**, oversees an orphanage that provides refuge to the city's most vulnerable. Captain Hawke, the legendary *Warden of the Seas*, is known for his strength, cunning, and love for those in his charge. As tensions between them simmer beneath the surface, a deeper bond is tested when Hawke returns home wounded and weary, leaving Cedric to question their place at Hawke's side.